SHARK SKIN
Suite

TIM DORSEY

SHARK SKIN
Suite

wm
WILLIAM MORROW
An Imprint of HarperCollins*Publishers*

SHARK SKIN SUITE. Copyright © 2015 by Tim Dorsey. All rights reserved. Printed in the United States of America. No part of this book may be used or reproduced in any manner whatsoever without written permission except in the case of brief quotations embodied in critical articles and reviews. For information address HarperCollins Publishers, 195 Broadway, New York, NY 10007.

HarperCollins books may be purchased for educational, business, or sales promotional use. For information please e-mail the Special Markets Department at SPsales@harpercollins.com.

A hardcover edition of this book was published in 2015 by William Morrow, an imprint of HarperCollins Publishers.

FIRST WILLIAM MORROW PAPERBACK EDITION PUBLISHED 2015.

Library of Congress Cataloging-in-Publication Data has been applied for.

ISBN 978-0-06-224002-6

18 19 OV/RRD 10 9 8 7 6 5 4 3

For Steve Yeaw

History doesn't repeat itself, but it does rhyme.

MARK TWAIN

SHARK SKIN

Suite

Prologue

My name is Edith Grabowski, I live in Florida and I'm old as dirt. Eat me.

Those last two words you just read? They're now on like a million T-shirts, along with my picture. There are other T-shirts with more photos from the rest of my gang: Edna, Eunice and Ethel. About 392 years of hard life between us. Everyone says we have spunk. Some claim we give them hope. There used to be a reason we made headlines and became famous, but who can remember? I think now we're in the news just because we're in the news, like half the nobodies on reality shows. The networks want to know every detail, especially the sex. They follow us into restrooms. Enough already.

We needed something to kill those high beams of publicity. So every time the TV people chased us down and turned the cameras on again, I'd say, "Eat me." We thought there were laws against putting such language on the air. But all that did was sell more T-shirts. And coffee mugs, and big foam hats with our names, and rear-window decals of four old ladies peeing on just about everything.

They never leave us alone, day and night. Then we remembered the big stink over Janet Jackson at the Super Bowl. So this morning when they turned on the cameras outside my condo, the four of us had our own wardrobe malfunction. Everyone acted like their heads had caught fire, and one of the reporters threw up on his microphone. And me and the girls laughed like motherfuckers.

So here we are again. Story time. Guess you want to know what happened, *again*. We landed in the middle of another huge Florida freak show that made the news all the way to Germany and Japan. How many times is that now? Four? Five? We're like geriatric Forrest Gumps.

Anyway, it all started back when everyone was hunting pythons in the Everglades, and some guy died at a cockroach-eating contest in Deerfield Beach, and this chick got arrested for riding a manatee like Seabiscuit, and a mysterious eyeball the size of a coconut washed ashore in Miami, and an entire trailer park crowded around the apparition of Christ in a power meter, and . . . *Shhhh! Shut up, Ethel! I'm talking to these people here!* . . . Sorry about that. Ethel says I'm senile and getting off track, but if she was telling the story, we'd now be tits deep in some long-winded nonsense about her great-grand-nephew who's trying to "find himself" but instead just finds all the food in her refrigerator and plays video games all day before locking himself in the bathroom for three hours with an old briefcase he won't let anyone touch and insists through the door that he's dealing with a fungus. Now *that's* off track. When I listed all those wacked-out news stories earlier, I just wanted to give you the latest lowdown on the Sunshine State to show what passes for normal around here, like residents strolling ho-hum along the shore, stepping over a big-ass eyeball and thinking: *Sure, why not?*

After you can grasp that baseline of weirdness, you'll understand how this story could actually happen. But only in the Sunshine State. It unfolded last year in the middle of the Florida Keys with the whole fore-closure crisis still gripping the nation. Except whenever something goes to hell everywhere else in the country, Florida puts it on roller skates with rocket thrusters. And whenever me and the girls get dragged in, there's always one name that takes it to the next level:

Serge.

Hold on a second. We're walking down the sidewalk right now. One of our fans is driving by in a convertible. He just honked at us and yelled "Eat me," like you'd shout "You da man" when someone tees off in golf.

Sure, why not?

Mahoney's the name. The chipped letters on my office window say I'm a private eye, private dick, gumshoe, hawkshaw, shamus, sherlock, sleuthhound, and the chair on the paying side of my desk is the last whistle-stop on the railroad of hard luck and soft dames.

The chair doesn't talk much but the people in it do: bankers, barbers, butchers, boozers, men-about-town, ladies-in-waiting, ex-husbands, futures traders, straight arrows, crooked cops, long-shot gamblers, nearsighted pimps, dark horses, alley cats, loan sharks, stool pigeons and Charlie Sheen.

Their accents are different but the story's the same, betting on the Chance Brothers, Fat and Slim. They hoof through my door from sunrise until the clock's big hand is on boxcars. Then I have a standing appointment with Harvey Wallbanger.

My bartender is a regular Joe named Louie who makes with the cocktails faster than the paint jigger at Sherwin-Williams. But my gut tells me you didn't come to hear me mumble about the social life of bookies and bangtails.

You want the lowdown on Serge? He's my factotum when things start to roll hinkey, and that's as often as "close cover before striking." It began like any other day, except this one was about to throw me more curves than a double-jointed hooker with a spitball. The case stunk worse than a Sterno bum with a pet skunk named Shooter, and by the time the fat lady warbled, the mouthpieces in shark skin suits were all over us like a zoo chimp on the flesh banana . . . and Serge A. Storms continued gathering force, about to make landfall . . .

Coleman!" Serge waved urgently. "Come here!"

"I'm busy." Coleman stood at the motel sink, pouring a palmful of suds into his other hand and back again.

"What the hell are you doing?" asked Serge.

"Handcrafted beer," said Coleman. "I still don't get it."

"You idiot, just come over here."

Coleman rinsed sticky hands and strolled across the room. "What's up?"

"I finally got published!" Serge clapped his hands like a windup toy with cymbals. "Dreams *can* come true!"

"But weren't you already published by that newspaper?"

"That's what I thought, too." Serge leaned toward his laptop screen. "I mailed in my manifesto, *Fixing the Entire World,* to their letters to the editor, and I thought they were amazed by my expository style and global management skill set."

"They weren't?"

"Turns out they were printing it in cooperation with the police, asking the public's help to track a serial killer. So that slightly taints its acceptance on literary merits . . . but not this time!" He turned the screen toward his pal. "Take a gander."

"You wrote a review on Amazon?"

"That's right," said Serge. "E-publishing is the future of the written word."

"But I thought you hated stuff people put up on the Web."

"That's how I used to feel. Until *I* got published." Serge pushed Coleman's head toward the laptop. "When the Internet first caught fire, they all said, 'Now everyone can express their opinion.' Then we saw the results and went, *ewwwww,* maybe not so great. And such a waste, too. We finally had this revolutionary new medium of communication to attain universal harmony, and people are posting videos of children hitting their dads in the nuts with Wiffle bats and writing one-star reviews shitting all over *Lawrence of Arabia:* 'Too long,' 'Too British,' 'What's the deal with all the Arabs?' . . . I decided to jump in and demonstrate the Web's true potential. Everyone else just reviews books and movies, so I went for my own niche."

Coleman looked up from the screen. "You reviewed duct tape?"

"They always say to write what you know." He grinned proudly. "I already have six hundred 'likes.'"

Coleman squinted as he plodded through the text:

> I'm here to say that duct tape isn't just for ducts anymore. I could not survive without it. I can't say enough about duct tape. One of the earliest versions was developed in 1942 by the good people at Revolite (according to Wikipedia, so who freakin' knows?) and later used extensively by the military and NASA. It even helped save the *Apollo 13* crew (wow!). I like duct tape for its soundproofing qualities when concentration and stealth are a priority. But don't go cheap, as the shoddier brands can easily be loosened with the tongue. In the home improvement universe, duct tape is *Sgt. Pepper's*, *Citizen Kane* and *The Great Gatsby* all wrapped into one. If I could, I'd give this review a hundred stars, but The Man has boxed me in at five. So in conclusion, even if you don't need duct tape, buy a roll today, "invite" some people over to your motel room, let your imagination run amok and surprise yourself!
>
> SERGE A. STORMS

Part ONE

Chapter ONE

THE MIDDLE OF THE FLORIDA KEYS

The invasion was under way. They hit the beach in overwhelming strength.

Thousands of giant iguanas, Burmese pythons and African land snails.

The iguanas basked along the grassy banks of the roads, for some reason all parallel, facing traffic like they knew something. The snakes wiggled through boat canals and curled up in the engine blocks of surprised car owners. The snails inspired the greatest disbelief, eating anything, including cement, and their baseball-sized shells punctured tires.

It was the attack of irresponsible pet owners who'd become mollified by exotic species that knew no local predators, found an abundant food source and grew to unnatural scale. The pets had either gotten loose or were deliberately released when the owners' motivation was required for more pressing matters of buying lottery tickets and fireworks.

One of the snails completed a two-day slime odyssey across a parking lot and began nibbling at the corner of a low-slung concrete building that sat quietly beside the Overseas Highway.

Above the automatic front doors was a colorful mosaic of tropical fish that fit together to form one large fish. To the right of the design: FISHERMEN'S HOSPITAL.

It was the main community hospital for long stretches of the Keys in both directions. No fishermen were inside.

The medical center resided in the city of Marathon. The city got its name because it was the midpoint in the marathon effort to build the overseas railroad just after the turn of the twentieth century. It was often erroneously called Marathon *Key,* when the city actually sat on the island of Vaca Key. Civic leaders constantly attempted to clarify the name to news organizations that continued dispatching stories datelined "Marathon Key" anytime weirdness happened, like when those barracuda fired themselves out of the water like harpoons, biting people in fishing boats. The injured fishermen were taken to a different hospital.

On the hospital's first floor, inside a sterile patient room, a thin line of blue light crossed the screen of a heart monitor, beeping each time the line spiked. Normal range. Of more concern on another machine were red blood-pressure numbers that loitered on the downside.

The patient's massive bandages concealed gender, but it was a woman. One arm in a cast, gauze on both legs, ribs taped and a head so completely wrapped in white that only the hole over the left eye hinted anyone was inside.

The hospital had that universal hospital smell, a bouquet of disinfectant and the funk in an old person's house. The Florida Keys added a briny tinge, like vinegar potato chips. The wrist of the arm not in a cast was handcuffed to the bed's railing.

A chart hung from the foot of the bed: *Campanella, Brook.*

A uniformed police officer stood outside the door. Three others in suits hovered around the patient.

Another man in a better-fitting suit pointed at the cuffs. "Is that really necessary?" Her lawyer.

Brook had been a well-liked paralegal at a large South Florida firm until disappearing several weeks back under murky details. When word first broke of her arrival at the hospital, the firm immediately flew in one of their best defense attorneys.

On the other side of the bed, detectives glanced at one another. Procedure required handcuffs, but discretion disagreed. And the cops needed cooperation that hadn't been forthcoming. A tiny key clicked in the lock, and a cuff snapped off her wrist. The detective looked up at the lawyer. "Good faith?"

"Even if we were inclined to talk, it's far too soon," said the attorney. "She just regained consciousness after surgery. Can't this wait?"

"Actually it can't," said the detective stowing cuffs. "Every second is critical right now."

His partner opened a notepad. "Serge is probably still somewhere in the Keys. We've rarely gotten this close to him."

"Your client's in deep trouble," said the first. "Participated in a three-hundred-mile crime spree, not to mention obstruction of justice for helping a person of interest in more than twenty homicides evade capture."

"For God's sake," said the attorney. "She was kidnapped."

"Maybe in the beginning," said the second detective. "But we've got a roomful of witnesses who saw her in public with Serge, free to leave but never trying to escape."

"He always had a gun on her," said the lawyer, "which he wasn't going to wave around for your witnesses. Plus she did try to escape, several times before she finally made it, and you're looking at the results. I mean, who jumps from a moving vehicle on the Seven Mile Bridge?"

"What about her fingerprints at the various locations?"

"But no gun-toting Patty Hearst photos or anything else connecting her to even one of Serge's crimes." The lawyer gestured toward his client. "Trust your own eyes. Does this look like a willing participant?"

The first detective sighed. "If we can just ask her a few preliminary questions, then we'll go."

"Questions?" said the lawyer. "She's got a tube down her throat and the rest of her mouth is bandaged shut."

"But she can blink," said the second. "One for yes, two for no."

"We'll be as brief as possible," said the first. "And you approve each question."

The lawyer exhaled hard. "If it will get you out of here. She needs her rest."

"Fair enough." The detective turned toward Brook. "Did Serge do this to you?"

The attorney squeezed her right hand. "You can answer that."

One blink.

"Did Serge kill those people?"

One blink.

"Do you know where he is?"

Two blinks.

"Where he might be heading?"

Two blinks.

"Did he mention any known associates besides Coleman?"

Two blinks.

"Can you remember—"

The attorney stepped around the bed. "That's it for today. I have to insist."

"Okay," said the first detective. "We'll pick it up tomorrow."

The investigators left Brook's room and stopped to congregate at a water cooler across the hall.

"What do you think?"

"Back when she was still missing, I would have bet my paycheck she was in on the whole thing."

"Me, too," said his partner. "I've seen this scenario before. No matter how many restaurant and convenience-store sightings of so-called victims smiling with their captors, they always later swear they were too scared to leave."

The other detective looked back toward the closed hospital room door. "But after seeing her in there, I have no doubt she was utterly terrified the whole time."

"So how do you want to play it? Tell her lawyer she's in the clear?"

The other detective shook his head. "We need to bluff a little while longer."

"What for?"

"I'm a hundred percent on her innocence, but there's still the Stockholm syndrome."

"Stockholm? After that beating?"

The detective shrugged. "In some twisted corner of her mind, she may still feel some screwed-up devotion to her tormentor."

"You think she knows more about Serge's whereabouts than she's letting on?"

"There's always the chance. That's why we need to keep the pressure on."

"I don't feel good about this." The detective stared at his shoes. "It was creepy enough questioning her just now with that blinking eye."

"I know it's a shitty thing to do," said the second detective. "I got a family just like the next guy. But I also want to protect them from all the psychos out there."

They both stopped and looked over again at the guarded door of Brook's room.

"God only knows what that poor kid went through . . ."

They heard a crash and ran outside. A Camaro with a snail-punctured tire had hit a utility pole in front of the emergency room. A stretcher came out.

Back inside Brook's room, the attorney patted her hand. "Don't think any more for today. Just go to sleep."

Brook's one visible eye slowly closed as she dozed into a deep morphine dream that seemed vividly real. Because it had been . . .

Chapter TWO

THREE DAYS EARLIER

The eye was large and wide and blue, with innocent lashes. Practically pressed against the wood, staring down into a tiny hole.

Brook Campanella stood back up and read the tiny brass plate nailed above the hole. "Who's Mel Fisher?"

"The famous treasure salvager," said Serge. "Discovered the wreck of the *Atocha* and about forty tons of gold, silver, emeralds and other goodies. Died 1996."

Brook pointed at the wood. "He's in there?"

"Part of him, supposedly."

Brook looked down the length of the polished bar. Numerous other half-inch holes drilled at precise intervals, each with its own accompanying brass plate. The contents of the holes were a light alabaster, in contrast to the dark, brooding wood, sealed with varnish. In front of each hole sat a stool.

Brook looked puzzled at Serge. "You mean to tell me people come in here and drink with someone's cremated remains right in front of their beers?"

"Don't forget the empty holes in between."

Brook glanced again. "What are they for?"

"The people sitting on the bar stools in front of them—bought burial slots in advance. They're obviously goal oriented." Serge smiled big. "There are bars and then there are *bars*. This one's the ultimate crusty-locals dive, where politicians and assorted characters have been coming for decades."

"And it's called?"

"The Chart Room."

"Why?"

"Nautical charts, like those hanging in that corner where Jimmy Buffett played for tips while still unknown," said Serge. "He arrived in the early seventies with Jerry Jeff Walker, and the Chart Room is the first place they stopped. The now-famous novelist Tom Corcoran just happened to be bartending at the time, and since Jimmy said he was new to Key West, Tom said the inaugural beer was on him, and then Corcoran went on to write a couple songs with Jimmy, 'Fins' and 'Cuban Crime of Passion,' and shoot photos for seven of his album covers."

They stopped to take in the hodgepodge of faded photos and newspaper clips tacked up behind the bar. A sign: TIP BIG!—above a fake million-dollar bill. Political buttons, business cards from defunct businesses. An actual coconut sat among a shelf of glasses without explanation. Some of the photos were of dogs and people mooning.

"I never expected a place like this when we walked up a few minutes ago," said Brook. "I just saw a giant luxury resort with everything perfectly manicured and polished."

"The Pier House," Serge footnoted. "North end of Duval."

"But how does the bar still exist?" asked Brook. "It's everything big corporations detest, as if the people who own this place don't know it's here."

"That's the reaction I always get when I bring people, voluntarily or against their will, leading them on the winding route through a Hawaiian-pastel landscaping maze with pasty northerners cannonballing in the pool, fiddling with drink umbrellas and feeding pet tarpon off the boardwalk—until we discover this joint tucked out of sight under the back side like it's janitorial storage. One of the tiniest bars, but pound for pound . . ."

Brook slowly began to nod. "I'm starting to get it. I see why you like the place . . ."

It was the perfect answer. The way to Serge's heart was through his trivia. And Brook wasn't like the others. She was pure and possessed historical stamina. Serge had tried vainly to teach previous love interests about his cherished state, but they just wanted to have sex.

"Oh yes! Oh yes! Oh, Serge! Harder! Faster! What are you thinking about?"

"Artifacts from the Seminole wars, agrarian pioneers at Cape Sable, Florida lighthouses in chronological order of construction . . ."

"To delay your orgasm?"

"No, to speed it up . . ."

But Brook was different. When the couple initially arrived in Key West, Serge had guarded expectations. He began his trademark A-tour of the island, a withering multiday quest of brutal attrition. To his surprise, Brook stayed with him stride for stride.

"Key West tip number 362: If you have to go to the bathroom on Duval Street, most of the restrooms are for patrons only, and the ones on the ground floor of the venerable La Concha hotel are locked and require a room key for access, so you just take the elevator to the observation deck, where the bathrooms aren't militarized."

Brook exited the ladies' room on top of the hotel. "That feels better. Where to now? Hey, how about that cemetery you were telling me about? I'll bet you'd like to take lots of photos . . ."

Serge thought: *Heart be still.*

They weren't just an odd couple but a freak pairing of nature, like those Internet photos of a mouse that thinks a cat's its mom. Serge was criminally insane, and Brook was Norman Rockwell territory. They'd met during one of Mahoney's cases. She was his client and in a serious jam, the proverbial damsel in distress. So Serge added more distress. "Get in the fucking car if you want to live!"

She got in.

Only because of the harrowing alternative. And once that danger had passed, the specter of Serge became even more terrifying. But Serge was an old-school criminal: Leave the vulnerable alone, or rescue if need be. To Brook's astonishment, he was a total gentleman and the ultimate protector. She felt completely safe for the first time since she could remember.

That was three months ago, a schoolgirl crush growing by the day. Brook had never laughed so much in her life.

"What's so funny?" asked Serge.

"Your new diet," said Brook. "Replacing the bulb in the refrigerator with a black light so everything looks like toxic waste."

"I'm totally serious. I could get a book deal."

And she couldn't get enough of his encyclopedic brain-evacuation rants. Their dynamic became a subtropical *My Fair Lady*, her Eliza Doolittle to his Henry Higgins by way of Speedy Gonzalez.

For his part, Serge slowly began to notice the sweet little flower by his side. She was the only uncontaminated thing in his life, and he decided to keep it that way. In the beginning, Brook had worried about sexual come-ons. Now she wondered, *What's he waiting for?*

And that's where it stood as she helped him photographically map every inch of the Chart Room. *Click, click, click.* "Serge, I think I'm getting the hang of this." *Click, click, click.* "Where to now?"

"How about Havana Docks? It's another bar behind this place up on piers with a great view of the harbor," said Serge. "One thing you should know about me: I'm all about drinking holes with views of water over the bottles."

"Sounds so romantic." She clutched his arm tighter. "And you were right about putting out of my mind that whole mess back in Fort Lauderdale. I'm definitely in the clear by now."

Serge stopped to photograph one of the massive tarpon awaiting tourist handouts. "As they say, worry is usually interest paid on a debt that never comes due."

They made more stops, admiring and snapping pictures of chromatic flowers, wading birds, flats boats and more fish. Brook snuggled into his side and stared up at him radiantly. Passersby would have guessed it was a honeymoon.

The couple finally climbed the wooden planks leading to Havana Docks. Brook made a prompt left after hitting the air-conditioning. "I need to powder my nose."

"I need to look at water over bottles."

Moments later, a carefree Brook emerged from the ladies' room, stowing lipstick in her purse. Something seized her arm from behind and yanked her back into the alcove.

"Oh, it's you, Serge." Brook took her hand off her chest. "Nearly gave me a stroke."

"We have to get the hell out of here! Now!"

"But we just got here," said Brook. "Why?"

"Because they have a TV."

"I know you hate network programming—"

He pulled her to the front of the short hall and pointed around the corner at the large-screen TV over the bar. "It's probably been playing all day." The volume was up loud enough for them to hear across the empty lounge.

"Hey," said Brook. "What's my photo doing on the news?"

"At this hour, authorities are conducting a massive search for this woman in connection with two brutal South Florida murders . . ."

Brook went slack-jawed. Another face filled the screen.

"Law enforcement suspect she is traveling in the company of this man, Serge Storms, wanted for questioning in at least twenty other homicides . . ."

The noise in Brook's head was an air-raid siren.

"The pair was last believed to be traveling toward Key West . . ."

Her legs began to buckle, and Serge caught her on the way down.

Chapter THREE

THE GULF STREAM

A catamaran sat anchored six miles southwest of Key West.

It had left the dock crammed cheek to jowl with fifty tourists who had suddenly decided to take up snorkeling. They were instructed how to fasten and blow up their yellow flotation vests, making the deck even more crowded. Locals called it a cattle boat.

It had a large sail that was stowed so it could quickly motor out to the reef and get those paying customers in the water. They now surrounded the boat, bobbing in the sea like a school of spastic lemon jellyfish.

A head rose from the sea and spit out a snorkel. "I think I saw a fish."

"Where?" said Ethel.

"Down there," said Edith.

"I don't see anything," said Edna.

"They promised all this fantastic marine life," said Eunice. "Why aren't we finding it?"

Because the best underwater viewing was at Pennekamp, Looe Key and the Tortugas. And the fiercely competitive Key West snorkeling racket depended on turnaround time, which meant the nearest reef, which was barren.

"I see some rocks," said Edna.

But it was still the Gulf Stream, and a few stray fish couldn't help but swim by. Then visitors from Indiana and Ohio who didn't know any better would go home happy. It was a sound formula: People not used to treading open ocean quickly tired of waves and tide, returning to the boat long before their snorkel time was up. On the way back to Key West they were served unlimited free Rum Runners that they lapped up in the manner of people offered free liquor everywhere, and by the time they staggered onto the dock, the four scrawny fish they had seen turned into a Jacques Cousteau expedition.

"I definitely see one this time," said Ethel. "That little guy."

"I see one over there," said Eunice. "That makes two."

Edith was looking the other way. "I think the guys running the boat are hotties."

"Edith, they're all seventy years younger than us."

"Exactly."

"I have to admit I'm with Edith on this one," said Edna.

"I'm exhausted," said Eunice.

"Me, too," said Ethel. "Let's go drink a shitload of those Rum Runners."

"What about you, Edith? . . . Edith? . . . What's that look on your face?"

"I have to go to the bathroom."

"So go already. It's the ocean."

"No, it's not—"

"Wait," said Edna. "You don't mean number two."

"I didn't plan it."

"Just hold it until we get back on the boat!"

"Have you forgotten?" said Edith. "At our age that's not always in the cards."

"No! Stop! Whatever you do . . ."

Edith closed her eyes, and exhaled with satisfied relief.

"Dear God in heaven!" The other three frantically splashed away from her.

Back on deck, the boat's crew circulated with giant red pitchers, filling dozens of plastic cups held out by the beckoning mob. The crew was motivated; it increased tips. Four crouched women with white hair elbowed their way through. Ethel held a cup over her head. "Hit me!"

"That's your fourth," said Edna.

"And this train ain't stoppin' now."

"Whoa!" Eunice jumped back, arms dripping with red liquid from the pitcher. "What's the deal?"

"Sorry," said the crew member. "Someone just pinched my ass." He spun around to see a giggling Edith worm her way out of sight into the crowd.

The anchor hoisted. Those with better cameras migrated starboard to shoot the setting sun through girders of the nearby Sand Key Lighthouse, which began service in 1853. Since it was a reef light, it wasn't one of those round concrete jobs but an iron skeleton in the shape of a steep pyramid. The sand of Sand Key was underwater. One of the shutterbugs with a Nikon pointed off the port bow. "A waterspout!"

"I've never seen a waterspout before," said Eunice.

"It looks so pretty," said Edna.

"You wouldn't say that if you saw it on land," said Ethel. "They're called tornadoes."

"Except this one's just harmlessly sucking up water."

"And some fish that don't like it," said Eunice.

"Maybe that's where all the fish went that we were supposed to see today," said Ethel.

"Have another drink," said Edna.

The crew started the engine. They had a strict no-ocean-littering policy, because of staunch fines from the ever-vigilant Coast Guard. So there was immediate concern when a passenger with a video camera panned wide-angle along the side of the boat. "What the heck is that floating over the reef? . . ."

A half hour later, the gangway lowered onto the dock, and the crew steadied its customers as they wobbled ashore. *"Here's ten bucks for your tip bucket! . . ." "Never seen so many fish! . . ."*

The old ladies climbed down next.

Eunice reached the dock and covered her eyes. "Jesus, Edith! I've never been so embarrassed in my entire life!"

"I don't see what you're so upset about."

"Edith! The first mate used a net on a long pole to fish your diaper out of the ocean!"

"Fuck it, let's find a bar."

"I know a good one." Edna pointed across a sunset crowd surrounding jugglers and tightrope walkers and a guy turning blue in a straitjacket wrapped with chains. "Just on the other side of Mallory Square."

The elderly quartet finally reached the top step outside their destination, and Edna grabbed the door handle. "What do you think?"

"Look at that view!" said Eunice.

"Told you it was a great place."

They went inside Havana Docks. Eunice stopped and pointed at the face entirely filling the flat-screen TV. "Look! It's Serge!"

"You're right!" yelled Edna. "It *is* Serge!"

"What's he done now?"

Serge's eyes flew wide at the sound of his name echoing through the bar. He pulled Brook deeper into the alcove outside the restrooms and urgently tapped her cheeks. "I know you're woozy, but we have to get out of here!"

A waiter passed by and stopped. "Is she okay?"

"Just needs some air."

The waiter was about to leave, but stopped again. "Do I know you from somewhere?"

"No!"

Brook managed to steady her legs. They hurried east toward Key West Bight. Every passing bar seemed to have a TV with their faces. "Wrong way." Serge jerked her south, ducking in the first souvenir shop they saw. The clerk rang them up. "Have we met somewhere before?"

"No!"

They ran out of the store with bright Conch Republic baseball caps pulled low over their faces bank-robber style. "This way . . ."

They reversed course, moving west on Greene Street. Up ahead, a large grouper marked their sanctuary. It hung over the doors of Captain Tony's Saloon, the original Sloppy Joe's where Hemingway used to kick back after his daily writing quota of five hundred words. A drunk tourist now stood on the sidewalk, throwing quarters backward over his head in a long-standing tradition of trying to get pocket change in the grouper's mouth for good luck. Serge knew that Tony's didn't have a TV and was cave dark. He also knew something else.

Quarters bounced and rolled on the sidewalk as Serge and Brook ran hand in hand into the bar, past pool tables, some real tombstones and the old lynching tree that grew up through the roof. They reached the back of the lounge; Serge's fist pounded a door that said PRIVATE.

From inside "What now?" It was opened by an extra-tall, lanky man who used to pitch for the University of Miami Hurricanes. His eyes bugged out. "Serge!" He quickly checked to see if anyone was looking, then pulled them both inside and slammed the door.

"Jesus, you're all over the news, every station. What have you gotten yourself into now?"

"I can explain."

The man held up a hand. "I don't want to know."

"I need a favor."

"That I knew."

"It's too hot for us in Key West," said Serge. "We need to get off the Rock, but people are starting to recognize us on the street . . ."

" . . . And you need to get to Big Pine."

"Can you help us, Joe?"

Joe rubbed his forehead. The full name was Joe Faber, who bought the bar from Captain Tony two decades back, allowing the local celebrity to remain on his bar-stool perch by the front door—right up to his death in '08 at the age of ninety-two—taking donations for autographs and, if the women were sufficiently hammered, getting in a little fondling. Faber also owned the infamous No Name Pub, a converted 1930s trading post and brothel back in the banana trees on Big Pine Key.

"Man, Serge, when you show up, you bring the band." Joe grabbed his keys off a hook. "We'll go out the back . . ."

Chapter FOUR

THE OVERSEAS HIGHWAY

Joe Faber loved his classic '96 Cadillac DeVille. Serge had also once owned a Caddy and was familiar with the roomy trunk, but this was the first time he was getting the ride.

"What are you doing?" Brook asked in the dark next to the spare tire.

"Counting bridges," said Serge. "That last one was Ramrod, and Little Torch is coming up. Then one more to Big Pine."

A couple minutes later: "We're stopping," said Brook.

"First red light since Stock Island after leaving Key West twenty-six miles back. Then we turn north into the backcountry."

Serge finally heard rocks under the tires. "We're here."

The car stopped and the trunk popped open in blinding sunlight.

Joe helped Brook climb out. "I pulled us around back by the gas tanks so nobody would see."

"I owe you," said Serge.

"I know." The Caddy slung pebbles and sped off.

Quiet again except wind and occasional cawing gulls over Bogie Channel.

Serge headed toward a whitewashed two-story clapboard building—the combination marina and motel office. The rear door opened before he could knock.

"Good God, Serge, get in here before anyone sees!" Hands yanked them inside. "You're all over the TV!"

"It's this crazy twenty-four-hour news cycle," said Serge. "When I was a kid, just three channels, the national anthem, a prayer, test pattern, go to bed. And the 7-Eleven closed at *eleven*. It was a healthier time."

"Don't change the subject."

"My manners," said Serge. "Brook, I'd like you to meet Julie. Julie, this is Brook."

"You're changing the subject."

Serge cleared his throat. "I need a—"

"Favor," said Julie. "Okay, we got a free cabin."

"Cabin number five?" Serge pumped his eyebrows. "You know how I feel about ol' *casa cinco*."

"Serge, you're not exactly in a position to be choosy."

"You're absolutely right," said Serge. "But if you have number five."

Julie sighed and pulled a plastic fob off a pegboard. "Here's the key. And can you come back sometime when you're not using my place as a fugitive hangout?"

"You say that like it's bad publicity."

"Because it is."

"Excuse me." Brook asked Julie, "How well do you know Serge?"

"Well enough not to get into a trunk with him. Girl, take care of yourself."

The pair pulled their baseball caps down again and walked briskly across a white gravel parking lot.

"How exactly do you know all these people?" asked Brook.

"I just have a knack for collecting friends," said Serge. "And they're always offering to do favors. It's odd."

They continued toward a row of tiny cabins. The Old Wooden Bridge Fishing Camp. The wood part of the bridge was gone, now a modern concrete arch festooned with fishing poles and cast nets, connecting Big Pine to the hardy residents of No Name Key and their thriving hermit village of generators, septic tanks and cisterns.

Serge reached the door. Since time was critical, he only briefly kissed the number five as he unlocked it.

It was a cozy cottage. Could easily have been a single room, but a thin wooden divider separated two small beds from the sofa and tube TV. Serge's favorite part was the full wall of windows along the front of the cabin that overlooked the magnificent waters of Bogie Channel. He could spend hours watching the rhythms of nature through that glass.

Serge quickly closed all the blinds and pulled Brook to the couch.

She looked searchingly into his ice-blue eyes. "What happens now?"

"Strategize," said Serge. "I've seen this movie before, and I know how cops tick. The first thing we need to do is split up."

"But, Serge, I want to stay with you!"

He shook his head. "I knew that's how you'd react, but it's nonnegotiable. This isn't your world."

"But why?"

"Operationally, it's a no-brainer. They're looking for a couple traveling together. More important, though, is your future. It's me they want, and the sooner we part, the better it will go for you."

"But I didn't do anything, and anything I did do was legally justified."

"You're fond of me?" asked Serge.

"So?"

"So we hung out. That's aiding and abetting a known fugitive." Serge got up and peeked through the blinds. "The longer police can't capture someone, the more pissed off they get. Go figure. Then they target anyone who might have helped you remain free. Usually it's relatives with addresses that have been under surveillance. The police know you haven't stayed there, but they fuck with them anyway, hoping to rattle their cages and get them to phone you on a wiretapped line. But you fall into a worse category."

"What's that?"

"Someone who's been seen rolling with me." Serge began pacing. "The only option is to immediately turn yourself in and minimize the damage."

"I don't want to turn myself in." Tears welled. "I mean, I thought you and me—"

"Stop!" He knelt in front of the couch and grabbed her by the shoulders. "Look, if I didn't also have feelings for you, I'd let you come along—"

"Serge!"

"Who knows what the future will bring? Someday down the road, long after you've gotten your law degree and have a corner office with a successful firm, the phone will ring out of the blue and it will be me, hopefully not because I need a lawyer."

"But there must be a way we can stay together."

"When I said there was only one option, there's another: You become a lifelong fugitive. Is that really what you want? Always looking over your shoulder, flinching every time a car backfires, running out the back door whenever there's a knock at the front, carrying bags of marbles to throw on the sidewalk in the event of a chase? Actually, I used to throw the marbles in general as a preventive measure, but that just *created* chases. Not to mention constantly escaping through Chinese kitchens with crashing food trays and Cantonese hysterics. Personally I couldn't live any other way, but are you prepared to pull all that chow mein out of your hair?" Serge idly grabbed the TV remote and clicked the set on. Brook's face filled the screen. He clicked it off.

She was crying now. "I—I—I don't know what to do."

"What you do is let me think for both of us from now on." Serge took a seat next to Brook and held her hand. "Right now I need you to compose yourself and pay attention. Can you do that?"

She wiped her eyes and nodded.

"Okay, the only way this will work is if I kidnapped you. Anything they ask about, pin it all on me. Tell them everything even if I didn't do it. Agree to testify."

"I can't do that."

"You have to," said Serge. "When you turn yourself in, there are only two untasty items on the menu: They'll either think you started out as a kidnap victim but I brainwashed you into becoming an accomplice. Or they might actually believe your story. But they'll still bluff as leverage for details to track me down."

"Then what do I do?"

"Give them details."

"Make them up?"

"No, tell the truth." Serge stood and stretched. "The point is you have to convince them, and they have this annoying way of figuring out when you're lying. So the more candid you are about me, the more it will buttress our kidnapping charade. Tell them everything: my routines, frequent haunts, jaunty attire, charismatic quirks, love of country, disdain for eleven items in the express lane, passion for folding road maps back correctly. Just stick to the story that I had a gun on you the whole time."

"But details will help them capture you."

"I can take care of myself." Serge checked his wallet for cash reserves. "Then it's settled."

"What about your car?"

"It's a memory. We have to wait while Faber gets me another ride with clean plates and retrieves our luggage from the Southern Cross. Man, he's going to hold this over my head so long it's almost not worth it." He stopped and tapped his chin. "But I have the oddest feeling I'm forgetting something. It's been nagging me all day. What could it possibly be?"

"Serge," said Brook. "Where's Coleman?"

Chapter FIVE

KEY WEST

Another anonymous fleabag motel on Truman Avenue. And what do we have behind door number three?

The third door flew open. A naked man ran across the parking lot with clothes bunched in his arms and a spiked dog collar around his neck.

Back in the doorway stood a curvaceous woman with an irrepressible mane of fiery red hair. A shiny Smith & Wesson .38 pistol gripped loosely in her left hand. "Come back! It was just role-playing!"

The fleeing man never broke stride through honking traffic. *"You're a crazy bitch!"*

The woman frowned and closed the door. She clicked on the TV. An episode of *Desperate Housewives* was interrupted by breaking news. Serge's face filled the screen.

"Cocksucker!"

A .38 bullet blasted the picture tube in a shower of glass and sparks. She casually stuck the gun in her purse and headed out the door.

Brakes screeched on Truman Avenue. A pickup rear-ended a Miata.

Frat boys on mopeds shouted propositions. Guys on bicycles turned around and doubled back.

The woman ignored them all and continued down the sidewalk in the kind of chin-up, aggressively sexual strut that made men forget the fear of death and glance over with their wives present.

She reached the entrance of a corner bar with all the windows open and wooden ceiling fans set on lazy.

A bartender happened to turn; his eyebrows jackknifed. He huddled with the others.

"You serve her."

"I'm not going to serve her. You serve her."

"Are you crazy? . . ."

She settled onto a stool at the far end. A salesman quickly moved to the stool next to hers and offered a drink. She slowly turned toward him. He abruptly left the building.

"What are you guys afraid of?" asked the newest bartender.

"That's Molly."

"Who's Molly? . . ."

The TV over the bar flashed a news bulletin. *" . . . Authorities are looking for this man . . ."*

Molly's hand swiftly went into her purse.

"Change the channel! Change the channel! . . ." yelled one of the bartenders.

Trembling fingers fumbled with the remote and clicked coverage over to a Belgian soccer game. Molly withdrew her empty hand.

"I still don't know who Molly is," said the clueless bartender.

"Serge's wife."

"Serge has a wife?"

"Been separated almost a decade, but she refuses to sign the divorce papers. Whatever else you do in this life, don't mention his name . . ."

Back on Big Pine Key:

"Coleman!" Serge jumped up. "That's right! We left that idiot in the Million Dollar Bar on Truman. See, that's the thing about my A-tour of Key West. Coleman's all cool with it at the beginning, but then, 'I just need to lie down a minute,' like when we lost him in the cemetery."

"And I found him snoozing between those crypts," said Brook. "You'd have thought those ant bites would have woken him up."

"Not when he goes to the dark side." Serge flipped open his cell. "So I figured we'd straighten him up with some *café con leche* and get him to the Million Dollar. At least I could count on him staying put there . . . Damn, he's not answering his phone."

"Why do they call it the Million Dollar?" asked Brook. "It's just a small locals' dive."

"Believe it or not, that's what real estate goes for down there." He dialed again. "Hello? Who's this?"

"Don. Who's this?"

"Serge. Is Coleman there?"

"Yeah, he's resting."

"Where?"

"On the pool table."

"I need to talk to him."

"Me, too. You know how hard it is getting urine out of green felt?"

Serge covered his eyes. "I'm good for it. Listen, can you get him in a cab for the Old Wooden Bridge? And pin a note on his shirt saying there's an extra key to cabin five waiting for him in the office."

"I want him out of here more than you do."

"I can understand," said Serge.

"No, you can't. Molly's here."

"Molly! What's she doing there?"

"How should I know? She's your wife. You almost owed me a new flat screen."

"Has she seen Coleman?"

"Hell no! I got Lubs and Boomer at the pool table shielding her view until Mike can drag him out the back."

"I'll make it up to you," said Serge.

"Expect a bill from the pool-table people."

The phone went dead.

Serge heaved a breath of frustration and turned around.

Brook was staring. "Who's Molly?"

"My wife?"

"Your *wife*!"

"Separated for years. Won't sign the papers." Serge grabbed his room key. "The important thing is they're retrieving Coleman."

"Where are you going?"

"I have to get out of here."

"But we're not supposed to show our faces," said Brook. "You keep checking out the blinds."

"Cabin fever is the natural enemy of strategic judgment. Plus there's a really cool place I want to show you!"

He opened the door.

"Serge, there's a tiny deer waiting at the bottom of the steps."

"It's one of the endangered miniature Key deer that only live on Big Pine and No Name Key."

"He seems to know you."

"His name's Sparky. He likes Cheetos." Serge petted the deer on the head as he went past. "You're not supposed to feed or touch them, but those big eyes wear you down."

He led her along the isolated street in growing darkness. Silent except for their footsteps.

Brook looked up at wild palms bending in the cool night breeze. "Where the heck are we going?"

"No Name."

"It doesn't have a name?"

"No, *that's* the name."

Brook chuckled. "Who's on first?"

"It's a pub."

She stopped on the center line. "We're going to a bar? Don't you think that's a little risky?"

"Relax, it's the No Name. You'll see . . ." Serge walked around the side of the building and grabbed the handle on a screen door. "This place is totally cool. They'd never rat me out, and everyone's sly enough not to attract any undue attention toward me."

They stepped inside.

"*Serge!*"

"*You're all over TV!*"

"*Did you really do all that shit?*"

Serge pulled out a stool for Brook. "Can you guys dial it down a tad? I think Interpol heard you."

Brook rotated in place where she sat. "Wow, the bar is completely wallpapered with signed dollar bills. Ceiling, too . . ."

"Mine's up over that little pass-through window to the kitchen where they send out the world's greatest pizzas," said Serge, looking out the screen door as a pink taxi went by.

The cab turned at the corner and parked in front of cabin number five. The dashboard air freshener was a tiny voodoo mask. The driver was from Senegal. "Okay, big fella, enough beauty rest."

"Wha—?" Coleman sat up in the backseat with caramel peanuts in his ears.

The driver steadied Coleman until they reached the picnic table in front of the cottage. Coleman climbed on top and went back to sleep. The cab pulled away.

Back at the No Name, Serge huddled with Brook. "The next step is to anticipate the cops' questions. So we need to rehearse your answers, which means remembering all the public places where there might have been surveillance cameras or witnesses."

"Let's see," said Brook. "We took the tram out to Pigeon Key, toured Fort Martello, went for a biplane ride over the Marquesas atoll, slow-danced in the Green Parrot, had ice cream at the southernmost point, you gave me a piggyback ride on Smathers Beach . . . what's the matter?"

Serge's forehead was on the bar. The same reel of images flickered inside his own skull: one long gooey montage from a chick flick starring Reese Witherspoon, who turns down the Stanford grad for true love with the hometown boy who grinds keys in the hardware store.

She leaned over and rubbed his neck. "Are you okay?"

Serge raised his head. "We have a problem."

"What is it?"

"The kidnapping jazz isn't going to fly."

Brook's face brightened with a big smile. "Then I get to stay with you?"

"No." Serge fiddled with the label on his water bottle. "There's only one alternative left."

"What is it?"

"I have to turn myself in."

"That's crazy," said Brook. "Why would you do that?"

Serge wouldn't look at her. "I've had a good run. No regrets. The sole way to get the heat off you is to give them what they really want."

"I won't let you do it."

"You won't be able to stop me," said Serge. "I'll tell them I lied and manipulated you. They won't go for it—not totally. So in exchange for details about certain cold cases, I'll demand immunity for you."

"Stop talking like that!"

"You're the most decent thing I've got going." Serge took a long sip and stared up at a collage of police patches from across North America. "It's more than worth it. You've got so much to look forward to, and my luck is long past the expiration date."

"There has to be another way."

He shook his head. "A moment comes in every life with a choice that defines who you are, and this is mine."

"But you'll go to prison for life, maybe even death row."

"I've always wanted to be an escape artist."

"Shut up! . . ."

. . . The moon rose behind cabin number five. Coleman pushed himself up on the picnic table. He groaned and pulled out a sticky peanut—"Now I can hear better"—then he looked down at himself.

"What's this?" He plucked the note off the front of his shirt, staggered over to the office and knocked. No answer. He pressed his face to the glass. No lights on. He stumbled back to the cabin and tried the knob. Locked. He sat back down on the picnic table. Something licked his hand. He fed the deer a peanut . . .

. . . Inside the No Name, Brook lit up and raised a finger of epiphany. "I've got it! I know another way out of this!"

Serge guzzled the rest of his water. "Like what?"

"Look at me."

"Yeah?"

Brook got off her stool and stood in front of him. "I want you to beat me up."

"This is no time to joke."

"I couldn't be more serious. Hit me. Hard!"

"What's gotten into you?"

"It'll make them believe the kidnapping tale," said Brook.

"There's no way I'm hitting you. That's final."

"I'll say it's what you did to me after my escape attempt," said Brook. "Then I tried again and succeeded the next day. That way you won't have to turn yourself in, and we can later secretly reunite and be together."

"Even if we did try your plan—which we're not—cops always see right through that," said Serge. "Someone makes a murder look like a robbery by giving themselves a flesh wound in the meaty part of their arm. Really convincing."

"It's convincing if you beat me badly enough."

"You're wasting your breath. My freedom is a small price to pay for your happiness."

"Serge, I love you and can't let you do this for me," said Brook. "Remember a minute ago when you mentioned a choice that defines a life? That's a two-way street, and I've made my choice."

"This conversation's over." Serge brusquely hopped off his stool and threw open the screen door.

The couple didn't speak on the trek back toward the cabin.

Suddenly, a whoosh of wind went by.

The sight stopped them. Flickering blue lights. A police car skidded around the corner into the fishing camp. Then another whoosh and more flashing blue.

"How'd they find us so quickly?" said Brook.

Serge didn't answer as he took off running toward the camp.

Brook shouted ahead into the night: "What are you going to do?"

Serge silently sped up.

Brook broke into her own sprint. "Don't turn yourself in!"

Chapter SIX

CABIN NUMBER FIVE

Serge reached the corner, and sure enough, both police cars were parked at impromptu angles in front of his cottage. The rest of the cabins had emptied a crowd of onlookers that surrounded the eventfulness.

He walked purposefully toward one of the officers.

Brook snapped a whisper from behind: "Don't confess or I'll get mad!"

Serge ignored her and strolled directly to the closest uniform. "Good evening, officer. Is there something I can help you with?"

"Actually there is," said the corporal. "Are you staying in this cabin?"

"Yes, I am."

The officer opened a notebook. "What's your name?"

"Serge A. Storms."

"We've been looking for you."

"I'm sure you have," said Serge. "I'll tell you everything. Where do you want to start?"

Brook stood horrified in the background. She made her right hand into a fist and gave her chin a light test punch. "Ow."

Serge pointed at the officer's belt. "Shouldn't you get out your handcuffs?"

"Depends on how things go."

"That's an enlightened view."

The officer waved. "Follow me."

They walked around the back of the cottage to a tipped-over garbage can. Above it was a jimmied-open window with a pair of thick legs protruding outside. The window had slid closed on the middle of a generous derriere, apparently trapping someone trying to get inside. Legs kicked with anemic energy and rhythm.

The officer looked back at Serge. "Recognize this man?"

He nodded. "I've seen those legs before, and in even less usual context."

A muffled voice from inside the cabin. "Serge, is that you?"

"Coleman, what are you doing?"

"Entering our cabin," said Coleman. "Looks real nice."

"What about your back half?"

"Still working on that." Feet wiggled. "The note on my shirt said there was a spare key in the office, but by the time I regained consciousness, it was closed. Luckily I found this window unlatched, and then it fell down on me when I was crawling through."

"How long have you been stuck?"

"Maybe a half hour."

"What are your plans?" asked Serge.

"Watch TV."

"Not later," said Serge. "I mean right now."

"I *am* watching TV right now. I was able to reach the remote on the arm of the couch." Fart. "You're all over the news, dude."

Serge turned and smiled at the officer.

The officer didn't smile back. "Is this man staying with you?"

Legs kicking harder.

"Unfortunately," said Serge. "Is that what this is about?"

"We got a couple burglary calls." The corporal closed his notebook. "Please latch your windows."

"I think I got it," said Coleman. "I'm coming loose."

"No," said Serge. "Let me come inside and lift it off you."

Crash, thud. The window busted out of its frame and the legs disappeared.

The officer headed for his car. "There goes your deposit."

"Not the first time," said Serge.

The squad cars backed up from the cabin and drove away. The couple went inside.

Coleman pushed the window off his head and got up. "What's for dinner?"

Brook tapped a fist to her nose. "Beat me up."

Serge turned his back and opened the door.

"Where are you going?"

"To get some air."

"Don't give yourself up," said Brook.

"Bring back something to eat," said Coleman.

C rickets.
  Bullfrogs.

Waves lapped a low-tide shore in moonlight. Seaweed wrapped the island-expanding roots of red mangroves that dangled and grabbed down into the surf. Overhead, stars. Billions. The Big Dipper. It told Serge midnight was afoot. He stared out across the black water from the dead end of the ancient ferry ruins at the far edge of No Name Key. He had a gift for reminiscing about times before he was born.

After the Labor Day hurricane of '35 took out the railroad, they decided it should be a highway, since automobiles were now around. Except it couldn't be built in a day. The last gap was the watery run from Marathon to the lower Keys, and for a time, all the cars heading to Key West had to be ferried ashore at this then-bustling port that had since been abandoned to nature. Today's so-called ruins were but strewn and somewhat-submerged concrete with rusty underpinnings. A bunch of boulders were placed on top, at the end of the road, by authorities who feared wrong-way departures from the No Name Pub would end up driving off the island into the drink, which they would.

Serge set a foot upon one of the large stones, an elbow resting on his raised knee. He gazed south at the string of tiny headlights racing down U.S. 1 across the Spanish Harbor Keys. When he left the cabin earlier, his brain was in a vise. But he knew his state's foolproof spots for emergency mental decompression. The foot came off the boulder, and he pivoted for the three-mile return walk to the cottage. After crossing the island, he headed up the incline of the Bogie Channel Bridge. The night fishermen were out in ritual, casting lines and spinning lead-fringed nets into the air. Serge eventually made out cabin five in the distance. "What in the name of—" A solitary porch light blazed. Two people dancing outside. The distant thumps of a cheap boom box skipped across the waves: *". . . Play that funky music, white boy . . ."*

Moments later, Serge strolled up to the scene. Coleman was on his back again, babbling atop the picnic table. On the steps, Brook swigged from a fifth of Jack Daniel's and let a tiny deer lap M&M's from her hand.

"Brook . . ." said Serge.

"Beat me up."

"Did you go somewhere?"

Another swig. "Coleman and me got a cab for Big Pine Liquors and the Winn-Dissy, I mean Dixie."

"You're drunk."

"That's the plan." Brook's attempt to stand landed her on her butt. "I'm not good with pain. And figured you wouldn't feel so bad hitting me if I couldn't feel it."

"There's no chance I'm hitting you."

"Then I'm going to find a flight of stairs or some shit." She raised the bottle again.

"I'll take that." Serge pulled the whiskey from her stubborn fingers. "Now let's get you to bed."

"Beat me up . . ."

Chapter SEVEN

THE NEXT MORNING

Sunshine streamed through thoughtful clouds over the Florida Keys, sending warm shafts into the blinds at the Old Wooden Bridge Fishing Camp.

There was never a gradual awakening for Serge. His eyes would just spring open and he was into the day. He looked through the open bathroom door where Coleman was still snoring. Then his eyes wandered toward the other bed.

Empty.

But how?

Brook had been pretty smashed when he'd tucked her in. He would have sworn she'd outsleep him by hours.

Serge searched the rest of the cottage. Then around the outside. Then around the fishing camp. The sky was clear and a stiff onshore wind cut the heat. Perfect day to be on the water. Serge stopped and scratched his head. Sportsmen fueled center-console fishing skiffs near the big Texaco gas tank. They clomped down the dock carrying fly rods and coolers and frozen bait. Others rented orange-and-yellow kayaks, paddling out of the still harbor and into the heavy chop of Bogie Channel that quickly swept them off with the changing tide whether it was their intention or not.

Serge climbed the wooden steps of a clapboard building and entered the bottom-floor marina and motel office. Customers stood in line for ChapStick and nautical maps, fishing weights and bobbers, coffee, postcards, polarized sunglasses, advice. Someone opened a refrigerated case for sodas.

The last angler left and gave Serge the counter.

Julie rehung a sun visor that someone had second thoughts about. She returned with a smile. "You seem lost."

Serge stared down in concern. He looked up. "Julie, did you happen to see the woman I arrived with yesterday? Maybe taking a morning stroll?"

"No, why? Another one get away?"

Julie had never seen Serge anything less than radiantly confident. Now he was worried. "It's probably nothing." He went back to the cabin as Coleman sat up dazed on the bathroom tiles.

"Coleman, you know where Brook is?"

He removed a Lincoln penny from his mouth and examined it. "She's gone?"

"Did you go anywhere last night besides the liquor and grocery stores?"

"No, I mean, yeah, we stopped back in the No Name Pub again."

"Anything happen?"

"Not really." Coleman put the penny in his pocket, where he discovered a melted Klondike bar. "I wanted to eat that."

"Think hard," said Serge. "This is important."

"Well, we met some of the regulars: Yulee, Fellsmere, Daytona Dave, Sop Choppy, Bob and Shirtless Bob—"

"Fine," Serge said impatiently. "Did anything happen?"

"She was chatting with a lot of people, but after all she's pretty cute." Coleman grabbed a bottle of hair of the dog. "Then some of them took a table in back and leaned closer like they had secrets and then Sop Choppy—that's the big biker—"

"I know who he is. What did they do?"

"He called someone on his cell and handed it to Brook, who talked like forever, but that's really all."

"And none of this seemed unusual to you?"

"Not really." Coleman reached in the fridge for a Schlitz. "It's the No Name."

"Great." Serge opened all the blinds and plopped down on the sofa; the water on the other side of the windows grew choppier, kayakers screaming in the channel as they were swept out to Florida Bay. "Where on earth can she be?"

Tires squealed as a muscle car whipped around the corner and skidded up in the gravel just before hitting the picnic table.

Coleman pointed with his beer. "Maybe that's her."

Serge bolted out of the cabin.

The driver's door opened.

Serge sagged. "Oh, it's just you, Faber."

"Oh, it's just *me*?" said Joe. "I was expecting a little more gratitude, like, 'Hey, I know you're running a couple of really busy bars, but thanks for risking your neck collecting the luggage of a known fugitive and throwing it in the trunk of a cool new ride you just hooked me up with.' It's a seventy-six Cobra, by the way. Next time a Pinto."

"No really, thanks," said Serge. "I just got my mind on something—"

Joe threw the car keys like he was still pitching for Miami. Serge ducked and Coleman grabbed his forehead. "Ow, shit!"

Faber stomped up the street to check on his bartenders.

Serge followed him, and Coleman followed Serge. "Where are you going?"

"To talk to Sop Choppy. He has some explaining."

The screen door flew open with a bang. "There you are!"

Sop Choppy looked up from a mug of beer. Eyes got big. "Serge, uh, what are you doing here?"

"Surprised to see me?"

"Yeah, you're supposed to be in hiding."

"You better start talking. Fast!"

"About what?"

"Last night, Brook."

"Oh, that." Sop Choppy relaxed and hoisted his mug. "Don't worry about it. All taken care of, just like you wanted."

"What are you talking about?" said Serge. "I didn't ask you for anything."

"Brook relayed your message. I thought I was doing you a favor. Why? Did I do something wrong?"

"What *did* you do?"

"Oh my God," said Sop Choppy. "Then this is bad . . ."

Faber was behind the counter filling out a vacation schedule. A beer mug shattered. He turned to see Serge jerk Sop Choppy off his stool and drag him toward the men's room. The owner threw up his arms and went back in the kitchen.

Several miles away, on the side of U.S. 1, a timid knock on a door at a signless motel. A man in shorts answered. Shaved head and prison tats running up his neck. More ink formed a teardrop next to his left eye. A scar from a box cutter ran from one corner of his mouth to his ear. He took a drag on the stub of a Marlboro pinched in his fingers.

"You Brook?"

She nodded. "You Bones?"

"Still time to change your mind."

Brook gulped and shook her head. "I got your money." She began opening her purse.

"Not here." He glanced outside, then waved her into the room. "You're going to want a drink first. Maybe a few . . ."

. . . A blue-and-white Ford Cobra raced south on Big Pine Key. Coleman made the rare decision to buckle his seat belt without being told. They went hard around a corner, and the shoulder strap cut into his chest.

"Serge, you might want to slow down. I mean you usually drive fast, but—"

"Shut up."

Serge quickly arrived at the motel room supplied by Sop Choppy. No knocking, just straight to kicking in the door.

Coleman moseyed up. "Where is she?"

"Too late," said Serge.

They looked around. The room would not be back in service for a while. Broken lamps and mirror, holes in drywall, legs busted off a chair. The blood might wash out of the sheets but not the mattress.

Serge smelled the air. Fresh cigarette smoke. "We just missed them."

They ran back outside and jumped in the car. Serge pulled to the edge of U.S. 1.

"What are you waiting for?"

"It's a fifty-fifty shot." Serge frantically glanced left and right. "Which way would I go? . . . I'd want an escape route."

He cut the wheel and sped east.

Coleman rubbed his shoulder. "Where are we going?"

"To where he's going to drop her."

"I don't know what's happening."

Serge's eyes locked on to the road with tunnel vision, weaving across the double orange line to pass slower cars and narrowly missing an on-coming dump truck. Bahia Honda, Ohio and Missouri Keys, Little Duck. They hit the Seven Mile Bridge, and the needle hit a hundred. Halfway across, with Pigeon Key in sight, dozens of red taillights came on. Serge slammed the brakes with both feet and skidded to within inches of a Mazda's bumper.

Traffic at a dead standstill and nothing coming the other way.

Coleman stuck his head out the window. "The road's jammed up forever. Think it's a wreck? . . . Serge? . . . *Serge?* . . ."

Coleman turned to see an open driver's door. He watched through the windshield as Serge sprinted up the center line. He ran past fifty cars until stopping behind the police line. He could do nothing as paramedics slid a stretcher into the ambulance.

Part TWO

ONE YEAR LATER

Chapter EIGHT

SOMEWHERE ALONG U.S. 1 IN MIAMI

And another thing that pisses me off," said Serge. "Ticket companies. Like when you go to buy your Skynyrd tickets online, they make you re-type some made-up security word that's written all crazy, like you're trying to read a newspaper through a motel-door peephole, and I can never figure out the fucking thing. Does that say 'Quittle shnatzume'? And then I get one of the letters wrong and they give me another chance. 'Xydolak prunsassi,' and I get that wrong. 'Btsabi glohelf,' 'Mentracu Twatinger.' And by the time I type it right, the only remaining seats are in the top row, and then I destroy another keyboard."

Coleman was wearing a felt jester's hat, and the bells jingled as he chugged a beer bong. "I hear they'll soon have pot vending machines in Colorado."

"Coleman?"

"What?"

"I was talking to you."

"Right, we're having a conversation. You said something and then I said something."

"No," said Serge. "What you said had absolutely nothing to do with what I just said. In a conversation, it at least has to be vaguely related."

"Really?" Coleman wiped foam from his mouth. "That would explain a lot."

"Like if I was at a black-tie charity ball with canapés and spinach dip, and I bring up the ticket bullshit to a socialite in a strapless gown with an apple martini, she'd volley back a cultured response about her favorite Skynyrd concert or motel peepholes or that she once employed a lotion boy of unknown origin named Mentracu Twatinger."

"That's why they're so rich."

"The whole key to social climbing is not having spinach in your teeth." Serge killed the rest of his coffee. "See, the beauty of a good conversation is that it may wander all over the place, and after numerous chess-move segues"—Serge made a gentle curving motion with his right hand—"then you can work the conversation back around to the pot machines. Let's try again."

"Okay," said Coleman. "Fuck ticket companies."

"That's better," said Serge.

"I heard they make us type the weird security words because robots were buying up all the best tickets."

"And what's with that convenience charge?" said Serge. "It's so big you'd expect the president of the ticket company to fly in and hand-deliver them himself."

"Except I've never seen robots watching a concert."

"Because they're all sitting in the front row," said Serge. "My thinking is if the robots have figured that out, then bad seats for Beyoncé are the least of our problems."

"And God forbid if they get to the pot machines," said Coleman.

"Now, *this* is a conversation," said Serge.

"How far is Colorado?"

Serge continued along Federal Highway, where the sidewalk hosted robust pedestrian traffic. Other places they're heading to work or home or lunch, maybe to pick up dry cleaning. Not here. Just walking, cutting through motel parking lots and alleys, stopping to meet on street corners and behind steel-barred convenience stores to form brief, random alliances for continuing adventures of backward progress.

A block west of the highway sat a three-bedroom bungalow. An extension cord ran from the blind side of the garage next door, through a chain-link fence and into a back window. A Cobra pulled up in the driveway.

Coleman strolled into the kitchen, where the extension cord made the refrigerator hum. He opened the door for a cold one. "The black light is trippy."

"It's for my new diet book," said Serge.

Knock, knock, knock!

Coleman jumped. "Who can that be?"

"I have a special technique to find out." Serge walked to the front door and opened it. "Hello!"

"Do you live here?" asked a dour man with a notepad.

"Yes, I do!"

"Do you plan on paying the bank any money before next Friday?"

"Let me think." Serge stared up and twiddled his thumbs. "Uh, no! You can write that down as a definite."

He handed Serge a court document. "Then you have eleven days to move out or the sheriff will evict you."

"Sounds fair to me." Serge grinned wide. "Have yourself a great one, douchebag!"

He closed the door and returned to the dining room, sitting cross-legged on the floor in front of an array of paperwork.

Coleman plopped down next to him, splashing beer. "Tell me again how we're able to stay here for free."

"Foreclosures are rampant in Florida, and it just takes a little records search and surveillance to find the people who have simply split and abandoned their house, wasting perfectly good digs that still have weeks left before the legal eviction deadline." Serge rearranged pages on the floor. "Don't get me wrong: I love our roach motels, but sometimes it's good to stretch out."

"What about that guy at the door?" said Coleman. "I can't believe he didn't throw us out or call the cops. We don't own this place."

"He didn't ask that," said Serge. "He just asked if we live here. We do."

"How'd you figure this scheme out?"

"It's been heavily covered in the news: People all over Florida are doing it since our skyrocketing housing defaults have ushered in the new age of squatters, and the police have essentially washed their hands of the whole mess, leaving it to the banks and process servers. One woman even had a lawyer cite a century-old homesteading law meant for pioneers driving cattle."

Coleman looked around.

"No cows."

"Right." Coleman uncapped a flask. "What's all those papers?"

Serge continued transposing their placement on the hardwood floor. "My renewed plan for global domination. Another reason for the house. When you invite the diplomats over to bend them to your will, an island kitchen says much more than Motel 6."

Coleman leaned forward with a jingle of bells. "How's it going?"

"Pretty good, actually." Serge picked up of one of the pages. "Here's the most recent findings of the blue-ribbon commission consisting of me: 'Economic turmoil, unstable foreign governments and fractured politics at home all combine to create a fertile window of opportunity for a new leader to emerge.'"

"Sounds like you're on your way," said Coleman.

Serge picked up another page. "Here's the downside: 'Extensive research shows we don't have jobs and are almost out of money.'"

Coleman drained the flask and made a face. "We've done all right before."

"That's the spirit." Serge stood and tossed Coleman a navy-blue windbreaker.

"What's this?"

"The key to cash flow. Put it on."

Coleman searched for an armhole. "How is this supposed to make us money?"

"The windbreaker is the natural extension of clipboards, orange safety vests and traffic cones," said Serge. "They're readily available, but everyone assumes that if you have one, you're officially authorized to be doing whatever it is you're up to."

"But it's just a jacket."

"Not just *any* jacket." Serge slipped on his own. "Read the back."

Coleman turned it over. In large block yellow letters: BAIL RECOVERY AGENT. "What's that mean?"

"Bounty hunter," said Serge. "I got to thinking. The legal system in our country is just spraying money like an oil geyser. How can we catch some of it?"

"Clipboards and cones are one thing," said Coleman. "But we could get in trouble for pretending to be these agents."

Serge raised a finger of triumph. "And therein lies the loophole. We could get arrested for impersonation if our windbreakers said FBI or ATF or police, but bounty hunters don't work for the government."

"That's some loophole," said Coleman, slipping his right arm in the left sleeve.

"Let me give you a hand with that." Serge turned the jacket around on Coleman's back. "It's just another glaring opportunity missed by the general populace. There's no law against pretending to be a civilian professional. For all the cops care, you can order as many windbreakers as you want that say 'Pet Grooming Agent.'"

Coleman poked a hand out the end of a sleeve. "Where'd you get *this* idea?"

"My new Master Plan. I've completely rededicated my life to the practice of law. Except they won't let me be a lawyer just because I forgot to go to law school."

"That's just not right."

"Tell me about it," said Serge. "If you practice law without a license, they arrest you. And *then* you're allowed to be a lawyer and represent yourself. What is that bullshit?"

Coleman burped with another jingle of bells. "Okay, so we're wearing jackets. Now what?"

"Continue my alternate legal education." He stuck a stun gun in his pocket. "I've been watching a lot of Florida movies concerning crime and punishment. Elmore Leonard's bestselling novel *Rum Punch* was set in Riviera Beach and the Palm Beach Gardens mall. In the film version, Tarantino resurrected the career of journeyman actor Robert Forster in the lead role of street-smart bail bondsman Max Cherry. So I figured I'd start there and learn American jurisprudence from the ground up until I'm ready to argue before a jury. Let's rock."

They headed down the street.

"Where are we going?"

"To catch a bail jumper."

"You know where one is?"

"Yes and no." Serge pulled a fake document from his pocket. "I don't have any particular suspect in my sights. But mathematically, at any particular time, there is the nearest bail jumper to you. Might be ten miles, might be one. Except the odds are much better in Florida, where you can throw a rock in any all-night waffle joint and it'll ricochet off three fugitives."

They turned the corner at U.S. 1 and headed up the sidewalk.

"I'm still worried about one thing." Coleman pulled an airline miniature from his pocket for nerves. "The impersonation might not be against the law, but we're both wanted. We'll be calling attention to ourselves."

"Another perk of the windbreakers," said Serge. "Who would ever expect fugitives to be posing as bounty hunters?"

TAMPA

The music came first.

It droned faintly in the distance, pounding, thumping rhythms. Drums and bass guitars from a large number of stereos.

As the sound grew closer, higher frequencies revealed themselves. Other instruments and vocals kicked in. Rock, rap, country, techno-dance, alternative FM, Christian rock. All growing louder in a swirling sonic mush, fusing themselves into a single new genre about partying all night with gangsta bitches screwing cowboys to the nasty beat that leads to Jesus.

Then headlights.

Halogen beams swung around the dark corner of a building, leading a massive flock of other lights. Expensive new cars, clunkers and in-between-mileage used models with encumbered titles. But everything sporty. No SUVs or boxy sedans. Nothing big except the Jeeps.

They fanned out and raced at uncoordinated vectors with disregard to the markings on the pavement. Several near misses as usual. Brakes screeched, steering wheels jerked, shouting and hand gestures out windows. Right on schedule. The regular Saturday-night landing wave of teens had arrived at the Macroplex 30 Cinema.

The cars spit out high schoolers with faces aglow in the light of a hundred cell phones. They texted and chatted across the parking lot as social gravity pulled them into naturally forming clumps. Jocks, stoners, brains, Goths, cheerleaders and gay kids, who suddenly found themselves 50 percent popular, which unfortunately was the average of only two levels of tolerance, zero and a hundred.

The respective groups commenced tribal rituals to create the illusion they were in demand. Guys did complicated handshakes and got themselves in occasional headlocks; girls shrieked and hugged and called out friends' names that could be traced to a paranormal event a decade and a half earlier, which tugged expectant parents toward the same hard consonant and diphthongs: Kaylee, Kylee, Casey, Caitlin, Kayla and another Kaylee but with a *C*. They bought tickets and popcorn.

The cinema was weighted toward movies starring young people who were vampires, could do ancient magic, paid off debts to the syndicate by street racing and went on spring break. The few adults at the theater filed into a pair of ill-attended movies about difficult choices made by three generations of estranged relatives and an Elizabethan costume-fest about a seventeenth-century British countess who feels drawn to Bavaria for some reason.

Outside in the parking lot, a few late arrivals straggled toward the ticket booth. But generally it was that calmed-down period between the movies' start times. A security guard drove by in a golf cart. He passed an empty Lexus and made a left at the end of the row. Three men in the Lexus sat back up. When the crush of kids had arrived fifteen minutes earlier, the telephoto lens of a digital camera had poked out the top of a tinted window. *Click, click, click.* Now it sat on the dash. The photos matched kids with cars. The man who took the shots studied the screen of his laptop, which displayed hundreds of downloaded close-ups. He wore Italian shoes, a breathable black polo shirt and the merciless thin line of a mouth. His coal-black hair was parted down the middle so that bangs covered forceps depressions from a non-glitch-free delivery forty-eight years ago. The name on the birth certificate was Linus Quim, but he recently started going by Bannon. He was the leader.

In the passenger seat sat another man named Bannon who wasn't allowed to use his name anymore. On his legs lay yearbooks from the two nearest high schools, along with parent-teacher directories of phone numbers. The public wasn't supposed to have the directories, but enough money to the wrong students made them available. The man formerly known as Bannon held an open annual next to the laptop. "I think this one's a match."

"You think?"

"Top row, middle. Virtually certain."

"You're right." Bannon pulled up another photo on the laptop and enlarged the back of the teen's car. "Mark it."

The passenger wrote *yellow Volkswagen Beetle,* then the license plate. He paged through the school directory and found the parents' home phone number.

"Next photo," said Bannon, scrolling through his laptop gallery.

The passenger began flipping through yearbooks again. Bannon looked back at a third person in the backseat. "Yellow Volks."

The man nodded without speaking and got out. He casually strolled toward the theater, stopping next to the Beetle to light a cigarette in a casual ruse as he surreptitiously glanced inside the vehicle for anything distinctive.

It was tedious work, and they mostly shot blanks. Many of the teens were from other schools. Plus yearbook photos were almost worse than driver's licenses. Plus the sheer numbers, which they winnowed however they could. The students in their photos were all driving, so that pretty much ruled out freshmen, and gender cut the rest in half. It still left more than five hundred photos to fish through for names. The one thing on their side:

Time.

Bannon checked his Bulova watch. Allowing for previews and commercials, the shortest movie that started around nine still had an hour left. He glanced toward the lobby. An eighty-year-old ticket taker tore another stub, wondering whether he had eaten the last piece of meringue in his fridge. Bannon squeezed Visine on his corneas and returned to the laptop.

Inside the theater, teenagers cheered for a street-racing vampire. The British countess discovered that Bavaria was cold.

Ten minutes later, Bannon checked his watch again and closed the laptop. "Time's up."

The passenger read his notebook. "We got five."

"Five?" said Bannon. "From over sixty kids we photographed?"

"I'd say that's good," opined a voice from the backseat. "We came up empty three weeks ago."

"I wasn't asking." Bannon put the Lexus in gear and pulled around the other side of the mall.

The theater idea had been a breakthrough. Until a month ago, their surveillance operation had taken forever. But now the parking lot generated a much higher sampling and extra good looks at the vehicles. Then there was the biggest advantage of all from working the movies.

"Let's get hopping," said Bannon. "We've only got a half hour until they start turning their cell phones back on."

Chapter NINE

MIAMI

Coleman unsnapped his windbreaker in the heat. "We didn't catch any bail jumpers today."

"I forgot they're nocturnal," said Serge. "Traveling great ranges on hidden trails through numerous habitats. Then they burrow in during the light of day and allow their brains to reboot from the last shift's chemical fog. But now that it's night again, our luck should change."

"You're really smart."

The sidewalks began to awaken again with the pedestrian subculture. Strangers continued meeting by chance and bonding like unstable, short-life molecules. It was a lifestyle that intuitively knew navy windbreakers had block letters on the back, and the oncoming stream of foot traffic split in half to give Serge and Coleman a wide berth.

"Hey!" Coleman pointed. "There's your car. What's it doing at that place?"

"I strategically positioned it ahead of time."

"In front of the dumpy motel we were going to stay at before we found the house?"

"Every budget motel in Florida is required to have at least one bail jumper." Serge unfolded a page from his pocket. "The ones with the most jumpers are those establishments whose guests pull furniture from the rooms and sit outside their doors to increase negative possibilities."

Coleman clanged an empty miniature into a garbage can. "So how do you plan to find this motel's jumper?"

"He'll find us."

Serge veered into the motel's parking lot and read the document in his hand. Then he reached in his pocket again and took out a photograph.

"But that's a picture of you," said Coleman.

"They don't know that." Serge produced another photo and handed it to his buddy.

"It's a picture of me." Coleman self-consciously squeezed his cheeks. "Is that how I look?"

"Just walk slow and keep glancing back and forth from that photo to each person we come across." Serge squinted at a group of shirtless men milling beside a low-riding pickup. "And keep turning around so they can read the backs of our jackets."

"Most of them are staring at us," said Coleman.

"And the rest are intentionally looking away," said Serge. "That means it's working."

A motel door opened near the pickup, and a man in a mechanic's shirt stepped outside with a quart bottle.

"Serge, that guy just took off."

"We've got a runner!"

The mechanic sprinted along the front of the motel, hurdling people sitting outside their doors. He kept glancing back at the self-appointed bounty hunter gaining on him. The man's feet slid in dirt as he tried to round the end of the building, and Serge dove for the tackle.

"All right, you!" Serge yanked him to his feet and poked the stun gun in his rib. "No funny stuff."

They marched back to the Cobra, where Serge popped the trunk. "In you go!" The hood slammed.

"Serge, you just threw a guy in your trunk in broad daylight."

"And normally that would attract attention." Serge opened the driver's door. "But look around. The overarching reaction is one of personal relief."

Coleman climbed in his side of the car. "Okay, you grabbed a guy who ran away from us. But I don't see the money part."

"Here's his wallet." Serge pulled out the driver's license. "Well, well, Mr. Nicholas Sharp, glad to have you on board . . ."

An hour later, a '76 Cobra rolled past the county jail featuring vertical window slits too narrow for a human. Surrounding the detention center was a scattering of squat concrete huts. Each had a phone number painted extra large so it could be read from the window slits.

Serge pulled up in front of Ricky's Bail Bonds. Dobermans barked and hurled themselves against the neighboring fence of a hubcap emporium. Next to the painted phone number was a large floating face with a broad smile, presumably Ricky, for the impression of a more upbeat business, like off-brand whole life insurance.

Coleman grabbed his door handle. "How'd you know to come here?"

"That phone call I made to Mahoney on the way over," said Serge. "Had him check around for outstanding warrants. Bondsmen now share Internet databases to cut losses."

Bells jingled and a prune-headed man looked up from a desk cluttered with courthouse forms, sandwich wrappers and crumbs. A rotating table fan whirred in the corner.

"Ricky?" asked Serge.

"No, Benny." The man stuffed a last bite of chicken salad in his mouth and hit one of the sandwich wrappers with a flyswatter. "Who the hell are you?"

Serge turned around to show him the back of his jacket.

"Bounty hunters?"

"Not really. We just bought the jackets at one of those police supply stores where police never shop, only weirdos who blog in their skivvies about the feds and black helicopters and go to those stores to buy nunchucks and samurai swords that you never see on a cop's belt, but then again I've never been arrested in Malaysia."

The swatter knocked over a bobblehead of a Miami Heat player. "Why are you telling me this?" The man stood up and went on a mission with the insect weapon.

"Because I'm just about to save you twenty grand."

Benny lost interest in the fly. "You got three minutes."

Serge took a seat and slowly looked around the single-room office. "This is just like *Jackie Brown,* the movie based on the classic Elmore Leonard book that was set in my hometown. Can I call you Max Cherry?"

"Two minutes."

"Talk on the street is you'd like to have a word with one Nicky Sharp."

Benny put the impatience on hold. "You know where Nicky Sharp is? That shitbag skipped out on twenty G's!"

"If I'm not mistaken, the standard fee is ten percent of whatever you stood to lose." Serge crossed his legs and interlaced fingers behind his head. "I can bring him in if you want."

"Can't do it," said Benny.

"Sure I can," said Serge. "It'll be easy."

"No, I mean it's against the law. You said you weren't a real bounty hunter."

"So?"

"So, under Florida statute you can't apprehend someone unless you have a bail-bond license. I could go to jail if I accept a capture from you."

"But I know a bunch of guys who are only bounty hunters."

Benny nodded. "A lot of guys get their bondsman license with no intention of opening a bail office, just so they can nab fugitives."

"That's legal?"

"Tell you what: Nicky's forfeiture put a big hurt on my monthly nut. So if you can provide a pinpoint location and it's an easy apprehension— and you're not involved in any way that would get me in trouble—I'll go that ten percent."

Serge stretched as he stood. "Oh, I think I might be able to pinpoint him for you."

A minute later, they stood at the Cobra's trunk.

"What are you doing?" asked Benny. "I thought you said we were going for a drive."

"I actually said we were going to the *car*." Serge popped the trunk. "Already in plastic wrist restraints. Is that an easy enough apprehension?"

"Jesus Christ!" Benny slammed the trunk and pointed toward the jail. "Are you crazy? They can see!"

"Okay." Serge shrugged and headed for his driver's door. "If you don't want him . . ."

"Didn't say that." Benny quickly glanced both ways. "Pull around back."

The '76 Ford Cobra cruised south on U.S. 1, Serge thumbing a wad of cash and swilling his new brand of Dunkin' Donuts coffee. He noticed something up ahead and handed the currency to Coleman. "Stick that in the glove compartment."

"Man, I can't believe this money was just sitting out there." He popped the latch. "And barely any work."

"But I still feel the process has too much fat on the bone." The muscle car jumped a curb and screeched to a stop.

"Another budget motel?" asked Coleman.

Serge jumped out and spun on one foot in a triple ballerina pirouette, brightly announcing the words on the back of his jacket as it flapped behind him. Then he fell to his right knee, closed one eye and pointed accusingly at each person outside a room.

A shirtless man took off running.

So did Serge. *"I love this state! . . ."*

Lights remained low inside a two-story Mediterranean Revival home on the west side of the peninsula. The owners had paid four hundred thousand when it was first constructed fifteen years ago, then watched its value rocket to seven-fifty, then fall back to four.

The dimness was cut by the flickering of a giant plasma TV in the living room. A married couple of nineteen years sat shoeless on the sofa watching an old James Bond movie where Paul McCartney sings the theme song. Two plates of mostly eaten rigatoni sat on the coffee table. The woman got up with an empty glass. "Would you like some more wine?"

"Sure." The husband hit pause as she took his glass and headed for the built-in, temperature-controlled wine cabinet with see-through doors.

The phone rang.

"I'll get it." She changed direction and picked up the receiver. "Hello?"

"Is this Mrs. Madison?"

"Yes?"

"Does your daughter drive a convertible yellow Volkswagen?"

"Uh . . . who is this?"

"There's been an accident."

"What! Where! Is she okay?"

"Not really. She's unconscious and bleeding. Doesn't look good."

Mr. Madison jumped up from the couch. "What's going on?"

"Caylee's been in an accident," said his wife. Then back in the phone: "Is an ambulance there?"

"No."

"How long ago did you call?"

"I didn't."

"Why not?"

"Because I personally don't have the need," said the caller. "I'm fine, but my passenger airbag failed to deploy."

"What's that mean?" asked Mrs. Madison.

"It means your stupid fucking brat blew a stop sign and killed my wife . . ."

"Your wife's dead?"

" . . . So now I'm standing here staring at your spoiled rich kid, wondering whether to call that ambulance. But currently I'm leaning toward wanting you to feel what I'm going through right now."

"Please!" shrieked Mrs. Madison. "You have to call an ambulance."

Mr. Madison got the drift and snatched the phone away. "Who is this!"

"Someone watching your daughter circle the drain."

"You son of a bitch!"

"That's no way to persuade me to call an ambulance."

Mr. Madison clenched his teeth with focus. "What do you want?"

"Ten thousand dollars wired immediately."

"Bullshit!" Mr. Madison whispered sharply to his wife, "Get my cell phone and call Caylee."

"Good thinking," said the caller. "That's what I'd do."

"How do I know it's really my daughter?"

"You don't. It could be any yellow Beetle with a sunflower in that stupid dashboard holder and some other girl wearing a tie-dye Smashing Pumpkins T-shirt . . ."

Mrs. Madison's panic in the background: "Bruce, she's not answering!"

"Bruce," said the caller. "I think I hear something. Sounds like a cell phone somewhere down on the floor of the car. Oh, and we're way, way out in the country down this farm road. I wouldn't be expecting any motorists to happen upon us anytime soon."

"Okay, listen," said Mr. Madison. "I'll get you the money."

"Thataboy, Bruce."

"But you have to call an ambulance in the meantime. I swear I'll still wire the payment."

"No dice."

"We don't have time!"

"Couldn't agree more, Bruce. So you probably want to stop wasting it on the phone. From the high school parking sticker on her car, I'm guessing there's a wire place open at this hour no more than five minutes from most of the homes in that district. Here's the address and the number you'll be sending to. I'll call your cell when it arrives. Got something to write with? . . ."

Mr. Madison reached the wire office in less than three minutes.

"Are you okay?" asked the clerk at the transfer desk.

"Here," said an ashen Bruce, slapping three credit cards on the counter and a piece of paper. "Try the Visa first and send ten thousand to this number."

The clerk stared at him.

"Hurry! It's important!"

"Okay, okay, Jesus . . ." The clerk rushed through the procedure and pressed a final button to complete the electronic marvel. "There. It's off. Would you like a receipt?"

Bruce jumped as a cell phone went off in his pocket. He got it out as fast as possible, momentarily fumbling it in the air, then pressed it to his head. "The money just went through! Call the ambulance!"

"What?" said a young female voice.

"Caylee?" said her father. "Where are you! What are you doing?"

"I just got out of the movie and turned my phone back on," said the teen. "Then I immediately called you like you always tell me to."

A total of five such calls shattered the evening in nice homes across south Tampa. One of the dads was a lawyer and figured out the scam in time. Another was able to reach his daughter by phone because she ditched the movie to make out with a boy she wasn't allowed to see. That left three payments totaling $30,000 that were picked up by an associate in Costa Rica. Not bad for a day's dirty work.

Bannon was already reclining on his own south Tampa sofa when he received the last confirmation from Central America. It came in on the same disposable cell phone that he had just used to give a bunch of parents heart attacks. "Thanks, Sanchez . . ." Bannon held a second, just-out-of-the-box disposable phone in his other hand. "Same time next Saturday. Take down this new number . . ."

Then he sank smugly into his couch and resumed watching the Golf Channel. Someone in knickers extolled the virtues of keeping knees properly bent in a sand bunker as Bannon broke apart a cell phone with his hands.

Chapter TEN

DOWNTOWN MIAMI

A run-down two-story office building stood in the shadow of a drawbridge on the bank of the Miami River. Junkyards and auto salvage and Jamaican trawlers moored to the shore. Unfed guard dogs barked. The drawbridge began to rise, and motorists cursed in six languages. The office building's population had dwindled to a handful of tenants in the heat of the summer.

The reason: no air-conditioning.

The building was circa World War II, and the original interiors had been accidentally preserved due to landlord neglect and depressed economics of the sketchy river district. Spiderweb cracks spread across the old lath-and-plaster walls.

As the sun reached its zenith, heat seemed to well up from the ground. One of the upstairs transom windows was open, and a large plantation fan whapped out of kilter. Below the fan sat a high-usage oak desk chronicled by numerous overlapping coffee-mug stains. Next to a half-empty bottle of rye were the current tenant's propped-up feet, wearing old oxfords with an Adlai Stevenson hole in the sole. The office

door had a pebbled-glass window with flecked gold lettering: MA-
HONEY & ASSOCIATES, PRIVATE INVESTIGATIONS.

A single fedora rested atop the hat rack in the corner.

Mahoney leaned back in his chair and flipped through a deck of
playing cards with girlie pictures. Attractive, topless women back when
their eating habits were healthy. He slapped down the queen of spades,
who covered her key parts with Japanese foldout fans.

A pith helmet Frisbee'd through the air and landed on the hat rack
next to the fedora. Mahoney peered up with a steely glint. "Doctor Liv-
ingston, I presume?"

"What, this?" said Serge, looking down at his new Rudyard Kipling
ensemble. His right hand held a capture pole with a rope loop. "It's my
new safari suit."

Mahoney flipped over the queen of hearts to find a pinup with a
feather boa.

Serge pointed. "Do I see coffee?" He reached for a cold mug atop
another brown desk circle, and drained it in one long guzzle. "So I
decided to treat myself to new threads. Bet you're dying to know
why I went with the big-game hunter look. I'll tell you! Every lawyer
and future lawyer needs an exotic sport to cement his image, and
I'm going on that big python hunt in the Everglades. But I know
what you're thinking: The python hunt is over—and what a travesty! They barely caught anything. Here we are supposedly in the
middle of some apocalyptic invasion of Burmese pythons slithering
through the suburbs in such staggering numbers that there must
be an eight-hundred-pound snake under every kitchen sink with
a poodle-shaped lump in its stomach, and state officials offer eye-
popping cash prizes to unleash our entire population, which mus-
ters at the rallying points like that scene from *Jaws* where they post
the bounty on the shark, and a million people show up at the docks
with ridiculous fishing equipment like axes and shotguns. And then
our great python hunt is over, and we only come up with sixty-eight
of the suckers. We've had more than our share of national shame
over the years, but sixty-eight is just embarrassing—"

Serge was interrupted by a heavy scurrying sound across the floor. Mahoney looked down at the edge of his desk. Coleman crawled around the corner and glanced up with a grimace.

"Don't mind him," said Serge, pouring another mug of coffee from Mahoney's checkered thermos. "He just received a shipment of drugs from the Internet. I warned him you never know what you're getting when you order off the Web."

Coleman emitted a panicked, scratchy whine, then spun around on his knees and scurried back out of sight.

Serge chugged the second mug. "I found the box Coleman received in the mail and looked at him: 'Dude, they're pet meds. You have heartworms or something?' But he just said, 'Fuck it. I'm taking 'em anyway.' And now we have this."

The scurrying sound disappeared down the hallway. The queen of diamonds flipped over.

Serge slammed the empty mug on the desk. "When we arrived at your office, I got worried because this place was built before modern code enforcement, which means the window ledges are really low and Coleman could easily tumble out. But then I started thinking about the meds he got in the mail and it reminded me of a trick you can play on cats. It's mean if you actually do it to animals, but it's an act of mercy where Coleman's concerned."

The scurrying returned from the hall. Coleman crawled back around the desk. Mahoney noticed he wasn't wearing a shirt. A long strip of duct tape ran down the length of his back.

"Serge, help!" said Coleman. "I'm stuck underneath something really low."

"You're doing fine," said Serge. "Just proceed as you are and you'll be out from below it in no time."

"Thanks, Serge." The crawling noise returned to the hall.

"No window falls for Coleman today." Serge stood and gathered his capture stick. "Well, snakes are a-waitin' . . ." He scratched his temple with the end of the pole. "But I'm a kill-free animal lover, so what will I do with the hundreds of Burmese pythons I'm sure to nab?"

He stopped scratching and grabbed his pith helmet off the hat rack. "Guess I'll mail them back to Burma."

A black rotary desk phone rang.

Mahoney let it ring at least nine times, as he always did, because an answered phone held finite possibilities. But a ringing phone was limited only by imagination, and Mahoney dreamed out loud: "Foggy piers, leggy dames, filterless cigarettes, brass knuckles, a lake being dragged, a villain with a monocle, a hooker trying to better herself with typing classes . . ."

"Jumping Judas!" yelled Serge. "Answer the thing already! You don't know how batshit that makes me!"

Mahoney sneered and grabbed the receiver. "It's your dime. Start gargling . . ."

"Please, we need your help. Last Saturday night . . ."

"The story had all the elements," said Mahoney. "Sympathetic victim, ruthless grifters, juicy revenge angle. I snagged a fresh toothpick and chewed on the tearjerker until my pie hole had the taste of a stripper's breath after a week's run on the broken dreams end of Reno, and my guts twisted up like the inside of the same stripper's stomach after the ninety-nine-cent sunrise special in a Hoboken hash house . . ."

On the other end of the line: *"What?"*

"We'll take the case." He hung up.

Serge was waiting. "Are you going to tell me?"

"Park the caboose."

Serge sat down again. Mahoney laid out the tribulations of his newest client.

Serge leaped to his feet. "That son of a bitch! Where did this happen?"

"Cigar City."

Serge ripped the duct tape off Coleman's back, and they split for Tampa.

An eighteen-foot fishing boat idled without wake down a canal that threaded between the backyards of some of the earliest ranch homes in the state.

The couple in the boat were the Loseys. The name on the boat's stern: THE LOW SEAS. Another day in retirement paradise. The couple chatted about an item in the morning paper on the death of an original Tarzan chimp near Orlando. They passed a home with a protest sign on its seawall: PICK ON SOMEONE IN YOUR OWN TAX BRACKET.

The boat reached the end of the canal and throttled up the Caloosahatchee River. "I didn't know chimps lived that long." The river led to the Gulf of Mexico and many of the finest mangrove fishing grounds surrounding the islands of Lee County, home of Thomas Edison and the "World's Largest Shell Factory."

More and more boats headed down the canals and merged in the tributary, which was spanned by several large bridges that connected Fort Myers to Cape Coral. Most local residents didn't even know it, but Cape Coral is the largest city between Tampa and Miami, in terms of square miles, which was 120. Of greater note are its 400 miles of canals, more than any other city in the world, including Venice. Pet reptiles have gotten loose and multiplied.

It was a planned city, designed to attract northern retirees with all those canals. About half the place was filled out by people who decided their golden years needed a boat. The rest of the city is still waiting. That's mainly the west side, where platted streets have occasional houses between large fields. It's also the part of town where the most well-known thoroughfare is called Burnt Store Road, lined with real estate signs selling fields popular among dirt bikers.

The name of that street comes from the city's rich history of real estate transactions. In 1855, a Seminole Indian chief called Billy Bowlegs saw land being cleared for American forts and settlements. Bowlegs was concerned that the government was about to evict his people. The government told him nonsense and kept saying, "Could you please move back a little more?" So the chief led a raid and burned down a trading post. Soon Indians had no land in the area. Bowlegs retired to Oklahoma.

Today, property is still being seized in Cape Coral. Florida has the highest foreclosure rate in the nation—one out of every thirty-two homes—and Cape Coral is among the hardest-hit cities in the state. Many causes are cited. Subprime lending, underwater mortgages, housing bubble, "What was I thinking?" Then a new reason emerged. In theory, banks don't want foreclosures because they lose money. Then the business model changed through federal bailouts and loose regulations that allowed bad risk to be sold off to government institutions. But mostly, banks knew how easily honest people can be frightened.

Greed snowballed as only greed can. Banks began sending out notices at the first possible second under the law, then before the property was in default, then, screw it, to anyone they felt like. It's surprising how many homeowners panicked and made disastrous decisions. Then again, maybe not. And it's all true. The banks could get away with it because they eliminated the paper trail by enrolling in their own private electronic filing system, facilitated by politicians with fat new campaign contributions. True again. It's why they're called banks.

So many documents were now moving around in the shell game that there weren't enough financial employees to verify them as required, so they just recklessly signed them.

Hilda and Vernon Rockford retired from Cedar Rapids because shoveling the driveway had lost its luster. Their Iowa home had been paid off years before from his job at the Quaker Oats mill. They rolled the sale of the house into their downsized villa in Cape Coral. Not a penny owed—their castle was free and clear. The Rockfords couldn't have foreseen it at the time, but they were about to make headlines across the country. If you didn't already know it actually happened, you wouldn't believe it. The Rockfords certainly didn't.

It was a Tuesday morning. The house had a cheerful breakfast nook overlooking one of those countless canals. The Fort Myers *News-Press* lay open to college basketball scores. Orange juice. Hilda brought in the mail.

"The Hawkeyes lost to Michigan State," said Vernon.

"That's nice." Hilda sorted envelopes and tossed non-essentials on the counter like a blackjack dealer. AARP, free heating and air inspection, oil-change special, Stanley Steamer, a government-looking letter that was a scam, and the *Saver's Gazette* newspaper with classified ads featuring used aquariums and discount treatment for diseased gums.

"The Cyclones beat Drake."

"Why don't the children write?"

Hilda was about to discard another official-looking envelope, because they never did any business with the bank it came from, but something made her open it.

"E-mail," said Vernon.

"What?"

"The kids use e-mail now."

"Look at this."

"What is it?"

"Just read."

Vernon pushed glasses up his nose. "Foreclosure?"

"What do we do?"

He turned to the comics. "Throw it away. It's a mistake."

Two weeks later: "We got another notice from the bank. What's going on?"

"Throw it away."

And so forth. Until they found the sheriff's notice on their door.

HIGHWAY 27

Bass fishermen stood atop the hurricane berm skirting the southern shore of Lake Okeechobee.

"How did you sink the boat?"

"I thought the bilge plug was in. Let's drink beer."

"Okay."

They climbed down the grassy incline as a '76 Cobra raced by with an empty coffee thermos on the dash.

"Here's another fun fact," said Serge. "Miami security companies began selling thumbprint-recognition pads for access to vaults, but they had to stop because executives were getting their thumbs cut off. Not a big selling point . . . I've decided I need a T-shirt gun."

Coleman packed a bowl. "You mean those things at sporting events?"

"I've never understood the phenomenon, but everyone absolutely loses their minds whenever they see someone pull out a T-shirt gun. It's a universal constant that transcends all cultural divides: Republicans, Democrats, rich, poor, glassblowers, Inuit Indians, Motown nostalgia acts: They all pay a fortune for their tickets and sit nicely dressed and civilized. Then the dudes with the T-shirt guns come out and everyone gets that crazy red demon glow in their eyes, ready to tear arms out of their sockets and dive off balconies for three dollars of cotton. On the other end, the guys with the guns are in complete control of the crowd and get a God complex, teasing them, faking shots and making thousands of screaming loons sway left and right with their slightest move. And yet nobody but me can see the potential, like the next time the rest of the world is giving America a bunch of shit, our president just goes before the UN General Assembly and busts out a T-shirt gun. Problem fucking solved."

"That would rule."

"I need a T-shirt gun."

They reached Tampa two hours later and pulled up to a shopping center. Serge knew that there were cops and then there were *mall* cops. It only took four hundred dollars of Mahoney's expense money to score a copy of the surveillance video, and only ten more to buy the pawned VCR that had been sitting for eight years with the toaster ovens.

Coleman waddled across the budget motel room with an armload of beer and pork rinds. He dropped down on the end of a bed. "What movie we watchin'?"

Serge inserted the tape and pressed play. "It's a documentary. *Death of an Asshole.*"

The video opened with the view of a parking lot outside a multiplex cinema. People came and went in black and white.

"This is boring." Coleman chomped with his mouth open. "Where are the good parts?"

"Just saw one."

Coleman leaned forward and split his pants. "Where?"

Serge reversed the tape, starting again in slow motion. "Right there. The guy pretending to smoke a cigarette when he's actually checking out the inside of that Volkswagen Beetle . . . Come on, come on, please be in the frame. Come *onnnnnnnn* . . ."

"What do you want in the frame?"

"The car he came in . . . Yes! There it is. That black Lexus." Serge pressed a button. "Now come to Papa . . ."

"Why are you fast-forwarding?"

"Because I already know the rest of the story and just want to watch the ending."

On TV, people walked in comical fast motion, like old newsreel footage of the 1919 World Series. Finally Serge noticed something on the screen and switched the tape to super slo-mo.

Coleman leaned closer to the tube. "What are we looking for?"

Serge ignored him. "Still too dark . . ."

The Lexus pulled out of its parking slot and made a patient left turn.

"There it is! The license plate." Serge hit pause. "Perfect. They drove under that crime light in the lot, knocking out the shadow."

Serge wrote down the number.

"Now what?"

"Time to spend a little more of Mahoney's cash." He picked up the phone. "It's Serge. I need a plate run for name and address. Here's the number . . . Yes, tomorrow will be fine."

Coleman changed the channel to cartoons. "I didn't know you could call and get info off a license plate."

"Most people can't, just because it's illegal," said Serge. "But with enough money, there are all kinds of hotlines around this state."

Chapter ELEVEN

BROOK

Ms. Campanella completed her law degree in record time at an unprestigious commuter college. She aced the bar exam and celebrated in her apartment with a frozen dinner and a video rental. The next week she joined a local legal aid center, which paid squat. But her dream had come true; she got her first case. They gave it to Brook because it was supposed to be easy.

Three months later, Brook stood on the edge of a commercial parking lot wearing a smart blue pantsuit put together from thrift stores, which was standard attire for the lawyers in her center. The office provided affordable assistance to moderate-income residents fighting the crushing gears of power and bureaucracy. They battled VA cases and untangling wills that people thought they could write themselves.

Brook checked her watch and stared across the parking lot. On the intersection's other three corners stood a Shell station, a Walgreens and a walk-in clinic. Her mind drifted back to the day she first met the Rockfords. They took her to the breakfast nook.

"I don't understand it," said Hilda. "We haven't even set foot in that bank."

"There was never a loan on this house," said Vernon. "We paid in full up front."

"The letters kept coming," said Hilda.

"What did you do with them?" asked Brook.

"Threw 'em out," said Vernon. "We don't know from those people."

Brook took shorthand on a legal pad. "And that's when you got the notice from the circuit court clerk that they had filed against your home?"

Hilda nodded. "The same day the sheriff tacked that thing on our door. And since it was now an official county government document . . ."

"Certified mail," added Vernon.

" . . . we figured we better call and explain it was all a big mistake," said Hilda. "They said they would check into it."

Brook continued writing. "Then what happened?"

"The notices kept coming. Except these new ones now stated how many days until we had to move out. Then the sheriff came." Hilda's hands started shaking. "We kept calling, and they kept saying they would check. It's like nobody was talking to each other."

Brook underlined the last part. "Did you ever send them anything in writing?"

"No, we just phoned them because it was a mistake and we're honest people."

Brook thought—but didn't say—honesty doesn't count. She removed papers from her briefcase. "I'll need you to sign some documents giving me power of attorney and access to financial records."

Vernon signed first. "Will this ever end?"

Hilda went next. "It's made us sick with worry."

"You can stop worrying now." Brook slid the papers back into her attaché and stood. "I'll take care of everything."

Brook had reason for confidence. She'd done homework before visiting the couple: County records showed no mortgage liens and an unclouded title. But there was the matter of a ticking clock. The Rockfords had relied so much on phone calls and trust in fellow man that they'd let the eviction train roll down the tracks until it almost reached the station. The young lawyer still had a couple days to file a last-second opposition to the proceeding, which meant working through the weekend at home in sweatpants.

The following Monday, Brook collected the final pieces of notarized evidence that a closing company had screwed up a mortgage on the next block and transposed street numbers. The verifying bank officers were under a monthly foreclosure quota and just scribbled their names again without verifying.

Since eviction was set for the following Friday, an emergency hearing hit the docket. A bored attorney stood on one side of the courtroom—annoyed that someone had the gall to fight a slam-dunk eviction and eat into his afternoon tennis time. He cavalierly opened a file of inaccurate documents.

Brook had the correct ones. They both gave their folders to the judge, who took all of ten minutes before removing his glasses and glaring at the bank's lawyer. "Anything else in that briefcase that might actually be accurate?"

The air went out of the attorney. "I request a continuance."

"Okay, sell me," said the judge, holding up the fruits of Brook's research. "If I grant a delay, what exactly do you plan to introduce to refute this?"

"I would, uh, need to confer first with house counsel—"

"Denied. First American Bank will pay attorney and court costs, and a cease-and-desist order will be filed forthwith."

The attorney was still stammering when the gavel banged. "Court's in recess."

Weeks passed, nothing from the bank. Brook sent a certified letter. The Rockfords called: "We got another notice."

"Don't even mail it," said Brook. "I'll come by and pick it up."

More weeks, no check, another notice, rinse, lather, repeat. Brook petitioned the court to enforce its decree. The bank received another order from the judge. Nothing changed. The bank was too big; unless it was the U.S. Justice Department, they didn't care who had to wait. With billions in assets, what could anyone do to them?

Brook told her bosses her next move. They laughed and gave her the go-ahead: *More power to you.* Brook filed her motion to show cause.

The same bored attorney stood before the judge. "Your Honor, it's an honest paperwork mistake. You have my word this will be rectified and prompt payment dispatched immediately."

The judge turned toward Brook for her response. She knew her play. Any major firm would have called it preposterous, because judges rarely go outside the envelope. But Brook knew something else: Judges also don't like to be ignored.

"Your Honor," said Brook. "As you can see in the certified receipts before you, as well as in the copy of your enforcement order, First American has uniformly ignored diligent efforts to seek compliance for almost two months. The only possible conclusion is they have no respect for this court."

The judge liked this. "What do you suggest?"

"May I approach?"

He nodded. Brook handed him her newest motion. As the judge read it, he couldn't prevent the corner of a grin from escaping. He handed it to the bailiff for the bank's lawyer.

The attorney read the motion and looked up in alarm. "Foreclosure? You can't do that!"

The judge raised his eyebrows. "Really? You do it all the time."

"But we're a bank!"

"And I'm only a judge?" He leaned back in his padded chair and swiveled slightly. "You should have already been intimately familiar with foreclosure law when you first appeared before this court, and now you will be . . . Order is entered: thirty days to comply or forfeiture proceedings will commence."

"To recover this tiny amount of money?" protested the attorney.

"No, to get your attention," said the judge. "I think I've got it."

The gavel banged.

The judge was wrong. All he'd required of the bank was to pay meager legal costs and leave the poor plaintiffs alone. Nope. They were a big bank, after all. The bowels of their bureaucracy even belched out another eviction notice.

So here it was, the morning of the thirty-first day. Brook stood waiting in the corner of the parking lot. A moving truck arrived at a local branch of First American. The truck had a mural on the side of the Empire State Building, Grand Canyon and Golden Gate Bridge. It blocked the whole parking lot. The security guard told the driver to move. Then two patrol cars pulled up. The guard went inside and got the manager.

"What's going on?"

A sheriff's deputy handed him the court's seizure order.

"There must be some kind of mistake."

"Apparently the judge thinks so," said the deputy.

The moving guys rolled handcarts up the walkway. The branch manager blocked them. "You can't take our stuff!"

"Move away," said the deputy. "Or be arrested."

Poetic justice is a term cheaply flung, but this was a sweet sonnet. Inside the building, a legal bank robbery. Deputies ordered all employees to move away from their workstations. The moving company began unplugging computers and loading furniture. The only thing they couldn't touch was the money, because it belonged to depositors. A clock came down off a wall.

Inside a glass office, the manager burned up the phone lines to district and regional headquarters. In the middle of a call, the manager stood because someone took his chair. Then someone else unplugged the phone and removed the receiver from his hand.

People began lining the sidewalk. News trucks arrived. Brook was soon joined by the rest of her staff from the legal aid center, which had closed early because this was just too good. As word of the foreclosure worked its way through the crowd of onlookers, laughter and applause.

The manager darted back and forth across the parking lot like an animal in a wildfire. He saw Brook standing with the sergeant.

"I can pay you from the cash drawers!"

Brook shook her head. "You of all people should know that isn't proper foreclosure procedure. Once seizure has commenced, it's our property. You can't suddenly run up and pay the balance due to stop everything. But you already know that because evicted homeowners have requested the same mercy from you, and what is your trained response? I'll refresh your memory: 'We have to raise funds from the auction of seized property to satisfy the judgment.'"

"But you're taking way too much to cover what we owe! It's not fair!"

Brook shrugged. "They're your rules. The best laws campaign money can buy. And you never know how little people are willing to bid for this stuff, so we have to take it all to make sure. But I promise to return the extra—*trust me*."

A special van arrived. Electrical workers propped ladders against the front of the building and climbed. The branch manager's eyes popped. "Not the sign!"

Emergency phone calls crisscrossed the state. "I'm watching it on the news right now," said an executive vice president. "What are we paying you for?"

Lawyers were dragged from lunch and golf courses. Soon they arrived in force, pulling up to the bank in a wing formation of BMWs and Jaguars. They surrounded Brook with checkbooks.

"Too late," she said. "But maybe you can go to the auction and be the high bidders."

"When's the auction?" asked a man in pinstripes.

"I can probably get it on my calendar for next month."

"But the branch will be closed all that time."

"Branch? Singular?" She pointed north. "We have two more scheduled today, and another three tomorrow."

The attorneys huddled. Eventually, they started nodding. The one with seniority deferentially approached Brook. "There's another way to resolve this outside of foreclosure. Without admitting any liability, what if we offered a settlement for your client's time and emotional suffering? In return, you stipulate to make a tax-deductible donation of the property, which is rightfully yours, to one of the bank's many charitable foundations."

"What kind of settlement?"

He threw out a number.

Brook did worse than reject it. She just stared.

So he doubled it. Then tripled.

No response.

"Be reasonable," said the attorney. "That's ten times what we originally owed."

Brook looked over his shoulder at burly moving men. "Nice conference table."

The lawyer turned and watched it disappear into the back of the semi. "Okay, here's my final offer . . ."

Brook scrunched her eyebrows, then looked up. "Add a zero."

"What?" More furniture clanged loudly into the trailer. "All right!" He got out his checkbook.

Brook shook her head. "I'm afraid it will have to be a certified check."

The attorney huffed and started toward the bank. He met the branch manager in the middle of the parking lot.

He returned to Brook. "You already took the printers they use to make the checks."

"Then I guess you'll just have to go to another bank." She checked her watch. "Better hurry. They close notoriously early."

"Can you at least stop loading until I get back?"

Another empty stare.

"Fine!"

By the end of the afternoon, Brook held a check for $850,000. She was interviewed by all three local TV affiliates as workers in the background unloaded the truck. Ladders went back up against the front of the building.

The Rockfords arrived.

"We can't thank Brook enough," Vernon said into a camera. "Me and Hilda would have been out on the street if it wasn't for—"

A loud crash made everyone turn. The electric First American sign lay in pieces. The worker on one of the ladders pointed at the worker on the other ladder.

It grew dark as the last news trucks pulled away. The legal aid team congratulated Brook and headed for their cars. They began leaving the lot en masse as a lone vehicle entered the other way.

The black stretch limo parked, and a chauffeur opened the back door.

A distinguished man with salt-and-pepper hair stepped out. "Brook Campanella?"

"Yes?"

"My name is Ken Shapiro of Shapiro, Heathcote-Mendacious and Blatt..."

Brook thought: *Jeez, you don't have to tell me. It's one of the biggest firms in the state, in all the Southeast.*

Shapiro looked around the parking lot, then shook his head with a smile. "Do you always cause such a fuss?"

"My clients required vigorous advocacy according to the canons—"

Shapiro held up a hand. "Relax, you already passed the bar. And banks are the ultimate passive-aggressives. You had to keep a full-court press." He smiled again. "Me and some of the partners were watching on TV. Priceless."

"You came here just to tell me that?"

"No," said the partner. "And we all truly respect the legal aid center. They do great work for people without deep pockets. But your time could be spent helping a lot more people. We do a lot of important class-action work."

"You're offering me a job?"

"Forgive me, but we'd like to know as soon as possible," said Shapiro. "Some important trials are coming up."

"But I just got out of law school," said Brook. "And I've never tried a case."

"We know that," said Shapiro. "You'd start as second chair and get your feet wet with some easy expert witnesses. You'll be fine."

"But, Mr. Shapiro, I don't—"

"I'll level with you . . . and call me Ken," said Ken. "Please don't take this the wrong way, because it bears no reflection on what we think of your legal mind, but . . . you just have the right look. Face, stature, television presence."

"Look?"

"Completely nonthreatening. To the point many people would want to protect you," said Ken. "When I mentioned the partners were watching you on TV, we also had our jury consultant with us, and he said, I quote: 'Go down there and hire her immediately before someone else does. I need to start getting her in front of juries.'"

"Sounds superficial," said Brook.

"It is," said Ken, handing her a piece of paper. "But we're fighting the bad guys. Think about it."

"Excuse me." Brook looked up from the note. "I don't think this phone number is from around here."

"That's not a phone number." Ken climbed into the backseat of the limo. "It's our offer."

The limo drove away.

Chapter TWELVE

SOUTH TAMPA

A pastel-green bungalow sat on the corner of a residential street. The green was pistachio. Drums and tubas carried faintly in the distance from a high school football game. Much closer, laughter and loud talk from the direction of the bungalow. But all the lights in the house were out; the revelry came from the backyard, where students had discovered that the foreclosed home was unoccupied and the perfect spot for kegs and joints.

Four hours went by. The party dwindled down as a blue-and-white Cobra passed the house and wound slowly through the upscale neighborhood. Mediterraneans and post-moderns and driveway basketball hoops. Someone still flew a silk porch flag for Romney.

Serge rolled to a stop at the curb and leaned for a better view three houses down. "Excellent, still asleep." He quietly opened the door. "Coleman, you know what to do."

"What's that?"

"I told you twice on the way over."

"You were talking to me?"

"Coleman, who else was in the car?"

"I thought it was another time you were talking to the world in general, screaming about courtesy and fabric of neighborhoods. So I drank beer like usual."

"You do not drink beer! You're in the world, too! I was just giving you context for tonight's maneuver . . . Screw it, just follow and I'll fill you in." Serge gently eased his door closed. "Right now the most important thing is to remain as silent as possible—"

Crash.

Coleman pushed himself from the ground and uprighted a trash can. "Could you repeat that last part? I couldn't hear because of the noise . . ."

Upstairs in the master bedroom of a stucco house with a barrel-tile roof, the soothing blue digits of a clock radio said 3:17. When they reached 3:21, the phone rang. The only person in bed tried to clear the haze as he reached and knocked over the clock. The phone continued ringing. He picked up the clock and looked at the numbers. "It's never good news at this hour. Who on earth could be calling?" He grabbed the phone. "Hello?"

A muffled voice with cellular static. "Is this Linus Quim?"

"Who are you?"

"There's been an accident. Since you're on the line with me, I'm guessing it's not you in the car."

Quim was sitting up straight now. "What are you talking about?"

"Do you own a new black Lexus with a yacht club sticker in the corner of the windshield?"

"Ohhhh." Linus began nodding to himself. "Sanchez, have you been drinking?"

"Whoever was driving your car tonight killed my best friend."

"Dammit, Sanchez! The joke's not funny. And don't be talking about this stuff on the phone. My *home* phone!"

"Your friend's bleeding out, but I'm not going to call an ambulance until you wire me—"

"Goddammit, Sanchez! We'll talk tomorrow, and if you call me back tonight, I'll kill you!" He slammed the phone down in the cradle. It bounced behind the nightstand, and he had to reel it back in by the curly cord. "I can't wait to get my hands on that putz."

He lay back down and closed his eyes.

His eyes opened. "I can't sleep."

Quim yanked the sheets off his legs. He always had been obsessively organized, which is why he was the only one in the gang who could map out their meticulous plans. And he couldn't go back to sleep as long as something was out of place.

The Lexus.

And the poor phone reception now left him unsure about Sanchez's voice.

He jogged down the stairs and through the kitchen to the garage's side door. When he opened it, the car was sitting inside just like he'd left it—just like he thought. Worried for nothing. Now he could go back to sleep. "That moron Sanchez . . ."

He was closing the door when a hand came out of the darkness and jerked him into the garage.

"There's been an accident," said Serge, bashing Quim on the head with a tire iron. "Oops, I slipped."

THE NEXT DAY

From the sidewalk, the view up the face of the thirty-story building was steep and bright. One of those all-glass designs with floor-to-ceiling mirror windows. The noon sun began peeking over the southwest corner, fracturing the light into sparkling rays.

Streams of pedestrians parted around Brook Campanella, standing in the middle of the sidewalk, craning her neck toward the Fort Lauderdale sky. Capturing the moment. And hesitating. Brook shielded her eyes as cotton-ball clouds slowly drifted over the roof, creating the illusion that the building was moving. Her stomach felt the unbalance of vertigo, but it was also nerves. She took a deep breath and went inside.

The open space of the lobby echoed the clatter of a marble floor.

Brook went through the metal detector, and her briefcase went through the X-ray. The reason for the precaution was that half the people liked what was going on in the building; the other half not so much. Par for the legal biz. Brook grabbed her attaché on the other side. The security guard expressed that he wanted her day to be good, but wasn't emotionally invested either way.

The high-speed express elevator opened on the top floor. Brook entered another lobby with a lower ceiling. Ahead sat a long cherry-oak reception desk. Behind the desk was a wall where recessed lighting emphasized the firm's logo: three interlocking letters, SH&B, forming a flat sculpture of glossy chrome. It was originally going to be brushed metal until someone said they weren't selling refrigerators. Hidden shims offset the sign two inches out from the wall so that unseen lighting could leave a shadow. About $80,000 had gone into this thinking.

Brook approached the desk and gave her name.

The receptionist smiled with on-command friendship. "They're already waiting for you in the conference room."

"Who's waiting? Where's the conference room?"

"Everyone. That way."

Brook walked hesitantly past private offices and the copy room and other doors leading to unknown activity. She suddenly stopped, and her tummy knotted again. Ahead, the windows of the conference room. Inside stretched the longest table she had ever seen, surrounded by dozens of people in suits that definitely weren't off the rack. At the head of the table, a well-tended man stood and made a gregarious waving motion for her to enter.

"Everyone," said Ken Shapiro. "This is Brook Campanella, our newest associate."

"Hello, Brook . . ." "Welcome . . ." "Have a seat . . ."

"You've already met me," said Ken, gesturing to his left. "This is Willard Heathcote-Mendacious and Shug Blatt . . ."

Each smiled and nodded in turn.

"You won't remember everyone else's names right now, but you'll like them," said Ken.

The rest smiled and nodded.

"We have high hopes for you," said Ken.

"Heard great things," said Willard.

"The future is later," said Shug.

Brook became dizzy. Outside those floor-to-ceiling windows on the east side of the conference room was the reverse of her sidewalk view: a steep drop down to antlike people, taxis and the Las Olas shopping district reaching toward the Atlantic beach along Highway A1A.

The table chirped to life with chitchat, everyone commenting on Brook's TV debut outside the foreclosed bank. Laughter. Brook was silent.

"Now down to business," said Ken. "We've already assigned your first case. *Sheffield et al v. Consolidated Financial*."

Brook's jaw fell. "That massive class-action mortgage suit against one of the biggest companies in the state?"

"Then you're already up to speed," said Ken.

"I don't even know where my desk is."

Ken casually flicked his wrist. "It'll all come naturally. The desk, the case. Relax."

"We're counting on you," said Willard.

"No rush, you can start after lunch," said Shug.

Her eyes ping-ponged between the partners. It was something weird. They looked very much different, hair color, face shapes. Yet they appeared the same, the way some dogs look like their owners. It was a combination of clothes, carriage and general aura from decades of building one of the most powerful legal firms in Florida, inbreeding their mannerisms and speech. When one reached for a water carafe, so did the others. Their sentences segued seamlessly.

Ken pressed a button on the intercom. "Nancy, eleven o'clock, take Brook shopping for some clothes."

Brook self-consciously looked down at herself, then pulled her chair up tight to the table.

"I know what you're thinking," said Ken. "*'I've just started.'* But according to TV, you're already a rock star at mortgage law." He strolled around the side of the table and placed a hand on a shoulder. "You'll be teamed with Shelby here . . ."

Shelby said hello by raising a single finger.

" . . . He'll teach you everything you need to know. We've decided you're essential for this trial. You're wondering why?"

Brook nodded.

"You're jury candy," said another voice.

Ken chuckled and placed a hand on another shoulder. "This is Dmitri Smoot, our jury consultant. He can be a little blunt."

Smoot was the only person at the table with a goatee and no sense of humor. "Do you wear glasses?"

"No," said Brook.

"You do now," said Smoot. "The lenses will be plain glass. Our focus groups selected rims that connect with sixty-five percent of the total population, and eighty-one percent of those who can't figure how to get out of jury duty."

Ken pressed the intercom again. "Nancy, twelve thirty, Vision Palace."

"Mauve scarf," said Smoot.

"Nancy . . ." said Ken.

Brook poured a glass of water. So did the partners. The room started to spin.

"That's about it," said Ken.

"That wraps it up," said Willard.

"Roll credits," said Shug.

Chapter THIRTEEN

THE EVERGLADES

A Ford Cobra raced east across a narrow two-laner with no shoulders called the Tamiami Trail. It passed a roadside attraction of airboats and gator nuggets.

They drove on in silence.

More boat docks, dams, spillways, panther crossing signs, people cane-fishing in straw hats, vultures working the road. Pickups parked along grassy embankments. Men in camo caps roamed with machetes and baseball bats.

Coleman turned his head as they went by. "Who are those dudes?"

"Python hunters."

"I thought the hunt was over."

"Only the contest part. The stupidness continues."

The pair completed eighty miles from the west coast. Just before reaching the outskirts of Miami, the Ford made a right at Dade Corners and sped south on Krome Avenue. After arriving at the end of the state in Homestead and Florida City, Serge took a fork southeast away from the rest of traffic, into sparser settlements and grids of agriculture until there was nothing. He threaded the Cobra onto the kind of solitary road that said *turn around*.

"What is this street?" asked Coleman.

"It's a dead end."

"Where's the dead end?"

"Forty miles."

Coleman whistled. "Now, *that's* a dead end. Why are we going there?"

Serge stuck a thumb over his shoulder. "To get away from all those python-hunting wannabe mooks. If I'm going to track giant constrictors, I need a sector all to myself so I can bag every last one."

The Cobra hadn't seen another vehicle in either direction for a half hour. Coleman was working a bottle of Old Crow with diligence when . . .

Splat.

Coleman leaned toward a dime-sized blotch on the windshield. "Serge, what was—"

Splat . . . splat, splat.

Serge turned on the wipers and fired a squirt of washer fluid. "Mosquito season."

"Those giant red stains are *mosquitoes*?"

"Where we're going is arguably the fiercest insect breeding ground in the entire nation, where you often need wipers in total sunshine."

Splat, splat, splat.

"Where *are* we going?"

"Flamingo." Serge hit the washer fluid again. "Most people think where we just came from is the last extreme stop on the bottom of the mainland, but our alternate destination is the real brass ring. So ridiculously remote that few ever make it or even know it exists."

"Anything out there?"

"A ghost town." Serge came around a final slow bend. "More than a hundred years ago, settlers had plenty of land upon which to raise crops and gather other staples to sail down to the wealthy wreckers and cigar kings of land-starved Key West. After the town disappeared, the Everglades National Park put in a remote visitors' outpost, with a few motel rooms, but that was canceled by Hurricane Wilma in 2005, and now only the most rugged tenters hammer their stakes in the sand. From an airplane, the virtually empty designated camping area looks like a big pineapple."

The Cobra parked outside the visitors' center. "They even sell mosquito lapel pins and bumper stickers and can coozies with drops of blood. It's reverse-psychology advertising: Embrace your biggest drawback and tourists think that if they aren't eaten alive, they've been gypped."

Coleman slapped his neck. "Like all those funky bars that say 'Warm beer, lousy service'?"

"True fact about those bars. The owners started getting complaints from British customers because they drink warm beer anyway, and when cold beer arrives, they say, 'What gives?' I guess bartenders in Liverpool are also rude."

They went inside and approached the info desk.

"May I help you?" asked a park ranger.

Serge opened his wallet. "Yes, one souvenir mosquito pin. Nice marketing tactic. With a name like Smucker's . . ."

"What?"

"Where's the tombstone?" said Serge. "I must touch it."

"Oh, the tombstone," said the ranger, ringing up the pin. "Right over there with the exhibits."

Serge snatched the souvenir off the counter and ran across the room. He placed his palms against a flat rock and closed his eyes.

Coleman bent down to read the artifact. "'Guy Bradley'?"

"Shhhhh," said Serge. "I'm channeling. For the entire time I'm here, I'm going to be Bradley and carry on his legacy."

"But, Serge—"

"I don't know anyone named Serge."

"Uh, but, Guy."

"Yes?"

"Who was he?"

"Just one of my all-time Florida heroes." Serge opened his eyes. A small tour group had arrived. He faced them and spread his arms. "Thank you for coming! Besides being a ghost town, Flamingo was also the Wild West. And Bradley became the unofficial sheriff, hired by the Audubon Society."

"We're from the Audubon Society," said someone in the group with big binoculars.

"And a fine group it is," said Serge. "Especially overcoming a scandalous past that you've been trying to hush up all these years."

"What are you talking about?"

"James Audubon visited Key West in 1832 and stayed at the landmark home on Whitehead Street, which is now a museum and gallery. He spurred conservation awareness of our feathered friends through his fabulous paintings. Ironically, in order to capture their majesty on canvas, he first had to kill the birds and prop them up in aesthetic poses with whatever they used before pipe cleaners were invented. You have to let him slide a little on that one because otherwise there'd be birds flapping around the ceiling of his studio, and all the paintings would have been blurry."

Murmurs in the group. *"I didn't know that."*

"Then in the early 1900s, rich dames in New York tried to outdo each other, strutting down Park Avenue with ridiculous Lady Gaga hats sprouting giant fans of bird plumes that soon became more valuable than gold, and poachers began shooting up entire rookeries in the Everglades. So Bradley single-handedly patrolled the entire bottom of the state from Ten Thousand Islands to Flamingo, valiantly battling the heartless hunters. Out west, gangs robbed trains; in Florida, they collected feathers, which is embarrassing on multiple levels, and in July of 1905, only a few steps up that beach outside, Bradley attempted to arrest the infamous Smith gang and was brutally gunned down. Then, in one of the most famous Florida legal cases that nobody remembers today except me because I'm putting myself through wildcat law school, the head of the Smith clan was found not guilty in a Key West trial. Bradley was buried on the shore behind this building with a dynamite view of Florida Bay, but his grave was washed to sea in 1960 by Hurricane Donna. They recovered the tombstone and put it on display here. You must touch it. Any questions?"

One of them looked up at Serge's pith helmet. "Are you one of the rangers?"

"No, just someone who roams from town to town, taking odd jobs, enlightening people, correcting others, then leaving quickly before they can say thank you . . . Come on, Coleman."

They ran out the door.

The Cobra drove west as far as the park road would go. "Fetch the camping gear in the backseat."

"Which is the camping stuff?"

"All of it."

"But there's also a lot of weird electric stuff that I've never seen anyone camp with."

"Because nobody's ever camped this way before." Serge gathered a spool of wire and armature switches. "I stopped while you were passed out in Naples and did some shopping at the twenty-four-hour home improvement store. Since we're on the great python hunt, I would be remiss not to conduct scientific experiments to further our awareness of the environment."

"But don't your experiments usually have a—"

Bang, bang, bang . . .

Serge popped the trunk.

"I'll kill you!" yelled Linus Quim. *"Untie me right now!"*

Serge swung the tire iron. "I hate city noise when I'm out in nature."

FORT LAUDERDALE

Four small white cardboard boxes sat on a table. Two pieces of wood went into one of them.

The wood came out with five lo mein noodles, and five lo mein noodles promptly fell off.

A man sighed.

Brook finished chewing and stuck a fork into her own order of chop suey. "Why do you keep trying to use chopsticks?"

Shelby stuck them back in his box. "Because I've never failed at anything. This is important."

Brook slid a different box across the table. "Fried rice?"

"Thanks."

Shelby. Shelby Lang, thirty-one, top of his law class and the fastest-rising star in the firm, mainly because of billable hours. That's why the conference room's wall clock now said 2:29, which was A.M. The law office had showers, an exercise spa, even a bunk room for catnaps. All about those billable hours. Shelby had on sweats with a Florida State Seminoles insignia.

Brook's hair was still damp from the shower. She wore light-green hospital scrub pants and a shirt with a picture of a bridge from a Brooklyn high school. Shelby decided that the dressed-down look wasn't bad on her. And those doelike eyes couldn't hurt with juries. But there would never be any untoward crossing of professional lines with Brook, because Shelby liked his roommate Jack better.

For her part, Brook was a bit surprised by the pairing with her new colleague. The biggest firms were notorious for depersonalization, the bottom line and pricks. Shelby didn't fit. He was funny, easygoing and devoid of arrogance. In other words, normal. Except for those damn chopsticks.

"Gimme those!" said Brook.

Shelby was working a single grain of rice toward his mouth. "Hey!"

She slapped something in his hand. "Fork!"

Shelby looked up and began to grin. So did Brook.

They were hitting it off.

She opened a folder of financial records. "How did your firm get this case anyway? I thought it was being handled by someone else."

"It was," said Shelby, finally able to eat. "But it was just this tiny one-man operation in Tamarac. A hand-painted shingle hanging outside a former used-car lot. Guy named Ziggy Blade."

"Is that a real name?"

"Even more bizarre is how he stumbled into getting the case certified as a class," said Shelby. "Started with a single raggedy-ass client that nobody else would help. And normally Consolidated Financial is connected enough through political contributions that a plaintiff can only get worthless crumbs of documents during discovery. But Ziggy pulled a decent judge, and after a million objections and appeals, Consolidated was ordered to produce. So they pulled the classic needle-in-a-haystack trick, and literally a forklift arrived at Ziggy's office with a teetering pallet of file boxes. They figured he's just one guy; there's no way he can sift through it all."

Brook opened the wonton. "Except they guessed wrong?"

"Don't know how the guy found the time, but he connected the dots and discovered such a large pattern of loan-servicing irregularities that it couldn't be anything but deliberate. The biggest case ever of its kind in the country. And usually a sure win on just those documents."

"Except?"

"You should see the legal team Consolidated is putting on the field." Shelby bit into an egg roll. "Riley, Moss, Bauer, Tripp and Phaul."

"The Death Star," said Brook.

"We had a meeting and tried to explain what he was up against, but Ziggy wouldn't budge. Until Riley went to plan B and buried him with another forklift. This time motions. Now there definitely weren't enough hours in the day, and Ziggy faced having the case dismissed for non-response. Only a firm of our size has the resources."

"So I'm guessing you paid all his back expenses, let him to stay on as consulting counsel and promised a cut if we prevailed that would allow him to retire five times over."

"At least," said Shelby. He handed two files across the desk.

Brook began flipping through. "I don't remember these people."

"New named plaintiffs to lead the class," said Shelby. "Our firm dug them up."

"Don't we already have enough?"

"You never have enough against Riley. And these are particularly sympathetic." Shelby grabbed a fortune cookie. "Dmitri Smoot said they tested well in front of a mock jury."

Brook stuck the files in her briefcase. "Guess we'll be making some house calls."

"Hope you have comfortable shoes." Shelby broke open the cookie and pulled out a tiny strip of paper.

"What's it say?" asked Brook.

"*'Help! I'm being held prisoner in a fortune-cookie factory!'*"

Brook cracked up.

"It's an old Alan King joke," said Shelby. "But a good one."

Chapter FOURTEEN

FLAMINGO

The sun rose and so did Coleman. He sat up in the backseat without memory. "What happened last night?"

"You took an early dive before we could establish camp, so we slept in the car. Just grab something and try to be useful." Serge set off with duffel bag in hand and a folded tent hoisted over his shoulder.

Coleman pointed the other way. "What about the campsites in the big pineapple?"

"Those are for people who don't know what they're doing." Serge headed down to the beach and walked between the waterline and sea oats. He got a contact buzz from the secluded, snow-white shore facing due south toward distant mangrove islets dotting the bay under a crisp sky that filled his polarized sunglasses. Perfection.

"Serge? Were you just messing with those bird freaks yesterday?"

"Every word was true. Guy Bradley's life even inspired the before-its-time 1958 environmental classic *Wind Across the Everglades,* starring Christopher Plummer, who tracks Burl Ives as the ruthless poacher

Cottonmouth." Serge stopped in the sand and nodded. "This is where Bradley made his last stand. Can you dig it?"

Bird-watchers strolled along the shore. Up ahead, they saw a man in a pith helmet drop his gear before being riddled by make-believe bullets, staggering backward into the surf and splashing lifelessly. They came running.

Serge popped out of the water with an ecstatic smile. "We hope you've enjoyed today's historic reenactment . . . Now, my impersonation of a snowy egret." He began jerking his neck and shuffling in the sand.

The group made a wide circle and ran off the beach.

Serge stopped twitching. "Time to establish the homestead and look for snakes . . ."

Hours passed. Serge pushed away branches and led Coleman back toward their campsite. They emerged from the scrubland into a small clearing with a tent and a small hole surrounded by stones for the evening's campfire. It was a nice big tent, the kind you can practically stand up inside.

Coleman slapped his neck.

Serge sat on the ground and frowned.

"You shouldn't be so hard on yourself," said Coleman. "The whole state only caught sixty-eight snakes."

"I could have sworn we'd be stacking them like cordwood."

"At least you tried." Coleman found a beer in his suitcase. "That one time you were wrestling in the water for almost a half hour."

"But it turned out to be a small log." He got up and listlessly gathered firewood.

Soon it was dark, and campfire flames flickered in a stout breeze off the water that kept the mosquitoes at distance.

The traveling pair sat cross-legged in the fire's warm glow. Serge's mood had boomeranged back to A-OK. The camaraderie, conversation and raconteur tradition of a campfire with a close friend had set his head right.

"And what's the deal with the emergency broadcast system?" said Serge. "I'll be listening to astounding dialogue in a Steven Seagal movie when the sound drops out and a red banner runs across the screen, followed by annoying blasts of static."

"Who needs it?" said Coleman.

"Someday when the shit really hits boil and it's not a test, then what?" Serge uncapped a canteen. "The sky's blood red, alien ray guns cutting people in half, the undead noshing on our slowest neighbors, and the government responds by hitting our TVs with obnoxious static."

"If you listen to static on mushrooms, it's a special language of the machines."

"But what about this?" said Serge. "What if all these years, the people sending the tests don't realize we're just getting static? It's a test, after all, which by definition means they're not completely sure it works. For all we know, they're sending critical verbal instructions that they just assume are getting through. And all because none of us calls to tell them, 'Hey, your shit's broken.' Instead we're like, 'The static again for the millionth time. Okay, we get it. Now can we get back to Seagal bending a guy's leg the wrong direction?'"

Serge reached in his duffel and pulled out a sheet of hard plastic with thin metal strips.

Coleman took a swig from a fifth of Jack. "What's that?"

"An electroplate. I made it myself." He reached in the bag again. "Here's a capacitor and solenoid and small motor."

"Your science project?"

"Yes, except I'm still working on the trigger element." He placed them back in the bag. "I decided to go organic this time and let my environment inspire me and fill in the blanks, but I'm still waiting for the vibe."

"What was that electro-thing for?"

Serge sat up and rubbed his palms. "Okay, during the summer season this park has like more mosquitoes than practically anyplace in Florida. The stories are legendary. You know how insects like flames? Pioneers from the 1800s reported that swarms of mosquitoes were putting out their kerosene lamps. Someone else saw them suffocate a cow.

So I was thinking I could work in the electroplate. When a mosquito hits, the current running through the metal strips will fry it like a bug zapper. But unlike a bug zapper, there's more: The plate has two separate circuits of alternating parallel strips. One is hot, the other has no electricity. When the mosquito meets its maker, the salty juices become an electrolyte and allow a tiny bit of current to jump the dead circuit that feeds the capacitor, which stores each charge until it builds up enough to fire the voltage. But why would a mosquito be attracted to the plate? And what will I do with the capacitor's charge? Therein lies the rub . . ."

Another swig of whiskey. "I'm sure it will come to you." *Slap*.

"Coleman, the marshmallow on the end of your stick is engulfed in flames, yet you're still leaving it in there."

"I know. Camping's cool!"

"How are you going to eat that carbon cinder?"

"Eat it? I thought we were just burning stuff up."

"What did you think I was doing rotating my stick until the marshmallow was gently brown and then popping it in my mouth?"

"Thought you were doing it wrong. Didn't want to say anything."

"Remember lying in the grass when you were a kid?" said Serge. "That was the best! Not a care in the world, just staring up at the clouds from a lush bed of Saint Augustine, thinking maybe later you'd run through a sprinkler or dig a mudhole."

"And then you'd go inside for some Hawaiian Punch," said Coleman. "And if you hadn't been wearing a shirt, your back would start itching like crazy."

"It's a kid's job to lie in the grass, but they don't warn you about the itching," said Serge.

"When I camped as a kid, we used to tell scary stories so we wouldn't be able to sleep," said Coleman. "They all had ax murderers. Know any?"

"Just the classics," said Serge.

Coleman set another marshmallow ablaze. "Hit me."

"Okay," said Serge. "Here's one every kid needs to know . . ."

Coleman sat with wide-eyed attention for ten minutes until Serge reached the conclusion: " . . . And then the police phoned the babysitter back and said, 'The calls are coming from inside the house!' "

Coleman covered his eyes.

Serge grabbed his checklist and marked an *X* next to *Scary stories*.

"What's next?"

"Campfire songs," said Serge. "Remember that Phil Collins tune at the end of the *Miami Vice* pilot?"

"Who can forget?"

They both cleared their throats for off-key harmony: *"I can feel it . . . coming in the air toniiiiiiight . . ."*

"Hey, Serge, remember the rumor about that song? Phil was up on an oceanfront balcony at night and sees someone drowning while this other guy on the beach just watches without helping . . ."

" . . . And then he writes a song about it," says Serge. "And gives the guy front-row tickets to his concert . . ."

" . . . And then Phil sings the song to him and the spotlight hits the dude and he's royally busted!"

"Great story."

"What do you mean 'story'?"

"It's a myth, like Mama Cass choking to death on a ham sandwich when she just had a heart attack."

"No sandwich?" Coleman sat up with concern. "Please tell me Keith Richards kicked H before a Stones tour by flying to South America and having all his blood replaced."

Serge shook his head.

Coleman stared at his flaming stick. "My life has been built on lies."

Serge grabbed an aerosol can and sprayed himself. "Want more repellent?"

"No, I'm cool."

"There's a couple mosquitoes on your arm. The breeze is keeping most of them away, but a few will always get through."

"I like it."

Serge got a funny look. "You like getting bitten?"

"I was slapping my neck earlier, but now I'm drunk."

"You mean you don't feel the stings?"

"No, I still feel them." Coleman grinned toward his arm. "It's this fun thing I discovered partying outside a few years ago."

"Please, illuminate."

"You know how mosquitoes suck a lot of your blood?"

"Right, some species are able to engorge themselves until it's the vast majority of their body weight."

"So if I have a high enough blood-alcohol content, the mosquitoes get seriously fucked up." Coleman smiled again. "Watch these little buggers."

One of the mosquitoes finished and took off, then the other. They flew normally for the first few feet, then began veering erratically, flying sideways and upside down before falling to the ground. They took off again and fell back to earth. One staggered into the campfire with a small flash.

Coleman grabbed his bourbon. "Camping is cool!"

Serge scanned down his camping checklist. "Marshmallows, childhood memories, horror stories, singing around the fire, Keith Richards transfusion." He folded the list. "Well, that about does it. Time for bed."

Serge poured his canteen on the fire, producing a column of ash and steam, then unrolled a fluffy bag on the ground.

"Don't the sleeping bags go in the tent?"

"Absolutely not." Serge wiggled inside. "You're supposed to sleep under the stars."

"Then why'd you bring the tent?"

"Because you're just supposed to pitch a tent when camping. Everyone knows that." Serge zipped himself up to his neck. "Better get some shut-eye. We've got a big day tomorrow."

Coleman shrugged and unrolled his own sleeping sack.

They stared up at bright constellations.

"Serge?"

"What?"

"I'm really hot."

"Me, too." Stinging perspiration rolled into Serge's eyes. "And the wind died down."

"There's a million more mosquitoes." Coleman slapped his sweaty neck. "I'm starting to really hate this."

"That's why they call it camping." Serge slapped his own wet neck. "Now pipe down and go to sleep."

They both zipped the bags up ever farther around their heads until only their noses were sticking out.

Billions of miles away, stars and nebulae moved across the sky. One inch away, a tiny *Culex biscaynensis* hovered for a landing and inserted a barely visible proboscis into a much larger proboscis.

"Ow!" Serge jumped up and grabbed his nose. "This is ridiculous!"

Coleman loosened the drawstring so he could see. "Serge, why are you hopping around in the sleeping bag?"

"Because the zipper's stuck."

"Ow! Damn!" Coleman jumped up. "They're swarming!"

"I forgot they're attracted to carbon dioxide." Serge hopped around the campsite. "What's with this stupid zipper?"

Coleman hopped next to him. "Mine's stuck, too."

They continued hopping frantically like giant inchworms encased in down and Gore-Tex. Serge bounded blindly into a tiny pit.

"*Yowwwww!* The embers from the campfire are still hot!"

"Where?" said Coleman. "*Owwwwww!* My feet are on fire!"

They fell to the ground. Serge violently broke the zipper and ripped the bag off himself, then flung it in the bushes.

Coleman rolled through the smoldering pit. "Fire again."

Serge grabbed the melted foot of his friend's bag and pulled him free.

Five minutes later, the front seats of a '76 Ford Cobra were reclined all the way. The engine idled so air-conditioning could run. Serge munched ridged potato chips and held a magnifying glass to his souvenir mosquito pin. Then he turned on the battery-powered travel TV sitting atop the dash. "I love camping."

Coleman poured whiskey shots. "How long can we run the air-conditioning?"

"There's a full tank, so it should last longer than we need to sleep." Serge popped a chip in his mouth. "But just in case, we have an alarm clock."

"I don't see any clock."

Bang, bang, bang . . .

"Oh, him," said Coleman.

Serge grabbed a tire iron from under the seat. He went to the trunk and came back.

"What did you just do?" asked Coleman.

"Hit the snooze button."

"I like it in the car," said Coleman. "It's much better than what was happening before."

"The key to enjoying nature is learning how to adapt." Serge turned up the A/C and bunched a T-shirt into a makeshift pillow. "I'm going to sleep."

"I want to watch more TV," said Coleman. "Camping's cool!"

Chapter FIFTEEN

MEANWHILE

The Sawgrass Expressway separates the Everglades from the western sprawl of Broward County. A white Toyota Camry headed north, a half hour after leaving downtown Fort Lauderdale. The Camry had the no-option package but the fabric seats were clean. A decal in the back window suggested that someone believed Florida State was "#1" at something.

"Shelby," said Brook. "Are we being followed?"

"Why do you ask?"

"Because you're constantly glancing in the rearview."

"That's how you have to drive down here." Shelby looked at the mirror again and leaned over the steering wheel. "South Florida drivers are the worst. They tailgate at eighty and change lanes without clearance. So if you just stay in the right lane and leave extra separation from the car in front of you, you'll be fine. As long as you keep watching—" He looked up again.

"The rearview?"

"In South Florida, all the trouble comes from behind." Shelby gave the Camry a brief burst of gas and swung over to the side of the lane. The shoulder's warning strips rumbled under his right tires. A black Corvette whipped around and blew by like they were standing still.

"Good God," said Brook. "If you hadn't sped up and scooted over, he would have clipped your back end."

"Got the address?"

Brook opened a file in her lap. "Why did Mrs. Wozniak want to meet at such an ungodly hour?"

"Says she's a night owl. Likes to watch infomercials and preachers." Shelby tapped the brakes and swerved. A Camaro whipped in front of him. "Maybe tomorrow we can go see Ziggy. He left a message."

"What about?"

"Didn't elaborate," said Shelby. "Or couldn't over the phone."

"Which is it?"

Shelby shrugged. "You'll just have to meet Ziggy."

"Why don't you simply call him back and ask?"

"You need to meet Ziggy anyway," said Shelby. "It'll eventually come up."

"What will?"

"Keeps calling with strategy and stuff. You'll start getting calls, too. Still thinks he's lead counsel on the case."

"But the firm absorbed it," said Brook. "That's standard. He just has to kick back and collect his fee."

"You have to meet Ziggy."

Moments later, the Toyota turned left into the Coral Shores trailer park, which was fifteen miles inland. The entrance had wooden signs with pelicans and an empty space on the pavement where a guard shack had once stood. A retired man on a three-wheel bicycle pedaled across the road in the dark. He wore a blue baseball cap that said he had served on the USS *John C. Calhoun*. In the bicycle's handlebar basket was a pet iguana that seemed to either enjoy the ride or was utterly confused by this turn in his life. Shelby continued winding through trailers, looking for the address. The park was still and quiet, except for all the other senior citizens with blank expressions and giant tricycles who slowly pedaled back and forth in the dark like a mellow zombie movie.

The Camry finally parked in the dirt next to a double-wide. It was one of those trailers where the front steps were surrounded with way too much stuff to compensate for it being a trailer. Flags, gnomes, dead potted plants, giant frog statues, tiny windmills, wind chimes, birdhouses and a signpost with various arrows indicating the mileage to London, Nova Scotia and Bangkok.

The lawyers climbed the steps and knocked.

A voice from inside: "Who is it?"

"Shelby and Brook."

"Who?"

"Your attorneys. We called."

"One minute."

Muffled sounds, glass clinking, shuffling, something fell over, coughing. Shelby and Brook glanced at each other. More coughs, a horribly violent clearing of a throat, then the door opened.

"Make yourself at home." An older woman in a nightgown turned and retreated back into the dimness of the trailer.

The lawyers took seats on a sofa covered in plastic. At the end of the couch was an embroidered pillow of a dalmatian. The beginning of a trend. The pair's eyes moved around the room: a giant floor-standing ceramic dalmatian; framed paintings of dalmatians; shelves filled with dalmatian stuffed animals, figurines and commemorative plates. A model fire engine had a spotted dog behind the wheel.

"Thank you for seeing us," said Shelby. "We won't take up much of your time."

"You're no bother. I'm glad to have the company," said Mrs. Wozniak. "It's been hard for me since the colonel passed away."

"Your husband?"

"No." She pointed. "My dalmatian."

The lawyers turned toward what they had previously believed to be another stuffed toy, but was actually the work of a taxidermist.

Brook whispered sideways, "Awkward."

"Mrs. Wozniak," said Shelby, "the reason we're here is that we need to go over your testimony for the trial."

"Call me Ruthy. I don't understand why I have to testify."

"Because you're a named plaintiff," said Brook.

"I still don't know what any of this means. What's a class action?"

"Remember when you talked to that other lawyer at our firm?" asked Shelby. "If the finance company only treated you badly, then there would just be your lawsuit. But we've found many, many other people that the company also treated unfairly—" Shelby stopped.

Mrs. Wozniak had begun petting something invisible in her lap. "Go on. I'm listening."

"Uh, anyway, so the judge considers all of those other victims part of the same class, which is why it's called a class action."

"Would you like some tea?" She stood up. She sat back down. "I don't have any."

"Ma'am," said Brook. "We just need to go over what you will say in court."

"Will all those other victims be in court?" asked Ruthy.

"No, they're not named plaintiffs like you are," said Shelby.

"I still don't understand."

"It means you get more money," said Brook.

"But I don't want to go to court," said Ruthy. "I want to stay in my trailer."

Brook got up and took a seat alongside Mrs. Wozniak, placing a hand on hers. "That's why we're here. Everything will be fine."

"You're so sweet." She began petting air again. "Okay, what do I have to do?"

Brook thought of the right way to say it. "First, it's best if witnesses keep their hands folded in their lap."

"Like this? That's easy."

"Good; now then, we're going to ask you some simple things, like what the mortgage people said when you were applying for a loan, and what documents they required."

"What about the other lawyers? On TV, they're mean and trick you."

"We won't let that happen," said Shelby. "We'll object if they try anything."

Brook stroked her hand. "Here's the important part. The lawyer is going to try to blame you."

"But I didn't do anything."

"We know that," said Brook. "Except a lot of people think you should have been more responsible for the amount of money you took out on the house."

"I just did what they said. I told them I didn't understand about money, but they were so polite and said they could get me a house much nicer than anything I ever dreamed of." She got out a hankie and dabbed tears. "Then they took it away from me."

"And that's all you'll have to say. We'll take care of the rest."

"Should I tell them about the colonel?"

"You might want to leave that part out."

Chapter SIXTEEN

FLAMINGO

It was darkest just before dawn. The overnight sky had undergone a shift change of constellations. Waves lapped the shore, mosquitoes buzzed, owls hooted, frogs croaked, a Ford Cobra idled.

An instrument gauge said the gas tank was half empty.

Bang, bang, bang . . .

Serge's eyes remained shut. "It can't be morning already."

Bang, bang, bang . . .

He opened one eye. Jet black outside. His glow-in-the-dark wrist-watch said five A.M. He closed the eye.

Bang, bang, bang . . .

"I don't want to get up." Serge shifted his weight. "He'll stop if I ignore him."

Bang, bang, bang . . .

Serge sighed and kept his eyes closed.

Then another sound. "Serge? Can you hear me?"

Serge groaned and adjusted the T-shirt pillow. "Coleman, go back to sleep!"

"Is it morning yet?"

"You idiot, can't you tell it's still dark?"

"I can't see anything," said Coleman. "Could you give me a little help?"

"Leave me alone . . ."

Then Serge realized the voice wasn't as close as it should have been. It was also quite warm despite the A/C, and mosquitoes were biting again. "What the hell?"

He turned and saw the passenger door wide open. In his stupor, Coleman had somehow spilled out of the car.

Bang, bang, bang . . .

Serge gave a heavier sigh. "Now I *have* to get up."

He grabbed the tire iron and made another pass by the trunk— *crack*—then continued around the car. "Coleman, where are you?"

"Down here."

"Where— . . . Oh, Jesus, don't move!"

"I don't think I can," said Coleman. "What's going on?"

Serge urgently reached in the backseat for tools. "The biggest freaking Burmese python I've ever seen has dislocated its jaws and is beginning to devour you headfirst."

"It's down over my eyes," said Coleman. "Can you do something before it gets to my mouth? I won't like that."

"Just hold still. The snake has rearward-facing teeth to latch onto its prey." Serge wedged implements on both sides of Coleman's head. "Since the jaws are dislocated, it doesn't have much clamping strength."

"Serge, why didn't it squeeze me to death first?"

"Normally, it would have." Serge gripped a pair of channel-lock pliers over the bridge of Coleman's nose. "Unless the snake thinks its meal is no longer alive, and you sleep like the dead."

"I thought I was too big for a snake to eat."

"You are, but it doesn't stop them from trying, like the one python in the news that ruptured itself trying to ingest an alligator. And this baby must have a huge appetite, because you've got one big-ass melon on your neck."

"I prefer 'special-headed person.' "

"It's starting to coil in defense," said Serge. "I'm going to have to finish fast, and as soon as you're free, I need you to find the tail."

"Why?"

"Because I'll be grabbing the neck. They don't have much resistance to humans stretching them out, but once they start to wrap, it gets ugly fast." Serge grunted and heaved a final last time with the pliers. "There! You're free! Find the tail, find the tail!"

"There's goo in my eyes."

"Hurry, it's got my arm!"

"Is this the tail?"

"No, my ankle! Find the tail!"

Coleman fell over backward. "But I'm still really fucked up."

"Can't fix that now." Serge flopped over on his back, wrestling with massive jaws trying to get at his face. "What's taking so long with the tail? It's got my other arm now!"

"Okay, I got a part of the snake. How do I find the tail?"

"Just keep going the opposite direction from me. And make it snappy. I'm losing feeling in my arms and won't be able to hold the neck much longer."

"I think it's working. I'm feeling my way along," said Coleman. "Spoke too soon. I can't go any farther."

"Why not?"

"It's got my leg."

Serge rolled over with the jaws. "So pull it loose."

"I need to do something else first."

"Coleman, what can be more important?"

"One of the coils is going around my neck."

Serge rolled the other way. "This is critical: As fast as you can, get one of your arms up next to your throat so when it starts squeezing you can breathe for a couple more minutes."

"Okay, now it has my leg, neck *and* arm," said Coleman. "Camping is starting to be bad again."

"Damn, it's got both of us," said Serge. "Forget the tail. Emergency

Notification System: We both start crawling as fast and hard as we can away from each other. That should stretch it out."

"I'm crawling," said Coleman. "But it's taking everything I got to just move an inch at a time. And it keeps flipping me over."

"Same here." Serge involuntarily rolled to his left and dug his feet into the ground. "Just don't stop."

Coleman clawed at dirt with his free hand. "Serge, when they announced the python hunt, wasn't there a safety class people were supposed to take?"

"That's for amateurs. Keep crawling!"

"I'm getting too tired . . . don't . . . think . . . I can . . . make . . . it . . ."

"You have to!" Serge realized Coleman was about to go down for the count, so he summoned his last bit of strength for a single burst. "Give it all you can one last time—now!"

Both yelled for that extra oomph and strained ahead.

"It's working," said Coleman.

"I know." Serge got one arm free. "He's starting to uncoil and deal with what we're doing to him."

"It let go of my leg . . . and my neck."

"Can you get to the tail?"

"I think so . . . yeah, got it!"

Serge yanked his other arm loose and stood with hands around the snake's neck. "Pull!"

This was a much easier task. The pair stretched the snake into a long reptilian rope.

"Good God," said Coleman. "It must be a hundred feet long!"

"Closer to seventeen," said Serge.

"What do we do with it now?"

Serge looked around. "Put it in the car."

The full moon was high, backlighting dragonflies and vultures as the swamp world made a sizzling racket. Serge pinned the snake's neck with his foot while he fished keys from his pocket and opened the driver's door.

"Coleman, I'm going to climb through the car with its head and go out the other side. Then we'll bunch him up and slam the doors. But he's going to coil, so it'll have to be a quick release."

They completed the task and stared through the windows.

Coleman slapped his neck. "It's exploring."

Bang, bang, bang...

Serge glanced at the trunk, then turned to Coleman with his mouth open.

"Why are you looking at me like that?"

"Eureka!" said Serge. "You're a genius!"

"I am?"

Serge ran to the campsite for his duffel bag. "You just gave me the last organic inspiration I needed for my science project!"

"You're welcome ... Where are you going?"

"To get your sleeping bag!"

Serge quickly returned with the sack, brushing dirt off the side. "None the worse for wear. And glad your zipper isn't broken like mine. Help me get the python inside this thing."

"I like him in the car better."

"Coleman! There's nothing to be afraid of. I've seen it on TV a million times. I'll grab the head and stick it down inside, and then you quickly feed the rest of the snake into the bag."

Serge opened the driver's door, where the snake was curled up nicely on the seat. "There you are! ..." Moments later, the snake's tail disappeared into the bag and Serge pulled the drawstring tight, locking it with a plastic snap.

Coleman panted with hands on his knees. "I need a drink."

"Good thinking."

"Are you serious?" Coleman dove in the car for his bottle. "Because usually you nag about me getting messed up."

Serge dragged the heavy bag. "Not this time. Bring the fifth with you."

Coleman stood next to the campfire pit, holding the bottle by the neck. Serge was inside the tent, connecting wires with a crimping tool.

He punctured a hole in the floor with an extra plastic stake, securing the tiny motor that was connected to the solenoid switch and an array of small dry-cell batteries. Another stake held the end of the sleeping bag in place.

"Serge," said Coleman. "You left the tent flap open. Mosquitoes are getting in."

"That's crucial to the plan." Serge ran another wire from the battery to the electroplate, then to the capacitor, which was routed back to the solenoid. "Just keep drinking."

"No need to tell me twice." The bottle went skyward.

Serge exited the tent and pulled a plastic box with a red cross from his duffel, removing a syringe and a glass vial.

Coleman took another slug and wiped dribble with the back of his hand. "What's that?"

"Some stuff I added to my first-aid kit because the ones in the store never come with everything you need, like a syringe and paralytic agent when you need uncooperative patients to remain still."

Serge jammed the needle in the vial. He pulled back the plunger to fill the chamber and ran toward the Cobra's trunk.

Bang, bang, bang . . .

The trunk popped open. Linus Quim thrashed like a landed fish, screaming under duct tape. Serge patted his head. "You're just going to hurt yourself that way." The needle stabbed Quim in the butt, and he fell inert.

Coleman continued chugging as instructed, watching Serge in the moonlight as he dragged their captive by the ankles. Then he carefully positioned Quim inside the tent.

Serge stepped back outside and beamed with satisfaction. "Coleman, what do you think?"

"I'm drunk."

"You have impeccable timing." Serge held the tent flap open. "Now get in there and do your thing."

"My thing?"

"Have another drink."

Coleman went inside the tent and sat cross-legged with his bottle. "Camping's getting better again."

Serge sprayed himself liberally with insect repellent, then stepped inside and took a seat beside his pal.

Coleman lowered the fifth. "What's going on?"

"Mother Nature taking its course," said Serge. "I just redirected the route a little."

A mosquito landed on Coleman's arm, then another, and another. They took off in wobbly flight as others found exposed flesh.

"Oooo, almost forgot," said Serge. "Stay here."

Coleman forged on into intoxication as mosquitoes flew away from him like children participating in that sadistic initiation of spinning around with their foreheads on the end of a baseball bat. Bugs staggered around the tent's floor.

Serge returned with a long, clear tube and a roll of duct tape. He inserted one end of the tube in Linus's mouth and taped it in place. The rest of the tube ran the length of Quim's body and was taped to one of his ankles. Serge sat next to Coleman again. "There, now nature has clear sailing."

"Getting a little wrecked here," said Coleman. "What am I looking at?"

The first mosquito flew in a corkscrew pattern and landed on the electroplate with a tiny flicker.

Serge canted his head. "There's the first charge to the capacitor."

"That means I'm seeing triple."

Flash.

"There's the second. I don't know how many it will take since this is all organic. But when it hits the tipping point, the capacitor will fire a charge to the solenoid, which will turn on the little motor . . . Hey, Linus!"

"He can't hear you," said Coleman. "He's out cold."

"No, that's the paralytic agent," said Serge. "He's fully awake and can hear fine. Just can't move . . . Yo! Quim! What kind of deranged upbringing would cause you to prey on parents' worst fears?"

"He's not answering," said Coleman.

"He can't talk either, but super fortunate for us it was a rhetorical question."

Flash, flash.

Serge snapped his fingers. "Quim, listen up, because this is your bonus round. I always give my contestants a way out. We're leaving soon to give you some privacy so you don't have to worry about any embarrassing photos ending up on Facebook. And after we do, a certain series of events will take place, ending with that little motor turning on. As you can see here, there's a wire running from its axle to the clasp locking the drawstring on the sleeping bag holding a big honkin' Burmese python. You definitely don't want that motor releasing the drawstring. Hoo-wee! . . ."

"Oh, I get it now," said Coleman. A mosquito took off from his arm and joined a small squadron flying inverted before stumbling around the floor.

" . . . Here's the thing about major constrictors: They often underestimate the size of dinner and try to tackle something too large."

Coleman nodded. "I would have ruptured him."

"He's right," Serge told Quim. "Coleman definitely would have given him a tummy ache. But you, on the other hand, are a sniveling, skinny little drink of water, so it's on the bubble."

"Is that the bonus round?" asked Coleman.

"You got it." Serge held his wristwatch toward Quim and tapped the face. "You're still almost sure to rupture him, but will it be in time? The tube in your mouth allows you to breathe and pray. Or maybe the paralytic will wear off and you can get those elbows working on the snake's insides to tilt the odds in your favor . . . But don't wait too long because it'll be digesting you the whole time. If you think getting pruny in the bathtub is bad . . ."

"Serge," said Coleman. "Will that tube really allow him to stay alive and awake while the snake sucks him in? Yuck."

"But if he makes it, think of the stories on his TV appearances! Another great weirdness headline for Florida!" Serge helped Coleman to his feet, and they stepped out of the tent. Before releasing the flap, Serge turned one last time. "Well, Quim, that's about it. But never forget: There's always hope."

Coleman belched. "Or the mosquitoes could sober up."

"He's right again," said Serge. "A double bonus round. It's your lucky day!"

A few minutes passed before Quim heard the sound of a Ford Cobra driving away and a tiny motor turning on. His transfixed eyes watched the drawstring on the sleeping bag slowly pull wide. A forked reptilian tongue twitched out the opening. The snake patiently slithered from the bag. Quim felt something on the top of his scalp. Then down to his forehead. Then down farther as goo dripped in the top of his eyes.

It went dark.

Chapter SEVENTEEN

THE NEXT DAY

Another trailer park. This one called Paradise Lakes. Brook looked at the tab on the next file: *Cooder Ratch*. They pulled up to a manufactured home with a Confederate flag in the window and a sign on the door illustrated by a gun: FORGET THE DOG, BEWARE OF OWNER. This time it was Shelby who took a deep breath before knocking.

The door opened and a shirtless man flicked a cigarette butt outside. "When do I get paid?"

"The trial hasn't started yet."

"Fucking lawyers." Cooder led them inside a trailer decorated with empty bottles. He grabbed a full one from the fridge, popped the cap and fell into a couch. "What do you guys want?"

"We need to go over your testimony—"

"I already told you: They screwed me in the ass!"

"We might want to soften that just a bit for court," said Shelby.

"Are you a faggot?" said Cooder.

"What did you just say?" Shelby started getting up.

Brook jumped to her feet first. "Mr. Ratch, you want to know when you get paid? The better question is how much, and I have some good news!"

"Really? . . ."

The Toyota Camry headed back on the Sawgrass Expressway. Shelby repeatedly hit gas and brake and swerved as traffic whizzed around. "Is someone playing a joke on us? These are the new named plaintiffs who are supposed to *help* our case?"

"It's your buddies at the law firm who added them," said Brook.

"I know, I know," said Shelby. "That was the jury consultant's idea."

Three sports cars whipped in front of the Toyota in an impromptu street race, forcing Shelby to ease off and reestablish distance.

"So what's the deal with the consultant?" said Brook. "He actually thinks these are good witnesses? Especially that last asshole?"

"Says it's all a matter of timing." Shelby fell back several more car lengths. "We're supposed to call Ruthy first and get the jury to start hating the defense attorney when they grill her on cross. Then we call Cooder, who in theory will act as proxy for the jurors' rage against their lawyers and strike a chord with certain blue-collar elements, at least according to his focus groups."

"Is this consultant any good?" asked Brook.

"We pay him like he is."

Shelby hit the brakes and dropped behind the newest cars in his lane.

Brook shook her head. "You were right about these drivers. If you don't stay right on the next guy's bumper, they keep cutting in until it feels like we're backing up to the last exit."

"Just have to let it roll off you," said Shelby. "That's life in general: Can't let jerks dictate your emotions."

"You make it sound like nothing bothers you."

"It doesn't."

"Then what about Cooder back there?"

"I think this is our exit."

The lawyers left for lunch and the courtroom became quiet. In one of the back rows, a young newspaper reporter gathered his notes and opened a cell phone.

" . . . Got the whole story. Prosecution rested. Looks like defendants will have to take the stand if they want a fighting chance. I'm thinking Metro front, maybe one-A, twenty inches . . . Could you repeat that last part? . . . Come back to the office immediately? But all the important testimony is this afternoon . . . Another mandatory meeting? . . . Larry, this is one of the biggest corruption cases in the state, millions in no-bid contracts and municipal-bond underwriting. Half the city council might go to jail . . . I know it's complicated—that's why it's essential we explain it . . . I disagree. The readers won't be bored once they understand the facts and how it undermines the very foundation— . . . What do you mean 'that doesn't sell ads'? Look, can I just skip this one meeting? We're having them every day now and getting scooped left and right . . . Uh, yes I like getting a paycheck. I'll be there . . ."

The reporter had five years of deep research reporting under his belt and an untucked shirt. His tie was loosened and, like his collar, sported tiny gnarls of fraying polyester. His byline read: Reevis X. Tome. Reevis thought that including the *X* was stupid, but his publisher insisted because it lent an air of integrity. His middle name was Paul.

Reevis reluctantly returned to his Datsun and caught the I-95 ramp north. He worked for one of the big South Florida papers, like the *Miami Herald, Fort Lauderdale Sun Sentinel* and *Palm Beach Post,* but not one of those. They were all currently locked in a fierce newspaper war. Except not against one another. Against the future. Everything was now the Internet. And the Internet had just announced, courtesy of Yahoo, the top ten most endangered jobs in the nation. And coming in at number two with a bullet was—drum roll—"newspaper reporter." Courteously, the article suggested alternative thriving jobs for each of the enumerated declining vocations. In the case of print reporters: Public relations was tomorrow's land of rainbows and Skittles. Reevis shuddered at the thought. To anyone with newspaper ink in their blood, this was like telling a Navy SEAL to become a birthday party clown.

It was inevitable. Newspapers, TV, radio and websites everywhere were furiously consolidating into mega-media conglomerates. News was heading in a fresh direction, and that direction was toward a plantation. The owners and top execs saw their compensation rocket, and top television anchors in each market signed guaranteed contracts in the upper six figures. Everyone else was told these were tough times. To save the companies from bankruptcy, they would have to absorb salary cuts, take unpaid furloughs and work harder. Reporters began shooting their own photos, photographers had to write stories, and both were required to appear on camera at ribbon cuttings and propane explosions, speaking into microphones as naturally as if they had just received involuntary sex reassignments.

Oh, but it gets better: the pedigree of the latest owners. News outlets used to be acquired by other media companies, or someone with at least a whiff of journalism background. Now the buying was done by venture capitalists, land consortiums, commodity traders and petrochemical distributors. Reevis's newspaper was bought by a thermometer factory.

The paper's hardened journalists had remained in denial about their profession's erosion, until a single watershed moment. The chief of photography went to his new managing editor, who had previously managed the entire southeast region fixing windshield cracks. The photo chief dropped stacks of pictures on the desk to illustrate the drastic difference in quality between his staff's efforts and those of conscripts from the news department. "They're just horrible! And not just exposure or f-stop, but chopping off legs and whole heads, and this last pile has one or more fingers over the lens to varying degrees."

The managing editor studied the images a moment before picking up the phone for security. "You're right, it's bad, but . . ."

The photo editor jerked his arm away from the guards escorting him out the front entrance. "I can leave on my own. Fuck you."

The editor's quote, in its entirety, went word-of-mouth viral, becoming the catchphrase of every frontline spear-carrier. Then, on a Tuesday, someone stayed late in the newsroom after the night shift had put the last edition of the paper to bed. The lights were off. In the dim glow from the hallway, the company's new mission statement hung proudly atop the front wall:

> To enhance our community's aggregate through multi-platform metrics of media synergy catalyzing integrated outcomes of macro-disciplines toward inclusive methodology paradigms generating positive algorithms of unwavering commitment to our children, the flag and God.

The next morning, reporters and editors filed in, stopped briefly, then took their seats and stared at computer screens as if nothing was different, grinning inside. Toward the front of the room, the publisher shouted at maintenance workers on ladders vainly trying to remove a roll of shelf paper glued over the sign with a new mission statement, courtesy of the managing editor's departing remarks to the photo chief:

> It's bad, but it's good enough.

Reevis checked his watch as he exited the interstate. He'd made good time from the courthouse. The Datsun raced a few short blocks and pulled into the company parking lot, which used to be free but was now deducted from each paycheck, whether employees used it or not.

Reevis raced through the lobby of the rechristened crystal news complex and caught the elevator for the fifth-floor auditorium. The meeting was about to start, just a few stragglers like Reevis looking for seats. He found one in the back row, where he always liked to sit, with the cynical old guard of journalism from the days of typewriters and indoor smoking. Though Reevis had a half decade of experience, nobody ever believed him. It had nothing to do with professionalism or performance; it was that cherub face. For him, shaving was an affectation. Whenever Reevis showed up to interview, someone always did the math: *You need a college degree to be a journalist, so he has to be at least twenty-one. Unless I heard him wrong on the phone and he's from one of the high school papers.*

And now, if one looked at the mostly veteran occupants of the auditorium's back row: *One of these things is not like the others.*

But the old gang roundly accepted Reevis, if for no other reason than he had still gone to journalism school long after it was well known to be economic suicide.

"What's this meeting about?" asked Reevis.

"Same as all the others," said a crusty crime reporter named Danning. "Pull us away from writing stories to tell us we're not writing enough stories."

The publisher climbed the steps to the stage, where the new ownership group stood in the wings. His most important contribution to the paper's top chair was a publisher's name—E. Strunkend White—and he moved among the well-wishers, shaking hands and making small talk with the only people in the room who didn't have ticking deadline clocks between their ears.

The back row squirmed and checked their wrists.

Reevis leaned forward and looked down the row. "Anything good happen today while I was out?"

Danning elbowed a thirty-year city-hall beat reporter named Mazerek. "Tell him about Chelsea."

"What about Chelsea?" asked Reevis. Chelsea Lane was the second-most-popular TV anchor from Miami to West Palm, rumored to have received a 27 percent pay bump since the last Nielsens, meaning she now made three times more than the entire last row combined.

"A thing of pure beauty," said Mazerek. "You know how ever since we merged with the TV station, she has to strut through the middle of the newsroom five times a day? Talking super loud so we all know we're in her presence? She comes through again this morning, shouting away, yada, and the rest of us are thinking, 'How much attention do you need? You're already *on TV.*'"

Danning elbowed him again. "You're burying the lead."

"Oh, right," said Mazerek. "Then in the middle of yodeling through the room, something gets caught on one of her ridiculous high heels—and she takes a world-class header!"

"No!" said Reevis.

"I shit you not!" said Mazerek. "But the best part is it wasn't one of those neat, graceful falls. It started with a half trip, which made her think she could correct it and not go down, so she's moving faster and faster, trying to get her feet back under her. Finally, after stumbling a good twenty feet, she goes flying with her arms out like she's sliding into second base. Of course nobody helps her up. And she gets to her knees and looks around, and everyone just continues typing and making phone calls like nothing happened, which makes her think we're all laughing at her inside . . ."

"We were," said a seasoned investigative reporter named Bilko.

"Anything else?" asked Reevis.

"After Chelsea left, someone found a piece of chalk and drew a crime-scene outline where she went splat, limbs bent at crazy angles," said Mazerek. "And someone else drew skid marks leading up to the site of the crash."

"Wish I could have been there," said Reevis.

"How's the photography coming?" asked Danning, tilting his head at a cynical angle. "Still in the car?"

Reevis sighed. "Nobody's noticed yet."

"What are you guys talking about?" asked Mazerek.

"You'll love this," said Danning. "Ever since our esteemed managing editor put the kibosh on photo quality, our boy here refuses to get out of the car."

"I'm not following," said Bilko.

"It's a matter of principle," said Reevis.

Danning put a hand on the junior reporter's shoulder. "He's taking a stand. All his photos will be shot from his driver's seat until someone catches on, but I don't think they're going to."

"What about mug shots?" asked Mazerek.

"From the car, too," said Danning. "He lures them out of their building with some medical excuse."

Bilko scratched his scalp. "So that's why all his head shots in the paper are of people looking down at something."

Mazerek put his hand on Reevis's other shoulder. "I'm liking the kid better and better each day."

Danning pointed forward. "Believe it or not, he's finally going to start."

A finger tapped a microphone. "Good afternoon," said the publisher. "I would like to begin by thanking all of you for the hard work during our restructuring designed to increase efficiencies by combining the efforts of our various media . . ."

The people on the side of the stage applauded. The audience gave him the stink eye.

" . . . However, there is still much to do."

Up to now, everyone had been wondering what was on the giant, sheet-covered easel behind him. The publisher turned toward an assistant, which was the signal to remove the sheet.

"Un-fucking-believable," said Danning.

"A giant thermometer?" said Reevis.

The red on the thermometer rose only a tiny bit from the bulb at the bottom, indicating the temperature of a patient going into hypothermic shock. The publisher aimed a laser pointer at the visual aid.

"This is our current average story output." The laser went to the top of the display, next to the large number 98.6. "And this is where we need to be to survive in this market . . ."

"I may throw up," said Mazerek.

E. Strunkend White had placed the laser pointer back in his breast pocket but forgot to turn it off. The audience didn't hear another word as they stared at the red dot coming through his jacket.

Danning fidgeted and glanced at his Timex. "I got two stories to file."

"What a farce," said Bilko. "I don't know how much longer I can take this."

Another easel was brought out, listing a series of consultant findings.

"Time-motion studies?" said Mazerek.

"They're tracking how we walk around the office?" said Bilko.

"We're approaching the iceberg," said Danning.

The publisher leaned into his microphone. "I know a lot of you are thinking you already have full plates, so we've come up with a set of streamlining prime directives." A fist pounded the podium. "First, cut the number of phone calls per story in half..."

And the fist continued to pound with the announcement of each new cost-cutting measure. Apparently that wasn't enough emphasis. From behind the curtains on the side of the stage, someone emerged and took up a position next to the publisher.

Every jaw in the audience fell.

"Did someone drug my coffee?" asked Danning.

Bilko shook his head. "Are we really seeing this shit?"

"Wish I had a camera," said Mazerek. "Nobody would ever believe this actually happened at a major Florida newspaper."

Onstage, someone in a Power Ranger costume stood beside the podium. Each time the publisher announced another directive, the ranger jumped into a new fighting stance and karate-chopped the air.

"No more investigative stories!" said the publisher. "If it's not breaking, it's not news!"

The Power Ranger's hands sliced and jabbed.

Danning turned to Mazerek. "We just hit the iceberg."

Chapter EIGHTEEN

MIDNIGHT

Hialeah.

A blinking neon sign behind barbed wire said that Roscoe's Haul 'N Scrap was still open for sudden vehicle-crushing needs. Next door stood a small concrete pillbox of a building the size of an office at a no-credit-no-problem used-car lot.

The name of the defunct car dealership remained faintly visible under a new paint job that now read: ZIGGY BLADE, ATTORNEY-AT-LAW (DUIs, TRAFFIC COURT, WILLS & DIVORCE).

All the windows had burglar bars, and a large steel plate protected the entire doorknob area from crowbars. The lone car out front was a purple Jetta with a COEXIST bumper sticker where each letter was a religious logo. The streetlights had the extra-yellowish haze that said you shouldn't be here. A pumping stereo went by on the next street, leaving a Doppler effect of barking dogs.

An index finger pressed the doorbell.

A long pause.

The doorbell rang again. And again.

"Maybe he's not here," said Brook. "I don't see any lights."

"That's his car. He's here." Shelby pressed the button again. "You have to know Ziggy."

Ding-dong. Another pause. Then from inside, barely audible through the door: "We're closed."

A fist pounded. "Ziggy, open up! It's me, Shelby. I brought my new partner."

"Oh, shit." Then a patter of footsteps running away from the door.

An exchange of looks between the attorneys.

In the back of the office, Ziggy threw open a window and flapped a towel to clear the smoke—"Be there in a second!"—a bottom desk drawer slammed shut with an ashtray full of roaches.

The sound of footsteps again. "Coming! . . ." Ziggy gave his mouth a burst of breath spray and opened with a big smile and bloodshot eyes.

"Ziggy, this is Brook Campanella . . . Brook, Ziggy."

They shook hands.

"Let's get inside," said Ziggy. "I don't like to leave the door open at this hour."

The pair entered. Ziggy stuck his head outside a final time, quickly glancing up and down the street, then slammed the door, bolting four locks and propping a chair under the knob.

The building was a single room divided in two with bamboo curtains. The front half consisted of the reception area. Cot, two plastic molded chairs and movie posters. *Twelve Angry Men, To Kill a Mockingbird, My Cousin Vinny.*

Ziggy parted the curtains and led them in back. "Sorry about the mess." He balled up a Taco Bell wrapper.

"You left a message?" said Shelby.

"That's right. Have a seat." Ziggy went to a corner table holding a boom box. "You don't mind, do you? I love music when I'm thinking."

Brook looked Ziggy up and down. Nothing working. Short and blubbery, with a scraggle of beard and uncombed hair sticking horizontally out over his ears. A negative genetic experiment crossing Danny DeVito and Allen Ginsberg. His too-tight T-shirt had a picture of Manson over the phrase CHARLIE DON'T SURF.

Ziggy decided the music wasn't loud enough and gave the volume knob an extra crank.

"... *Send lawyers, guns and money!* ..."

"That's better." Ziggy walked back to his desk with a slapping of flip-flops and opened a bottle of aspirin.

Brook looked around. The wood-paneled walls were actually rolls of contact paper. A diploma hung crooked. It was a Xerox.

Ziggy pulled some handwritten pages from the top drawer. "I wanted to try out my opening arguments on you. It's just a rough draft, so don't hold back on the criticism ..."

"Ziggy ..." said Shelby.

"Hold on, okay ... Ladies and gentlemen of the jury, you may think this is just a mortgage fraud case, but jettison that thought. It is much, much more: the death of the American Dream! The sovereign individual thrown against the gears of the industrial complex!" Ziggy threw an arm in the air. "The McCarthy hearings! Vietnam! Watergate! ..."

"Ziggy ..."

"... J. Edgar Hoover! Iran-Contra! The CIA and LSD!—"

"Ziggy!" shouted Shelby.

Ziggy lowered the arm and looked up from his papers. "You want me to change something?"

"Ziggy, what are you doing?" asked Shelby.

"Giving my opening statement. I just told you."

"But I'm giving the opening statement," said Shelby.

"Really?" said Ziggy. "You like it that much? Okay, you can read the first half and I'll—"

"That's not what I meant."

"I'm not following."

"My firm has the case now. I've already written my opening remarks."

"Nobody told me."

"Jesus, Ziggy, we tell you every time you call the office. You're not involved in the trial."

"This is fascist bullshit!" said Ziggy. "I don't blame you, but you're going to lose this case because the soul of sixties free-verse oratory has been corporatized."

"Ziggy, foreclosure has nothing to do with dropping LSD."

"Yes, it does." Ziggy shuffled his papers. "You didn't let me finish. It all ties together. The universe is one."

"Look," said Shelby, lowering his voice. "I don't know who else would have had your kind of passion to pull this case together. I mean those forklifts full of documents . . ."

"I did a little speed."

"Whatever. The point is, you've already contributed more than anyone could remotely expect. Now it's time for our area of expertise. Unfortunately trials have become a sterile science, and you did willingly sign that contract turning the matter over to us. We've already paid your back expenses, so we now have risk exposure, too."

"But it's the biggest case I'll ever have," said Ziggy. "One of the only cases. Most people just call here for a used car."

"We'll give you all due credit in the newspapers and legal journals."

Ziggy's eyes became glassy, and his lower lip stuck out. "Can I at least sit at the table? I promise not to say anything."

"Jeez . . ." Shelby took in the visual totality of Ziggy, thinking, *The jury consultant's head would melt off his neck.* "I . . . mm . . ."

"Excuse me," said Brook, "but there are only two chairs."

"Uh, that's right," said Shelby. "The table's just so long. It's how they built the courtroom, but otherwise you'd be our first choice . . ."

"You really mean that?"

"Absolutely," said Shelby, nodding with vigor. "How about we instead keep you apprised of all developments as we lead up to the trial?"

"I'd really appreciate that," said Ziggy. "It's always nice to have you visit."

Beep-beep-beep-beep . . .

"Well, that's my car's burglar alarm," said Shelby, standing up. "Guess we better be going."

Ziggy followed them to the door. "Nice to meet you, Brook . . . Don't be strangers . . ."

Whatever had sounded the car's alarm was gone, and the lawyers drove off without incident.

Ziggy locked back up and grabbed the ashtray from his bottom drawer, poking around for something roach-worthy. He stuck a burnt nub in an alligator clip and blazed it. Then he leaned back in his chair, kicked feet up on the desk and grabbed a manila file. The folder had an adhesive label on the tab: *Grand-Bourg Holding Group.*

He flipped through impenetrable spreadsheets and photostats of bank records from murky consortiums incorporated in the Lesser Antilles. He reached one of the last pages and stopped with a perplexed look. He flipped back toward the front of the file and pulled out another page, setting them side by side in his lap. He took a long, thoughtful toke on the roach. Eyes moving back and forth. Addresses, dollar figures, doing-business-as. Another toke, scratching his stomach.

Suddenly his feet dropped off the desk. He grabbed the phone and dialed.

"It's me, Ziggy . . . I think I might have some work for you . . . I'm sorry, I can't understand anything you're talking about . . . Yes, it's some private-eye work. Got a pen handy? . . . Mahoney, you'll have to speak English . . . Okay, here's what I need you to find out . . ."

THE NEXT AFTERNOON

Somewhere in the middle of Florida, a tremendous roar echoed from the far side of one of the state's few hills.

"What the hell is that racket?" said Coleman. "Oh, shit, damn!"—slapping his chest and clutching between his legs.

Serge glanced over from the driver's seat. "What did you do now?"

"Dropped my joint. The sound startled me." Coleman bent forward to check the floor.

"You better hurry up and find it! I don't want to deal with another pot-related car fire." Serge accelerated east on Highway 44. "The last blaze was so huge local TV covered it with aircraft."

"That time it wasn't my fault." Coleman pushed himself up and twisted around in his seat. "Your gunfire made me jump."

"Oh, it's always my gunfire, like I'm supposed to put the Second Amendment on hold while you get baked."

"Loud sounds disturb me."

"What are you, a nervous poodle hearing a blender?"

"Oh, shit! That hurts like a bastard!" Coleman took off one of his sneakers and looked inside. "I found it."

"Hope you didn't burn anything in here. I just had the upholstery done."

"No." Coleman stuck a finger through fabric. "Just my sock . . . That roaring sound is getting louder."

"Because we're in God's country now."

"What does that mean?"

"Just keep your eyes where the highway crests that distant hill."

Coleman leaned toward the dash. "I see them. Jesus, look at all those Harleys."

"Bikers always bird-dog the best scenic drives showcasing the state's natural bounty. They aggressively shun interstates, suburbs and any place that even hints there's a mall within twenty miles."

Coleman pulled out rolling papers. "I've never seen a Hells Angel in the food court."

Serge stuck his arm out the window, giving the bikers a big thumbs-up as they passed.

"What's that strange look they're all giving you?"

"It means we're brothers of the road," said Serge. "Hand me my assault rifle."

Coleman turned around on his knees and reached in the backseat. *Bang.*

"Crap!"

Bang.

Serge looked up at a pair of holes in the roof. "Coleman, I can understand accidentally firing once . . ."

"Not my fault. The sound of the first one made me jump."

"Give me that thing!" Serge snatched it away and clicked on the safety. "You just better hope those bullets don't come down anyplace important."

The Cobra raced past pristine pastures, lakes, barns. Herons and egrets went about their business. A windmill creaked.

Coleman twisted up a fresh one. "What do you think about all this screaming lately on gun control?"

"Everyone's lost their minds." Serge rammed a high-capacity magazine in his weapon. "Who the hell needs an assault rifle to hunt deer?"

"But you have an assault rifle."

"I don't hunt deer."

"What about your jumbo magazine?"

"I need that, too, in case I'm facing overwhelming odds." He reached under his seat. "In fact, I need an extra one, which I plan to duct-tape inverted to the first one so I can just flip it over."

Coleman toked and thought. "So bikers tell you when you're in God's country?"

"That or billboards."

"Billboards?"

"There's no middle ground with billboards in God's country. Half of them advertise the road to avoid the eternal fires of damnation; the rest the road to topless truck stops."

Coleman held his joint toward the windshield. "What's that big thing up ahead?"

"Looks like one of those giant balloons for roadside advertising, except this one's in front of a church."

"What's it say?"

Serge turned as they went by. "Something about gay marriage ruining everything."

A preacher barked into a bullhorn. Two bullets came down from the sky and popped the balloon.

Coleman turned around in his seat. "It deflated on top of the preacher. The others are trying to pull him out."

"The Lord works in mysterious ways."

Coleman sat back around. "Where are you going today?"

"Still working on my new Master Plan, platinum edition." A sign went by, proclaiming the city limits of Leesburg. "I've always wanted to be a lawyer."

Coleman made a face. "But everyone hates lawyers. You've heard all the jokes: 'Why does New Jersey have so much toxic waste and California so many lawyers?'"

"And?"

"And what?"

"The rest of the joke."

"That's it," said Coleman. "It means lawyers blow."

"New Jersey got to pick first."

"What do you mean?"

"Forget it." Serge took a bend in the road as more bikers thundered by. "See, lawyers are another example of me zigging when everyone else zags. Sure, a bunch of them are parasites, maybe most, but just like in your intestines, there are a lot of good parasites doing some heavy lifting. And when push comes to shove, and the common man is up against powerful interests, guess what his last line of defense is?"

"Intestinal parasites?"

"I just remembered another Florida legal movie," said Serge. "This one focused on punishment. It's where we're heading now."

"To watch a movie?"

"No, where it happened. Or rather where the real events happened. But they went and filmed it again in Hollywood. Don't get me started on that."

"Which movie?"

"Okay, here's the best part!" Serge took his hands off the wheel and cracked knuckles. "It's the all-time 1967 American rebellion classic *Cool Hand Luke,* starring Paul Newman."

"You mean the chain-gang movie?" said Coleman. "But I thought that was Mississippi or Georgia."

"And that's what everyone thinks," said Serge. "It drives me crazy, yet another example of other states stealing our props. But it really happened in Florida. And not just North Florida, where everyone scoffs and says, 'Well, that's really Georgia anyway.' This was way down in the middle of the state right around here. I just need to drive a little farther and turn south at Tavares."

"You mean the band that sang 'Heaven Must Be Missing an Angel'? That really would be punishment."

"No, you idiot, the city." Serge cut the wheel and made a right onto U.S. 19. They had already been driving through rural outskirts, and now they left even that behind. "I got connections at the library and told them I needed some historical research, and they said they'd get right on it." He uncrumpled a ball of paper on the steering wheel. "Received rough directions to put me in the ballpark, but said they weren't sure what I'd find."

"So we're going to hang out in the middle of another field again?"

"Something wrong with that?"

"It's boring."

"Don't poop on my moment."

"But we're always standing in weeds and sticker patches while you tell me to 'dig it.'"

"You should be thanking me. Even if everything's gone, just standing in the spot of such momentous cultural significance and intrinsically soaking it in is more than one could ask for." Serge pointed up at two circles of light coming through the car's roof. "And don't think we're not going to discuss those holes."

The Cobra cruised a few more miles before pulling onto the dirt near an easily missed sign that said CAMP ROAD. Serge kept it under five miles an hour as he craned his neck left and right. They passed a tiny church, then some trailers and a woman walking barefoot with a vegetable basket. The Cobra disappeared into the woods.

Ten minutes later, Coleman looked ahead at the ever-narrowing road, branches scraping both sides of the car as the sun went down. "Where are we?"

"Probably missed the place. Better go back."

"But we can't turn around."

Serge threw his arm over the back of the seat and faced out the rear window. "Time once again to practice backing up several miles."

"Hey," said Coleman. "There's that barefoot woman we passed earlier. She's looking at us weird."

"Probably just nerve damage to her face. I'm sure she see Cobras backing through the woods at forty all the time."

"She's waving like she wants to tell us something."

Serge eased to a stop and rolled down the window. The woman set her basket on the ground and stared inside the car with puzzlement. "Can I help you fellas find something?"

"Yes!" said Serge. "Donn Pearce wrote the novel *Cool Hand Luke* after serving a stint at Road Prison Number Fifty-eight, but the suits changed the number to thirty-six and moved it to Hollywood."

"You're trying to find the old chain-gang place?" She pointed over the top of the car. "Used to be right there on the other side of all that brush. Just keep backing up until you get to the fork and take the other spur."

"The foliage in California looked different," said Serge. "So they stole a bunch of our Spanish moss and mailed it to the left coast to hang it on the trees. True story, look it up." The Cobra departed with backward spinning wheels.

Serge whipped around at the fork and zoomed up to a locked fence with a KEEP OUT sign from the state of Florida. Which meant bolt cutters. The Cobra bounded across an empty expanse of earth. "Coleman! Dig it!"

"Whoopie, another field."

The muscle car continued across the grassy flat. Along the south side ran a row of crooked old wooden posts and barbed wire covered with vines. Nature has its own way of foreclosing. Decades of creep from reeds, palmettos, overgrown underbrush and weed-covered dunes from some kind of soil upheaval. In the distance, a rare sign of man's former endeavor.

"Check out the corroded three-sided metal shed over there, or what's left of it." Serge got out his camera and turned on the flash. "Maybe, just maybe, it stored tools that the chain gangs used to work on nearby roads. One can only hope. Don't get me wrong—I'm perfectly content to be in this field."

"Hooray."

Serge suddenly hit the brakes, pitching Coleman forward into the dash. "What'd you do that for?"

"Those oaks with a bunch of scrub that's taken root." Serge grabbed his heart. "I think I see something, but it's way too dark from over here."

The Cobra circled west for a better view. The car stopped. Serge got out and fell to his knees.

"God loves me."

Chapter NINETEEN

MEANWHILE

A clear tube of red light gradually phased to green and blue. The tube stretched for miles, if you didn't count breaks in the white-washed balustrade running between the beach and Highway A1A. Traffic practically didn't exist since it was after three A.M. on a week-night, or make that morning.

Back toward the city, Fort Lauderdale's skyline stood mostly dark except for some widely spaced office lights scattered across the faces of the high-rises. Most of them were cleaning crews. Except one office on a thirtieth floor.

"I can see the red tubes from the beach," said Brook. "Now it's green."

"It's a beautiful state," said Shelby, standing next to her at the floor-to-ceiling windows. "I actually grew up right down there near the river."

"Where?"

"It's now a martini bar."

The conference room's table was again covered with files and cold take-out food. Mexican, this time.

Brook yawned and stretched.

Shelby walked back to the table. "I think you should handle Ruthy on direct."

Brook spun in alarm. "What?"

"Our jury consultant thinks so, too."

"You want me to question a witness at the beginning of my very first trial?"

"Got to start sometime, so best to get it out of the way." Shelby idly moved refried beans around a plate. "Besides, you and her are a much more sympathetic fit than if I do it."

"But I get . . ."

"Get what?"

"When I'm super nervous, like just before speaking to a large group—"

"You throw up? That's normal."

"No, diarrhea."

Shelby stared.

"But that's not the bad part," said Brook. "It's lead-up panic: Can I run out of the room and make it in time?"

"We've definitely been putting in too many late hours together." Shelby grabbed a Q&A script. "Let's go over direct again. I'll play Ruthy this time . . ."

An hour later, the sound of vacuum cleaners outside the conference room. Brook yawned again as she strolled in a circle around the table, reviewing documents interspersed with notecards of legal strategy. "I think we've covered it all."

"You can go," said Shelby. "I just want to look back over a couple more things."

"But you need your sleep, too." Brook tossed half a burrito in the trash. "Opening arguments are in two days, and we need to get our body clocks back among the living."

"I said you could go."

She pulled out a chair. "Then I'm staying."

Shelby held a manila folder with an adhesive tab. *Grand-Bourg Holding Group*.

"What's that?" asked Brook.

"I don't know." Shelby flipped through papers. "These are the discovery documents that don't fit any other category. They don't fit anything, almost as if they're from another case that accidentally got mixed up down in the mail room."

"Looks like financial spreads and random international corporate recordings."

"Ownership issues, but it's gibberish." He reached one of the last pages and stopped. Then he flipped back to the front of the file and pulled out a page. He held them side by side.

Brook leaned over his shoulder. "Notice something?"

"Not sure." One was printed on rice paper and the other had an official-looking stamp from Aruba. "Why would that money . . . ? And then over here . . . ?"

"The mortgages?"

"No, Consolidated itself."

"I don't understand."

"Neither do I." He picked up the phone.

"Who are you calling at this hour?"

"Just leaving a voice mail with our firm's private investigators." A finger pressed touch-tone numbers. "I won't be getting up till at least noon, and I'd like them to start looking into this first thing."

"What do you think they'll find?"

"Who knows? The point is, I don't want any surprises in the courtroom." He inexplicably hung up.

"Why'd you do that?" asked Brook. "You didn't leave a message."

"If it's something we could use, then our investigator poking around might tip them off." Shelby slapped his cheeks to restore alertness. "I'm half-loopy from lack of sleep. It's probably nothing." He began dialing again . . .

SOUTH OF TAVARES

Serge slowly rose from his knees in religious awe.

"It's just a building," said Coleman. "Like a little house."

"Get a grip," Serge told himself. "I need a positive ID before I let myself become effectively excited." He grabbed a piece of glossy paper from over the sun visor.

"What's that?" asked Coleman.

"Screen grab I printed out from *Cool Hand Luke*." Serge walked to the front of the building and raised the picture for comparison. "The film crew took meticulous sets of photos out here before constructing an exact replica of the prison camp out in Stockton."

Coleman leaned over. "Your picture looks the same as the building. What's it mean?"

"Time to get excited!" He chugged a travel mug and slipped on mirrored sunglasses.

Coleman sluggishly followed Serge to where he repeatedly ran up and down four blue steps to a porch.

"Okay, this field also has a house," said Coleman. "I've dug it. Can we go to a bar now?"

"Not just any house! It's where the warden lived." Serge turned at the top of the steps and ran back. "Can't believe it's still standing. Strother Martin paced right here on this porch, except in California."

"I'm still bored."

"Coleman, we're working."

"Running up and down steps?"

"I'm in training to be a lawyer." Serge panted as he completed another short lap. "Everyone else just goes to law school. That's why I'll have the edge. That's enough running."

The air was still, nurturing the kind of humidity that made people taste their own salt. Serge stood with hands on hips and stared silently across the dark field from behind mirrored sunglasses.

"Can you see anything with those things on at night?" asked Coleman.

"No." Serge maintained his gaze with a stone face. "These were worn by Morgan Woodward, who had one of the greatest nonspeaking roles in film history as Boss Godfrey, who shot Luke in the climactic scene."

"That's nice," said Coleman. "But what's any of this have to do with being a lawyer?"

"This is what." Serge popped the trunk and grabbed a shirt collar. "Out you go!"

A bound and gagged man flopped to the ground. "Since I don't have a law degree, I can't practice in court. But I found a giant loophole that says I can be a fixer." Serge dragged the man up the steps and hand-cuffed him to a railing.

"What's a fixer?" asked Coleman.

"Every gigantic law firm has one." Serge retrieved a cooler from the backseat. "It's a lawyer who's a breed apart: somebody with a law school education and the balls of a bounty hunter. So they pull them out of the courtroom to work in the field."

"What do they do?"

"A fixer is a one-man rapid-response team that gets his arms around a crisis before it blows out of proportion, like if someone's being black-mailed or throws a punch at a formal gala, or if a political rival mails a box of his own doo-doo to the mayor before realizing the idea isn't as sparkling as it first seemed. They deal with the chaos of reality as op-posed to the artificial order of the courtroom."

"You're going to be a fixer?"

"I finally realized it's what I was destined for my entire life." Serge stared down through his sunglasses at the hostage. "I know the law and the street. As long as I stay out of the courthouse and only practice in the field, I'm not committing any crime." He kicked the whining cap-tive in the ribs. "Well, you know what I mean."

"Who is that guy, anyway?"

"A particularly ugly case." *Kick, slap.* "Did you know that lawyers have created a legal form of blackmail? It's true. What you do is sue someone over an insignificant pretext—like a limited-partnership glitch or intellectual-property theft—but there's an overt hint that certain embarrassing evidence will inevitably surface. That's the real issue. Those revelations won't prove anything illegal but will be abso-lutely catastrophic in terms of reputation and income, like all those

Christmas-party cell-phone videos floating around the Internet involving candy-cane dildos."

"I'm collecting those."

"Then the suing party offers to settle and includes a confidentiality clause, which is really a de facto bribe to keep silent, and it's all legally bulletproof."

"This is really going on?"

"More than you'd think," said Serge. "There was actually one case in the news where these lawyers forgot the confidentiality clause and simply faxed a monetary request to keep quiet. Naturally they were arrested for extortion, and the TV legal pundits had a chuckle-fest: 'Ho-ho-ho, they didn't understand how to work our tricky little bribe scheme.' And the rest of us are watching at home with disgusted looks: 'This is what flies for okay in your culture?' . . . Coleman, get my stopwatch from the glove compartment."

Coleman wiped his brow as a bird of prey circled overhead. He returned from the car. "Here you go, Serge . . . How'd you land this case, anyway?"

"Mahoney. The big firms have in-house fixers, but the smaller ones outsource on an as-needed basis. He was skeptical when I suggested the fixer gig, but business is starting to trickle in." He bent down and glared into the captive's eyes from a range of three inches. "I'm going to remove the duct tape now and I expect you not to scream."

Rip.

"I'll fucking kill you!"

Serge bashed him with a wicked uppercut, then applied fresh tape. He climbed the porch steps and stared out at nothing particular. "*'What we have here is failure to communicate.'* . . . I've always wanted to say that."

"What did this dude do?" asked Coleman.

"Fooled around on his wife and got divorced. Then he wouldn't pay child support, so she almost went broke and started a home-based business. Apparently she had a knack for it because it took off and money came pouring in. Something to do with party planning."

Coleman's ears perked. "People actually pay you for that?"

"Not like you think. Anyway, the ex-husband gets wind and wants a cut and threatens to show some private bedroom photos they had taken during better times, which wouldn't go over big with the soccer moms at little Tommy's birthday. Enter the confidentiality clause."

"So this is the ex-husband?"

"No, that would be witness-tampering, which is wrong." *Kick, kick.* "This is the lawyer." Serge crouched again in front of his guest. "Will you keep quiet this time if I take off the tape?"

The attorney had had enough. He nodded weakly with blood streaming from both nostrils.

"Great! Because we're coming to my favorite part of the movie!" Serge hopped with joy as he placed his cooler on the porch between them.

Rip.

A brief cry. Serge opened the thirty-six-gallon insulated box and removed a tray. The captive's eyebrows twisted in confusion. "Please don't hit me, but I have no idea what's going on. Who are you?"

"I'm a fixer, and we're going re-create the Paul Newman scene where he takes a bet to eat fifty hard-boiled eggs." Serge pulled the first egg out of the tray. "I know it's not how fixers usually operate, but there's a new breed of cat in town . . . Oh, and I couldn't lay my hands on that many hard-boiled eggs in a pinch, so I went to the deli at Publix and bought deviled eggs . . . Coleman, ready?"

Coleman nodded and clicked the stopwatch.

"Open wide!" Serge crammed the first egg into the attorney's mouth. He grabbed a second egg and popped it in his own mouth, licking his fingers. "Actually that's pretty tasty . . . Open up again . . ." Serge detected another question on the attorney's face. "What? You didn't think I was going to let you have all the fun? See, this is what's happening here. We're forming a bond. And I'm hoping you're a movie buff, because I can get pretty hung up on my favorite flicks. If you are a buff, we've got hours of fun ahead. Well, maybe not hours. Forget I said that. Did you know some of *Cool Hand* was actually shot in Florida? The bloodhound chase through the woods used a body double for Newman up at the Callahan Road Prison just north of Jacksonville. Open wide!" Serge continued feeding the captive as he chewed his own eggs. "We're doing it together, 'Kumbaya'-style, and if you reach Luke's record with me, I'll let you go. That's my bonus round. More on that later . . ."

The captive swallowed hard. "That's it?"

"Well, there is one little catch." Serge jammed another egg in his face. "Drop the lawsuit with the confidentiality clause. And persuade your client not to file with anyone else."

"How am I supposed to do that—" He was cut short with another egg.

"Come up with some kind of lie. You're a lawyer." Serge chomped and swallowed. "But if you don't, we'll keep coming out here until you either see the light or start liking eggs with paprika . . . Coleman?"

"What? Oh." He looked down at a sweep second hand. "Twenty minutes . . ."

Twenty minutes later:

Coleman giggled at Serge, laid out on the warden's porch. "You look pregnant."

"It's not a joke," said Serge. "My tummy feels all fucked up. What was I thinking?"

"The other dude looks in worse shape. Listen to him moan."

"That's because he doesn't have my warrior constitution." Serge slowly pushed himself into a sitting position. "Prussian stamina is essential to reenacting classic Florida movies."

"Is he going to die?"

"No, but he might wish he would."

"You're not waxing this dude?" Coleman sulked. "I thought this was another of your science projects."

"It is."

"Just eggs?"

"Maybe I'm losing a step with age." He reached into the cooler again for a cocktail mixer, deftly adding a menu of ingredients before vigorous shaking.

"What's that?" asked Coleman.

"Something to wash it down. It's not healthy for him to eat that much without a beverage." He poured the shaker's contents into a martini glass and took a seat on the porch next to the prostrate lawyer. "Hey, film buddy, this will make you feel much better."

The attorney held his bulging stomach and grimaced. "What are those fumes coming out of the glass?"

"A little dry ice. I saw it in the Tom Cruise movie *Cocktail,* and I'm a sucker for panache."

The barrister hesitated.

"Listen," said Serge. "If I wanted to kill you, there's a whole arsenal in my car."

The lawyer looked in the drink again. "You say this is okay?"

"I guarantee you'll feel totally different after drinking that."

"I'd do anything to get rid of this stomach ache . . . Here goes . . ." He drained the conic glass.

"Guess that wraps it up here," said Serge. "I know I mentioned hours of stimulating movie conversation, but I just remembered I have to go watch *Absence of Malice,* another Paul Newman Florida flick about the law and journalism. Am I jazzed!" Serge unlocked the handcuffs and headed back to his car. "Well, toodles!"

The longest pause. "Just like that? . . . You mean I'm free to go?"

"Free as a naked jaybird." Serge pointed toward his car with a thumb. "Unless you want to join us for the Miami *Absence of Malice* tour."

"No, I'm good."

The Cobra began driving away from the warden's residence. Coleman looked out the back window at the attorney staggering from the porch holding his stomach. "I don't believe it. You actually let someone go."

"There's a first time for everything."

"But what if he tells on us?"

"Let him try." Serge angled his muscle car toward the vandalized entrance gate. "That's one of the keys to my new breed of fixer: Make the intimidation so weird and embarrassing that even if it is revealed, it'll be laughed out of the room: 'I want to report a stomach ache because a Paul Newman fan made me eat deviled eggs.'"

"And we used mirrored sunglasses at night and a stopwatch."

"Exactly." Serge uncapped a bottle of Pepto-Bismol.

"By the way . . ." Coleman cracked a warm Schlitz. "What did you give him to drink?"

"That? Just a belly-soothing mixture of banana extract, guava, soy, virgin olive oil for the stomach lining and . . . oh, and just a tincture of pool chlorine. Those were the fumes, so I had to fib and say it was dry ice."

"Pool . . . ? Isn't that poisonous?"

"Oh, no! I mean maybe . . . well, yes—but only in a severely higher dosage than I administered—we swim in chlorinated pools all the time and swallow a lot of the water with little effect."

"Hey, the dude back there is grabbing a tree. He's starting to vibrate. You sure the chlorine didn't poison him?"

"Without a doubt." Serge turned the steering wheel toward the chain-link opening. "I checked all the swimming-pool concentration tables to be safe."

"Then why did you put it in at all?"

"Yeah, why did I?" Serge asked himself. "Uh, right. Did you know that each individual egg has one hundred and ninety-eight milligrams of phosphorus, one hundred and thirty-eight of potassium and one hundred and thirty-two of sodium, plus a bunch of sulfur?"

"No."

"And that's just a single egg." Serge shook his head with disbelief. "If you eat fifty—and who in their right mind would do that?—the last thing you want to drink is chlorine."

"Why not?"

"The valence of the outer electron shell. I know I'm talking to a wall here . . ."

"You are."

" . . . But all those chemicals in eggs react aggressively with chlorine, releasing a tremendous amount of heat and creating sodium chloride, potassium chloride, et cetera . . . Very gaseous in the reaction."

"Never heard of them," said Coleman as a tiny man in the background burped with violence.

"Trust me: Those chemicals are out there." Serge stopped at the gate and turned around in his seat. "Besides rocketing internal temperature, all those just-created salts would throw electrolyte balances off the chart, nervous system going haywire, organs shutting down, violent tremors, unconsciousness, worse."

"Electrolytes?"

"Very important to keep your precious bodily fluids in the safe zone. For instance, doctors about to perform some surgeries had to stop recommending certain hilariously aggressive bowel-evacuating solutions for the night before—if you're out there in our audience and took them, you know who you are—because people were dying from electrolyte crashes. And that was from a well-trusted over-the-counter product."

"Electrolytes are that important?"

"Damn straight. You can actually kill someone with too much constipation relief remedy." Serge stopped and tapped his chin. "Note to self . . ."

"Look!" Coleman pointed at the man flopping around in front of an oak tree. "Now he's tearing off all his clothes and running around the porch screaming."

"Must really be into *Cool Hand Luke*," said Serge. "Some people are way too obsessed with movies. I don't get it."

"He's stopped moving," said Coleman. "What's that mean?"

"Either he's performing the Paul Newman death scene or it's my first success as a fixer." Serge mashed the gas pedal. "Let's find something else that's broken."

Chapter TWENTY

FORT LAUDERDALE

Shelby Lang swiveled on the steps. "What are you stopping for?"

Brook stared up at the Broward County courthouse. She took a shallow swallow of air and pushed ahead.

Shelby emptied his pockets for the metal detector. "You sure you're okay?"

"I'll be fine."

They were by far the earliest to arrive in the courtroom. Before the next soul appeared, all was ready at the plaintiff's table. Files, notepads, water. Brook nudged a pen that was a half inch out of alignment.

After a nervous spell of stillness, the bailiff entered, followed by the court stenographer and a cast of local residents unconnected to any case who came to the courthouse each day because it was better than TV.

The double doors in the back of the courtroom swung open again. Brook turned around and gulped. In marched four strikingly hand-some men in identical black suits and black hair. Yale, Brown, Dart-mouth, Harvard. Blue tie, red tie, blue tie, red-and-blue. The imposing legal team of Riley and company took seats and opened briefcases in unison. An assistant wheeled in a handcart of file boxes. Someone else set up a giant easel for oversized, dry-mounted exhibits.

Brook elbowed Shelby. "Were they raised in test tubes?"

"Yes."

Finally another door in the front of the room opened. From the judge's chambers emerged a burly man in a black robe, a shade over six-five.

"What do you know about him?" whispered Brook.

"Judge Kennesaw Montgomery Boone?" said Shelby. "Let's put it this way: We couldn't have gotten a worse draw from the rotation. Totally sympathetic to corporations."

"That bad?"

"He didn't think the Supreme Court went far enough in *Citizens United*. Get ready to be overruled."

They sat without talking. A single rhythmic sound bounced off the walls, Brook clicking a pen open and closed. She noticed Shelby staring. "Sorry . . ." Then curiosity: "Where's the jury pool?"

"Won't be one today," said Shelby.

"Why not? Trial's supposed to start."

"It's been delayed," said Shelby. "Motion hearing. Just got a text."

"What kind of motion?"

Shelby told her what he expected.

"But they were supposed to do that a long time ago. It's unheard of at this stage."

"Anything to disrupt us," said Shelby. "Welcome to the opening shot in the psychological war."

A gavel banged. "I'm ready to hear motions."

A man stood at the defense table and told the judge what he wanted.

Shelby jumped to his feet. "Objection!"

"Overruled."

"May I cite precedent?"

The gavel banged. "Court is in recess." The black robe disappeared into chambers. Four men at the defense table simultaneously snapped briefcases and marched out of the courtroom with North Korean military precision, followed by a handcart of unopened boxes and an easel of unexhibited exhibits.

"That could have gone better," said Brook.

"Short and sweet." Shelby gathered stuff from their table. "Nothing I didn't expect."

"What do we do now?"

Shelby stood with his own briefcase. "Gas up the car."

A newspaper reporter in the back of the courtroom watched Shelby and Brook depart. He opened his cell. " . . . Boone granted the motion. I'm going to need some travel expenses approved and at least a week— . . . What? *Another* mandatory meeting? . . . But I have to hit the road . . ."

A half hour later, a blue Datsun entered the company lot.

Reevis spotted a trio of crusty journalists heading back from lunch. "Guys, wait up!"

Three men on the opposite sidewalk stopped and turned. Ill-fitting jackets and threadbare shoes. Bilko wore his trademark porkpie hat. Danning's jacket featured a bunch of thin blue-and-white vertical stripes like a southern lawyer. Mazerek had Brylcreem stains on his collar.

Reevis trotted across the street and caught his breath. "Going to the meeting?"

"It's mandatory."

The quartet strolled for the elevator. Danning stopped and pointed at a side door. "Let's take the stairs."

As they headed across the lobby, an unnaturally large number of colleagues began funneling toward the stairwell.

"What's going on?" asked Reevis.

"The roach," said Bilko.

"Roach?" asked Reevis.

Danning entered the stairwell. "You'll see . . ."

In the latest wave of austerity, Reevis's paper had cut two-thirds of the janitorial staff because shareholders never set foot in the building. Filth grew like weeds. Then came the roach . . .

Reevis trudged up the steps. "I still don't know what's going on."

"One more flight," said Mazerek.

Few had ever used the stairs until now. Foot traffic became thicker and thicker until it clogged to a stop on the third landing.

"I can't see," said Reevis. "Too many people."

"They'll move on," said Danning. "It's well worth the wait."

It was. Other journalists satisfied their curiosity and resumed their ascent toward the meeting.

Reevis wormed his way to the front for a view. "What the hell? When did this start?"

Mazerek stared down at an overturned bug. "Reliable reports pin the roach's death about a week ago, but nobody can be sure because the only people who take the stairs are the ones on diets."

"A sports guy started it," said Bilko. "He realized he'd seen the same roach for three straight days. And since it was so big, he couldn't believe it hadn't been cleaned up . . ."

" . . . Then he remembered most of the janitors were let go," continued Mazerek. "So the next day he made a tiny little cross for the roach. Journalists are already a strange lot, and sportswriters even stranger . . ."

" . . . The next day he came back to see if the roach was still there, and someone else had left flowers," said Danning. "Word started getting around and more and more people began taking the stairs. Next came some little candles, and the crime-scene tape went up. That was a week ago, and now we have this"—waving his hand over a bed of roses and baby's breath.

Reevis bent down to look at a tiny framed tribute photo of the roach in happier days. "Looks like a mini version of that outpouring for Princess Di."

"Frustration vents in weird ways," said Bilko.

"These are fucked-up times for our business," said Danning.

Mazerek pointed his cell-phone camera. "This time they'll have to believe this is going on at a major Florida newspaper."

"Better get to that meeting . . ."

They exited on the next landing and found the conference room. Smaller than the other venues, maybe thirty seats.

Bilko jerked his thumb. "Get a load of this too-cool-for-school punk."

At the front of the room, a lean young man fiddled at another easel. Skinny jeans, loafers with no socks, untucked black dress shirt, spiked hair.

"Looks like some spoiled movie director's nephew," said Mazerek.

"Got the whole L.A. thing going on," said Danning.

"*That's* our consultant?" said Reevis.

The easel held a giant flip pad. The consultant folded the first page over the top. "If you will all take seats, we can begin . . ."

They started with a fever chart comparing revenues of various newspapers. Far below the rest was a dotted line tracking their own paper's dismal performance. Another large page flipped over: a bar chart of anemic company stock. Another page: a pie chart from depressing ad sales . . .

Reevis whispered out the corner of his mouth, "What's this got to do with reporting? I thought the consultant was supposed to teach us the latest journalism techniques, like advanced computer public-record searches."

Danning leaned back smugly and folded his arms. "The whole object of this travesty is to shame us."

"No, seriously . . ." said Reevis.

"Seriously," said Bilko. "Just in case we get any headstrong notions about the added workload, they sling these belittling statistics at us."

"The irony is that a prime job requirement for newspaper reporters is ultra-sensitive bullshit detectors," said Mazerek. "And then they send in these bozos with see-through turds."

"And notice how they've chopped us up into small groups?" said Danning. "Studies show that larger audiences risk a group contagion of mutiny. So just sit back like everyone else and let this jerk talk himself out about how we're supposed to be doing our jobs, and then we can go back to the real job of putting out a paper."

"*Excuse me?*"

The guys in the back of the room looked up.

The consultant was staring at them. "Am I boring you? Is there something you'd like to ask?"

"No," said Mazerek. "We're fine."

Reevis's hand went up. "Actually, I do have a question."

Three heads in the back row snapped toward him. "What are you doing? Just shut up."

"What's your question?" asked the consultant.

"You make a lot more money than us, right?" said Reevis. "And you're explaining how we need to be better journalists?"

The consultant couldn't have been happier with the challenge. He grinned condescendingly: *I am going to put this twerp out like a wet cigar.* "Are those real questions or just rhetorical?"

Mazerek elbowed Reevis. "Will you shut up already?"

"Those were rhetorical," said Reevis. "Here's my real question: What's an inverted pyramid?"

"What?" asked the consultant. He was the only person in the room who didn't know where Reevis was going.

"An inverted pyramid," the young reporter repeated. "What is it?"

The rest of the audience knew two things: One, they loved this. And two, Reevis was knotting his own noose.

The consultant grew red-faced. "I don't have time for this nonsense." He turned back to the easel. "Now, if you'll take a look—"

"You don't know, do you?" said Reevis.

Bilko covered his face. "Jesus, just drop it."

"No!" snapped the consultant. "Why don't you tell me what it is?"

"How to prioritize facts for the most basic news story," said Reevis. "It's one of the first things they teach in your freshman year of J-school."

The consultant took a deep breath and exhaled hard out his nostrils. "Are you finished?"

"No," said Reevis. "What's *New York Times v. Sullivan*?"

Danning smacked himself in the forehead.

The consultant placed his hands on his hips. "Why don't you tell me?"

"The most important libel case ever decided by the Supreme Court," said Reevis. "Established standards of public figures and 'absence of malice.' Also taught freshman year."

"What's your point?"

"Just wanted to clarify something for myself," said Reevis. "I picked the two easiest questions that even the worst journalists in America could answer. Please, continue telling us how to do our jobs better."

The consultant stared at Reevis with a squint of rage, then knocked over the easel and stormed out of the room.

Danning raised both eyebrows high as he stood. "Didn't know you had it in you."

"Kid, you got a pair of brass ones," said Mazerek.

Bilko grabbed his porkpie. "Lunch is on us tomorrow."

Like most newsrooms, the *Journal*'s was a large, wide-open space with columns holding up the ceiling over the sea of crammed desks. No cubicle walls, so reporters didn't have to get up to shout to each other. Because it was the news biz. Along the south wall ran a series of glassed-in offices for upper editors. They had a view of the parking lot. The paper was approaching the early deadline for zoned neighborhood editions. Phones rang, keyboards clattered.

Three veteran reporters typed with urgency. They kept glancing over the tops of their screens toward the final office at the end of the floor, which belonged to the managing editor. Seated inside with his back to the glass was Reevis. The veterans shot silent glances at one another.

The door at the end of the room finally opened. They couldn't get a read on the young reporter's face as he returned to his desk.

"What happened?" asked Mazerek.

"They put a note in my file." Reevis sat down at his computer. "And told me not to bother the consultants anymore."

"That's not so bad," said Bilko.

"We admire what you did," Danning said with a chuckle. "Just try to keep a lid on it at the libel class this Friday."

Chapter TWENTY-ONE

SOMEWHERE ELSE IN THE MIDDLE OF THE STATE

Oak trees ran the town; the people just lived there. They grew everywhere, forming shade canopies over roads and obscuring buildings. Anyplace you walked, massive lengths of Spanish moss draped from overhead branches like an endless cavern of ZZ Top beards.

The moss hung in front of the barbershop, the wood-shingled railroad warehouse, a trading post, the Garage Café and a short row of early brick buildings that formed main street, which was called Cholokka Boulevard. Four elegant white Corinthian columns held up the two-story southern veranda of a plantation-style mansion.

Except for the late-model SUVs and coupes parked in front of the antiques shops, it could have been 1898. The mansion was now a bed & breakfast.

An arm extended from the driver's window, snapping photos as the '76 Ford Cobra headed north. The arm came back inside. "I can never get enough of Micanopy! It's the oldest inland town in Florida, and also the oldest overall that was settled by Americans, as opposed to the Spanish in Saint Augustine."

"What's it named after?"

"The Indian chief who had to move to Oklahoma."

The Ford continued north toward Gainesville on U.S. 441. Serge toyed with his ammo magazines as he drove. "And for those playing along at home, we have a new number one for the oxymoron files: death benefits."

Coleman took a big hit. "That's messed up . . . Can I have the extra ammo clip? I've got a cool idea."

"But I need it."

"You already have one."

"What if I'm up against more than thirty people?"

"I just thought it would be a cool place to hide my dope."

Serge lit up in thought. He quickly passed the clip across the front seat with a sly grin.

Coleman glanced warily, then began packing it. "What changed your mind?"

"You know what a fan of irony I am," said Serge, turning off the highway. "I'll give it to you under one condition. If you're arrested for possession you have to plea-bargain, and during your allocution, you must say this to the judge: 'I admit I was the guy who removed all the bullets from the assault rifle's extended magazine and then filled it with pot. But now I realize that was wrong because marijuana is dangerous.'"

"Righteous."

"Make no mistake: I'm all about guns! I just love the legal incongruities our national discourse has spawned, like I can buy a shotgun any time of day without a serious background check, but if I need something for my sniffles, it's six forms of ID and complete school transcripts. The government has essentially created a system where if I want to clear a head cold, the easiest cure is to blow my brains out."

Coleman looked around the thickening woods. "Where are we?"

"Paynes Prairie." Serge parked the car near a trail sign. "To the observation tower!"

Serge ran ahead and bounded up the steps. "I'm all about observation towers! I climb them even when they're not technically for observation, like billboards, cellular relays and lighting structures at high school fields. Because the key to achievement in life is not letting others define your towers." He looked down from an upper landing. "Coleman, what's taking you so long?"

Coleman was bent over a railing, wondering if he was going to retch, and wondering if that would be a better thing.

"Coleman!"

He stood and grabbed his stomach. "How much farther?"

"Look up!" Serge yelled down through the middle of the pressure-treated staircases. "To the top!"

"Crap." Coleman resumed slogging a step at a time.

Serge reached the observation deck and stood paralyzed in a balloon of his own intoxication. A whisper: "It's beautiful . . ."

Coleman clomped up the last few steps and collapsed on the planks. Serge looked toward his feet. "What are you doing down there?"

"You know how I need to take regular breaks from the vertical world."

"Stand up and check this out!" Serge extended an arm like he was posing for a painting of an explorer. "Most people would never expect this in Florida!"

Coleman struggled to his feet and joined his buddy at the railing. He slowly turned his head toward Serge.

"What?"

"It's a field."

"Right," said Serge. "But this one is a *great* field. Look at that panorama to the horizon, a lush savanna like you'd expect to find in the Mauritanian plains of East Africa."

"It's just bushes and a bunch of grass sitting still."

"No, it's not," said Serge. "There's a serious amount of shit going on down there. Miocene Epoch remnants of limestone basins collapsing in sinkholes to the Floridan aquifer, creating an insane irrigation and drainage system for a thriving balance of ecological interaction between swamp and arid scrub. How can you not get a boner?"

"Serge, you already know how I feel about fields, so a super big one isn't better. It's like I don't enjoy being pushed down into a pile of dog crap, so I won't love being pushed into ten."

"Don't you call Paynes Prairie ten piles of dog crap!"

"It's worse," said Coleman. "You can put dog crap in a paper bag and set it on fire on someone's doorstep. *That* I'd stay to see."

"Where are you going?" said Serge.

"Back down. This sucks."

"Wait, I've spotted a longleaf-pine sand hill!"

"Meet you back at the car."

Serge ran across the deck. "You're not leaving until you dig the prairie."

"Watch me," said Coleman. "Hey, let go of my hair!"

"Are you going to stay? . . . Ow, my ear! I'll put you in a headlock!"

"I'll grab your nuts!"

"Ow, the headlock!"

"Yowch! My nuts!"

They crashed to the deck and rolled violently. Pinching, pulling, bending fingers back and screaming . . .

Serge suddenly froze and poked his head up in alertness.

"Why'd you stop?" said Coleman. "We were having fun."

"Listen. Do you hear that?"

"Sounds like some chick talking at the bottom of the tower. Except she's using the extra-loud cell-phone voice."

Serge pushed himself up. "How inconsiderate! She's shattering our tranquillity."

"Where are you going?" asked Coleman.

"The bottom."

"To confront her?"

"No, my work here is finished. It's back to the Master Plan . . ."

Fifteen minutes later, and a few hundred yards down a walking trail, Coleman looked around as they entered a short concrete tunnel. "What's this thing?"

"The remains of an ancient railroad trestle," said Serge. "They abandoned it in place to preserve history. Nothing left on either side but the strangling roots of nature reclaiming her turf."

The trail opened into a wide raised causeway of grass. On one side, a drop into thick vegetation; on the other, a marsh. Serge grabbed Coleman's shoulder. "Don't get too close."

"Holy God, there's a bunch of huge alligators on the banks of this trail!"

"There used to be alligators *on* this trail," said Serge. "The key features of Paynes Prairie are its sinkholes. Usually rainwater is absorbed into the ground and filters through a stratum of porous rock until it reaches the aquifer. But if you see a body of water out here, like the famous Alachua Sink coming up on your left, it has a number of holes collapsed through the rock, which is what drains the rain and keeps this prairie from filling with water. But over centuries, the holes have become clogged from time to time with rotted plants and stuff, creating a massive lake like the one Hernando de Soto found in 1539. The last time it happened was in the late 1800s, when a clog again put the whole prairie underwater, and for a couple decades, steamboats were sailing back and forth right where we're walking."

"What happened?"

"Here's where history has a sense of humor." Serge pointed toward a rock formation in the water. "The clog gave way and a giant sinkhole reopened with such ferocity it was like putting a foot-wide drain in a bathtub. The water disappeared so fast that some of the steamboats were left out in the mud."

"What's the problem with that guy walking up ahead of us?" asked Coleman. "Keeps looking around all nervous like he's not having a good time."

"He's missing the whole concept of hiking. You have to get into it for its own sake." Serge gestured at himself and Coleman. "Take us, for example. We're becoming one with nature, unlike that uptight city guy who looks as if he's on a forced march through Florida's magnificence at gunpoint." Serge walked up and pressed a gun barrel into the man's spine. "What are you slowing down for?"

Chapter TWENTY-TWO

CHANGE OF VENUE

The afternoon sun danced off whitecaps in the Gulf Stream. Along the mangrove shorelines, fly-fishermen cast hand-tied lures into the shallows, hoping for the Florida Keys Grand Slam of bonefish, permit and tarpon.

If it were a movie, a camera-laden helicopter would swoop over the Seven Mile Bridge, filming a white Jetta crossing the hump of the span at Moser Channel.

Inside the car: "Change of venue?" said Brook. "That's pretty rare in a civil case."

"Except the Broward jury pool is crammed with foreclosures, even higher among those who can't get out of jury duty. But Judge Boone would have granted whatever they asked for anyway."

Brook had her hand out the window, catching the breeze like a child. "At least we get to go to Key West."

"I've never been," said Shelby. "You know the area?"

"Actually, I do . . ."

Soon they were wheeling luggage down Duval Street. Coming the other way: a tourist stream of floral shirts, sandals and Rum Runners in to-go cups. A barefoot man sat on the curb, weaving a hat from palm fronds. A local rode by on a bicycle with a cockatoo on his shoulder. A guitar case sat open on the sidewalk with loose change and dollar bills. "'*Wastin' away again . . .*'"

Shelby stopped wheeling his Samsonite in front of a clapboard building and looked up at an old neon sign of yellow on green. SOUTHERN CROSS.

"How'd you pick this place?" he asked.

"It's a spit away from the courthouse on Whitehead. That's the next street," said Brook, wheeling past him and leading the way down a side path to registration. "It gets noisy at night on Duval, so I booked our rooms upstairs in the back. But that's nothing compared to the racket just before dawn."

"Why?"

"Roosters," said Brook. "That's why you avoid ground-floor rooms on Duval if they face an alley."

After dumping off luggage and locking up their respective rooms, the lawyers regrouped in the hallway. "What's the matter?" asked Brook.

"We're going to be stuck down here for who knows how long," Shelby said with a touch of melancholy.

"I get it," said Brook. "You're going to miss Jack."

Shelby shrugged. "I got a job to do." Then he brightened with a smile. "We have a little downtime before the witnesses get here. Know anything good to do?"

"Come on." Brook headed for the stairs. "I'll give you the tour . . ."

In quick succession, Shelby was shown the cremation holes in the bar at the Chart Room, Jimmy Buffett's secret recording studio at Key West Bight, the hanging tree in Captain Tony's, pressed cheese bread in 5 Brothers Grocery, the cemetery . . .

"What's the matter?" asked Brook.

"I have to go to the bathroom pretty bad, but no public restrooms for the last ten blocks."

"Follow me."

They entered the venerable La Concha hotel. "Ah, there's one."

"No," said Brook.

He tried the handle. "It's locked."

"You need a room key."

"But I thought you said there was a restroom."

"This way." She led him to the elevators. The doors opened in the rooftop lounge surrounded by the observation deck. "There you go."

"Yessss!"

He reemerged a minute later with relief. They went outside for the view, leaning against a ledge of orange barrel tiles. "Wow, you can see everything from up here."

"Tallest building in Old Town, built 1926. There's a big sunset ritual up here each night, second only to Mallory Square. That way is the lighthouse near Hemingway's, and the redbrick building in the other direction is the historic Customs House—"

"Excuse me," said Shelby. "Did you used to live here?"

"No. Why?"

"All the trivia you were rattling off on the drive down here, then that off-the-grid tour this afternoon and now all these facts," said Shelby. "I can't understand how someone who never lived in a place could know so much."

"I had a good teacher."

"Brook . . . *Brook?* . . . Now *you* have a look like you're missing someone."

Silence.

"I'm sorry," said Shelby. "I shouldn't have . . . Listen, my feet are pretty tired. I'll bet you know a funky little spot to relax and have a drink."

"Got just the place." Brook set off for the elevator. "But we have to get off Duval with all the tourist noise and Buffett clones. So it means a little more walking."

"I'm up to it."

Duval is a narrow street shared by a spectrum of incompatible transportation. People who have never ridden a moped rent them by the hundreds, then gun the throttle after drinking and zip between cars, bicycles and pedestrians. A yellow moped took a tight corner at Truman, sending a bicyclist ramming into the curb. The next moped ran the red light and cut off the tourist trolley, scooting between families in the crosswalk.

"Jesus," said Shelby. "I can't believe nobody gets hit."

"They do," said Brook, turning up Truman. "Key West has one of the highest non-car road-accident rates in the country."

Shelby watched as a moped hit an African land snail, flipping a frat boy over the handlebars. "So where's this place you're taking me?"

"The Million Dollar Bar, also known as Don's Place. Only locals and well-versed visitors."

A few more blocks and they were there. The entrance sat on a diagonal at the corner. All the windows open for sea breeze. One of those narrow joints defined by length.

As soon as she walked in the door: "Hey, Brook, great to see you."

"Hi, Don." She turned to Shelby. "That's the owner."

"I guessed."

From behind the bar. "Brook!" "Where you been?"

"Hey, Kurt, Boomer."

From a stool at the end of the bar: "Brook, where's Serge?"

The bar went silent.

The customer on the next stool nudged him.

"What? What'd I say?"

"Just shut up!"

Shelby looked at Brook and opened his mouth, then closed it.

"It's okay." She headed toward the pool room in back. "Sometime when I get enough drinks in me, I'll tell you a story."

"No rush."

"Hey, Don," yelled Brook. "What's this big stain on the pool table?"

"Coleman. Tried everything to get it out."

Brook racked the balls in the triangle.

"We're going to play?" asked Shelby.

She chalked a cue stick. "Unless you just want to watch me."

"Yo!" yelled the bartender. "What are you having?"

"Uh, Budweiser," said Shelby.

"Jack," said Brook.

Shelby raised his eyebrows.

"Not your Jack," she added. "Daniel's."

"I figured that," said Shelby. "You're full of surprises . . ."

There was a commotion toward the front of the bar. Four old ladies with black wraparound glaucoma goggles stormed in like they owned the place.

"The G-Unit!" yelled the bartender.

"Wild Turkey!" yelled Edna, raising a thumb. "Up!"

The gang climbed atop four stools, and the bartender came over with the bottle. "What's new with you gals?"

Eunice set her glasses on the bar. "Edith crapped herself again."

"Wasn't my fault. It's that stupid trailer I rented on Stock Island."

Eunice looked at the bartender. "Can you believe she forgot to seal the doggie door when the weather started turning?"

"What?" He lined shot glasses in front of the gang and began pouring. "Everyone in the Keys knows to seal doggie doors before winter."

"I didn't," said Edith. "Then, in the middle of the night, something lying on my chest woke me up. And I open my eyes and there's this big fucking iguana. *You* try not crapping yourself."

"Reptiles are cold-blooded," said the bartender. "When the temperature drops, they try to get in houses because they sense the air inside is much warmer than outdoors. Then they go looking for the warmest spot in the home, which is usually a sleeping resident."

Edith tossed back a shot. "Now somebody tells me . . ."

Shelby stared curiously from the back of the room. "The G-Unit?"

Brook lined up a shot. "Regulars. *G* for 'grandma.' Says it makes them sound def." The five ball slammed into a pocket.

Someone else entered from the street and took a stool. A bombshell redhead with a musk of spring-loaded violence. The bartenders retreated and huddled. *"I'm not serving her." "Neither am I." "One of us*

better get over there soon because she's getting pissed." "Okay, I'll go first,
but if anyone mentions Serge, I'm hitting the ground..."

The bartender named Boomer forced a smile. "What can I get you?"

She idly twisted a curly lock of hair around a finger. "Has Serge
been around lately?"

The bartender hit the ground.

The woman stood and leaned over the counter. "You okay down
there?"

A couple drinks later in the pool room, all the striped balls were still
on the table. The only solid was a black one numbered eight. Brook tapped
a side pocket with the end of her cue and sank it. "Want to play again?"

"Rack 'em up."

Brook grabbed the triangle. "What still baffles me is why a financial institution as big and well known as Consolidated would try to
pull these stunts. I could understand some fly-by-night little loan office
on the back side of town."

"The surprising thing is how few *don't* do it," said Shelby, striking
the cue ball.

Brook chased down the ball as it bounced across the floor. "But
they have so much to lose."

"You'd think," said Shelby. "Except regulations are only as good as
enforcement, which is gutted by lobbyists and campaign cash."

Brook sank a wicked bank shot. She walked around the table
and tapped another pocket. "The biggest fraud to me is in the court
of public opinion. They've actually convinced a lot of people that the
buyers share equal responsibility." She dropped the four ball. "They'd
have us believe that spontaneously, millions of first-time home buyers
ran into mortgage offices and were savvy enough to trick financiers into
lending them too much money." Chalking her cue and rounding the
table. "I have one answer to equal footing: Go to a house closing. When
my dad bought his condo down here, his arm was practically in a sling
after signing that mountain of documents."

"I have another answer to who's responsible," said Shelby. "Who
ended up with all the money?"

Something suddenly knocked Shelby into the table. A shouting bartender: *"No! Not again!"*

Brook turned as Eunice ran past her, followed by Edith, who had grabbed a cue stick off the wall. "I'm sick of the diaper jokes! . . ." *Swing.* The stick missed Eunice.

"Ow!" Shelby rubbed his shoulder as the women raced in a circle around the table.

On the next pass, Eunice grabbed her own stick and turned. "Then stop shitting yourself!" *Swing.*

The stick smacked the Jägermeister lamp over the pool table before a pair of bartenders finally separated the women and escorted them away. "No more Wild Turkey for you."

Shelby raised an eyebrow at Brook. "This happen often?"

Brook was already lining up her next shot. "More often than not." She sank the eight ball again. All the striped balls were left again. "Another game?"

Shelby just held his beer and stared at the table. "How'd you learn to play pool like that?"

Brook shrugged and finished her current drink. "I'm from Brooklyn."

Shelby narrowed his eyes a moment. "Brooklyn . . . Brook?"

Another shrug. "Dad was a Dodgers fan. Claimed we were related to the catcher, but I doubt it."

"Where's your dad now?"

"Let's sit down," said Brook. "I'll tell you a story."

They grabbed a pair of stools and the bartender produced another round of drinks.

"You can't tell anybody this," said Brook. "It could ruin me."

"You mean get disbarred?"

"Go to jail."

"You trust me that much already?"

"Yes, but even friends can be subpoenaed by grand juries." She handed him a dollar.

"What's this?"

"I'm hiring you as my attorney," said Brook. "That makes everything I'm about to say privileged communication."

Then she gave another dollar to the guy sitting on her other side. "I'm in." The patron passed her a foam can coozie. She shook it and dumped six dice on the bar.

"Damn." "She did it again." "Why do we let her play?"

"What are you doing?" asked Shelby.

"Friendly local tradition called 'ship, captain, crew.'" She passed the coozie down the bar. "Now back to consulting with my new attorney. It all started shortly after I moved down here to take care of my dad . . ."

Shelby remained uniformly silent for the next half hour as Brook spun her inconceivable yarn. She finally reached the end. "And I've never seen Serge since . . ."

Shelby didn't know what to say, so he didn't.

"Say something," said Brook.

"I had no idea."

He was looking at her, but she could tell his gaze was slightly off. She touched the side of her neck. "The scar?"

"Didn't mean to stare," said Shelby.

"The guy I paid went a little overboard," said Brook. "I told him to be convincing, but . . . I later found out he's in it for more than the money. He likes his work."

"So that's why the jury consultant suggested you get a scarf."

Chapter TWENTY-THREE

PAYNES PRAIRIE

Please don't shoot me! I swear I'll never do it again." The man's hiking pace became motivated.

Coleman sucked on a tube from a hiking hydration vest filled with vodka. "What are you trying to fix with that guy?"

"The scumbags of Florida keep lowering my bar of expectations." Serge sucked his own hydration vest of coffee. "First came the housing bubble and its burst, which pulled back the curtain on a whole viper pit of predators: subprime lenders, appraisers, speculators, politicians, brokers . . . Then, when all is done, and hardworking Americans are about to be forced into the street wearing pickle barrels, in comes the lowest of the low."

"Dope dealers who short you on weight?"

"Dishonest mortgage-modification companies," said Serge. "It's an evil so beneath everything that it staggers the conscience. These new suckerfish target old people and families with kids who are desperately trying to keep a roof over their heads. Their house is already upside down and they're six months behind on the loan. So these companies promise they can restructure the mortgage to make payments afford-able. Then they take all kinds of up-front fees and advance closing costs—and don't lift a finger. So not only do the families get foreclosed upon anyway, but their savings are now depleted."

"And they need a fixer?"

"This guy ahead of us took a friend of Mahoney's for almost eight grand. So I worked the numbers and intend to make him a restructur-ing offer he can't refuse." Serge poked the gun barrel in the man's back again. "My new breed of fixer must be prepared to do complex math on hiking trails."

The man in front of them stopped and wiped his face with his shirt. "I need to rest. Just a minute."

"Why?" asked Serge. "You've reached the finish line."

The man turned with skepticism. "What do you mean?"

"You're free to go."

He stood quiet a second. "Is this a trick? You aren't going to shoot me in the back?"

"Absolutely not." Serge tucked the gun away under his tropical shirt. "I think you've learned your lesson. My clients will be expect-ing a refund check this afternoon, unless you've taken a likin' to hikin'. The Florida Trail runs the length of the entire state. I could always use a nature buddy like you for whole adventure because Coleman would never make it."

"No, I'll cut that check the moment I get to the office." He began walking around the pair to head back the way they'd come.

Serge stepped sideways and blocked his path. "Not that direction. It's the one we'll be taking, and I've been known to change my mind."

"Then how do I get out of here?"

Serge pointed into the distance. "Just keep following the path. It's much longer and you'll cover most of the prairie, but it will eventually circle back around. I think you'll like it better . . . Oh, almost forgot: one more thing before you go . . ." He handed the gun to Coleman. "Keep him covered."

Serge removed his coffee-hydration backpack and unzipped a

pair of utility pockets. He approached the man with an electric razor. "Hold still."

"What are you doing?"

"Just a little trim on the sides of your head. A small price to pay for your freedom." When Serge finished creating twin bald spots on the temples, he grabbed a pair of scissors and two strips of leather. "If you're a dog lover, you'll recognize these. But we don't need the ends . . ." *Snip, snip, snip . . .*

"W-w-what are you doing?"

"Hold still again if you want to get away." Serge liberally applied super glue to the shortened pieces of leather and pressed them against the sides of the man's head. "There, that should stick. When you get back to civilization, they have solvents at the hardware store, but I'd wear a hat because you look kind of funny. Now skeeee-daddle!"

Coleman sucked another swig of vodka. "Wow, he really took off running. I think he likes hiking now."

"What's not to like?" Serge reached in his backpack again and removed two short plastic spikes with small cylinders on the end. "It's all about taking the time to notice the little things." He hammered the stakes into the ground on each side of the trail. "That about does it. Time to head back."

Coleman turned around, still sucking.

Serge yanked him by the arm. "Watch where you're stepping!"

"Whoa, thanks." Coleman took the hydration tube out of his mouth and aimed it at the ground. "You just stopped me from stepping in the hugest pile of dog crap I've ever seen."

"That's because it's not from a dog. Something much bigger." Serge bent down to take a picture. "And it's not baked dry, so it hasn't been here long."

Coleman scooted to hide behind his friend and peeked over his shoulder. "What the hell's out here?"

"Relax, it's just free-range horses. They live all over the prairie." Serge walked a few more yards and pulled out his camera again.

"That's even a bigger pile," said Coleman. "How large do these horses grow?"

"This one didn't come from a horse." *Click, click, click.* "Which is another bonus about Paynes Prairie. It's the perfect place for the neophyte to learn animal tracking. In other areas, you need at least a rudimentary background to differentiate the scat of cougars, bobcats, foxes, panthers. But out here, the beginner need only gauge the scale. Smaller piles are horses."

"And this bigger one?"

"Buffalo."

"Get out of here," said Coleman. "There aren't any buffalo in Florida."

"Au contraire," said Serge. "Buffalo in great numbers roamed the grasslands of central Florida until they were wiped out in the nineteenth century. But conservationists reintroduced them forty years ago to establish the original natural balance."

Coleman slid behind Serge again. "Are they dangerous?"

"Sure, if you're an idiot." Serge took several long sucks on his coffee tube. "But play it smart and don't approach them or make wacky faces—and remain perfectly still—they're willing to live and let live."

"What about running away?"

Serge continued sucking and put up his arms. "Definitely not that! Especially out here in such an open expanse. If you're ever going to run, do it where you can get into some trees, like way over there. I'll let you in on a secret about buffalo, which reminds me of what I really hate about action movies. How many times have you seen some film where the killer is in a car chasing some woman on foot through a multi-deck parking garage? And you're leaping out of your seat yelling at the screen: 'Veer off and dive between the parked cars! Dive between the parked cars!' But no, they keep running straight down the middle of the concrete ramp, turning the corner and scampering down the middle of the next level—"

"Serge, what does that have to do with buffalo?"

"Wait! Wait! So then the car is gaining and about to run over the woman, and she turns down the next level, and that's when she always falls and loses a high heel, but now the car is suddenly farther away in order to give her time to get up and start running down the middle again. What is that bullshit? That's what I say! But sometimes I say it too loud and have to leave the theater—"

"Buffalo . . ."

"What?" Serge looked up. "Hey, our friend is coming back. I didn't get the sense he could run that fast."

"There's a whole herd behind him."

"And yet he's staying in the middle of the path."

"There are no parked cars," said Coleman. "Only that pond with the alligators and the sinkhole."

"He just fell and lost a shoe."

"Now he's back up again, but still running down the middle," said Coleman. "By the way, what were those things you glued to his head?"

"You've heard of invisible fences?"

"No."

"If you don't want to build a real fence but need to keep your dog in the yard, you buy a special collar for Fido. Then you hammer stakes in the ground at the edge of the property. The stakes have tiny transmitters on the ends, and if the dog goes too far, it makes the collar give him an electric shock. It's not a huge shock, but the dog gets the idea pretty fast. It should be an even faster learning curve for our friend up there, because I glued the leather straps with the shock units to his temples, and the voltage will seriously screw up the tiny electric signals that all our brains operate on."

"I think he just hit your invisible fence," said Coleman. "He's making wacky faces."

"Now he's looking back up the trail, and in the marsh and at my transmitters," said Serge. "Interesting call: buffalo, gators or electric shock? Only in Florida are you faced with such daily decisions."

"He's trying to get through your fence again but it's not even close," said Coleman. "Oooo, he's really spazzing out this time. Now he's flopping on the ground tearing at those things on his head."

Serge held an arm out across Coleman's chest. "Step back slowly to the side of the trail. Here they come . . ."

"Man, that first one got him right in the face," said Coleman. "And all the rest are hitting him, too, like it's on purpose."

"They just stampede in tight formations from safety instinct."

"He's starting to come apart."

The herd thundered by as Serge snapped photos.

"What now?" asked Coleman.

"Those vultures circling above will clean up the human vulture." Serge stowed his camera and began walking. "There's always a balance in nature."

Part THREE

THE TRIAL

Chapter TWENTY-FOUR

KEY WEST

The briefcases were sore thumbs on tourist-jammed Duval Street. Shelby and Brook made the short stroll from the Southern Cross to the Monroe County judicial center in under five minutes.

Shelby stared up at a big clock. "Wow, what a cool courthouse."

"It's the old courthouse," said Brook. "The new one's in back."

He turned another way. "Look at the rust on those bars. That jail is absolutely medieval."

"It's the old jail. The new one's on Stock Island."

Shelby reached the courtroom door and grabbed the handle. "Ready for the big day?"

"As they say, most trials are won and lost during jury selection."

They went inside and set up at the plaintiff's table. Team Riley was already there with the boxes and easel.

Brook unloaded her briefcase. "Why do they need all that stuff for voir dire?"

"They don't," said Shelby. "It's BS."

Brook laid out her own paperwork in a neat array. "So how many cases have you tried anyway?"

Shelby set a pen on a fresh legal pad. "This is my first."

Brook froze. "Your first? But it's my first, too. They said I'd be paired with someone who had a lot of experience."

"I do. Record amount of billable hours, just not in a courtroom."

"But why would such a big firm put two rookies on such an important case?"

"Because I've been bugging them like crazy to get jury face time," said Shelby. "Don't worry—I've got this."

A door behind the bench opened. Out came a large black robe filled with Judge Kennesaw Montgomery Boone. "Bring in the prospective jurors."

A bailiff opened another door, and the first round of candidates took seats in the box. It wasn't a group seen in most other courtrooms. Because it was Key West. Heavy tans, shorts, sandals, hangovers.

"Where's our jury consultant?" whispered Brook. "He was supposed to be here a half hour ago."

Shelby read a text on his cell. "On his way."

"What's taking him so long?" She pointed. "Theirs is already here."

A professorial man in a navy blazer sat in the first row, leaning over the railing to confer with his team.

The judge looked impatiently at the plaintiff's table. "Is there a problem? You have done voir dire before, haven't you?"

"No," said Shelby, "but I'm ready."

He approached the box and asked questions of integrity. Could they set aside personal bias and follow the law?

The defense went next. How much did they make? Had they ever missed a house payment? What did they think of people who did?

The defense huddled again with their consultant and offered its peremptory challenges.

Brook leaned sideways. "They're striking all the poorest people from the pool. It's class warfare."

"I know," said Shelby.

"But that'll force us to strike all the rich people, and that's not right either."

"I know."

"Where's our jury consultant? Cases are already won and lost—"

Shelby looked at his phone. "Stuck behind a crash on the Overseas. Road's closed."

"Just great."

The judge cleared his throat. "Your turn. Anytime you're ready."

"Sorry." Shelby approached the box. "Are you related to or do you know anyone currently serving in the military? . . ."

A defense attorney whispered over his shoulder at their consultant. "Why is he asking that?"

That night in one of Key West's most exclusive resorts: The screaming could be heard through the walls of the most spacious suite.

"You had no fucking idea why he was asking about relatives in the military?"

Four lawyers sat demurely in a row of comfy chairs.

One of the Riley partners continued pacing in rage. "What about you!"

The jury consultant fidgeted on the end of a bed and shrugged.

"Does anyone in this room besides me know the makeup of the plaintiff class?"

Blank stares.

"They've got dozens of National Guard reservists who were called up for active duty, and when their tours were extended, the pay cut from their regular jobs forced them into mortgage default—while they were fighting for our country! And then all those other questions: surgeries, 401(k)s, CD rates. You didn't have a clue where any of this was going? For God's sake, he handed you a treasure map for your own peremptory challenges. Instead you blindly used them to strike poor people."

The consultant raised his hand. "But our research shows—"

"Your research should have shown that half the poor people in this country hate the other half! Just listen to talk radio for five seconds."

A timid hand went up. "Why do they hate each other?"

"Because it's how rich politicians get elected these days! Don't you understand the whole divide-and-blame game? 'Pay no attention to my campaign donors, lobbyists and gerrymandered voting districts that have rigged the system. All your problems are really caused by that other poor asshole standing next to you, getting a free ride and hating Christmas.' . . . But did you take advantage of that windfall? No, you just gift-wrapped half your challenges for this Shelby guy, then he parsed through your prized keepers! And don't even get me started on the challenges for cause. This wet-behind-the-ears kid kicked all your asses. I should be paying *him*!"

"There's still a lot of time," said the boldest lawyer. "The trial hasn't even started."

"Is it more or less than a thousand times that you've heard the saying 'Trials are already won and lost—'" The attorneys ducked as a lamp flew over their heads and shattered on the wall. "Out! All of you! Get out of my sight!"

They never moved so fast. The partner slammed the door behind them and grabbed a tiny bottle of Chivas from the minibar. He opened his cell. "It's Moss . . . I know it's late. We have a problem . . . Who would have guessed the kid was this good? He's smarter than our whole team combined . . . I know. We'll just have to nail our opening arguments with everything we've got . . ."

Chapter TWENTY-FIVE

DOWNTOWN ORLANDO

Traffic grew thick on northbound I-4 as the skyline came into view.

"I don't remember that big building," said Coleman.

"Fairly new," said Serge. "The Amway Center."

"They need all that room to do their thing?"

"Coleman, that's the basketball arena where the Magic play. Amway just bought the naming rights."

"Oh." Coleman reclined with a crack-style beer-can pipe for his pot. "I've never figured out Amway people. I thought they were just trying to sell you vitamins and cleaning products."

"And you're their anti-market."

"I know, so I got the vibe something else was going on."

"It's like the Mafia without the murders," said Serge. "Families around dinner tables in hushed tones: 'Son, you're old enough now to know the truth. Your cousin's in the Amway.'"

The Cobra coasted down the exit ramp for Central Boulevard and stopped by a curb. Coleman stared up at a steep granite building with columns. "Another courthouse?"

"Another *old* courthouse," said Serge. "It's now the local history center."

They headed down a hall, and Serge opened a door. "I think this is the right courtroom . . . Yep, it is. See that venerable wooden defense table with the triangle of Plexiglas protecting the corner?"

"Why is it only protecting the corner?" asked Coleman.

"Because of what's under it."

They marched up the aisle to the table and Coleman bent down. "Hey, someone carved his name. It says . . . *Ted Bundy*. That's far out."

"Here's what's really far out: What the hell is Ted Bundy doing in court with a knife?" Serge snapped photos. "I can possibly accept him smuggling it through security in those days before metal detectors. But what were they thinking when he pulled the damn thing out and started chopping up a table? 'Well, I hear woodworking is one of his hobbies, and he's not bothering anybody.'"

"What now?" asked Coleman.

"To the next courthouse! . . ."

. . . The clock-tower dome had faded to verdigris like the Statue of Liberty. Both the big and little hands were on eleven, which was correct. The cornerstone of the tan brick building read: 1912. A pair of Canary Island date palms grew symmetrically on each side of the entrance.

A Ford Cobra sat on the corner in the middle of Citrus County as a pair of men headed up marble steps. Coleman pointed at the clock. "This one goes to eleven."

The courthouse stood on a centerpiece block of land platted diagonal to the rest of the street grid in the city of Inverness. Serge opened the front doors. In the middle of the floor was the seal of the state of Florida. Next to the seal stood a life-size cardboard cutout of a man wearing a gold tuxedo. Serge took a photo; Coleman took a swig. They climbed stairs to the second floor.

Serge opened another door. A gasp.

"You okay?" asked Coleman.

"I've only seen it in the movie." Serge rushed toward the railing separating the gallery from the trial area. He swung open the wooden gate and ran toward the defense table. "Coleman, get over here and take my picture in the Elvis chair."

"Elvis?"

"The 1962 box-office smash *Follow That Dream,* based on the novel *Pioneer, Go Home!* It's one of the few Florida movies actually filmed in Florida." Serge ran to the bench and spoke quietly to an invisible judge. "Also the only film where Elvis was a lawyer. Not a real one, but he represented himself as defendant in a homesteading eviction, which is a government form of foreclosure. And in the courtroom finale, Elvis whispers a gambit to the judge and wins the case for the Kwimper family."

Coleman looked around as Serge's voice bounced off the walls. "Where is everybody? I didn't see anyone on the way up the stairs either."

"It's a museum now. One of the librarians in town told me some cool trivia about this place." Serge rubbed his hands on wooden finials, scrollwork and other architectural flourishes. "Over the years, they tore out the courtroom's interior and modernized it, except it was like that seventies modernism, with drop ceilings and all the tasteless bullshit that must follow drop ceilings. When calmer heads finally prevailed and the restoration committee was formed, they realized they had blueprints, but no record of the courtroom's interior design and furniture. So they printed out screen shots from the Elvis movie and put it all back together. Like the cool balcony seating up there that conjures Atticus Finch."

Serge sprinted by.

"Where are you going?" asked Coleman.

"To the balcony. I must sit in a seat." Serge ran up the steps, sat down, stood up, ran down the steps. "Whew! That's off the checklist. And here's extra credit: One of Florida's favorite sons, Tom Petty, got to see them film the movie, as a boy of course, because his uncle was on the film crew, and Elvis inspired him to hock his baseball cards for a guitar. *'Runnin' down a dream'* . . . Let's rock! . . ."

One block over stood something more contemporary: an architecturally sterile brick box with an afterthought of shrubbery and a tiny gazebo that looked like it came from a bargain kit purchased by people who enjoy aboveground pools. The interior was furnished with durable, cost-saving materials that created all the drama of a cafeteria.

"The new county courthouse," said Serge. "Let's see what's on the menu!" Serge stuck his head in a half-open door. "Nothing in there but small claims." He ran for another courtroom.

Coleman caught up to him in the hallway. "What are you doing?"

"Searching for the best real-world legal education money can't buy. Screw *The Paper Chase*."

"Yeah," said Coleman. "Fuck that shit."

"Do you even know what it is?"

"No," said Coleman. "I just wanted to be supportive."

"It's a movie that's the ultimate representation of traditional legal learning. Remember when Hank Aaron broke Babe Ruth's record with his seven-hundred-and-fifteenth home run? And those two guys jumped out of the stands and slapped him on his back between second and third base?" Serge stuck his head inside the next door. "A friend said they were refugees from *The Paper Chase*. That's all you need to know about law school."

Serge withdrew his head from the proceedings of a mutually agreeable divorce. "These are the genuine legal classrooms, and I'm looking to audit a course." Another door. "Ahhh, here's what we're looking for!"

"You can just go right in?"

"And plenty of box seating." He raced for the front of the gallery. "The best entertainment value in America."

Coleman followed. "But why'd you pick this courtroom?"

"Because I saw a reporter with a notepad. That's a blinking red arrow that something juicy is afoot." Serge shuffled sideways down the first row and took the chair next to the journalist. "What's up, scoop?"

"What? Huh?" The reporter looked over. "Who are you?"

"The fixer."

The young man stared a moment. "Oh, you mean you do fieldwork for a law firm. Which one?"

Serge gazed off coyly. "Rather not say. Very sensitive case. High-profile stuff."

The reporter put pen to paper. "Anything I'd want to know about?"

Serge angled his head closer so he wouldn't be overheard. "*Cool Hand Luke.* That's all I can say. What's your name?"

"Reevis."

MEANWHILE IN KEY WEST . . .

"All rise," said the bailiff.

Judge Boone took his seat.

Brook turned around. "Who's that guy? Looks like he's ready to strangle ten people."

Shelby glanced back. "It's Red Moss, one of the Riley partners."

"Think he didn't like how yesterday went?"

The judge banged his gavel. "Your opening statement?"

Shelby set down the cram notes he was still reviewing at the last second. "Here goes nothing."

Brook held her breath as Shelby approached the jury box.

"Good morning, and I first want to thank you for your civic service here today. You're about to hear a very complex foreclosure case that will take a lot of time to explain and test your patience. I didn't even understand it myself for weeks. There will be many financial statements and confusing foreign terms used by the industry. But for all that, it boils down to a very simple case. Now, the defense will get up here in a moment and say that this case is a matter of responsibility, and they will be absolutely right. It's how we were all raised. Our parents taught us to treat others with honor, and when you give your word, you take responsibility for it and you honor it . . ."

Brook noticed some of the jurors begin to faintly nod in assent.

" . . . So when you take out a loan for a house, you agree to pay. And the mortgage company agrees to let you have the house based upon a fair deal. That's honor. However, I will do my best to present evidence that the original deal, as well as foreclosure action, was based upon collusion and dishonest financial procedures. And the defense will argue that I'm mistaken in my interpretation. Then you will use your judgment from your life experience and evaluate who is correct. I could be wrong about my case. I don't think I am, but that's not my decision. It is yours. That's our system. It is fair, and it is honorable. Not because it's the law, but because it's based upon American citizens such as you, who are fair and honorable, or you would have tried to get out of jury duty..."

A smattering of light laughter among the panel.

"... As you hear the evidence, keep in mind the defense counsel's upcoming words: 'It is a case of shared responsibility.' But that means on both sides. As each fact is introduced, please ask yourselves this: Did their client behave with honor? If they just get up here and try to distract you by only talking about the failed responsibility of the homeowners, then I submit that they, like their client, are not acting in honor. Thank you."

An attorney from the defense walked toward the jury box as Shelby sat down.

"Good morning..."

Shelby and Brook took notes as the opposing lawyer wound through his opening spiel for over an hour.

"... But in the end, this all comes down to a case of these homeowners not living up to their responsibility. Thank you."

Chapter TWENTY-SIX

CITRUS COUNTY

The judge called a recess and Serge tapped Reevis's shoulder. "I always wanted to be a reporter. It's true! As a small child, I'd cut up the *Palm Beach Post* with safety scissors and glue my own newspaper back together on construction paper. Then I learned more about the industry and started my own paper when I was five. Knocked on all the doors on my street, but the only person who would buy a subscription was this sweet old lady who lived alone, and I'd deliver one handwritten paper each week for a dime. Of course all I could write was my family life: all our secrets, money problems, fights, weird habits and other dirty laundry. I thought she just wanted to be cheered up by little kids coming around, when she actually turned out to be the biggest gossip on the block and everyone started staring at our house. Then I gave up the journalism bug when I was six. Didn't know at the time that it would be the last edition of my paper, but I felt circulation needed a boost, so I went around the side of the house and loosened all the fuses in the electrical box, but just a little so it wouldn't be noticed. It was July and hotter than hell, the air-conditioning is out, food spoiling in the fridge, and my folks are on the phone screaming at the power company and calling neighbors, but everyone else had power, and they're scratching their heads, asking what could possibly be wrong. Then I came running out of my bedroom yelling, *'Read all about it!'* And I hand them a paper with a giant outbreak-of-war headline: 'Massive Power Outage Strikes 431 West Thirty-second Street.' And they both smacked themselves in the forehead: 'Of course, little Serge again!' Apparently my folks weren't fond of journalists because that's one spanking I'll never forget. And that's why I'm not a reporter." Serge grinned.

Reevis apprehensively stared back, then looked down at his pad.

Serge scooted closer. "So what's the current state of print journalism?"

"Doomed." Reevis flipped his notebook closed. "TV only wants stuff blowing up or on fire or interviews of local sports fans who are drunk. Newspapers were the last resort for in-depth perspective and details. You'd catch a few seconds of something on television, then read the paper for the full verified facts. It was dry but it was important."

"And now?"

"Mainly rewrite press releases, and then we have to tweet."

"You're kidding?" Serge offered a swig from his hydration vest.

"What's that?"

"Coffee."

"Got mine right here." Reevis raised a giant travel mug from the floor. "You're not supposed to have beverages in court, but nobody cares."

They paused to chug in unison.

"We also have to blog, and then readers post comments that we must respond to."

"What do they say?"

"Primarily that we blow, but there are variations on the theme."

"Why?" said Serge. "Because of the decline of the profession?"

"No, because we're the biased lame-stream media. And that's the response when we're just covering celebrity golf tournaments. Then, regardless of the story, the thread of reader comments invariably veers off into a food fight over health care and homosexuals." Reevis gulped from his mug again. "The downward spiral began when conglomerates started buying up outlets and fusing various media together—TV, print, Internet, radio, all in one building—until you've got an information plantation. I'm having nightmares about cockroaches, thermometers and Power Rangers . . ."

Serge put a hand over the top of the reporter's coffee mug. "You might want to go easy on the stuff. And that's a lot, coming from me."

Reevis shook his head and chugged it dry. "Slit any journalist's wrist and coffee will come out."

"So I've heard."

"Photographers now have to write stories, and reporters take photographs, which none of us can do because we're always attending meetings reminding us of all the work we're not doing because we're at meetings. We've stopped running corrections because they eat up ad space, and I'm just waiting for the day they strap a battery belt on me for satellite reports."

"How on earth do you keep your chin up?"

"Whenever I have to take a photo of anything, I never get out of the car."

"Why?"

"To prove that quality in the newspaper business is now like tits on a bull," said Reevis. "I've been waiting for someone to say something, but so far just crickets."

"What if you have to shoot a mug shot of a public official?" asked Serge.

"I make some excuse for them to meet me in the parking lot," said Reevis. "All my mug shots are of people squinting down at sharp angles, and they all go right in the paper without a word. So I've started leaving the window up and shooting through the glass. It's a small protest, but it gets me by."

"There's one thing I don't understand," said Serge. "You mentioned media conglomerates, yet this is such a small market."

"I don't work here," said Reevis. "Drove over from the coast."

"Must be an important case."

"Just the opposite," said Reevis. "I told them I had several breaking stories that were much more important than this superficial nonsense, but they wanted me to write about one of the latest cultural crazes, Florida Man."

"What's that?"

"A fad like 'jump the shark' or the Kevin Bacon game," said Reevis. "Florida Man is a mythical superhero who represents how weird everyone knows Florida has become. So they Google the term 'Florida Man' and it keeps bringing up a list of fresh headlines: 'Florida Man Calls 911 Eighty Times for Kool-Aid and Weed.' 'Florida Man Impersonates Cop to Get Discount Waffles.' 'Florida Man Drops Acid and Asks Police to Cut Off His Penis.' 'Florida Man Breaks into House, Plays with Toy Helicopter, Masturbates.'"

"You're making this up," said Serge.

"Do the searches," said Reevis. "Every word is true."

"So tell me." Serge pointed at the judge's empty bench. "What's the legal system *really* like? Are the preconceptions accurate?"

Reevis shook his head. "A while back they polled a bunch of cops about the most realistic police show on TV, and they said *Barney Miller*. Same thing here: It ain't *Law & Order*."

"Then what is it?"

"Madness," said Reevis. "That's why I'm for the death penalty in theory and against it in practice. If you saw the day-in-day-out shit that goes on, your head would spin."

"Examples?"

"Two young prosecutors were chronically overloaded with cases and wanted to plead some out, which their boss rejected, so they pleaded them anyway, and six months after the guys left, the staff discovered all these case folders they had dropped behind every filing cabinet in the office. One judge's secretary always worked late so she could raid the judge's evidence safe for marijuana, because what's the defense going to say: 'My client had more pot than that'? After another trial, the stenographer showed me a legal pad from the judge's bench with so much religious doodling that he couldn't have heard a word of testimony. Another time, the police department didn't like how a cop was prosecuted for brutality, so when the D.A. was out of town, they went in his house without a warrant and took apart the bathroom plumbing looking for cocaine residue, which is why the D.A. only did cocaine out of town. It's all common knowledge in the courthouse halls, but the public never hears. And outside the building is Lady Justice with the scales."

The judge returned from recess. Testimony resumed and Reevis lowered his voice to a whisper. "Someone even created a Twitter account for Florida Man. Others have started their own twists, adding search terms. The most popular subthread is 'Florida Man Defecates': in department store, backseat of police car, motel pool."

"Taking a dump is like buying real estate," said Serge. "It's all location, location, location."

"I shouldn't even be here."

"What's this case about?" asked Serge.

"The newspaper wants a strong lead-in for their feature 'Florida Man Crashes Through Skylight of Couple's Residence, Goes on Defecating Rampage in Living Room.' This is where four years of journalism school has brought me?"

Serge patted him on the shoulder. "Keep the flame burning." He turned toward Coleman sitting on the other side. "What do you think of the testimony?"

"Let's get out of here."

"Of all people, I thought you'd get a big kick out of this case."

Coleman stood up. "Hits too close to home."

They checked out the action in the other courtrooms. Various writs and motions. Serge made notes of how the attorneys spoke.

Just before five o'clock, the pair left the building and drove away in the Cobra, passing a parked Datsun where the driver prepared to take a photo of someone standing on the sidewalk: *"Hold on a second while I put up the window."*

Another lamp shattered in a spacious resort suite.

"I couldn't believe my ears this morning!" screamed Red Moss. "Was I the only person listening to their opening argument?"

A hand raised timidly to shoulder level. "I was listening."

"Shut the hell up!"

The attorney from Dartmouth cleared his throat.

"What!" snapped Moss.

"But we spent weeks extensively scripting our opening, and all the partners approved it. Then we rehearsed day and night."

"Ever watch boxing?" asked Red. "You start with a game plan, but then you move when you see a goddamn fist. He anticipated your opening, and then you got up and stepped right into the punch! These are two rookies, for Christ's sake!"

"But we haven't shown them our easel yet. It's expensive."

"Out! Before I kill you!"

Another miniature stampede.

Another trip to the minibar. A disposable cell phone was dialed. "Yeah, it's Moss again . . . You wouldn't believe what happened in court this morning. Thank God it's Friday and we have the weekend to recover . . . What do you mean you have even worse news? . . . He asked a private investigator to look into what? Grand-Bourg Holding? Damn! That changes everything . . . Yes, I'm calling from an untraceable phone . . ."

Chapter **TWENTY-SEVEN**

DOWNTOWN MIAMI

It was the type of thick metal sign with raised letters that suggested it weighed a lot and that the building behind it was on some kind of historic register. They laid the cornerstone in 1925. Used to be the tallest thing in town.

Today it's in the shadows. If you've never seen the Miami-Dade courthouse, think of old cop shows like *Dragnet* and *Adam-12* where the police badges featured Los Angeles City Hall with a tower capped by a pyramid.

The foot traffic was determined in the midday heat. Folded newspapers, briefcases, take-out bags with Cuban sandwiches. A teenager sprinted up the middle of the street with a fistful of wristwatches. A whiskered man on the corner of Flagler had been screaming and kicking his own bicycle for five minutes. A shopowner chasing the shoplifting teen was hit by an ambulance. One of the folded newspapers told of a mysterious eyeball the size of a cantaloupe that had washed up on the beach. Everything was normal. Pedestrians continued chatting on cell phones.

At the courthouse curb stood a row of satellite trucks. Somewhere near the middle was a seventeen-year-old blue Datsun. Half the paint job had been baked off, with fluttering, ragged flaps along the edges of each blotch that made people think they could easily peel off the rest. Behind the wheel sat a young man with a loosened polyester tie and a white dress shirt with frayed collar.

"Sure you don't want to get out of the car?" asked the city councilman.

Reevis shook his head. "Hip dysplasia, comes and goes." *Click, click, click.*

Behind them, an ambulance loaded an expert at timepiece repair who now mainly just sold weird batteries.

The politician maintained an awkwardly frozen smile. Then, like a ventriloquist without moving his lips: "Are you done yet?"

"We're good."

The official headed down the sidewalk; the reporter jumped out of the car and ran up the courthouse steps.

The judge was already on the bench, an avuncular type who had seen everything. He sighed and glanced over at the plaintiff's table.

"Your Honor," said an inexperienced attorney, "if you can just give me a few more minutes."

"You said that an hour ago when I called a recess."

"But my investigator will be here any minute with key evidence that is the whole foundation of my case, which is part of a vast pattern across the state where the powerful have exploited some of our finest citizens."

From the other table. "Your Honor, this is highly unfair to my client, who is an upstanding member of the business community, as opposed to the plaintiff, who falsified her loan application and is here solely in an onerous shakedown that offends the sensibilities—"

"I did not!" shouted a delicate widow across the aisle. "That man stole my life savings!"

The judge banged his gavel. "Ma'am, no more outbursts or I will be forced to hold you in contempt . . . Counsel, control your client."

"I've got it," said the attorney. He put a reassuring hand on the widow's shoulder and whispered in her ear. She sobbed into a handkerchief.

"Your Honor, I have a motion before the court," said the defense attorney. "Summary dismissal."

The judge nodded and held up a hand for everyone to stop talking. It meant he was ready to sit back and mull his decision. The nameplate on the bench said COOLIDGE. The judge tapped his fingers. He chewed a forty-five-year-anniversary fountain pen from the state bar. He didn't like what the law required him to do next. The people coming before the court sure had changed since he became a jurist. At least back then most of the crooks had a code of honor. But these defendants today were smooth-palmed, no-dirt-under-the-nails country-club cowards who targeted the weakest first. The judge thought: *What is happening to my country?* He looked down. He touched his mouth. His pen had leaked ink on his lips. *Crap.*

He looked up again and held a hand over his mouth like he was coughing. "Under the circumstances, because the plaintiff has failed to produce certain promised evidentiary documents, I am left with no choice but to . . ."—he raised his gavel high—" . . . dismiss this—"

Both doors in the back of the courtroom dramatically burst open. *"Yo! Beak! Ice the gavel."*

The judge's head jerked back. *Beak?* He hadn't heard that slang for a judge in decades. He studied the man marching up the center aisle, waving a stack of papers over his head, wearing a tweed jacket and rumpled fedora. His necktie had a pattern of derringer pistols. He continued approaching the bench, talking loudly to himself as he walked.

"It was a bona fide Perry Mason moment. Mahoney's baby blues glommed the defense table like a bagman putting the arm on a dice-fiend holding the vig. The paperwork bombshell itched in my hand like a case of crabs you swore came from the mattress of a fleabag joint called the Night Owl, but the wife kept packing her bags for Poughkeepsie anyway." He reached the front of the bench.

The judge stood and leaned forward. "What are you mumbling about down there?"

Mahoney tossed the papers upward and pointed at the defendant.

"Robo-Hancock shyster bread-crumbed the *res ipsa loquitur* like a bloody *West Side Story* switchblade."

Judge Coolidge picked up the pages. "'Robo-Hancock'? You mean 'robo-signed'?" Another slang the judge recognized, but this one much more current, from the new tongue of foreclosure fraud. Housing defaults weren't flowing furiously enough for the most predacious, and courts began seeing a proliferation of mortgage assignments and affidavits from the same loan officers who couldn't possibly attest to the volume of facts they were autographing. So they just signed as fast as they could. The judge flipped through the stack of identical signatures and looked up. "Where'd you get these?"

"Dealt Franklins to the flunkies."

"What?"

"Paid a few hundred dollars to some low-level employees."

The defense attorney sprang to his feet. "Objection!"

"What is your objection?" asked Judge Coolidge.

"Your Honor, these so-called robo-documents, or whatever they're alleged, are completely inadmissible as stolen confidential company property. This fedora-wearing jester just admitted to bribing employees . . ."

Mahoney's toothpick stopped wiggling in his teeth and snapped in half.

The judge turned toward the plaintiff's attorney. "Son, what do you have to say?"

"Well, uh, I believe that the probative value of those documents outweigh any—"

The judge shook his head. "Wrong argument. Probative value is weighed against unduly inflaming a jury. Want to try again?"

The rookie looked down at his shoes and scratched his head.

The judge waited longer than was fair, then took a deep breath of reluctance. "In that case, I must rule that this evidence cannot be admitted—"

The doors in the back of the courtroom burst open again. "Hold everything! Did I miss any good parts? Could you have the court stenographer read back the juicy stuff?"

Defense counsel spun around. "What the hell's going on? First the fedora and now this joker. Who are you?"

The judge repeated the question with emphasis. "Yes, who *are* you?"

"Serge A. Storms, attorney for the plaintiff."

A front-row reporter looked up from his notepad. "Serge?"

"Shhhhh! Play it cool, Reevis."

The judge removed his glasses. "But the plaintiff already has an attorney."

"Just hired as co-counsel to assist with the admittance of the dynamite evidence recently discovered by my associate." Serge extended an upturned palm toward the private eye.

Mahoney tipped his hat in return.

The judge pointed at each of them. "You know each other?"

"Worked together many years."

"Who's that behind you?"

Coleman smiled and waved at the judge, wearing a T-shirt: ALSO AVAILABLE IN SOBER.

"My paralegal," said Serge, plopping his briefcase on the plaintiff's table. "Now, if the court would indulge me a brief moment to confer with my legal colleague."

"You have exactly one minute."

"Thank you, Your Honor." Serge turned and smiled at the young attorney. "Scoot over, bright boy. I need some elbow room."

The lawyer looked at Serge like he was a space alien. "Who are you?"

"The guy who helped Mahoney steal those documents. I'm not about to go through all that work and have them thrown out."

"Are you really a lawyer?"

"Not remotely." Serge flipped open the latches on his briefcase. "But you can't tell anyone because of attorney-client privilege."

"You're not my client."

"My word against yours. And who's going to believe an attorney who broke the privilege?" A sideways grin. "Have to admit I'm good."

The younger man stared in mute shock.

The judge tapped his gavel. "Can we?"

"Just another sec," said Serge.

"Make it quick."

Serge leaned into his new partner. "Where did you leave off just before I came in?"

"Defense objected to the new evidence because it was stolen . . ."

"Exactly what I'd expect," said Serge.

" . . . So I said the probative value—"

Serge shook his head. "Wrong argument. That's for inflaming the jury . . . Okay, I'll take it from here. Just dummy up and nod along with everything I say."

The gavel banged hard several times.

Serge beamed his biggest smile. "Ready, willing and able!"

The judge rolled his eyes at the ceiling. "Could the stenographer please tell me where the heck I was before all this?"

"Your Honor, you were just about to disallow the evidence because it was stolen."

"That's right," said the judge.

Serge sprang to his feet. "I object."

"You can't object." The judge pointed with his gavel. "*He* objected."

"I mean I have another argument you must consider before rendering your decision."

The judge fell back in his chair and let his chin sag to his chest. In a listless voice: "What?"

"Your Honor, stolen evidence is admissible if the parties involved were not agents of, or acting in concert with, the plaintiffs."

The judge pinched his upper lip in thought. "Interesting theory . . . what's your citation?"

"John Grisham's movie *The Rainmaker*." Serge gleefully stomped his feet. "There was a totally excellent marathon on cable last week, and in this movie the same thing happens except with an insurance company, and Danny DeVito calls Mickey Rourke, who's hiding out in Florida—that alone made my day!—and Rourke tells DeVito—"

"Stop!" said the judge. "Just stop! You can't cite a movie!"

"Why not?" said Serge. "It's precisely on point."

"It's a *movie*!"

"And a great one. If you haven't seen it already, do yourself a favor—"

"Are you really a lawyer?" asked the judge. He turned the other way. "Bailiff, check his credentials."

A thick-armed sheriff's deputy stepped forward from the side of the courtroom.

It didn't slow Serge: " . . . then Mickey Rourke cites *U.S. v. DeSoto*."

The judge did a double take. "Wait, I know the DeSoto case. It's exactly on point."

"That's what I've been trying to say all along," replied Serge. "Grisham does his research."

"As you were, bailiff." The judge turned to Serge. "But didn't your associate say he paid for the documents? That would make him an agent of the plaintiff."

"Not if the documents were already stolen by someone else," said Serge. "The whole foreclosure-fraud epidemic has sired an avalanche of outrage, in this case disgruntled employees who read the papers and spend lunch breaks at the copy machine."

"On point again," said the judge.

"This is a farce!" said the defense.

"Counsel!" snapped the judge. "You know the proper way to address this court."

"Then I object."

The gavel slammed. "Overruled! And the evidence is in. And your motion to dismiss is denied." Another gavel slam. "Court is in recess until tomorrow morning at nine." The judge looked toward the defense table a final time. "Given the turn of events today, I strongly suggest you consider working out a settlement." He disappeared into chambers.

The reporter checked his wristwatch and ran out of the courtroom.

Serge caught up to him near the street and stopped in puzzlement. "Reevis, what the heck are you doing?"

Reevis finished strapping on a battery belt for the TV people. "I don't want to talk about it."

"Fair enough," said Serge. "So what's next on your calendar?"

Chapter TWENTY-EIGHT

MONDAY MORNING

A fist banged on an upstairs door of the Southern Cross Hotel.

"Are you in there?" Brook checked her watch. "We're going to be late."

She pounded the door again and dialed Shelby's cell phone. No answer. "Where is he?"

More waiting and knocking until there wasn't any more time. "Maybe he already left." Brook headed down the stairs and over to the courthouse alone.

When she arrived, the defense table was empty. She got out her cell phone again. This time it rang before she could dial. "Hello?"

"Hi, Brook, this is Ken Shapiro. Hate to throw you a curve like this, but Shelby had a family emergency. His mother."

"Is it bad?" asked Brook.

"Don't know. The family called him and he called me. That's all I got."

"What about the trial?"

"We're sending another attorney down to assist you. Don't worry, he's intimately familiar with the case."

The bailiff opened a side door.

"When's he supposed to get here?"

"Shouldn't be long."

"But they're already bringing the jury in."

"Relax, you'll do fine."

The bailiff looked in her direction. His eyes telegraphed: *No cell phone in court.*

"Got to go." She closed the phone.

The doors in the back of the courtroom opened. *"Brook!"*

She turned around. A man smiled and waved.

Brook grabbed her stomach. "Holy Jesus, this can't be happening."

The man strolled to the plaintiff's table and set his briefcase down.

"Ziggy!" said Brook. "What the hell are you doing? This table is just for the trial lawyers. The substitute attorney will be arriving any second."

"He just did." Ziggy took a seat and inched up. "Your firm called and said they needed someone to fill in until Shelby got back . . . Are you okay?"

Brook doubled over with cramps. "Oh, no." She jumped up and ran out of the courtroom.

Ziggy followed and knocked on the door of the women's room. "Are you all right in there?"

"No. Go away! . . ."

Eventually the door opened and a pale-white attorney emerged.

Down the hall, the bailiff motioned from an open door. "Judge is waiting."

The mixed pair reentered the courtroom under the gamma-ray gaze of Judge Kennesaw Montgomery Boone. "Call your first witness!"

Brook opened a file. "Plaintiffs call Mrs. Evelyn Rogers."

A sweet little retiree climbed into the witness box with the bailiff's assistance. "You're such a polite young man."

Brook reached in her purse and handed something to Ziggy. "Use this?"

"Visine?"

"Your eyes are bloodshot. They look like road maps of Cleveland."
Brook snapped her purse shut. "You're high, aren't you?"

Ziggy held two fingers a short distance apart. "Just a teensy bit. But
only to get my head centered for cross-examination."

"You're not saying anything."

The judge cleared his throat. "There a problem?"

"No, Your Honor." Brook stood and approached the witness stand
with a warm smile. "Good morning."

Mrs. Rogers smiled back. "You're awfully young to be a lawyer."

"Yes, I am . . . Now, I'd like to talk about when you first applied for
your mortgage . . ."

A line of genteel questioning followed as Brook walked the retiree
through the process of the home appraisal and income qualifying.

"It was such a nice house," said Mrs. Rogers. "I couldn't believe they said
I would have no problems paying for it. It was almost too good to be true."

"No further questions," said Brook.

"You're such a nice young lady."

The defense attorney from Dartmouth got up. "Good morning,
Mrs. Rogers."

"Who are you?"

"An attorney for the mortgage company."

"Oh."

"I just have a couple simple questions. Did you sign an agreement to
make your payments each month?"

"Yes."

"And did you?"

"At first, but then something called a variable rate changed the
amount—"

"Did you sign an agreement to pay a variable rate?"

"Yes, but I didn't understand—"

"No further questions."

"You're not a nice man."

Laughter from the gallery of locals attending for their morning entertainment.

The gavel banged. "Order! There will be no more reactions from this audience."

Brook stood. "Redirect." She approached again with a document in a plastic bag. "Do you recognize this?"

"Objection!" said the defense. "That should have been handled on direct."

"Your Honor, he opened the door by asking what she agreed to," said Brook.

The judge leaned forward. "What is that?"

"One of the documents Consolidated filed with the foreclosure."

"Objection!" the defense repeated. "That's not related to the agreement."

"It's my first trial," Brook pleaded.

The judge noticed sympathy coming from the jury box. "The foundation's questionable, but since it's your first case, I'm willing to see where this goes before ruling ... this time."

"Thank you, Your Honor ... Now, Mrs. Rogers, if you'll look at this part—"

"I can't see without my glasses."

"I'll help you. Is your middle name Mary?"

"No, Marie."

"Is your address three-one-nine?"

"No, three-nine-one."

Brook established several other discrepancies, then turned to the judge. "Plaintiffs would like to submit this exhibit as an example of robo-signing—"

"Objection! She's characterizing!"

"Sustained. The jury will disregard that last remark."

Brook maintained poise. "I would like to submit this as our exhibit A."

The judge raised his eyebrows toward the defense table.

An attorney jumped up on cue. "Objection! Is plaintiffs' counsel prepared to present an officer of Consolidated to testify that he actually signed that document?"

"Actually, no," said Brook. "As a matter of fact, if defense will stipu-late, I'll agree that this document *wasn't* signed by the person whose name is at the bottom, and therefore prevents me from admitting it as evidence—as well as that whole box of other damning documents under my table that I'd love to get in. But then, if they weren't prop-erly signed, it means Consolidated filed fraudulent documents with the court. And since the foreclosures were based on said documents, we can all go home. Except the defendants, who will be back in *criminal* court."

The opposing attorney stared into high beams. " . . . Objection withdrawn." He sat meekly and folded into himself.

So went the rest of the tedious day, Brook methodically laying the premise for the class action.

A gavel banged. "Court is in recess."

The defense team stood and repacked their briefcases.

"How do you think it went?"

"Hope that suite at the resort doesn't have many more lamps."

Chapter TWENTY-NINE

THE *JOURNAL*

Reevis crossed the newspaper's lobby and approached the security desk. "He's with me."

"Name?"

"I'm Serge A. Storms! . . . Oooo, can I keep the visitor's badge as a souvenir? . . . No? Can't blame me for asking . . ." Serge pulled out his camera. "Where do you keep the Pulitzers?"

Reevis led him into the paper's auditorium. "I thought Coleman was coming."

"On a bender back in Miami. It starts innocent enough, and then the motel room is full of his 'new friends from the underpass.'" Serge stopped and watched a loud mass of people file down rows of folding chairs. "When I asked if I could attend your libel seminar, I was expecting a small classroom."

"No," said Reevis, heading for a long table against the back wall. "It's the quarterly libel tutorial conducted by the big Shapiro law firm."

"But I thought the paper was slashing costs everywhere."

"It's no charge because we have the firm on permanent retainer."

Reevis grabbed a Styrofoam cup. "And the lawyers don't mind because all the new inexperience at the paper has created a windfall of libel suits and billable hours."

Serge raced for his own cup. "Free coffee!"

They filled to the brim and took seats in the back row.

"Who's that guy?" asked Bilko.

"A friend," said Reevis. "He's going to be a lawyer and wanted to observe our libel class."

The veterans disapprovingly appraised Serge's tropical shirt with hula dancers, but didn't say anything for Reevis's sake.

An index finger tapped the microphone, signaling that it was time.

"Good afternoon. My name is Kent Pickering, and I'll be conducting our seminar today. As you probably know, some of your co-workers have been keeping our firm pretty busy . . ." He stopped to chuckle and the audience laughed with him.

Danning elbowed Mazerek. "Check out that Italian suit."

"It's half my salary," said Bilko.

Pickering walked out from behind the podium and leaned casually against its side. "I'd like to begin with two specific cases that we handled for the *Journal* in the last few months. The first involves a little mistake in a story about a vehicular homicide, which was generally correct except the article identified the driver as the suspect's son, Junior. Now, we could have argued that reasonable people would recognize it was actually the father, and the 'Jr.' at the end of the name was a simple clerical error. Except the reporter, armed with the wrong name, also interviewed neighbors and printed quotes about the son, including his fondness for the *Fast and Furious* series of street racer movies . . . That last part was a nice detail, especially since it made my firm a nice chunk of change . . ." Chuckles rippled through the audience.

Danning folded his arms. "I fail to see the humor."

Bilko folded his own. "This is what happens when you make photographers write stories."

Pickering strolled around to the other side of the podium. "Now, I can't stress enough the extra care we need to take concerning minors, as well as insulating ourselves with official police reports instead of just talking to bystanders. As an aside, please ask to see the driver's license of any witness who says his name is Mike Hunt or Dick Swells. They've been quoted nine times in the last year and I'm guessing it's not just two guys . . ." Another wave of chuckles. " . . . Anyway, in the case I was talking about, we had to set up a little college fund for Junior . . ."

Danning looked around at his laughing colleagues. "What is this, a comedy club?"

"I agree," said Serge. "It's a pox on your whole profession. Would you like me to take action?"

The trio looked down the row with twisted expressions. "Reevis, who exactly is this guy?"

"Relax, he's harmless."

Back up front: "Our second case went a little better. It involved your highly rated TV news segment, 'Gotcha Live!' . . ."

"Oh, this ridiculousness," said Bilko. "We can't write any more investigative pieces because they take too much time . . ."

"Except TV still can," said Mazerek. "Because they only take ten seconds."

Serge leaned toward Reevis. "What are they talking about?"

"Here's TV's idea of investigative reporting," said Reevis. "Hide a film crew, then throw a wallet out in the middle of a mall and see what people do."

Pickering slid back behind the podium. " . . . As you know, our ticket-scalping report . . ."

"Scalping?" asked Serge.

Reevis leaned and lowered his voice. "Another gem. Two of our TV reporters stood fifty feet apart outside the stadium. The first was selling fifty-dollar tickets, and the second wanted to buy tickets for a hundred. So some guy who is just taking his kids to the game notices them and takes the bait, buying from one reporter and selling to the other. Of course we also contacted the police in advance so we'd have great footage of them swooping in to arrest the dad . . ."

Pickering wrapped up the story from the podium. " . . . After our story aired, the case was thrown out of court for entrapment, but the father had already been fired from his job and sued us. Unfortunately for him, there's a little thing we call the First Amendment."

The attorney smiled and laughed, and the audience laughed with him.

When the laughter died down, a hand went up in the back row.

"Reevis," snapped Danning. "Put your arm down!"

"Are you crazy?" said Bilko.

Pickering peered over the podium. "Yes, you in the back row. What's your question?"

Reevis stood up. "Why are you laughing?"

"What?"

"You were laughing. Why?"

Mazerek covered his eyes. "Jesus, kid."

Pickering was stumped. "I don't understand your question."

"I appreciate that you have to represent us, even when we're wrong," said Reevis. "But do you have to make jokes about shoddy journalism that embarrassed an ordinary citizen in front of the entire community and cost him his livelihood?"

"Well, I, uh . . ."

"Have some shame." Reevis sat down.

The auditorium was uncomfortably silent, especially the stage. The collective thought: *Holy shit*.

An hour later, a crowd had gathered around Reevis's desk: Danning, Mazerek and Bilko, plus Serge and an equal number of security guards.

Reevis quietly emptied the belongings from his desk and placed them in a cardboard box.

"We're real sorry, kid," said Danning.

"Anything you need," said Bilko. "References . . ."

"Are all the libel classes like that?" asked Serge.

Reevis examined a small plaque for third place from some forgotten article, then into the box it went. "I'll be fine. I just couldn't work here anymore if it meant keeping quiet."

"What are you going to do now?" asked Mazerek.

"Don't know." Reevis picked up the box. "Maybe freelance."

"I got an idea," said Serge. "Follow me down to my car."

"Why?"

"Let's go for a ride."

SUGARLOAF KEY

A married couple strolled down a secluded path, arguing about the husband watching too much football.

"But it's the play-offs!"

"I have needs, too!"

"We'll go out to dinner tonight. Someplace nice."

"Are you going to wear that stupid Giants jersey again?"

"You don't like it?"

From another direction. "Mildred, what are you doing?"

"Watching *Law & Order*."

"You watch that stupid show too much. Come out here."

"It just started. This couple is arguing in Central Park."

"That's how it always starts. Get out here!"

"But they're just about to find a body in the bushes."

"Mildred!"

Mildred and Gerard Lapierre, seasonal residents from Canada, owned a stilt house on the channel overlooking Cudjoe Key. It was a balmy day and all the Bahama shutters were propped wide. Mildred stepped out onto the wraparound porch. "What's so important that I have to miss my show?"

"Will you look at that!" Gerard said with disgust. "Even way out here in nature, some jerk has to litter."

"Where?"

"Those shoes down in the mangroves."

"That's what's so important?"

"To me it is. The pristine view is why we picked out this place—"

"Gerard . . ."

"Then some idiot—"

"Gerard!"

"What?"

"Those shoes. They still have feet in them . . ."

An hour later, the Lapierres watched from their veranda as crime-scene technicians swarmed the shore. A black bag was zipped up over a face. A detective from Key West arrived and approached the medical examiner. "What are the details?"

"Adult male about thirty, single gunshot to the left temple."

A police diver rose from the water. "Got something." He held up a clear bag with a .38 revolver.

The coroner turned to the detective. "The stippling at the wound indicates the muzzle was in contact with the head. I'm guessing we'll find residue on his left hand."

"Suicide?"

"Here's his wallet. Three hundred in cash, which pretty much rules out robbery," said the examiner. "We won't be missing dinner over this one."

Chapter THIRTY

Reevis Tome sat with a cardboard box in his lap, staring out the windshield of a '76 Ford Cobra. "Where are we going?"

"Someplace cheerful!" Serge hit the gas and slalomed through city traffic. "You just got fired, so I'm on the case . . . Coffee?"

Serge poured himself a cup and passed the thermos. The car shook from an overhead roar as the shadow of a United jet swept across the road.

Serge smacked the steering wheel with joy. "Don't you just love it when you time the airplane shadow perfectly?"

"Are you okay?"

"Drink more coffee. Life will snap into focus." The Cobra whipped around a cement mixer on Belvedere Road. "Oooo! Oooo! Over there! The sign! Check out the sign!"

"You mean the old neon thing on Airport Liquors?"

"No, the other excellent sign. That retro job with interlocking orange shapes over a galloping greyhound. I *love* the Palm Beach Kennel Club!" *Click, click, click.* "Oh my God! They opened a poker room!"

"You play poker?"

"No."

The Cobra skidded up in front of the entrance, and Serge killed the thermos. "Let's get our cheer on!"

Serge ran inside, and Reevis raced to catch up, finally reaching him in a sprawling card room crammed with type A personalities and fevered intrigue. Cowboy hats, sunglasses, bolo ties.

Serge stood at a cashier's window and removed a single dollar bill from his wallet. "I'd like a chip please."

The cashier paused. "Just one? How do you expect to win?"

"It's all I'll need."

She shrugged and handed over a round piece of plastic.

Serge held it over his head. "I won! I won!"

Reevis caught up again as Serge sprinted down a grandstand aisle and out onto the open spectator apron surrounding the track. "Hurry up!" Serge yelled and waved. "The only way to watch a race is standing right against the fence at the finish pole. I'm always surprised everyone isn't down here."

"What's the deal with the poker chip?"

"The new card rooms have been a game changer in my life." Serge opened his palm in reverence. "Instead of buying some expensive keepsake from their gift shop, these chips are durable, with all the requisite imprinted data of a righteous souvenir find. And I trick them into giving it to me for only a dollar. Then I walk away. They never expect that."

Handlers emerged from the paddock and led a parade of athletic dogs with colorful numbers on their sides.

"Now *this* is Florida!" Serge waved an arm across the milieu. "Old-growth palms towering over the manicured infield with majestic lake and fountains. The rest of the world is making themselves crazy, stuck in office buildings and turning fluorescent under fluorescent lights. But we're out here in paradise, the sun on our necks, enjoying fresh air and the smell of cut grass with hundreds of other people who don't have jobs." He turned and grinned awkwardly. "Sorry, that topic's probably still a little raw for you. My point is, there's something special about Florida's betting palaces—horses, dogs, jai alai—frozen in time, like the old days when the Social Register would dress up and make a night of it. Can you believe that four thousand people packed this place on February seventeenth, 1932, to watch Broom Boy win the first race ever here? True story: Later that night one of the dogs actually caught the mechanical rabbit, causing parimutuel chaos and emotional turbulence."

"Serge." Reevis stared down at his shoes. "I know you mean well, but I really need to get going on résumés. Reporters don't get paid enough to have savings—"

"Your résumé's already in." Serge squinted at passing greyhounds for clues. "And you've already been hired."

Reevis looked up. "By who?"

"Me!"

The journalist sighed. "Listen, and don't take this wrong, because I actually find you entertaining in a charmingly eccentric way. But I have to start getting serious about this."

"Is this serious enough?" Serge pulled a fat wad from his pocket and peeled off large bills. "How's five hundred to get you over?"

"I can't take that!"

Serge shook his head and peeled off more bills. "Okay, seven hundred. And I'd heard beggars couldn't be choosy."

"No, I mean it's too much," said Reevis. "And you don't have any work for me."

"Oh, I've definitely got some work for you!" Serge tucked the cash in Reevis's shirt pocket. "Consider that a bridge payment until you land another newspaper gig. You can start with me this afternoon."

"Start what?"

Serge climbed up on the fence and pointed at a dog with a yellow flag on its side. "What do you think of number six?"

"I don't know anything about greyhounds," said Reevis. "This job you mentioned—"

"I don't know greyhounds either." Serge began doing jumping jacks. "So I never bet on the dogs. Instead I study the odds board and bet *against* the crowd."

"Win much?"

"What? Why am I jumping?" He stopped. "The dog business is extremely delicate. Everyone huddled with programs and pencils, performing complex logarithmic calculations, then on the way to the starting gate one of the dogs poops, throwing the odds board into pandemonium, people leaping out of their seats screaming in terror, clawing each other on their way back to the ticket windows, time ticking down like an H-bomb: 'For the love of Jesus, don't close the booth yet!'" He nodded to himself with the wisdom of experience. "That's when you make your move."

"Serge, back to this new work I'm supposed to do..."

"Requires your specific investigative skill set." Serge got out his poker chip for luck. "Involves some kind of big legal case. This private eye I know named Mahoney needs some legwork for an attorney in Hialeah..."

Number six pooped. Horrified screams. Serge winked. "Wait here."

He ran back in the clubhouse and quickly returned with a newly printed stub. "They're loading them in the gates! This could be the race of my life!"

Reevis took a saddened breath and joined Serge at the railing. "So what's the name of your dog?"

"No idea." Serge craned his neck toward the gate. "I always make up my own names anyway. That's the key to respect at the track: calling out nicknames not on the program like you have inside dope from knowing the dog socially . . . Here comes the rabbit . . . And they're off!"

"I guess we'll talk later about the new work."

"What work?" Serge pushed himself high up on the fence to see the back stretch.

"You just gave me seven hundred dollars."

"I did?"

"Look, if you want it back..." Reevis reached for his pocket.

"No, no, no. I'm sure it was about something... They're in the final turn! Number six takes the lead!" Serge hopped down in excitement and pulled hard on Reevis's shirt. "He's three lengths ahead . . . Come on, Turds O' Plenty! . . ."

"I don't believe it," said Reevis. "He's actually going to win."

"I know how to pick 'em!" Still hopping and pulling the shirt. "Fifty yards to go! . . . Come on, Turds!"

Thunderous cheers rose from the crowd as the dogs neared the finish line.

Then silence.

Serge hung over the fence. "What the hell just happened?"

"Your dog tripped and went nose down in the dirt," said Reevis. "Taking out the next three behind him."

Quiet was replaced by boos and other mob sounds. A blizzard of torn-up tickets fluttered down. *"Son of a bitch!" "This is fixed!" "Why did I bet on that dog?"*

Serge headed back to the clubhouse. "So anyway, Mahoney gave me this supposedly important legal file that allegedly is the key to some big case, but it just looks like mundane documents to me. Figured I'd give you a look-see before I gave up. Something called Grand-Bourg Holding . . ."

Serge stopped at a ticket window and handed over his stub.

Reevis's eyes widened as large bills were counted out in Serge's hand. "But number six lost."

"Exactly." Serge pocketed the cash. "I didn't bet on six."

FORT LAUDERDALE

A thirtieth-floor conference room filled with concerned people. Ken Shapiro was on the phone.

"I know it's difficult, but try to calm down. I can't understand anything you're saying."

Brook did her best. Through sobs: "I just know Shelby didn't kill himself!"

"Brook, you're upset," said Ken. "I talked to the police and all evidence points to suicide. Found the gun with his body in a tidal channel off Cudjoe Key. They say it's open-and-shut."

"I've been with him all week," said Brook. "He was in great spirits. Something's not right."

"I think we should take you off the case," said Ken. "At least temporarily."

"And leave it to Ziggy?"

"If you're worried about— . . . Listen, nobody at the firm will question this. We couldn't expect anyone to continue under these circumstances."

"But the trial is the whole reason he got killed," said Brook. "I'm sure of it!"

Someone at the conference table: "She's hearing hoofbeats and seeing zebras."

Ken made a slashing gesture across his neck to shut up. "Brook, if it helps you accept it, something else was going on. He lied to us when he called and said he had a family emergency. His mom was home and fine."

"Did you talk to Shelby?"

"No, he texted me."

"See?" said Brook.

"See what?" said Ken. "I want you to come back here."

Brook took deliberate breaths. "Okay, I promise I'll be fine. It's just that I only heard the news a few minutes ago. I'll get a good night's sleep. Shelby would want me to continue the case—he felt so strongly about it."

Ken closed his eyes for a long thought, then opened them. "All right, but if you feel the slightest reservation, contact me immediately. Take care of yourself."

He hung up and dialed again. "Who are you calling?" asked Shug Blatt.

"Our investigators. They have carry permits."

"What for?"

"It's nagging me. I talked to Shelby all week, everything upbeat. And I did only get a text."

"You really think she's right about a connection to the case?"

"Doubt it, but I'm not taking any chances," said Ken. "We're sending someone to watch her back."

Chapter THIRTY-ONE

PALM BEACH COUNTY

Serge glanced over from the driver's seat. "What do you think?"

"What do I *think*?" Reevis said sarcastically. "You won't even let me look at the legal file."

"I told you: because it's not time yet." Serge aimed his camera out the window. "So what do you think? In general?"

"About what?"

"Your new job."

"How should I know? You refuse to tell me anything about the damn thing."

"Exactly." *Click, click, click.* "Consider this like the movie *Training Day* with Denzel Washington, where all is slowly revealed to the new guy in due time. Except by then a bunch of bad shit hits the new guy. Hope that doesn't happen. Forget that reference. What I'm trying to say is you first need to get into my flow, like Hilary Swank following Clint Eastwood in *Million Dollar Baby*. Except that ended even worse than *Training Day*. Cancel that thought." Serge turned and grinned. "How do you like what I bought you?"

Reevis stared down at himself. "I never wear tropical shirts."

"Tropical shirts are critical in your new line of work." Serge slipped on dark sunglasses and turned south at Dixie Highway. "You can hide things in your waistband."

"Hide—?"

"We're here!" Serge leisurely turned the wheel again as they approached Lucerne Avenue and pulled into a parallel slot on the street. Another off-kilter grin and a slapping of palms. "Ready to start?"

"I honestly don't know what to say."

"That you like seven hundred dollars." Serge handed him the thermos. "Drink that. And I'm not asking. Since I'm your boss now, it's an order."

Reevis twisted off the cap. "I like coffee anyway."

"Then you're halfway home." Serge climbed out the driver's side. "What a beautiful day! Dig the clear blue sky. Follow me. Forget those movies."

Reevis stepped onto the sidewalk. "Is this Lake Worth?"

"That's what the sign on the old city hall across the street says." *Click, click.* "But for a brief period in 1980 it read 'Miranda Beach.'"

"But Lake Worth was never called Miranda Beach." Reevis finished off the thermos and handed it back. "It's not even a beach; we're on the mainland."

"Except in the movie."

"Movie?"

"Florida classic, easily in my top five."

Reevis snapped his fingers. "Miranda Beach. That was in *Body Heat*. I loved *Body Heat*. It was like L.A. noir meets Hitchcock by way of *The Palm Beach Story*. Kathleen Turner in that white dress was the new Bacall. Her best line to William Hurt: 'You're not too bright. I like that in a man.' Plus the arsonist was a young Miami native named Mickey Rourke, who also had a part in that Grisham film you mentioned . . ."

"Coffee kicking in?" asked Serge.

"Sorry, it's just that I'm a movie buff and you mentioned one of my all-time favorites. Guess I was babbling a little."

"Babbling is underrated." Serge headed toward the side of the road.

"You're off to a flying start, grasshopper." He reached under his shirt and handed over a large brown envelope.

Reevis peeled open the top of the sealed package and slowly flipped through the contents in confusion. "These are photos I'm supposed to investigate?"

"Not remotely." Serge tapped the pages in the reporter's hands. "Screen shots from *Body Heat* that I grabbed off a computer." He stopped at the intersection and checked his camera. "Whenever a great movie is made in Florida, I'm compelled to track down filming location so I can stand on the same spots as the stars and absorb the silver-screen magic."

Reevis held up an eight-by-ten glossy. "This one's the Mediterranean house where Turner and Hurt had their affair."

"The Scotia mansion in Hypoluxo on Periwinkle Drive, built by the city's first mayor in 1922. But it burned down in 1999, so I stood on the spot and went on a hunger strike for ten minutes."

The reporter held up another photo. "And this is the historic band shell where the couple met for the first time. I've been there. It's on the boardwalk in Hollywood."

"Possibly my easiest find to date. Take a look at the next one."

"Hey, that's William Hurt crossing the street toward his law office."

"Had a devil of a time finding it."

"It looks like this road." Reevis glanced around. "You found Hurt's law office?"

"Not yet." Serge licked his mouth. "I wanted you to be with me for the climax. I studied that film frame by frame for years, making notes of any possible clue: business names, traffic lights, the way the trees are planted along the road, but no luck. The closest I got was a distant street sign behind Hurt, but it was way too small, so I went over to a friend's house to blow it up on his sixty-two-inch flat screen. And my friend comes running down the stairs: 'Serge, it's three A.M. How'd you get in? We thought you were a burglar.' And I say, 'I turned the sound down to be polite,' then I point and ask, 'Can you read that street sign?' And he's like, 'Are you shitting me?' Then his wife comes down in a nightgown screaming like a banshee, so I guess they had been fighting just before I arrived, and I suggest marriage counseling, and they haven't talked to me for eight years."

Reevis had a blank look.

"I know what you're thinking." Serge began walking again. "Standard DVDs are insufficient resolution to read street signs. But then Blu-ray came out and the sign was in perfect focus, except it said 'Dixie Highway,' which is like a hundred miles long and doesn't narrow it at all, so I went to look at microfilm in the library because Hurt walks by this restaurant called Le Cyrano, and sure enough, on page B8 of the *Palm Beach Post* from February 26, 1982, there's a feature article about a great French restaurant on the northeast corner of Dixie and Lake Avenue." He stuck his arm out to the left. "It's now this gym that we're passing, which means"—Serge dramatically pivoted ninety degrees to his right—"there's Hurt's place."

Reevis glanced at the photo, then up at the building. "You're right, it matches. That's pretty impressive."

"Check out those three arched windows on the second floor. The last one says 'Law Office' in your picture. And at the crest of the building's roof: 'Rowe, 1923.' I'm guessing it's the Rowe building."

"But if you're this good at research, why do you need me?"

"It's a matter of focus." Serge looked up and down the street. "About three minutes into poring over dry documents on a computer, all I can think about is the next location I want to find, and then I'm hovering over the state with Google Earth . . . Let's go touch the building! You always have to touch the building!"

"Uh, okay."

Serge checked the road again.

"The street's clear," said Reevis. "What are you waiting for?"

Serge shook his head. "In the movie, Hurt runs in front of a car that hits the brakes and honks at him. We have to wait for a car . . . Here comes one . . . Now!"

Serge dashed into the street. Tires squealed, a horn honked. *"What's your fucking deal?"*

Serge raised a victory salute to the driver. "Film preservation!"

Reevis waited until the coast was clear, then jogged to the other side.

Serge touched the building. "Tag! You're it!" He spun and sprinted for his car.

Reevis was breathing hard when he climbed in the passenger seat. "I think you better take me back now."

"Why?" said Serge. "I just got you properly warmed up for your first assignment."

Reevis sighed. "So now you're finally going to let me see that legal file?"

"*Allllllmost . . .*" Serge threw the car in gear. "If you're a movie buff, how many James Bond films had scenes in Florida?"

"Ummm, three. Silver Springs, and two in Miami."

"Not bad, but four," said Serge. "You missed the one in Key West, where Timothy Dalton is reading *The Old Man and the Sea* on the balcony of the Hemingway House . . . More coffee! . . ."

A couple hours later, a pair of vehicles took Dixie Highway south through Miami before swinging east. They cruised slowly out along a curling spit of land surrounded by water below Coral Gables. The road came to an end overlooking Biscayne Bay. One of the cars stopped. The other, a '76 Cobra, turned around and came back in the opposite direction, pulling up so the drivers were window to window.

Serge bounded gleefully in his seat. "What do you think?"

Reevis glanced around the deserted waterfront. "I still don't understand why you had to rent me a second car."

"Because there were *two* cars in the movie! And I can't get enough of this place! Matheson Hammock Park, the actual filming location where Paul Newman passed documents between cars in the Sydney Pollack 1981 tour de force *Absence of Malice*—another classic Florida legal movie, *and* a journalism movie . . ." Serge produced a brown envelope and handed it through the window to Reevis. "Then someone in the distance with a zoom lens photographed Newman making the exchange . . ."

Someone in the distance with a zoom lens photographed Serge and Reevis making the exchange.

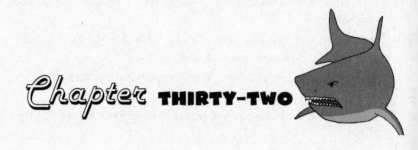

Chapter THIRTY-TWO

THE NEXT MORNING

Flip-flops slapped into the courtroom. The regular gathering of local busybodies began taking their seats in the audience for their morning show.

Brook remained out in the hall, swiveling her head. "Where are all our witnesses?"

"I checked on them last night at the hotel," said Ziggy.

"Check again."

Ziggy pointed. "There's two now."

"But we're not supposed to use those particular ones until the end. And even then, only if our case isn't strong enough."

"So we call them out of order."

"Check the hotel again!"

"Okay, okay." Ziggy got out his cell.

"I have to go to the bathroom." Brook ran down the hall. People turned around at the clatter of her shoes. A man in a golf shirt looked up from his newspaper at the fuss, then returned to the crossword.

The jury was led in, followed by the judge. He stopped and stared down at Ziggy sitting alone. "Where's your partner?"

"Right here!" said Brook, pulling a piece of toilet paper off her shoe and rushing to her seat. Out the side of her mouth: "Anything?"

"Nobody's answering," said Ziggy.

The judge pulled the shoulders of his robe out for comfort. "Call your first witness."

"Plaintiffs call Ruth Wozniak."

Ruth put her hand on the Bible and swore up and down to tell the truth.

Brook led her through the same line of testimony that they had rehearsed, except she had to move around the side of the stand to block the jury box when Ruthy began unconsciously petting an invisible dalmatian.

" . . . No more questions."

A defense attorney stood. "Good morning."

"Good morning," said Ruthy.

"You've sworn under oath to tell the truth. Is that correct?"

"Yes."

"Do you know the penalty if you don't?"

"I . . . could go to jail?"

"Correct again." He turned his back to the witness and faced the jury. "Could you tell the court where you work?"

"I retired two years ago."

"And you got your mortgage three years ago, is that correct?"

"Yes."

"Now, when you applied for your mortgage, you had to supply recent pay stubs, didn't you?"

"Yes."

The attorney walked back to the defense table and grabbed a notebook. "Mrs. Wozniak, isn't it a fact that you didn't retire two years ago, but were laid off shortly before getting your loan?"

"That was a long time ago," said Ruthy. "And I got a temp job a little later."

The attorney handed her a sheet of paper. "Here's a copy of the most recent stub you submitted for your loan. Can you read the date?"

"Not without my glasses."

"November fifth." He took the page back and waved it at the jury. "Isn't it a fact that you had already been laid off when you lied about your income to get your loan?"

Brook jumped up. "Objection, leading."

"Overruled. He's allowed to lead the witness. It's his cross."

"But—"

"Sit down."

The Yale attorney leaned against the railing across the front of the jury box. "I'll repeat the question. And remember, you're under oath. Didn't you lie about being employed to get your loan?"

Ruthy looked down. "Yes."

"No more questions."

Brook wrote on her legal pad: *fuck*.

Ziggy elbowed her. "What do we do now?"

She slumped. "It means we have to rehabilitate our case with the only other witness we have today . . ."

Cooder Ratch took the oath and reclined inappropriately in the witness chair.

Brook kept her questioning uneventful, but the witness's presentation wasn't wearing well with the jury. She decided to cut her losses and bail out early.

"That's all you're going to ask me?" snapped Cooder. "After I drove all the way—"

"I said no more questions." She took her seat and mumbled, "Can this get any worse?"

Ziggy felt something vibrate in his pocket. He checked his cell and recognized the number. "I need to go out in the hall . . ."

The Harvard attorney stood. "Your name's Cooder, right?"

"Weren't you listening earlier?"

"Have you ever been arrested?"

"That was a long time ago."

"Three years is a long time?" said the lawyer. "Meth possession, wasn't it?"

"Charges were dropped."

"Let me get this straight: You don't have enough money to pay your mortgage and yet you can afford methamphetamine?"

"That was way before . . . And it didn't happen."

"Which is it?"

"Both."

"Why were the charges dropped?"

"I was innocent."

The attorney read from his legal pad. "Didn't you offer jailhouse testimony against your cell mate? So you're a rat?"

"I'm not a rat!" said Cooder. "I was just doing the right thing."

"Was your cell mate convicted?"

"I don't remember."

"I have court records here to refresh your memory. He was found not guilty. Why was that?"

"Don't remember."

"I have court records for that, too. You were charged with perjury for what you said in that trial. Do you always lie when you get on a witness stand?"

"I can explain—"

The attorney was already walking away. "No further questions."

Brook underlined the word "fuck."

Ziggy ran back in from the hall with his cell phone. "Brook—"

"Not now."

Cooder climbed down from the witness stand.

"Brook, call him back on redirect!"

"Are you insane?" said Brook. "There's no way I'm putting that disaster on the stand again for more questions."

"Hurry, he's about to leave the courtroom."

"No way!"

Ziggy jumped up. "Your Honor, we'd like to call our witness back for redirect."

The judge pointed, and the bailiff blocked Cooder at the back doors. "What now?"

"Ziggy!" snapped Brook. "Have you lost your mind?"

"I got this one. Trust me."

"Ziggy!"

He ignored her and approached the witness box. "Your Honor, permission to treat this witness as hostile."

"You called this witness, so you better lay a darn good foundation."

"I plan to, Your Honor." Ziggy looked at Cooder. "What do you think of me?"

Cooder looked the lawyer up and down and snickered. "You're a fuckstick."

Ziggy gestured toward the bench with a pair of upturned palms.

Judge Boone rolled his eyes again. "Permission to treat as hostile."

"You don't have a job, do you?"

"So what?"

"Where'd you get the money to buy a Jet Ski last week?"

"Investments."

"Have you had any recent contact with those defense lawyers seated over there or any other representatives of Consolidated Financial without me or my partner's knowledge?"

"What of it?"

The gavel banged and snapped. "All attorneys! In my chambers, now! . . . Bailiff, get the jury out!"

Good thing the jury left. The shouting could clearly be heard through the walls. The court stenographer typed furiously.

"A Jet Ski!" yelled the judge. "My court!"

"It's not what you think," said the Dartmouth attorney.

"It's exactly what I think," said the judge. "Give me a reason fast why I shouldn't have the bailiff come in here and handcuff you all for witness tampering!"

"Because it was a loan."

"Your client made a Jet Ski loan to someone they'd already foreclosed on?"

"It was a different department. They didn't know."

"Don't insult me!" yelled the judge. "It's still a bribe. I'm getting the bailiff."

"Wait, no, it's not," said the attorney. "He was a late addition to their witness list, and the loan was made before. See the dates?" He held out two pages.

"You just *happened* to have the loan documents on you today?"

"We always research opposing counsels' witnesses, and when we found this . . . well, we decided to be prepared because it might look bad."

"Might look bad? It's a flaming abortion! And what about the other witness? Don't tell me the same thing!"

The lawyer opened his mouth but was cut off.

"Your Honor," said Brook. "I request special jury instructions, and for the transcript of everything said in here to be read in open court, and a public censure—"

"Hold your horses," said the judge. "I am going to read special instructions, but everything in chambers is sealed for now. That's an official gag order."

"But, Your Honor—" said Brook.

"Take half your loaf and be happy." Then he aimed an iron glint at the defense. "And you'll be hearing from the ethics committee . . . Back in court! . . ."

Judge Boone resumed the bench and waited until the jury finished seating. "Legal matters have arisen that you need not be concerned about. But I am instructing you to disregard in their entirety the testimony of the last two witnesses and to hold nothing that either of them said against the plaintiffs . . . Court is in recess." He reached for his gavel but forgot it was broken—"Shit"—and stormed back into chambers.

Ziggy began packing his briefcase. "At least we got the judge on our side now."

"More like neutral," said Brook. "How on earth did you know about that testimony?"

"I always vet witnesses with a private investigator I know," said

Ziggy. "Except I forgot to make the call then got busy with other things and one thing led to another."

Brook filled her own briefcase. "You mean one joint led to another."

"It happens. Anyway, I just got the callback while he was being cross-examined."

"Better late than never," said Brook. "What I don't understand is how they gave them those additional loans before we even knew they were going to be our witnesses."

"This *is* your first trial."

"What do you mean?"

"We were set up from the beginning," said Ziggy. "They somehow managed to plant those new plaintiffs with your firm, knowing they had baggage and would self-destruct under cross. All of our other legitimate witnesses probably got phone calls this morning saying the trial was postponed and they were offered a free sailboat trip out to the reef . . . If I'm late tomorrow, start without me."

"Why, what are you—?"

"Have to drive back to Miami and check into this further."

"Can't it be handled over the phone?"

"Not something like this."

Brook gathered up papers from the table. "Hope the rest goes a little better than today."

"I know. I could kick myself for not listening to my gut about Cooder. He just wasn't right." Ziggy clasped his briefcase shut. "Old lady Ruthy, on the other hand, I never would have suspected in a million years."

"What did *she* buy?"

"A Jet Ski."

That night, a finger pressed buttons on a cell phone.

"It's me, Moss . . . I know we're still getting our asses handed to us . . . Will you stop yelling? . . . Yes, I realize it was supposed to be fixed by those two bogus witnesses. Who could have thought that stupid girl and Ziggy would find out about the bribes? . . . What? Miami? Last I heard, our man photographed them passing the files between two cars near Biscayne Bay . . . How should I know who they are? Our guy just followed them for two days after the first one left the office of some private eye. And let me tell you, he had one hell of a time following them: They drove all over the place like they knew they were being tailed . . . No, I can't deal with that! I've got my hands full right here in Key West. You handle whatever's going on in Miami . . . As a matter of fact, I do have an idea. Remember our ace in the hole in case something like this happened? . . ."

Chapter THIRTY-THREE

MIAMI

The moon rose over another run-down motel along U.S. 1. This one had a row of hand-glued seashells along the trim of the roof, but most were just empty glue spots now. Headlights, blaring horns, pedestrians screaming about the coming of the cashless society, bus benches with humps in the middle to fight an epidemic of napping.

Another person started screaming, this one with reason. He ran in and out of an open motel room door, then in circles across the parking lot. "Coleman! . . . *Coleman!* . . . Coleman, where are you? . . ."

Serge began shaking in panic like a parent with a missing child in the lingerie department. "Coleman! . . ." Serge felt a certain custodial responsibility when Coleman was in his care. He once tried using a harness with a leash on the back, but Coleman always managed to wiggle out.

"What's the matter?" asked Reevis.

"Can't find Coleman!" Serge spun in alarm like an ice skater. "Whenever I return to collect him from a bender, he's either on the bed or under it, occasionally in an overflowing bathtub but always in the room. A bender is better than a leash . . . *Ahhhhh!* Where is that idiot?"

"Wow, you really care about him."

Serge nodded hard. "Okay, freaking out never helps you find anything. Calm down and go through the Coleman checklist . . ."

Serge spent the next two hours leading Reevis around local bars, Dumpsters, lifting up mattresses in alleys, calling emergency rooms. He stopped and scratched his head. "Dang, that usually turns him up. Where did that idiot go?"

"What about the underpasses?"

"Good thinking! . . ."

Five minutes later: *"You looking for Coleman?" "Our buddy!" "Stand-up dude!"* The homeless platoon hunkered up under the highway and passed around malt-liquor forties. *"Give him our best . . ."*

Serge stomped with impatience. "But where is he?"

"Don't know." A whiskered stickman flattened out a bedroll. *"Staggered off that way around noon."*

"Damn!" Serge and Reevis began making ever-widening concentric sweeps around the motel until Serge looked at his watch. "And now I have to take you to that meeting in Hialeah . . ."

"Serge, I haven't figured out anything yet."

"But you're making *some* progress with that file I gave you, right?"

"Yeah, dots are starting to connect with some LexisNexis searches." Reevis pulled the packet from the brown envelope. "And I have some promising requests in with the courts."

Serge threw the shift in gear. "Then what's the problem? Just give a status update."

"But investigative reporting is like watching a house being built— looks like crap until the last week when they paint and sod."

"Trust me." Serge floored the gas. "It won't matter where we're going."

The '76 Cobra sped west on the Palmetto Expressway. Serge took an anonymous exit down into the deserted industrial wasteland south of the Opa-Locka Airport. A crumpled scrap of paper was flattened on the steering wheel. Serge checked street signs and made a left, slowing as he searched for a building number. Not a soul around except distant silhouettes of the undead trudging across the street under harsh yellow crime lights.

The Cobra rolled past a blinking neon sign for a scrap yard and pulled up to a squat concrete pillbox of an office. Serge pressed the doorbell and heard it ring inside. No answer. He rang again without result. He cupped his hands around his face to peer through burglar bars over the windows. "All the lights are out. That's weird."

"I thought I heard music when we first arrived," said Reevis.

"Me, too, but now it's quiet." Serge looked up at the number over the door and checked the paper scrap again. "Did he give me the wrong address? . . . No, it's the right one." This time he repeatedly pressed the doorbell like Morse code. "Don't tell me I drove all the way out here for—"

Noise. A slight shuffling of feet inside. Serge pressed his eye to the peephole.

The person on the other side gasped at the sight of a giant distorted eyeball.

A fist pounded the door. "I know you're in there! Come on, open up!"

Nothing.

"Look, gas isn't free! Open the door!"

A long pause. Then: "We're closed."

"You're not closed!" Serge pounded louder. "Mahoney called and said you'd be waiting for me."

Another pause. "Mahoney?"

"Will you open up? The zombies are out here."

"Zombies?"

"Not the real kind." Serge turned and gave one of them a dollar to go away. "Just night crawlers who wander barren parts of the city after dark for anti-reasons. I'm sure you've seen them."

Silence.

"Look, why would I mention the name 'Mahoney' if I wasn't supposed to be here?"

Seconds ticked. "How do I know it's the same Mahoney?"

"You fucking idiot! Open up right now or I'm kicking the door in!"

"I have a gun."

"No, you don't."

"How'd you know?"

"Will you open up, for Christ's sake?"

There was a prolonged fumbling with several locks before the door finally opened three inches on the chain. The narrow slice of a face appeared. "Who are you?"

"Serge! Are you on drugs?"

"How'd you know?"

"Step back." Serge easily popped the door open with his shoulder.

"My chain!"

"Buy yourself another." Serge threw a fiver on the floor. "Are you Ziggy Blade?"

He nodded.

"Are you going to continue wasting my time?"

"Time? How much time has passed? How long have you been standing there?"

"What in the hell did you take?"

"Nuthin'." Ziggy turned and headed toward his back office.

Serge looked around and was actually impressed by the framed movie posters.

Ziggy grabbed a bottle of Patrón tequila next to the boom box on a corner table. He chugged from the fifth and cranked the volume knob back up. "I don't usually drink like this, except when I've dosed and the setting becomes unnerving. Your big eyeball sent me in a bad direction."

"... One pill makes you larger ..."

Serge grabbed a chair. "I still don't understand the drug culture."

From another direction. "Can I come out now?"

Serge jumped up and reached for the pistol beneath his tropical shirt. "Who else is in here?"

"Nobody you need to worry about." Ziggy bent down behind his desk. "The coast is clear. You're among friends."

The person crawled out from underneath and stood up.

Serge fell back against the wall. "Coleman!"

"Hey, Serge, what are you doing here?"

"I was just about to ask you the same thing. I've been worried sick looking all over for you."

"Not the leash again."

"Relax. I know you're tripping . . . I just don't understand how you got to our appointment before me. Did you get a call from Mahoney when I wasn't around?"

"What do you mean appointment?" Coleman brushed dust bunnies off his legs and turned up the stereo even louder.

"*. . . Go ask Alice . . .*"

Serge pulled his head back. "Have we entered the Twilight Zone? I was dashing around crazy trying to find you, and then, of all places, you turn up at the site of our next appointment. And you say you had no idea Mahoney set up a meeting with Ziggy?"

"None whatsoever."

"Then what on earth are you doing in this fleabag lawyer's office?"

"Well, my brother called me up . . ."

"Who's your brother?" asked Serge.

Ziggy raised his hand. "Older brother."

"Hold the fucking train." Serge shook his head vigorously like a cartoon character. "He's your older brother?"

Coleman grabbed the bottle of tequila. "Unless there's some way to overtake him."

Serge displayed unaware palms. "I never knew."

"Told you a whole bunch of times." Coleman inserted a new music disc. "Said he was a big lawyer in Miami."

"*. . . Strawberry fields forever . . .*"

"Yeah, I recall, but . . ." Serge slowly scanned the office walls of faux paneling. "I was expecting F. Lee Bailey, and that you were the aberrant spawn of some kind of ectopic accident where your mom conceived before bungee jumping. I figured your brother would be completely normal."

"No, it runs in the family."

"But the last name's different," said Serge.

Ziggy inserted the *Electric Ladyland* disc. "Changed it to live up to my marketing image."

"Image?" asked Serge. "Not answering doors and cowering in hallucinatory paranoia?"

"It's a bigger market than you'd think."

Coleman nodded.

"Uh, excuse me," said Reevis. "I don't mean to interrupt, but you wanted a status report on that document file? Grand-Bourg Holding Group?"

"Who's the kid?" asked Ziggy.

"An ex-reporter I took on to help decipher the documents you gave Mahoney to investigate."

"I remember now. It's why I left Key West to come back here." Ziggy poured another stiff tequila. "Lay it on me."

"Seems very complicated," said Reevis. "I'd love to report that I'm farther along, but right now it's just a lot of slow plodding through data correlation—"

"Perfect!" Ziggy downed his drink with a sour face. "Say no more . . . Where were we?"

Serge pointed in two directions. "Brothers."

"I was there when Dad stuffed Coleman in the cooler during the football game." Ziggy replaced the bulbous cork in the bottle. "But Pops was no picnic on me either. Check these scars." The attorney turned and dropped his pants for Serge.

"Please!" Serge raised a hand to block the view. "I get it and I'm sorry. It's all a crapshoot, and some kids get terrible rolls of the dice. I feel sickened that it affected how you guys turned out . . ."

Ziggy swung his head to Coleman, then back at Serge. "But we turned out fine."

"Sure," said Serge. "So let's get back to why Mahoney sent me to meet with you—"

"Manners first," said Ziggy, raising his briefcase onto the desk. "Check this out!"

He reached for one of the brass hinge rivets on the side of the attaché, which had a rubber plug on the end instead of metal threads. One of the latches flipped open. Ziggy flicked a Bic lighter next to the hinge, and his mouth went over the open latch.

Serge and Reevis glanced at each other. Then a strange bubbling sound. Ziggy raised his head and exhaled a thick cloud of smoke.

"You made a bong out of a briefcase?" asked Serge.

Ziggy prepared another hit. "Have to be extra careful near courthouses."

"But how?"

"Easier than you'd think," said Coleman. "All you do is drill two holes and slide an airtight Plexiglas shim under the leather with a self-contained bowl from a pet-store fish feeder. Then remove the brass hinge-plug for the carburetor because, as everyone knows, shit can't blaze in a vacuum, and the latch—"

"Enough already," said Serge. "You're definitely brothers. No DNA test necessary to match the bong-savant gene."

"Your newspaper guy?" said Ziggy.

"Still needs a couple more days," said Serge. "In the meantime, I'm about to get my hands on some legal assets that should hold our enemies at the gate until we learn more about this Grand-Bourg business."

Ziggy flicked the lighter again. "I'm all ears . . ."

Chapter THIRTY-FOUR

THE NEXT AFTERNOON

Brook checked her watch: 1:01 P.M.

The doors in the back of the courtroom flew open.

"Where have you been?" Brook demanded. "You were a no-show all morning!"

Ziggy jogged up the aisle, out of breath, sweating. "Sorry, been working on something."

"I'm really going to need your help," said Brook. "Yesterday was a nightmare with our two witnesses, and we don't have much time left to catch up."

"But the judge sided with us and gave those special instructions to ignore the testimony—"

Brook shook her head. "One of the biggest rules of trial work is just get the damning statements in front of the jury. No matter how honest they are in following rules, they can't get it out of their minds. And the judge issuing those instructions to forget it almost makes it worse. It's like saying don't think of a three-headed polka-dotted elephant. Then that's *all* they can think about. We're screwed unless we can make a comeback with our final witnesses."

"I've been working on something that I think will—"

"Shhh!" Brook pointed. "The judge."

Boone seated himself behind the bench. "Call your witness."

Brook questioned a retiree from Michigan. Then ones from Indiana, Ohio, Pennsylvania and Manitoba. All of them sunburned from the previous day's free sailboat trip.

She returned to the plaintiff's table.

"Why so down-in-the-mouth?" asked Ziggy. "I thought you did great."

"And as dull as watching paint dry. Jurors three, nine and eleven kept blinking hard to stay awake. What sticks out most in deliberations is the sexy stuff, like yesterday. I'm afraid I let Shelby down."

"But this thing I'm working on . . ." He turned around to check the courtroom's doors. "I really think it could help us."

Brook shook her head again. "Too late. That was our last witness. We have to rest our case and can't present any more evidence except on rebuttal. And their side is too smart to give us any openings."

Ziggy nudged her. "The judge is getting pissed again."

"Oh."

Boone tapped his fingers on the bench. "I'm not interrupting anything, am I?"

"Sorry."

"Any more witnesses?"

"That was the last one."

"Are you resting your case?"

With great reluctance and fallen crest: "We rest our case."

"All right, then," said the judge. "Defense, call your first witness."

The Yale attorney stood. "We call Consolidated COO Heinrich Neff."

A short older man in a three-piece suit headed toward the stand. His coat had a pocket-watch chain. He took the oath with an Austrian accent.

"Now, Mr. Neff," said the attorney. "As COO—"

Suddenly the back doors of the courtroom flew open with a flourish, and a man ran up the aisle, dramatically waving a fistful of papers over his head. "Hold everything!"

Brook turned around. "Dear God!"

Ziggy smiled. "Told you I was working on something."

The man in the aisle came to a screeching halt. "Brook!"

"Serge!"

Ziggy looked back and forth. "You know each other?"

"What are you doing here?" asked Brook.

"Just dropped by with some total bombshell evidence is all." Serge grinned big.

"But it's too late. We already rested our case," said Brook. "And how are you even involved in this case?"

Ziggy: "He's a field man for Mahoney, my private eye."

The judge had been vainly banging a new gavel to get their attention. He banged it once more, super loud. "What is the meaning of this disruption in my courtroom?"

"Your Honor," said Ziggy. "Plaintiffs have new evidence and would like to confer with our paralegal."

"*He's* a paralegal?" said Boone, pointing his gavel at Serge's tropical shirt covered with toucans.

"One of the best," said Ziggy. "Works for a private investigation firm on retainer. We'll only need a moment."

The defense attorney from Dartmouth was on his feet. "Objection! We're required to receive advance notice of anything they wish to admit. And it's moot anyway because they rested their case."

"You did rest your case," said the judge. "I can't allow whatever you've got there."

"We just received it," said Ziggy.

"There are some special exceptions," said Brook. "May I have a moment to research precedent? At the very least I'd like to get it on the record in case of appeal."

"Very well," said the judge. "We'll take a short recess for you to confer . . . Bailiff, remove the jury and make some copies for me and the defense to examine." He banged the gavel and disappeared into chambers.

As soon as he was gone: "This is great," said Ziggy. "I told you I was working on something. We hired an investigative reporter to look through some weird documents, and last night I showed him some other files . . ."

But nobody was listening. Serge had taken a seat in the first row of the gallery behind the plaintiff's table; he and Brook stared at each other in a trance.

Ziggy snapped his fingers between their faces. "Hello? Anybody home?"

Serge pushed his hand away. "How have you been?"

"*Where* have you been?" asked Brook.

"Some history?" said Ziggy.

Both of them: "Shut up!"

"Why haven't you called?" asked Brook.

"I've been looking high and low," said Serge.

"Me, too."

"Brook."

"Serge."

They took each other's hands.

The bailiff returned with the set of original documents for the plaintiffs and copies for the defense.

"Excuse me," said Ziggy, jerking a thumb toward the door of the judge's chambers, "but we have a lot to go over before Boone gets back."

Serge's eyes lingered on Brook another moment, then: "He's right. You have to take a look at these."

"What have we got here?" Brook grabbed the stack of papers. "Think it's important?"

Serge looked sideways. "Judging by their reaction, I'd say it is."

Across the aisle, Team Riley was huddled in furious discussion over the pages. They didn't even wait for the judge to get to the bench. As soon as Boone opened his chamber door, all four were on their feet. "Objection!"

The judge eyed them as he moved slowly toward his chair. "I take it you have strong feelings about something."

"Your Honor," said their lead counsel. "These are confidential internal documents containing proprietary trade secrets. What's more, they've all been passed through our legal department, which covers them under attorney-client privilege. The only possible way plaintiff could have gained possession of these is by theft."

The judge turned to Brook. "What do you have to say? Where did you get these?"

Serge leaned over the railing behind Brook. "Tell him they *were* stolen."

Brook turned around. "What!"

"Go ahead, tell him."

"I'm not telling him that," said Brook.

"Just trust me."

The judge softly tapped his gavel. "Well, does anybody have an answer?"

Serge hopped up and wildly waved an arm. "Oooo! Me, me, me! Pick me! . . ."

MIAMI

The waiting room had no magazines or other comforts. The molded plastic chairs were designed only for durability. The people in them weren't.

It was a high-mileage crowd, and the room was chatty, like a human bullfrog pond. Most were on cell phones: gossip, making plans that were the opposite of thought out, arguments about paying the cell-phone bill. At the front of the room was a locked door with reinforced glass. On the other side, more stagnation. A line of people at a counter, waiting their turn to sign forms.

The door opened. A sunburned man with uncombed hair emerged. A woman stood up from her molded chair and marched out of the room in a huff. The man ran after her. "It wasn't my fault . . ."

Waiting resumed in the processing-and-release center of the city jail.

The next man signed his name on a form and was handed a Ziploc bag with wallet, cell phone and keys. The door opened again.

Someone in another plastic chair stood up. He sported a black guayabera with yellow palm trees. "Tennessee? Tennessee Knox?"

The man with the Ziploc analyzed the face. "Do I know you?"

"I'm the guy who just bailed you out."

"Figured that," said Knox. "But why?"

"What's the matter?" asked the stranger. "You'd rather be back in there?"

Knox fished his billfold from the clear bag. "No, I appreciate it. But when it's someone you don't know, there's usually a catch."

"There is," said the man. "But it's a good one. Why don't we have lunch?"

"You paying?"

Forty minutes later, another cruise ship that would soon make feces-related headlines sailed away from the port and through the jetties that split Fisher Island from Miami Beach. A block away, at the southern tip of Washington Avenue, an eager line of people wrapped around a building that had been in business since 1913.

Inside, Tennessee Knox sat with a wax bib and a nutcracker. "Joe's Stone Crab! I could never afford to eat here. Man, when you said you were taking me to lunch . . ."

"Just a down payment of thanks."

"Hope it's not for nothing." Crabmeat splashed into a bowl of butter. "I haven't heard your proposal yet. Plus I still have charges pending."

The benefactor flicked his wrist. "Don't give it another thought."

The nutcracker busted a shell. "What are you, some kind of lawyer?"

"Yes, with one of the biggest firms."

"You still haven't told me your name."

"And I won't." The man leaned back from his untouched food. "I work in sensitive areas for powerful people."

"So what do you want me to do?"

"A burglary."

Knox squirted himself in the eye with lemon. "I'm just a small-time second-story man. If you want to take down a heavy score for corporate espionage, I'm afraid someone gave you bad information."

"Actually it won't even be a real burglary. All part of a complicated legal caveat. We just need to borrow your fingerprints."

"Now I'm confused."

"Will five thousand be sufficient illumination?"

"I'm starting to see clearly." Knox noshed another cold claw. "But why me?"

"You have a lengthy rap sheet for B-and-E. So they should quickly match your prints for what we're planning. But as I said, don't worry." The man snapped his fingers for the check. "And, waiter, can you box these up for us?"

Knox held a claw out from his mouth. "I've just gotten started."

The mystery man stood from the table. "We have to leave right away for the Keys."

"But I have to be in court tomorrow."

"Those charges are being dismissed as we speak."

Knox took off his bib and got up. "You're a fixer, aren't you?"

Chapter THIRTY-FIVE

BACK IN COURT

Serge continued bouncing on the balls of his feet and waving at the judge. "I know the answer!"

"Not you," said Boone. "An attorney has to respond. You're just a paralegal."

"And yet I'm allowed to be a lawyer if I'm arrested. Can we skip the arrest part if defense doesn't object?"

"Will you stop talking and sit down!" said Boone.

"Right, shutting up and sitting down now, in the paralegal seat."

"Are you finished?" yelled the judge.

Serge made a motion like he was closing a zipper across his lips.

"Good," said Boone, "but I still don't have an answer."

Serge poked Ziggy, who slowly stood. "Your Honor, they *were* stolen."

"Thank you," said the judge. "In that case it's an easy call. The evidence is inadmissible."

"Not so fast!"

The judge was apoplectic. "I can't believe you're still talking!"

"Oops, was that me?" said Serge. "Dang, another outburst. And I was trying to watch that. It's been a lifelong struggle, thinking I'm talking inside my head when I'm actually just blurting away. I've even tried working with a service dog."

"Shut up or I'll hold you in contempt!"

Serge grabbed Ziggy by the rear of his collar and jerked him backward. Urgent whispers.

"Your Honor," said Ziggy. "I'd like to cite Rourke."

"I'm not familiar with that," said the judge.

Another whisper.

"Mickey Rourke," said Ziggy.

"The actor?" said the judge. "I'm going to fine both of you for contempt if this foolishness doesn't stop immediately!"

A longer set of whispers.

"What I mean," said Ziggy, "is that in this movie, Rourke plays a lawyer faced with stolen evidence, and he cites the DeSoto case."

"Of all the crazy . . . wait," said Boone. "I've heard of *DeSoto*. A professor of mine was even a counsel in that trial, and I'll be damned if it isn't precisely on point."

From the other table. "Your Honor! This whole exchange has gone completely awry of any acceptable judicial procedures!"

"I will decide what's acceptable in my court," said the judge. "And you will sit down. Now!" He turned back to Ziggy. "If the party stealing the evidence is not working as an agent of, or in concert with, the government or plaintiffs . . ."

The plaintiff's table sat mute. The judge raised his eyes toward Serge. "Well?"

Serge overdid his mime act of pursing lips like they were superglued shut.

Boone squeezed his gavel in exasperation. "*Now* you can talk!"

Serge had also been holding his breath. He heaved out air and panted strenuously to restore oxygen. "Thank you, Your Honor. Things were getting sparkly."

"Who gave you these documents?"

"A whistle-blower."

"Who was it?"

"I don't know," said Serge.

"I'm going to make it simple," said the judge. "You can stay where you are, but you're under oath just like if you were sitting in the witness chair, with all perjury ramifications attached. Swear to tell the truth?"

"For you, anything."

The judge reclined. "Then tell me how you came into possession of these papers."

"They were slipped under Ziggy's door after he left Miami this morning."

"And any vague idea what precipitated this moment of serendipity?"

"I know exactly what did it," said Serge. "Mahoney's client needed a breakthrough, but our normal methodology of research hadn't borne fruit, so meanwhile there's this public courtyard where a bunch of Consolidated employees eat lunch with fountains and pigeon shit, and I stood up like a preacher and said right at the beginning—as a legal prophylactic—'I don't want to know your names, but your employer has made a lot of people suffer, including some who have died prematurely, and I need your help with the class-action lawsuit that I'm sure you all know about from the news. So if any of you has a throbbing conscience or is just a disgruntled asshole who can get your mitts on any unflattering company documents, please slip them under our door. But I'm definitely not asking you to steal anything, and don't let us see your face or give any other details because the judge would require me to disclose them.' . . . Then I threw a bunch of Ziggy's business cards in the air and made it rain, like in a strip club, except they came down on bologna sandwiches instead of boobs."

The judge shook his head with a grudging smile. "That's totally devious and legally brilliant. You should go to night school and make the leap from paralegal."

The other table was livid. "Your Honor! You're rewarding criminal behavior!"

"No, I'm not," said the judge. "Would you like to renew your other objection?"

"I don't remember."

"That they already rested their case," said Boone.

"That's right! They already—"

"Sustained. The documents are out," said the judge. "You're welcome."

"But, Your Honor!" said Brook.

"Sorry, it doesn't meet any threshold," said the judge. "Should have done your homework earlier . . . Defense may resume its direct of their witness."

Yale approached the stand again. "As I was *saying* . . ."—he gave Brook a shit-eating glare, then turned to the witness—"your position with Consolidated affords you great overview of the entire mortgage industry. In general, what happened a few years ago?"

"Something nobody could have ever foreseen," said Neff. "The housing bubble was a hundred-year-storm event. I feel just awful about all those hardworking people losing their homes."

"Is it the fault of the mortgagees who were foreclosed upon?"

"Absolutely not."

"Your fault?" asked Yale.

"No."

"Then if you had to put your finger on it, whom would you blame?"

"Wall Street."

"Wall Street?"

Neff nodded, working his gambit to distract the jury with an even more unpopular villain. "All their exotic investment instruments took down the market and sent investor money elsewhere. Plus an unprecedented number of speculators entered the housing market, artificially driving up prices without an actual underlying demand."

The attorney began walking along the front of the jury box, making eye contact. "So in a fair world, the plaintiffs would be suing Wall Street and vulture capitalists?"

"But it's not a fair world," said Neff.

"That's right," said the attorney. "They're suing you instead."

"I don't blame them," said Neff. "I'd be upset, too . . ."

Ziggy nudged Brook. "Why aren't you objecting and stopping this? There's no foundation."

"Giving him rope," said Brook. Then to herself: "Come on, come on, just a little more . . ."

" . . . But we're victims of the stock market and speculators as much as they are," said Neff. "Unfortunately, we both signed those loans, and we have shared responsibility for what happened, even though neither of us caused it."

"One last question," said the lawyer. "Did you treat all your customers honestly and with good faith?"

"Yes, I did," said Neff. "And under the circumstances, I wish I could have done more."

"No more questions," said Yale.

The judge turned to Brook. "Your witness."

She arose and walked toward the stand with a handful of documents. "I'd like you to look at these and tell me if you recognize any of them—"

Four Ivy League lawyers on their feet at once. "Objection!"

The judge made a beckoning motion with both hands. "Approach."

They all lined up in front of the bench. A defense attorney snapped in a hushed tone: "You already ruled on this, Your Honor. The evidence can't come in. She rested her case."

"That's right," said Brook. "But defense's witness just stated that the company acted in good faith. Your Honor knows what's in those documents. They're necessary for my rebuttal to the credibility of the witness about his good faith."

"Your Honor!" said Yale. "This is just a cheap attempt to circumvent your ruling and get inadmissible evidence in through the back door."

"That's exactly what she's doing," said the judge. "And it's a back door you just kicked wide open with your line of questioning. You knew what she had. I'm surprised you nibbled anywhere near that opening where she could take advantage."

"But—"

"Documents are in," said Boone. "Step back."

Brook strolled to the witness stand. "Do you recognize these?"

Heinrich Neff pushed reading glasses up his nose and glanced over the pages. "Not specifically, but they look like the sales of properties that were previously foreclosed. Fairly standard."

"And what about these?" asked Brook.

"Roughly the same thing." Neff attempted to hand the pages back.

"More than roughly the same," said Brook, stepping away. "Wouldn't you agree?"

"What do you mean?"

"Most of the addresses are the same."

"So? The same houses got sold again."

"Feel free to correct me," said Brook, "but there's a whole pool of your foreclosed properties whose values were set by the same small handful of appraisers."

"If you find people who do good work—"

"Interesting you should say that," said Brook. "Because I'm prepared to present expert witnesses who will testify that when the homes were sold the second time, you issued mortgages based on ultra-high appraisals far out of line from any comp properties or accepted industry practices."

"It's a subjective area," said Neff. "We use sound safeguards."

"Sound?" said Brook. "But you already knew these were high-risk properties, and yet you re-issued loans for amounts higher than what you had just foreclosed upon. Why would you do that? Is it because you could avoid all risk by bundling these off to Freddie Mac and Fannie Mae and stick the taxpayers?"

"Objection!"

"Overruled."

"I don't know in these specific cases," said Neff. "But yes, we do sometimes resell the loans to those agencies. That's the whole reason the government set it up. Very standard." He tried to hand the documents back again but Brook intentionally returned to her table, leaving him with an awkwardly outstretched hand, wanting to rid himself of evidence. It was a well-known jury tactic, like getting a murder defendant to hold the knife.

She grabbed a notepad and walked back. "Now let me ask you this: Is it unusual for someone to stop payments on a home within six months of purchase?"

"Not at all. People lose jobs, get unexpected medical bills. Happens all the time."

"What if it happened in every single case you're holding in your hands?"

"I don't know," said Neff. "I'd have to review the documents."

"Please do," said Brook. "And take your time."

"Uh, well, if you say so." He conducted a theatrical examination of the paperwork again and passed it back.

Brook flipped through the stack for the benefit of the jury. "Isn't it a fact that your company colluded with appraisers to jack up values before you enlisted straw buyers who intended all along to default, making millions for your company from the sale of those loans to the government?"

"Objection!" said Yale. "She's testifying and speculating and . . . and—"

"Your Honor," said Brook. "I intend to bring in my own giant easel with flow charts and experts to explain to the jury exactly how the scam worked."

"Objection to characterization of scam!"

One of the judge's arms disappeared inside his robe to scratch himself. "Jury will disregard that last description. As to the other, the witness may answer."

Neff looked back at the judge. "I don't remember the question."

"Would you like me to repeat it?" asked Brook.

The defense lawyers urgently shook their heads at the witness. Once was enough for the jury to hear that.

"I remember now," said Neff. "I don't remember."

"The question or the answer?" asked Brook.

"The answer."

"And nobody can ever prove whether or not you remember something," said Brook. "So did anyone advise you that if you don't want to answer an incriminating question and don't want to be charged with perjury, you should say, 'I don't remember' or 'I don't recall'?"

"Objection!" said Dartmouth. "That would be covered as privileged under attorney-client communication."

"I never said anything about an attorney," replied Brook. "But opposing counsel has just answered the question concerning who told him to say 'I don't remember.'"

"Objection!"

"Withdrawn. No more questions." Brook strolled triumphantly back to the plaintiff's table.

The judge turned the other way. "Would you like to examine your witness any further?"

The defense saw the faces in the jury box. Even a perfect redirect of their witness would fall on deaf ears right now. So, like a basketball team on the south side of a 16–0 run, they called time out.

"Your Honor," said Harvard. "In light of this last-second evidence, we request a recess until morning to examine these documents and prepare additional questioning."

"Granted."

The gavel banged.

Furious hands dialed a number in Fort Lauderdale. "It's Moss, dammit! Who else? . . . I know she ate our attorneys' lunch today. But how did those documents get loose in the first place? . . . All I can say is it's tit for tat. Time to give our standby player the green light . . ."

Chapter THIRTY-SIX

THE NEXT MORNING

Two early birds sat alone in the silent courtroom.

"We've got the momentum back," said Ziggy. "I'm starting to think we're actually going to win this thing."

"Brook really deserves this," said Serge.

They high-fived.

The doors in the back of the courtroom opened.

"Brook!" said Serge.

Brook got a funny look on her face. Then she ran back out the door.

Serge turned to Ziggy. "Something I said?"

Ziggy shook his head. "Nerves. They should charge her rent for that bathroom stall."

Brook sat indisposed in the tiny space. A personal pep talk. "Get it together, girl. This is the big day. You're in the homestretch now . . ."

Footsteps from the sink. "Brook? Is that you in there?"

Brook thinking, *What's a man's voice doing in the women's room? It's not Serge or Ziggy.* "Who's out there?"

"I have something for you."

A legal-sized envelope slid under the stall's door. Footsteps ran away.

Brook reached down and picked it up, removing photos and a typed letter. As she read: "Oh, dear God, this isn't happening. How did they find out?" Her stomach became a free-falling elevator. She would be spending some extra time this morning familiarizing herself with the porcelain.

Back in the courtroom: "This is getting exciting," said Ziggy. "What can that executive possibly say today to dig himself out of that hole Brook put him in?"

The doors opened again. "Brook," said Serge. "You're all flushed. Let me get you a chair."

"I'm fine." She steadied herself with the edge of the table and eased down into a seat. "Just some bad shrimp I got last night."

The judge and jury came in. The defense called Heinrich Neff back to the stand.

"Concerning these so-called straw buyers. Were you at all aware?"

"Absolutely not," said Neff. "If I'd had even the slightest notion, I would have immediately called authorities."

"And those appraisers who set high prices?"

"We don't use them anymore," said Neff. "Some unethical appraisers are always trying to drum up business by qualifying unrealistic amounts for loans. As soon as we saw the foreclosure rate, we dismissed them . . ."

"Brook," Ziggy whispered. "Why aren't you objecting?"

She just sat dazed.

"You look like you're feeling worse than you're letting on," said Serge. "Why don't we have Ziggy ask for a recess?"

"No, I'll be okay . . ."

The defense called more Consolidated officers to the stand, who explained in highly technical obfuscation why everything was on the up-and-up. They were polished and handsome and scoring points.

"It was our duty to the shareholders, many of whom are senior citizens with our stock in their retirement portfolios, who depend on us to put those houses back on the market and get the highest price."

The judge looked toward Brook. "Cross-examination?"

She shook her head again.

And so it went, through the rest of the morning and into the afternoon. The defense systematically chipping away at everything Brook had constructed the day before.

The defense finished with another witness. The judge looked toward the plaintiffs' table again with skepticism.

"No questions," Brook said in a vacuum of energy.

"Brook," said Ziggy. "You haven't cross-examined a single witness today."

She sat.

Ziggy stood. "I request a recess."

"Why?"

"Medical."

The judge didn't need to be told something wasn't right, and he didn't need any more details. "We're in recess."

They left the courtroom, and Brook immediately ran to the restroom.

Ziggy and Serge waited outside and knocked. "You okay in there?" They pressed ears to the door. Water running.

"Something's wrong," said Ziggy.

"And I don't think it's her regular nerves about the trial," said Serge.

The door finally opened and the guys quickly pulled their ears away. Brook's face still dripped from splashing at the sink. She silently led them out of the courthouse and toward her motel room. At the corner of Southard Street, she glanced back. A man in an aqua golf shirt looked up from a newspaper, then down. Brook's heart raced. She picked up the pace, looking around every ten yards.

They reached the Southern Cross Hotel. "I think I need to be with Brook awhile," Serge told Ziggy. "Can you check on Coleman back in our place and make sure he isn't tearing it up?"

"You got it."

At the top of the stairs, Brook pulled Serge into her room and quickly slammed the dead bolt. Then she hugged him with the biggest squeeze. His arms slowly wrapped around her in a light embrace.

"I know you're happy to see me," said Serge. "But what's really going on?"

"I think I'm being followed."

"I picked up on that." Serge calmly caressed her hair. "But I didn't see anyone. And I'm pretty good at that sort of thing."

"He had a golf shirt and was reading a newspaper."

"Where?"

"Outside the courthouse."

"Did you see him anywhere else on the way back to the motel?"

"No, but I saw him yesterday." Brook burrowed her face into his shoulder. "Also reading a newspaper. Different shirt."

"Brook, people have daily routines." Serge held her out by the arms. "It's all in your head."

"Is this in my head?" She opened her briefcase and handed Serge the legal envelope.

He read the contents. "You're being blackmailed?"

"It's not just disbarment—I'll go to jail."

"The guy in the golf shirt?"

She shook her head. "I think it's a different guy."

"Why do you say that?" asked Serge.

"Just look."

Serge pulled a photo from the envelope. A battered woman's face, barely recognizable as Brook's. "So it's the dude who you paid to beat you up? Now it all makes sense."

"Bones's note says he saw my name in the newspaper from the trial."

"Bones?"

"Who knows what his real name is." Brook poured herself a glass of water from the bathroom tap and sat down. "Wants fifty thousand or he'll call in an anonymous tip with all the details."

"First thing: Just relax," said Serge. "I'll get my arms around this and it'll all be fine."

"What's your plan? He says he'll only meet with me, and if he even suspects anyone else—"

"Like I said, just relax."

RAMROD KEY

Two concrete ovals in the middle of the parking lot said the building used to be a gas station. Painted over the garage doors: PARADISE REALTY.

Inside, on the walls where the fan belts and wiper blades used to hang, were glossy photos of cozy little Keys abodes. *Summerland Key, $189K; Sugarloaf, $179K; Boca Chica, $199K.* All the properties featured palms, poincianas and other tropical landscaping strategically placed to create the illusion that these were not mobile homes.

The company's sole agent sat behind a desk. There was a water-cooler, an empty box of doughnuts and a chew toy for an unseen dog. On the customer side of the desk sat a man in a black guayabera with yellow palm trees. "You also rent?"

The agent nodded. "Or rent to own. It's a good deal." It wasn't.

The customer pointed at one of the photos on the wall. "I'd like to rent that trailer."

"We prefer the term 'manufactured living.'"

"It's for my nephew. He's getting out of the service in a few weeks. How much?"

"Eight hundred a month, first and last and another for damage deposit."

"Sounds reasonable."

"But you do realize that since you'll be signing for it, you're the responsible party."

"No problem."

The agent pulled rental forms from a drawer and clicked a pen. "When would you like to start the lease?"

"Now. If I could get the keys today."

The agent raised his head. "But you said he isn't getting out for a few weeks."

"I'd like to spruce up the place for his welcome home."

"That's very nice," said the agent. "The only problem is we need to wait for the rent and deposit checks to clear."

The customer pulled a roll from his pocket. "Cash clear faster?"

The agent's eyes bulged at the size of the wad. "As long as you have a valid driver's license."

"That I do." He handed over a non-valid license with a fake name.

"Then just sign here and here and initial by these three X's." The agent stood up and arched his back to get out a crick. "I'll just make some copies and get the keys."

A half hour later, bells jingled at the front door of Paradise Pawn & Laundry.

The owner arrived behind the counter and wiped soapsuds off his hands. "Can I help you with anything?"

The customer's eyes were up on the shelves. Both arms began pointing. "Those TVs, a few laptops, silverware, the video games, clock radios, electric drills, the popcorn machine, the bullhorn, and that whole shelf of microwaves."

The owner chuckled. "What are going to do, open your own pawnshop?"

"Something like that," said a man in a black guayabera. "You give volume discounts?"

The owner's mouth became a straight line. "You're actually serious?"

The guayabera pulled the roll from his pocket. "Does this look like a punch line?"

The owner took a deep breath. "In that case, I can put a great package together for five thousand."

"Throw in the trombone and it's a deal."

Chapter THIRTY-SEVEN

MILE MARKER 26

Strands of cirrus clouds formed crimson streaks as the sun set over the gulf. Headlights came on in a chain that traced the Overseas Highway. A '76 Cobra crested the bridge to Little Torch Key.

"Where are we going?" asked Brook.

"He wants you to meet at his motel?"

"Right," said Brook. "But you're not seriously thinking of going there?"

Serge shook his head. "There's a place across the street with a perfect view of where he's staying."

"What are you going to do?"

"Not pay blackmail, for one thing." Serge turned into a narrow parking lot that ran between two rows of tiny stucco villas. They checked in and sat across from each other on the pair of beds.

"But I already have a motel room in Key West," said Brook. "I'm simultaneously staying at two places?"

"I've done it a million times," said Serge. "And from here forward, you're going to have to do exactly as I say without any questions, because there might not be time. I really wanted to leave you in Key West, but if you were being followed, this could be a ruse to lure me away from you. You're staying on my hip . . . until I make my move. Then we'll find out where this leads."

"What are you talking about? It leads to the guy who beat me."

"Brook, he's only asking for fifty K, when how many millions are riding on this trial?"

"You're not thinking the defense put him up to this," said Brook. "Even if they did want to intimidate me, they'd never get involved with a character like that, because he could just turn around and blackmail *them*."

"The scenario's wide open until I get him to answer a few questions."

"He's just going to spill everything to you?" She noticed the bullets in Serge's hand as he loaded a .380 automatic. "Oh."

"Don't leave the room." He went to the door. "And don't open unless you're absolutely sure it's me."

"What about staying on your hip?"

"I'm just going to the edge of the parking lot for recon of his place across the way." He turned around in the door. "But your room here will never be out of my view. *When Polly's in trouble, I am not slow! . . .*"

The door closed. Brook turned on the TV and surfed local news. Crime, crime, more crime, torso found in the mangroves. Head found in the salt flats. She turned off the tube. Her heart rate began coming down. She trusted Serge.

The door burst open and she jumped. "He's on the move! Get in the car!"

The Cobra raced east until they finally spotted an old Pinto several cars ahead. Serge let off the gas as they hit Big Pine Key.

"Traffic's stacking up," said Brook. "You're losing him."

"I know," said Serge. "As soon as you come off the bridge over the channel, it's the endangered Key-deer zone, which drops to thirty-five miles an hour at night. All these good citizens are living up to the social code, but that asshole's whipping around them like a maniac."

Brook pointed ahead to the island's only traffic light. "He's turning north."

"I see it. But it will take forever to get up there behind all these cars." Serge smacked the dashboard in frustration. "Now the light's changing, and it's a long one."

Serge eased up behind the line of vehicles waiting for a green light to turn onto Wilder Boulevard. "The good news is the island just goes back and stops at the water. There's no way out except returning to the Overseas Highway. His end destination is somewhere up there."

"If this is the only way out, then why don't we just wait here for him?" asked Brook.

"I said this *highway* is the only way out, but there are a number of other roads on the island that connect back to it." Serge watched the light turn green, then clenched his teeth as a number of drivers took their time making the left turn. He began banging his forehead on the steering wheel.

"Serge," said Brook. "It's just the coffee."

"I hate it when other drivers make the left turn super slow with big gaps, as if they're the only person trying to catch the light. Me? Total courtesy. I pretend the guy behind me is on the same team and it's my mission to get him through the light as well, like a fullback blocking in the red zone. I often wave them on with my arm out the window. 'Come on, you can make it! There's plenty of time!' Sometimes there is; other times not so much. But I've done my job."

"Serge, the light's been yellow a long time," said Brook. "And there's a cop parked on the corner."

"And that fucker left three car lengths in front of him." Serge screeched up to red and sulked. "He'll never be a fullback."

"Serge, try to focus." Brook massaged the back of his neck. "We need to find the guy in the Pinto."

"Don't worry. I know the island and we'll do a slow grid search through the neighborhoods."

They turned past the grocery store onto a long isolated stretch of road.

Serge pointed northwest. "We'll try to flush him—"

Crash.

Glass exploded as the rear window blew out. Serge checked the side mirror and noticed a black Camaro barreling down on them.

"Someone's shooting!" yelled Brook. "Is it him?"

"No, my wife."

Bullets whizzing by the car.

"That's the woman you said you were married to?"

Serge gestured back at the shattered glass. "If you call that marriage."

A last bang. "Excellent," said Serge. "She's out of bullets."

The Cobra skidded to a stop.

"What the hell are you doing?" said Brook.

"Just hand me what's in the glove compartment."

Serge jumped from his car and promptly shot out one of the Camaro's tires. "Molly, can you please sign these papers? I need to move on."

"I'm not signing any divorce papers," said the redhead. "I think we should get back together and give it another try."

"Molly, stop reloading and listen: We gave it more than a fair shot."

"You don't love me anymore?"

Serge shrugged. "All your shooting. A guy needs to relax when he comes home from work."

"I also have my needs. I slaved to keep a clean house, but Coleman always fucked up our guest towels."

"That's another thing my married friends mentioned: No history is too ancient."

"You never listen!" snapped Molly. "They were the guest towels!"

"Coleman *was* a guest."

"What don't you understand about the guest towels?"

"My ignorance is apparently total on this one."

"I could never have nice things." She clicked the chamber closed and began raising the gun.

Serge snatched the barrel, flinging it into the woods. Molly ran after the weapon and Serge bolted for the car.

Brook stared in shock. "What's all that gunfire about?"

Serge stuffed unsigned papers in the glove compartment. "Bathroom linen."

The Cobra scoured the mangrove country and took the Bogie Channel Bridge to No Name Key all the way to the ferry dock ruins. On the return trip he checked in with his eyes and ears at the Old Wooden Bridge Fishing Camp office and the No Name Pub, then made a last sweep past Blue Hole nature preserve before heading back to the Overseas Highway.

"Can't understand where he could have gone to." Serge slowed as a small deer crossed the road. "I switchbacked east and west as I worked my way north on the island like I was popping a pimple."

"What do we do now?"

"Return to our cottage and keep an eye out."

Fifteen minutes later, they rolled into the parking lot. "Remember to stay hidden," said Serge. "He knows what you look like, but I'm free to keep surveillance."

He unlocked the door and they stepped inside. A crinkly sound under their feet. He flicked on the light. "What the hell? Where'd all this plastic sheeting on the floor come from?"

Serge immediately recognized the source of the feeling he'd just gotten in the middle of his back.

"Don't try anything funny," said the man, poking Serge with the gun. "Both of you move to the middle of the room nice and slow."

The floor crackled as they walked past the dresser.

"Now stop and turn around." The man grinned lasciviously at Brook. "Bet you didn't expect to see me again."

"Look," said Serge. "There's no need for the gun. We were getting together your fifty thousand."

"No, you weren't," said Bones. "You were supposed to be at my motel room an hour ago. Instead you followed me up to Big Pine and back. You didn't think I'd simply plant myself in that room all fat and happy like a sitting duck?"

"So you expected us to do recon on your motel, and secretly positioned yourself until we revealed our location? Then you took us on that wild-goose chase of a drive up the islands in order to beat us back to *our* room?" Serge snapped his fingers and winced. "The old double-reverse surveillance sting. Should have known."

Bones raised his gun. "Say your prayers."

"Whoa!" said Serge. "Aren't you being a little hasty? You're going to shoot us just because we're late with the fifty G's?"

Bones shook his head. "I already have the fifty thousand. Plus a bonus when I'm done."

"Wait, what?" said Serge.

"You actually thought this was about blackmail?" said Bones. "That was just the bait—it was a hit all the way. Apparently a lot of money is riding on her trial, and she's a much better lawyer than anyone expected. So someone decided to take her off the case. And you, fella, are at the wrong place at the wrong time." He gave Brook an expression of disapproval. "You really shouldn't have stolen their confidential files. That's just not right."

Serge was careful to keep his eyes straight ahead as he used peripheral vision to gauge the distance to the open thermos of coffee on the dresser. "Hold on! I got a great story . . ."

"No use trying to stall."

"Really, it's an excellent Florida legal tale, totally true," said Serge. "This guy tried to frame someone for murder by sticking a tiny tape recorder in his jacket pocket and going to the observation deck atop the La Concha in Key West. He calls out the name of someone who wasn't there and says, 'Please don't throw me off the roof!' Then he jumped off the roof. Didn't work, but have to give him credit for commitment."

"Actually that's not a bad story," said Bones.

"Think so?" said Serge. "Then I got a million of 'em. Like the drunk driver near Duval who handed the police officer a taco instead of his license—"

"Shut up! I'm late for dinner, so it's time for good-byes." He looked over at Brook. "I hate to do this because you can take a beating better than most men. So I'll give you the courtesy of shooting him first. Then you might want to close your eyes."

"Fuck you," said Brook. "I'm not going to let you shoot me like a coward. These eyes will be staring straight into your sorry soul."

"Suit yourself."

Serge used the momentary distraction to move like lightning, grabbing the thermos and splashing the contents in Bones's eyes.

Bones looked mildly annoyed as brown drops trickled down his cheeks.

"Damn," said Serge. "It got cold."

"Changed my mind," said Bones. "I get the drift you're somewhat fond of Brook, so I'm shooting *her* first, just to piss you off."

In less than a nanosecond, Serge's brain rampaged through all possible options. Bones aimed his pistol just as Serge sifted the alternatives down to the only one left: He jumped in front of Brook as a human shield.

Bang.

Serge gritted his teeth as he reflexively jerked back like taking a punch in the gut. A second later he opened his eyes and stared curiously down at himself—then up at Bones, whose expression seemed off-center before he toppled facedown on the plastic sheeting.

"What just happened?" asked Brook.

Serge stared at a hole in the cottage's front window. "Stay here." He grabbed his own gun and went outside. Standing before him was a man in an aqua golf shirt. Curled inside the shooting glove on his right hand was a .45 automatic. He patted Serge on the shoulder as he hurried inside. "Might want to close that door."

Brook pointed. "That's the guy I told you about. Reading newspapers and following me. I wasn't imagining things."

"Who are you?" said Serge.

"Explain later. Right now we need to work fast." He handed Brook the gun—"Hold this"—then he grabbed one edge of the plastic sheet. "Serge, give me a hand. I'm guessing you know your way around this neighborhood."

Serge didn't move. "I need to know who I'm dealing with before we go any farther."

"Okay." The man let go of the sheet and stood up. "Name's Clint Racine. Brook's law firm sent me to watch out for her."

"That's why I thought I was being followed," said Brook.

"Because you were," said Clint.

"So you work for her firm?" asked Serge.

"Not exactly," said Clint. "They hired a private investigations company who hired me. That way they'd have a buffer of deniability on the off chance that their suspicions were correct—which they were—and things got messy." He looked down. "Which they have."

"So you're a private investigator?"

"No, a fixer. Actually have a law degree, if you can believe it." He bent down and grabbed the plastic again. "But I like the adrenaline."

"I hear ya." Serge knelt next to him. "Just one question: The shooting was totally justified, so why are you wrapping the body instead of calling the police?"

Clint rolled Bones over on the bloody sheet. "Because I did some background checking on Brook and learned the reason behind the ostensible blackmailing: her involvement with you, the fake beating. If I call the police, it'll all come out and she'll be ruined, not to mention the firm's reputation and—most important of all—losing the class-action case against Consolidated. I specialize in protecting clients when there aren't any solutions in a courtroom."

"Does her firm know about all this?"

"They know that they *don't* know. That's why fixers are paid so well. Anyone can fix a problem, but I make it totally vanish. I never tell them how I handled the job or even that it's done, and they never ask." He reached across Bones's chest. "Now grab the other edge . . ."

Serge helped Clint roll Bones into a neat package, then wrapped him again in a bedspread.

"I'll pull my van up," said Clint. "There's this incinerator. You don't need to know where. All that's important is you'll never see me again, and nobody will ever miss this dirtbag, so you can both sleep well." Clint noticed Brook holding his gun at arm's length like a scorpion. "And I'll take that back now . . ."

In short order, the body was loaded under cover of darkness. Clint climbed into the driver's seat and stuck his head out the window: "Remember, this never happened." Then he drove off into the night.

Chapter THIRTY-EIGHT

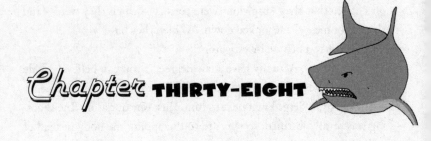

THE NEXT MORNING

The clock in the Monroe County courtroom was broken. Ziggy stared at it.

Brook had that weight-off-her-shoulders spring in her step as she approached the plaintiffs' table. "Good morning."

Ziggy continued staring.

Brook slowly unlatched her briefcase. "You okay?"

"Shhh! The clock . . ."

She looked up. "It's broken."

"Are you sure?" asked Ziggy.

"Are you high?" asked Brook.

He tilted his head back and dripped Visine. "I thought time was folding over on itself again."

"Great." Brook sighed. "Just don't say anything today."

The back doors flew open. Serge bounded up the aisle with an irrepressible grin. "How's it going?"

"He's high."

"So what?" said Serge. "You're back on the case! Can't wait to watch you beat 'em to a pulp. Start with a combination *corpus delicti, ad hominem, ipso facto, nolo contendere*"—throwing quick boxing jabs in the air—"a big *ad hoc* in their face to set up a final flurry of *quid pro quo, pro forma, pro se, pro bono, Sonny Bono . . .*"

"Are you okay?"

"I drank coffee. They've got the radioactive-strength Cuban kind down here."

"Wonderful." Brook grabbed her stomach. "I'll be right back."

Serge took the vacant seat next to Ziggy. "Is Brook okay?"

"She seems a little weird today."

"Did you notice the clock?" said Serge. "Either it's broken or we've just found an opening to the fourth dimension."

Ziggy stared up at the wall. "Existentially, the clock isn't completely broken. It's actually correct twice a day."

"Those are the wormholes. They're your secret escape hatch if things get sticky in here today." Serge picked up a pen. "The defense will never know what hit 'em."

"What are you doing?" asked Ziggy.

"Writing a reminder note on your forehead."

Down the hall in the ladies' room, Brook doubled over with cramps inside her favorite stall. She heard the outer door open.

"Brook?"

A man's voice in the women's room again. What the hell? Then she realized she recognized it. "Clint? Clint Racine? Is that you?"

"You honestly don't think that's my real name."

"Why are you here?"

"To tell you that you're withdrawing from the case."

"I don't understand," said Brook.

"Because the police just found Bones's body in Blue Hole up on Big Pine."

"But I thought you were—" She moaned with another cramp. "Did something go wrong?"

"No, it went exactly as I planned it."

"Planned—?"

"Shut up! Soon they'll be pulling a bullet from Bones that will match the ballistics of the gun that you handled and got your fingerprints all over. You know that cottage you rented yesterday? They should seriously consider getting those locks changed because they're so easy to pick. The gun is in a case hidden somewhere inside that you'll never, ever find. Also in the case's accessory pouch is a thumb drive describing your whole saga with enough detail to put you away for three lifetimes. Stay away from that courtroom and it remains hidden. If not, evidence has a way of being found."

Brook began shaking like a cicada. "But you can't count on getting a warrant from just an anonymous tip anymore."

"Who said anything about a warrant? Stolen evidence cuts both ways . . . Remember, not a toe inside that courtroom."

She listened as the footsteps faded.

Moments later, a door in the back of the courtroom slowly creaked open. "Pssst! Serge, Ziggy, come here."

"Brook," said Serge. "Why are you whispering? And why won't you come in the courtroom?"

"Yeah," said Ziggy. "You're acting strange."

"Just get out in the hall and I'll tell you."

They joined her. "What's the matter?"

She explained the whole story.

"But he told us he was working for your firm," said Serge.

"I'm guessing that was a lie," said Brook. "What do we do?"

"The obvious," said Serge. "Get back to that cottage."

"What about the trial?"

"Ziggy's got it," said Serge. "Don't you, Ziggy?"

Ziggy held his right hand in front of his face. "Far out."

"See? Nothing to worry about," said Serge. "Now let's get moving."

ALONG THE MIAMI RIVER

The drawbridge was up. A long line of stationary drivers cursed, changed radio stations and talked in Spanish on cell phones. A trawler sailed underneath on its way to Bimini with pallets of bulk food and toiletries from Sam's Club.

A few blocks away, the downtown library stood next to a stately piazza on Flagler. Upstairs, a row of academic types sat diligently before a row of microfilm machines. A motorized spool spun in one of the consoles, where ten boxes of previously viewed reels were stacked next to a sandwich. The film stopped and backed up. The person in the chair leaned closer. "I don't believe it."

Reevis pressed the print button, then held half a tuna sandwich in his mouth as he quickly gathered up notepads and files.

BACK IN THE KEYS

The motel office counter had a map of the property laminated on top with overlapping Scotch Tape. Next to it was a bell if someone wanted service.

Ding, ding, ding, ding, ding, ding, ding . . .

"Yes, yes . . ." A woman in curlers rushed out of the back room. "Good God, what is it?"

Ding, ding—

Serge's hand grabbed the bell to still the after-ring.

"Uh . . . you need something?"

Serge tapped the map. "We want the cottage we were staying in yesterday. Fourteen."

"Fourteen, fourteen . . ." said the clerk, flipping through a dusty index-card system. "Fourteen's taken. But we're pretty empty. We have others. One to thirteen, in fact."

"I must have fourteen," said Serge. "Sentimental value."

"But I already told you there are other people in fourteen."

"For now." Serge rushed out of the office and ran across the parking lot.

Knock-knock-knock.

A bleary-eyed tourist from Wichita opened the door a crack. "No maid service."

"I want your room!"

"What?" The door started closing.

Serge blocked it with his foot and opened his wallet. "The place is fifty a night. I'll give you three hundred. Deal?"

"You want to pay me three hundred to give up my room?"

Serge flapped the cash through the opening in the door.

"Sure," said the tourist. "It's a deal."

"Great," said Serge, forcing the door open the rest of the way and grabbing the man by his arm. "Out you go!"

"Hey, what about my luggage?"

Two suitcases flew into the parking lot and the door slammed.

"Okay," said Brook, looking around. "What now? He told me we'd never find it."

"He said *you* would never find it." Serge began unscrewing wall outlets and other things that were meant to stay screwed. "But I know how he thinks: I've hidden a ton of stuff in motel rooms, and I'm so good I haven't been able to find half of it. Still wondering where I put that snorkel."

"Why would you hide a snorkel?"

Serge lifted a mattress. "Met this chick who was a sexual three-ring circus, day and night. At first any guy would say, hot damn, yeah I can do that, I can wear that, I can talk like that. Then three weeks into a wholesale downward spiral of health, you're forced to start hiding her equipment." He lifted the other mattress. "Where can that gun be?"

A cell phone rang.

Serge pulled a painting off a wall with one hand and answered with the other. "What's shaking? . . . Oh, hi, Reevis. Totally forgot about you . . . The library? . . . What do you mean, 'I finally found it'?"

Chapter THIRTY-NINE

KEY WEST

Judge Boone stared at an empty plaintiffs' table.

In the men's room, pungent marijuana smoke wafted out the top of a locked stall. "I definitely need this." Ziggy continued sucking on his briefcase, then closed the latch and stood. "Whoa." He sat back down. "I keep forgetting how strong they're crossbreeding weed these days . . ."

The judge turned to the side of the room. "Bailiff?"

"I'll go look for him."

Before he could, Ziggy ran in.

The judge didn't care much for tardiness. He sarcastically pointed up at the clock.

"It's broken, sometimes." Ziggy stared down at his notepad.

"Would you like to cross-examine their last witness?"

"Definitely." He approached the stand.

"Excuse me," said the judge. "Do you have something written on your forehead?"

"It's just a reminder."

"What for?"

"I don't know. It was backward in the bathroom mirror," said Ziggy. "May I proceed?"

"Uh, sure."

Ziggy turned to the witness. "Do you work for the CIA?"

"No."

"Involved in the bombing of Cambodia?"

"No."

"Ever taken LSD?"

"No."

The judge raised his hands. "Attorneys approach."

They formed another line in front of the bench. Boone looked at the defense. "I normally don't ask this, but why aren't you objecting?"

"What for?" asked Yale.

"Relevance," said the judge.

"We're more than delighted to let him continue this line of questioning."

"All right, then." The judge made a shooing motion with his hands. "Step back."

Ziggy leaned against the witness stand and smiled. He looked down at the wooden railing and marveled at the lives of trees and carpenters throughout history. He looked up. The witness's head began to shimmer. *Wow, this must be that new hydroponic strain of killer weed going around.* Ziggy started to open his mouth. He suddenly realized the room was exceptionally bright. The sound of his own heartbeat pulsed in his ears like the beginning of a Pink Floyd album. A trickle of sweat ran down the side of his nose. He became concerned that his eyes were betraying the thoughts behind them: *Why is the guy in the black robe staring at me like that? And the woman behind the typing machine? And those twelve people in the box? In fact, everyone in the whole room is staring at me. What the fuck is that about? I'm minding my own business, not hurting anybody, unless . . . they all know. I hate it when they all know. Jesus, I have to get the hell out of here. Okay, be cool, ride it out. Just stand here perfectly still and eventually they'll all ignore you and go back to whatever it was they were doing before.*

"Hmm-hmm-hmmmm-hmmmm—"

A loud crack of a gavel.

Ziggy jumped back and spun. "What!"

"Any more questions?" asked Boone.

"Questions?"

"For the witness."

"Oh," said Ziggy. "*Ohhhh,* right." He stepped back up to the box. The witness stared at him. But not in his eyes. Above them.

Ziggy gripped the railing with white knuckles. "What are you looking at?"

"Something's written on your forehead."

"What's it say?"

" 'They all . . . *know.*' "

"Ahhhhh!" Ziggy ran out the door.

A gavel banged.

"Recess!"

Two hours later, Serge stopped in the center of the room and folded his arms. "That's it. Can't find the stupid thing."

"I have to go to the bathroom." Brook went in and turned on the light. Her voice echoed out: "Did you check the toilet tank?"

"Twice."

Brook finished her business and turned the light back off.

"It's driving me crazy," said Serge. "Just like that snorkel . . ."

Another echo. "Serge . . ."

" . . . and then I walked over . . ."

"Serge, come here."

He arrived in the bathroom doorway. "What is it?"

"Look."

"Turn on the light so I can see."

"No, that's the point," said Brook. "Something's glowing behind the mirror."

"That's where I put the snorkel!" Serge ran for his travel tools and began prying up an anchor bolt. "These old places have some funky conduits and shoddy plaster."

"The gun is in a conduit?"

"No, but that's where the glow is coming from. The conduits rust or crack and light from wherever bleeds in the walls." Serge freed a second bolt. "I got this end."

"I got the other," said Brook.

"Lift slowly out of those bottom two brackets and set it on the floor."

They stood in a moment of silence. The drywall had been broken out behind the mirror and the leather case hung by plastic ties from a framing stud. Serge slashed the straps with a pocketknife. "What exactly did Clint say again when you mentioned a warrant?"

"That stolen evidence cuts both ways . . . why are you smiling?"

"I know what they have in mind . . ."

Brook stuck her head out the bathroom door as a soft melody began coming from the front of the room. "Is that the theme from *Flipper*?"

"My cell," said Serge, grabbing it off the dresser. "Just got an e-mail. Perfect timing."

"What e-mail?"

Serge scrolled through his in-box. "This young reporter I hired to look into some of Ziggy's documents that had us stumped. Said he'd be sending an e-mail with attachments that would make everything clear. About a file called Brand-Gourd Holding or something."

"Stop right there. Could it instead be 'Grand-Bourg'?"

"Yeah, that's it. Why?" said Serge, distracted by his smartphone. "Heard of it?"

"Oh my God! Shelby was wondering about the same file," said Brook. "Then it could mean he—" She closed her eyes.

"What's the matter?" asked Serge.

"Let me see that e-mail."

Serge handed her the phone. Brook began shaking more and more as she read down. "Looks like it is true. There isn't any better explanation."

"What's true?" asked Serge.

She handed back the phone and let him read as she spelled it out. ". . . Except it's all circumstantial. We just can't prove it."

Serge stopped and stared off at a random point in space. He slowly began nodding to himself. "Then let's make it true."

"What do you mean?"

"I have a plan." Serge grabbed his wallet. "Do you have any blank stationery from your firm?"

"Sure, in my briefcase. What for?"

"Remember when I said I knew what they were up to?" said Serge.

Brook looked at the car keys in his hand. "Where are you going?"

"Shopping. We need a printer and a document scanner."

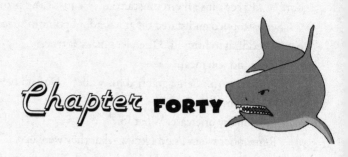

Chapter FORTY

THE NEXT MORNING

A Mount Rushmore portrait of the Ivy League sat at the defense table. Great spirits. From here on out, it would just be that imbecile Ziggy on the other side of the aisle.

The judge was going to cite Ziggy for contempt over the previous day's antics, but the defense implored Boone to accept his explanation of "rare seizures."

Ziggy continued sitting alone, chomping breath mints.

The doors in the back of the courtroom opened.

Dartmouth was still all grins when he idly turned around. His mouth fell open. He elbowed the lawyer next to him. No response. He elbowed again.

"Knock it off," said Yale. "I'm trying to tell a joke here."

A harder elbow.

"Hey, that hurt! What's the deal?" Yale turned around, then the rest of the lawyers.

"What the hell is she doing here?" said Harvard. "I thought they told us she wouldn't set foot again in this courtroom—"

"Shut up!"

Brook confidently took her seat at the plaintiffs' table and opened her briefcase.

Yale glanced at the others. "I need to call this in." He got up and went out in the hall.

"All rise," said the bailiff.

The judge appeared from chambers. "Call your first witness."

The day's proceedings took on a weird rhythm. The defense stalled and drew out every line of questioning into painful tedium. Brook was on the fast break.

They recessed for lunch.

Out in the hall, the defense team faced disarray. "What's taking them so long?"

"Be cool," said Dartmouth. "We can't let on."

Yale's cell rang. A short, clipped conversation and he hung up. "It's all good. Right after we reconvene . . ."

At the other end of the hall, Ziggy got a case of jitters. "What if it doesn't work?"

"Have faith," said Serge. "It can't fail . . . Brook, what's the matter? Don't tell me you're beginning to doubt my plan?"

"No, that's the problem." She uncharacteristically bit her nails. "It *should* work, but the whole thing is so volatile that the outcome could explode in any direction. You need to get as far away from here as possible."

"But it's going to be so priceless," said Serge. "Not a chance I'd miss this."

"It could backfire or worse." She worked her way across her fingertips like a cob of corn. "If you go back in that courtroom, there's a good chance you'll be in jail before dark."

AFTER LUNCH

The respective esteemed parties climbed the steps of the Monroe County judicial complex and filed back into the courtroom.

The first defense witness of the afternoon was a low-level junior accountant whose purpose was to put the jury to sleep.

Dartmouth leaned with an unhurried air against the railing of the witness box. "Please explain again the depreciation schedule."

"You take the original purchase price and determine the applicable number of years from the tax code . . ."

One juror held his eyelids up with index fingers.

" . . . Then you apply the bracket rate . . ."

The back doors of the courtroom burst open. A new character rushed up the aisle to the defense table. *Great,* thought the judge, *more drama.*

"Your Honor," said the lawyer questioning the witness. "A brief moment to confer?"

"Granted."

The defense team grouped around their table like a rugby scrum. Then they broke. "Your Honor, may I approach?"

Judge Boone waved him forward.

The lawyer carried a plastic bag containing a small leather case.

"What the heck's that?" asked the judge.

"If it pleases the court, one of our private investigators has uncovered a murder weapon."

"Murder?" said the judge. "This is a civil case about foreclosures."

"I know it's highly unusual, but if I may have some latitude to explain."

"Bailiff, take the jury out." The judge turned back to the attorney. "This better not be another waste of the court's time."

"I assure you it isn't."

"Okay," Boone said with mild sarcasm. "Who's the killer?"

"She is."

Boone's head jerked back. "The plaintiffs' attorney? Is this some kind of joke?"

"I couldn't be more serious."

"Then who did she kill?"

"A man named Bones Dickel. Deputies just pulled his body out of Blue Hole. Had to get it away from an alligator."

"Up on Big Pine?" asked the judge. "But why would she kill him?"

"He was blackmailing her."

The judge turned to Brook. "Is it true you were being blackmailed?"

"Your Honor, in light of these bizarre tactics by an obviously desperate defense, I must refer all questions on this matter to my lawyer."

"Can't say I blame you one bit." The judge's eyes returned to the defense. "Where are you getting all this?"

The lawyer pointed behind. "One of our private investigators."

"Step up," said the judge. "What's your name?"

A sallow individual with sun blotches came forward, wearing a black guayabera with yellow palm trees and dandruff. "Tommy Corona." He handed the judge a business card for redundancy.

Boone rested his chin atop folded hands. "Where did you get your information?"

"Someone called in an anonymous tip."

"What a surprise there," said the judge. "Why did he call *you*?"

"I hand out a lot of business cards." He gave the judge another one from habit. "A lot of people I approach refuse to speak to me, and others act like they have no idea what I'm talking about. But if you spread enough cards around, people who don't want to be identified will give you a ring . . . If you'll just order a ballistics test on that gun."

"You're getting ahead of yourself." The judge reclined in his padded chair. "I may regret this, but back up and start at the beginning and go slow."

"I was tracking a bail jumper for a bondsman in Miami. Goes by the name Tennessee Knox. Word on the street was he fled for the Keys. So I talked to relatives, known associates, unsavory types, handing out more cards, and the next day I got a call that he was supposedly living in a trailer on Boca Chica near the naval air station. But here's the strange part . . ."

"We're already at that dance," said the judge.

"The caller said I'd find a murder weapon in the trailer, and I asked who the bail jumper had killed, and he said, not the jumper—the killer was a female attorney who's trying a case against one of my other clients, the Riley firm, which was quite a coincidence."

"Too much to be a coincidence if you ask me," said the judge. "Continue."

"The caller said the gun's ballistics would match the bullet they're about to pull from the dead blackmailer at Blue Hole, and that the female attorney's fingerprints would be on the handle. So I go out to the trailer and case the place for back exits. I get a lot of runners. And I'm ready to knock on the front door and it's ajar. I called inside for him but no answer."

"Let me guess," said Boone. "You went in. You trespassed."

"I'm allowed to. Have a bail-bond license and he was a fugitive." Corona ran a hand through oily hair. "So I get inside and the place is stacked with all these TVs, computers, DVD players, microwaves, construction tools, a trombone. Then I saw a leather case on the coffee table, just like the one the anonymous caller had described. The one I just gave you."

"You removed evidence from a crime scene?"

"Technically it wasn't a crime scene yet," said the private eye. "Sure, it looked like a burglar's stash, but for all I knew, he enjoyed collecting stuff. Still, I felt it my duty as a citizen to report what I had discovered to the sheriff's office, and then I came right here."

"After stealing the gun?"

"Excuse me, Your Honor," said the Dartmouth attorney. "Right now the only person with standing to accuse Mr. Corona with theft of the gun is the bail jumper, who would be required to step forward—"

"A fugitive coming forward," said Boone. "Isn't that convenient? Just like having a bondsman's license to trespass. I smell a fixer in the brush pile."

"And as far as taking evidence," continued Dartmouth. "He immediately produced it here. People are always bringing evidence to the police department—or in this case your court."

Boone stopped and looked at Brook. "Is this your gun? Was it stolen?"

"My attorney . . ."

"Understandable." The judge swiveled in his chair and stared in thought at the broken clock. Then he swiveled back. "Well, this is a matter for law enforcement to investigate anyway."

"And concerning opposing counsel?" asked Yale.

"What do you want me to do, have her arrested?"

"Yes. She's a murder suspect."

"Out of the question," said the judge. "There's not remotely probable cause—just the craziest story I've ever heard in all my years on the bench. Still, I'm bound to have them run fingerprints and ballistics . . . Bailiff, take this gun to the sheriff's—"

"Your Honor," said Harvard. "Before you release the gun, there is one other thing the anonymous caller told our investigator."

"What's that?"

"There's a computer thumb drive in the gun case's accessory pouch."

"So?"

"It reportedly contains information about opposing counsel's prior involvement with the deceased concerning other crimes and her motive to silence him."

The judge waved the bailiff forward. "Still a matter for law enforcement, not a civil court."

"It also contains evidence of her misconduct in this case, suborning perjury from multiple witnesses and collusion in the theft of documents submitted earlier. It will clearly demonstrate that the previously admitted stolen papers from Consolidated should now be suppressed. I make a motion that the thumb drive be removed from the gun's case and submitted as evidence in this trial."

Brook's eyes flew open. "Objection! Any digital files relating to me are my personal property!"

The swing in events grabbed the judge's attention. "Do you realize what you're saying? If the thumb drive is yours, it connects you to the gun."

"I'm not saying that at all," said Brook. "My objection is limited solely to stolen evidence being admitted."

"Your Honor, the DeSoto case," said Dartmouth. "It's only fair. She used it to get in her stolen evidence against us. What's good for the goose—"

"Objection!" said Brook. "The precedent only applies if the thief wasn't an agent of the attorneys, and by their own admission the private investigator is on their payroll."

"She's wrong," said Yale. "*DeSoto* applies only to the original thief, which was the bail jumper living in that trailer. Anything after that..."

"He's right," said the judge.

"Objection!" said Brook. "I'm being set up. The court must weigh the impossible number of coincidences. If the evidence was just taken from my rental cottage by their investigator, it would be inadmissible. They needed an intermediary. Isn't it convenient about that burglar and the anonymous call? I'm guessing the next thing they'll say is the fingerprints of Tennessee Knox will probably be found all over my cottage after breaking in."

"Actually we were," said Yale.

"Your Honor," said Brook. "If we can be given a couple days for the sheriff to find this Mr. Knox, I believe he'll have some interesting things to say about opposing counsel. Once he realizes how he's been used and how deep they've gotten him, he'll have no trouble loosening his tongue."

"Everyone stop talking," said Boone. "I find this whole matter most disturbing. It strains credibility that there wasn't some teamwork involved here. But at every turn, the actions walk right up to the line without legally crossing it"—he turned with a glare toward the defense—"almost as if lawyers had been advising the players."

The attorneys looked at the floor.

"However, my primary concern is the trial currently before this court," said Boone. "And I take matters of suborning perjury and evidence tampering very seriously. Therefore I'm ruling the thumb drive admitted as evidence, pending my own review of its contents."

"Objection!" said Brook.

"Counsel, it won't kill you for me to look at the files," said Boone. "I've made my ruling."

"Objection for the record," said Brook.

"So noted." The judge surreptitiously pressed a hidden button under the edge of the bench. "In the meantime, everyone in this court-room will be guests of the county tonight."

The back doors of the courtroom flew open as a half-dozen deputies arrived in response to the judge's panic button.

Boone held up a hand to signal it was a low-level event. "Take them all into custody as material witnesses. Before we get this straightened out, I wouldn't want anyone to suddenly visit a sick relative out of state."

Dartmouth began stuttering. "Y-y-you're going to make us sleep in jail tonight?"

"Whether you sleep or not is your business." The judge vanished into chambers.

NEAR MIDNIGHT

An adhesive seal stretched across the edge of a door. The sky roared as an F-14 Tomcat from the naval base kicked in its afterburners over the Gulf Stream. Then quiet again on Boca Chica. The seal on the door told anyone reading it that the double-wide trailer was an active crime scene.

A rumble of tires as two patrol cars and an unmarked vehicle from the sheriff's office returned to the residence.

"Which way?" asked a detective.

"At that end of the canal," said the sergeant. "Fisherman said he spotted it tangled in a crab-trap line."

They headed around the side of the mobile home. "Why were there two crime-scene seals on the door?" asked the sergeant.

"The second one's for the *doggie* door," said the detective. "Should have been sealed anyway since it's getting colder near winter and they seek heat."

"Who seeks heat?"

"Long story."

They reached the shore and shined a searchlight. It swept mangrove roots. The beam stopped on a tiny reflective circle. The eye of a blue heron working the shallows. The beam continued on.

"There it is." The detective pointed at a human face bobbing in the tide, bleached, distended, hosting a school of tiny fish. "Better get one of the boats out. And bag the hands before those fish do any more damage. We still might be able to match prints to the all-points bulletin we got this afternoon."

"You seem happy," said the sergeant.

"Looks like we'll be calling off that search for Tennessee Knox."

Chapter FORTY-ONE

THE NEXT MORNING

Steel mesh covered the windows of the sheriff's prisoner van. It stopped in front of the courthouse, and Brook and Ziggy got out first, none the worse for wear. Next came four Ivy League lawyers who looked like refugees from the movie *Midnight Express*.

Everyone filed into the courtroom and took their usual seats. But it was all different: deputies stationed every few feet along the walls. The judge was waiting behind the bench, more serious than anyone had ever seen him.

The defense team nodded among themselves. This looked very positive, especially the added police presence. Brook and her case were obviously going to take a big fall.

The judge glanced toward the court stenographer, who said she was ready.

"Ms. Campanella?"

"Yes, Your Honor?"

Boone looked down over the top of his reading glasses. "That was a mighty interesting little thumb drive of yours."

She remained a stone.

"Evidence of falsified documents and attorney misconduct . . ."

The defense table: Yes!

"In fact I've never seen such a wholesale fraud upon the court. As I speak to you now, events are unfolding at several other locations around the state . . ."

Miami.

A convoy of dark vans screeched up to the curb. Side panels flew open. Thirty agents jumped out wearing dark windbreakers with big letters across the back.

FBI.

They rushed into the downtown high-rise offices of a major law firm. The agent at the front of the pack held a warrant. "Everyone step away from your desks and computers!"

The door of a corner office opened. "What's the meaning of this outrage?"

"Put your hands behind your back!"

For the record," said Judge Boone, "I've released the jury and am issuing a summary judgment . . ."

Ivy League defense team: Yes! Yes! Yes!

" . . . In favor of the plaintiffs."

Four lawyers sprang up. "What!"

"Wait," said Boone. "It gets better. I'm now turning this entire matter over to the Justice Department for criminal prosecution by the U.S. Attorney. And I'm reserving judgment on punitive damages in this mortgage case pending the outcome of those charges."

"Whose prosecution?" asked Harvard.

The judge turned toward one of the walls. "Deputies?"

They headed for the defense table.

"But the gun's ballistics," Yale said as he was seized by the arms. "And her prints?"

"Didn't match, none of it."

Boynton Beach.

Five black Suburbans screeched up to the curb. Agents poured into the posh offices of Consolidated Financial.

"Nobody move!"

But what about the thumb drive?" asked Dartmouth as he was about to be led away.

"Yes, the thumb drive," said Boone. "It paints an interesting story, which began when some genuine victims of foreclosure fraud retained the services of Mr. Ziggy Blade. To the surprise of the defendant, Mr. Blade was able to get the case certified as a class action. At such times, it is perfectly normal for a much larger firm with infinitely more resources to absorb the case with an agreed-upon split. In this case, however, documents on the thumb drive show a much different motivation for the arrangement. When the housing bubble burst, some people saw gold in the streets, primarily by defrauding the government through the use of straw buyers and bogus appraisals . . ."

"But that wasn't on the thumb drive!" said Dartmouth.

"How do you know what was on it?"

The attorney shut up.

"Exactly what I thought," said the judge. "As a result, Consolidated Financial acquired a number of silent partners, whose identities were intentionally clouded through a series of offshore subsidiaries, all leading to Aruba and something called Grand-Bourg Holding, that essentially laundered the money in a loop through the Caribbean before ending up back in South Florida . . ."

Fort Lauderdale.

A wave of dark windbreakers emptied file cabinets on the thirtieth floor of a downtown office building. Handcarts wheeled out piles of evidence boxes.

On the other side of the glass in a massive conference room, the partners of Shapiro, Heathcote-Mendacious and Blatt heard handcuffs click behind their backs.

But when the case became a class action," said Judge Boone, "it threatened to expose the hidden straw-buyer deals and, of much greater concern, the identities of those silent partners. So one of those secret partners—the Shapiro law firm—absorbed the case from Mr. Blade, not to win it for their clients but to assign a pair of rookie lawyers to the trial in order to tank it. It's rare, but it happens: Defense and plaintiffs conspired to fix a case. Only one problem. The rookies were better than anyone thought. And their discovery of the Grand-Bourg file was the proverbial smoking gun."

The deputies led the Ivy Leaguers away. "I want to call a lawyer!"

"Good idea," said the judge. He turned and dismissed the court stenographer.

The back doors closed behind the deputies and then it was down to just Brook and Ziggy. Boone had a smile as he shook his head at the odd couple. "There's one last thing that bothers me."

"What's that?" asked Brook.

"There was no smoking gun."

She wore her best poker face.

"If someone was super smart, I mean really clever, that file from Aruba *maybe* led them to *suspect* that the Shapiro firm was in bed with the defense team. But there was nothing remotely approaching probable cause for any kind of warrant." The judge bore down specifically on Brook. "Now, what would a lawyer do if they knew someone committed a massive crime but couldn't prove it?"

Ziggy raised his hand. Brook pulled it down.

"You have wise counsel." Boone smiled again. "The Grand-Bourg documents might have given a hint to the shenanigans, but there were major gaps in the evidence trail that prevented any prosecution."

Brook's lips were drying from the granite facade.

"Let me speculate, hypothetically of course," said Boone. "Say some attorney knows her firm is dirty and sabotaging her case—and heaven knows what else from that pistol they brought in. How could such an attorney point law enforcement in the right direction? How would someone go about filling in the Grand-Bourg evidence gaps and supplying the missing links?"

The courtroom's back door opened. Serge was ready to bound in, then saw the tension of the moment, waved his apology and let the door close back on its own.

"They might buy a document scanner and printer," continued Boone, "and fabricate documents to fill in those missing links. Essentially framing the guilty . . . That's right, we've already determined those documents were fake, but not before they led to the real documents and the coordinated raids this morning. And it's all legitimate: The FBI acted on good faith from what I gave them last night—I'd personally swear to that in any court."

"Interesting," said Ziggy.

"Yes, it is," said the judge. "But here's something even more fascinating to me. Now, it's perfectly legal for a person to whip up all the fake documents they want in order to incriminate the law firm that employs them—as long as they keep them at home and don't try to pass them off. They can wallpaper the den with 'em for all the law cares. What *would* be highly illegal is to, say, introduce the documents as evidence in a trial such as this."

Brook just stood there looking innocent, and Ziggy didn't.

"But a funny thing happened on the way to the courthouse," said Boone. "If someone steals those false documents that you're keeping at home—or in a rental cottage—you're not responsible for what they do with them. And if an attorney, such as yourself, wants to introduce false documents without committing a crime . . . and knows that somebody might try to steal something from you and submit it to this court to damage your case . . ." Judge Boone took off his glasses and bent forward toward Brook. "Tell me, are you really that smart?"

"I got okay grades."

A brief grin from the judge before the glasses went back on. "One last question. What was originally on that thumb drive?"

Brook just stood mute and cute.

"Right, ask your lawyer." Judge Kennesaw Montgomery Boone stood and stepped away from the bench. He glanced back one last time. "I truly hope I get the chance to see you practice before me again." Then, still shaking his head with amusement, disappeared into chambers.

Part FOUR

FANTASY FEST

Chapter FORTY-TWO

KEY WEST

A giant mutant crab blocked the road in both directions.

It stood upright, giant spiny legs reaching, twitching twenty feet into the night sky.

People screamed.

Then came a massive spider with even longer legs. And a peacock with a plume span that reached both sidewalks. A lobster with claws the size of refrigerators. A twelve-foot conch shell with a human face in the middle.

The screaming continued, along with laughter and applause, as each of the costumes passed down the middle of Duval Street. Music blared, liquor flowed. Many of the spectators on the sidewalks were also dressed—or undressed—for the occasion. They had paid handsomely for meticulous body-paint jobs that covered topless breasts with images of tigers, skeletons, devils, tropical fish and most of the characters from *Avatar*. For some reason, many decided their costumes needed large insect wings.

Serge threaded his way through the sardine crowd. He'd rented a white suit from *Scarface*. Brook was right behind, holding his hand, dressed as a Miami Dolphins cheerleader. Ziggy had Bob Marley dreadlocks, a Jamaican-flag shirt and a real spliff. Coleman brought up the rear; the only difference in his appearance was a cheap beard held to his face with a rubber band.

"I've never seen so many people crammed in one place," said Brook. "We can barely move."

"It's like this every year," said Serge. "Since 1979, when merchants decided to juice the off-season local economy each October, this monster has grown. Mardi Gras and Carnival in Rio might be bigger, but Fantasy Fest is exponentially more intense."

"Why?"

"Geography," said Serge. "Over a hundred thousand revelers—quadruple the normal population—descend on an island only four miles long and a mile and a half wide. Then all that is funneled into a mile stretch of Duval."

Out in the road, four human dung beetles rolled a ten-foot brown ball.

"Everyone's hammered and out of control." Brook stared at a woman with a clownfish design that placed the eyeballs over her nipples. "Not to mention all the public nudity. Why aren't they arrested?"

"A splash of paint and the police look the other way," said Serge. "The rest of social norms are chucked in the sea as well, releasing an eruption of bizarreness you could never imagine, let alone actually see."

"That's hard to believe."

"True story: A totally naked woman left one of the body-paint boutiques, approached a cop on the street at noon and asked, 'Am I legal?' He said, 'Put on a bikini bottom,' and walked away."

A parade float called "A-Cock-Alypse Now" went by. Then another float dubbed "The Big Lewinsky," populated by White House interns.

"Comin' through!" yelled Edith.

"Out of the way!" yelled Ethel.

Four topless old ladies body-painted like the band Kiss pushed their way up the sidewalk with open containers.

Someone pointed at them with a power salute. *"Eat me!"*

Brook froze as she watched the women pass. "Jesus."

"No, Jesus is over there," said Serge. "In that formation of mopeds with his disciples."

"Serge," said Coleman, tugging the back of his white jacket. "Why do I have to carry your tote bag?"

"Because it would clash with my Tony Montana image."

"Can we stop for a drink?"

"We're not really moving anyway," said Serge. "And could you possibly have put any less effort into your costume?"

"You don't like it?"

"It's just a beard on a rubber band."

"I'm that guy from *The Hangover*."

"Nobody's going to make that connection."

Coleman pouted. "I like it."

The old ladies came back the other way, followed by Spider-Man, the Creature from the Black Lagoon and a dozen Hemingway look-alikes.

Brook clutched Serge's arm. "All this weirdness. I'm . . . getting dizzy."

"It's still early," said Serge. "Nobody's gotten killed yet."

"Killed?" said Brook.

"Here's one story that will tell you everything you need to know about Fantasy Fest," said Serge. "Remember that great bar on Truman called Don's Place?"

She nodded.

"Last year, some guy was drinking in there wearing a full-body leotard and giant butterfly wings. Then he leaves the bar and just disappears."

"Where'd he go?"

"From what the police were able to put together, the dude apparently had an altercation on the street and suffered a brutal beatdown but was able to escape by crawling under a parked van. He was afraid to come out and didn't realize he'd already received fatal injuries. Nobody noticed for like half a day, and then late the next morning someone had to go to work or something and casually drove off in the van. Then these tourists out for a stroll notice a dead human butterfly lying in the street next to Don's Place. Only in Key West."

"Hey," yelled a frat boy. *"It's that guy from* The Hangover.*"*

Coleman saluted.

They pushed on.

"But all this is tame next to the little adventure we just had," said Serge. "You've got one hell of a legal career ahead."

"I still can't believe it," said Brook. "And I don't understand why they didn't just let Bones shoot us in that cottage and avoid all that complicated nonsense."

"A couple very good reasons," said Serge. "First, they'd already killed Shelby, so two dead lawyers on the same case is too much heat. Second, once they'd gotten in bed with Bones over the blackmail deal, there was no way they could let someone like that live. Too much of a loose cannon. And killing him dovetailed nicely into not only framing you but also planting evidence of attorney misconduct that would win the case outright."

"I still start shaking if I think about it too much."

"Don't," said Serge. "It's all over now. Relax and have some severely deserved fun."

Across the street, a femme fatale came dressed as the Lady in Red from the Dillinger shootout. "Molly!" someone yelled. She spun and reached for her purse. The guy dove inside a T-shirt store.

"This way," said Serge. "Let's get over to that side street and out of this mob."

They fought their way through breasts and floats and female impersonators on unicycles, until they reached the west edge of Southard. The crush of humanity began to uncoil on the dark block. Little knots of people in the shadows, the pungent whiff of marijuana, someone throwing up in a flowerpot. By the time they reached Whitehead Street, it was clear and mellow.

"This is much better," said Brook. "You can only take that in small doses."

"Serge," said Ziggy. "Me and Coleman are just going to slip into that narrow alley, but we're not doing anything suspicious."

"Don't lose my bag!" yelled Serge. "It's got the key element to my costume."

"Right here." Coleman raised the canvas tote by the handle before disappearing between buildings.

Serge shrugged and grinned at Brook. "So what now for you?"

"I was thinking more like us."

"Don't mean to be rude," said Serge. "But that cheerleader outfit is working."

She smiled and playfully shook her pom-poms. "We're already in paradise. Why don't we spend a few days together, now that all the excitement's over?"

A cell phone rang. Serge flipped it open. "Florida headquarters, Serge here."

"Listen carefully, motherfucker!"

"There's no need for potty mouth. Who is this?"

"We spent some quality time together rolling Bones up in a plastic sheet."

"Oh yeah," said Serge. "The guy in the aqua golf shirt. Clint Racine, was it? I've been meaning to kill you."

Brook got a strange look. *"Who is it?"*

Serge held up a hand for quiet.

"Shut up!" yelled the phone. "I want my money!"

"What money?"

"The million-dollar contingency fee I was supposed to get if we won the case! You ruined everything!"

"My sincerest apologies," said Serge. "Let's meet and discuss the arrangements, and chat a little about Shelby. I'm guessing that was also your work."

"I don't seem to have your serious attention," said Clint, backing off his tone with a splash of cockiness. "Wasn't someone else supposed to join your party for Fantasy Fest?"

"What are you talking about—?" Serge stopped as the meaning clicked. He closed his eyes. "I'm listening."

"Your little reporter pal Reevis is here with me. I snapped some nice long-range shots of you two exchanging documents at that park in Coral Gables."

"What do you want?"

"I told you, the money!"

"How do I even know you even have Reevis?" said Serge.

"You want proof of life?" said Clint. "How's this?"

Clint handed the phone over and snapped one of Reevis's fingers back.

"*Ahhhhhhhhhhh!* Stop! . . . Serge, don't listen to him! He'll double-cross you! This isn't a James Bond movie—"

Clint snatched the phone back. "Ready to stop fucking around with me?"

"Just don't hurt him! . . ." Serge's eyes flickered as the mental gears spun in his head. That Reevis was sharp. The four Bond movies with Florida scenes they'd discussed, specifically *License to Kill,* where Timothy Dalton comes to Key West for a wedding and reads *The Old Man and the Sea* . . . on the second-floor balcony of the author's house.

"Hello?" said the phone. "You still there?"

"Yeah, I'm here." Serge took off running south on Whitehead Street. "But you're going to have to give us a few days. We're not even close to getting the money yet."

"Bullshit," said Clint. "You're resourceful enough with your buddy's life in the balance."

"Okay, let me think . . ."

Brook ran after him. "Where are you going?"

Serge sprinted around the corner at Angela Street, running along the brick wall surrounding the Hemingway Museum.

"You still there?" asked Clint.

"Yeah," said Serge, returning to Duval and looking for motels closest to the Hemingway house. "I'll pull out all the stops and get the money ASAP. You just tell me what to do. Name it."

"That's better. So I'm going to take your friend for a little ride where you'll never find us, until you get the money together. But don't drag your feet because he has nine more fingers, and then other stuff . . ."

Serge crashed through people on the sidewalk, staring up at rooms and drunk people screaming down to the parade from their balconies.

Frustration. Over the phone, he heard a background of festivities, and was trying to match it with the noise around him on the street. But the sounds were too much of an indistinguishable drone.

"I'll call tomorrow," said Clint.

"Wait!" Serge kept running and glancing up at hotels. He needed more time. "Why don't you call later tonight in case I can come through early?"

"Not even you are that resourceful. Stop stalling!"

Out in the street, a float went by full of penguins blowing long, loud vuvuzela soccer horns.

"Just don't do anything crazy . . ." Serge heard the horns' viciously annoying blare in stereo: from his phone and the float directly behind him. He hit the brakes and turned to face a clapboard motel called the Queen Angel. "Excellent."

"Huh?" said Clint.

Serge hung up.

Brook reached him from behind. "What's going on?"

Serge's eyes scanned upper-floor windows. "He kidnapped Reevis."

"Who's Reevis? Who kidnapped him?"

"The reporter who figured out the money laundering for us. He was grabbed by the guy who shot Bones and Shelby . . ." Serge ran to the edge of the motel and found an alley. A quick nod to himself. "I'd run out the back."

"You'd run where?" asked Brook.

"Can't explain now. I need you to cover the front: Just stay at the end of this alley and keep your eye on the main entrance. If you see the guy who killed Bones come out with a young kid, yell to me at the other end of the alley."

Brook cupped her hands around her mouth as Serge took off. "But how do you know they'll come out? . . ."

Serge ducked inside a service door.

Brook strained to see on her tiptoes as a herd of topless unicorns passed between her and the alley. "Where the hell did he go?" More floats and screaming inebriates. Then people screaming for real, furiously trying to escape out the front entrance of the motel, which was blocked by the mob. Others poured from the service door into the alley. Somewhere in the middle of the alcohol cacophony, Brook heard the faint ringing of the building's fire alarm.

At the motel's front entrance: *"Fire! Let us out!"*

The mob thought it was some kind of game. *"Fire! Back in you go!"*

Eventually enough panicked guests had piled up in the doorway that they were able to ram through the sidewalk revelers. The evacuation dribbled off until it seemed everyone was in the clear. Then two last calm people strolled out as if everything was normal.

"Serge!" Brook yelled into the alley, pointing down Duval.

He sprinted back to the street. "Where are they?"

"In that crowd at the end of the block!"

"They're disappearing!"

Serge abandoned all civility as he crashed headlong into the crowd, swimming through a sea of shoulders. Brook stuck close in his wake. A mild breeze suddenly became a stout onshore wind as breezes are known to do without warning in the Keys. Serge looked up at clouds swiftly crossing the moon.

Clint had Reevis by the collar with a gun in his back. That fire alarm was too convenient. He kept checking behind and finally recognized Serge's head bobbing taller than the rest of the mob. Now it was Clint's turn to start crashing through people. He jabbed the gun barrel hard. "Move it or I'll drop you right here!"

Reevis flailed ahead of Clint, and they actually began to pull away from Serge. Only one problem. They were running out of Duval Street, which meant running out of island. The foot traffic thinned near the base of the road, and the wind whipped violently into a gale. Thunder. They made a hard right and ran toward an isolated gathering of people lit up by perpetual camera flashes. Visitors took turns rotating for photos at the seawall next to the massive red, yellow and black concrete thimble marking the southernmost point of the continental United States.

Clint didn't know Key West, or he would have known that the

other side of the tourist touchstone was fenced off by a military intelligence station listening in on Cuba. Clint was cornering himself.

Serge knew Key West, and he approached in a wide arc to Clint's north, making sure the corner stayed sealed. Lightning laced the blackness.

The ocean responded to the violence in the air, smashing the seawall behind the marker and shooting a salty wave over the crowd and their soon-to-be-repaired cameras. Clint had picked up Serge again and tracked his steady advance. He desperately looked left and right, backing up with Reevis in front of him as a shield until he had cut into the photo line.

"Hey, buddy, what's the freakin' deal?"

"Shut up!"

A wave of the gun spoke even louder, and the shutterbugs vanished with alarming efficiency.

It was now down to today's finalists. They were all alone, just Reevis and Clint against the concrete landmark, and Serge and Brook out in the open in the middle of Whitehead Street, blocking escape.

Clint wrapped a forearm around Reevis's neck and pressed the gun to his temple. "Get out of here or he's a dead man!"

Serge aimed his own pistol that he had pulled from his *Scarface* jacket. "Just let him go, and I'll let you go."

"Not a chance."

"Look around you," said Serge. "You're cornered."

"You're the one who's cornered."

"What are you talking about?"

"We may both have guns, but you have two people here you care about," said Clint. "If we decide to wrap this up here, Reevis is dead for sure . . ."

"Then I shoot you," said Serge.

"Maybe, but before I go down, it's better than fifty-fifty that I can take Brook out first, even if she's standing behind you," said Clint. "This baby in my hand is a forty-four, well known for its through-and-through capacity."

"You're dreaming," bluffed Serge. He knew Clint was right. Knight to bishop-four, check.

Reevis's head began tilting from the pressure of the barrel. "Start backing away now!"

Under Serge's breath: "Please, God, do something. If You're up there listening, this is a peachy time to make Your presence known."

Brook tugged the back of his shirt. "What are you doing?"

"Praying."

"Do you pray?"

"Not usually, because God's too busy helping people find lost wallets . . . Dear God, I know my record isn't spotless, but just this one time if You could—"

Splat.

Serge looked down at his feet and a large fish. "God, I didn't say I was hungry."

Splat, splat, splat.

"Serge," said Brook, "fish are falling all around us."

Splat, splat, splat, splat, splat.

They began flopping all over the street.

"What the hell?" Serge looked directly up into a giant full moon and saw hundreds of fish high above them on their way down from the heavens. A mackerel smacked his shoulder. "Take cover!"

He grabbed Brook by the hand and ran for shelter under a nest of coconut palms. Fish continued crashing around them as they peeked out from behind one of the tree trunks.

Clint wasn't doing so good, trying to flee the exposed point while controlling a hostage. They were both getting clobbered by seafood until a well-placed grouper knocked the gun from Clint's hand.

Reevis saw the pistol skitter away and made a break for it.

"Over here!" yelled Serge, waving him toward the palms.

The reporter veered in their direction as Clint reached his gun and took aim at Reevis's back. Serge jumped out from the tree's cover and aimed his own pistol. They were both simultaneously hit by mullet.

Serge pulled Reevis back behind the palm, and Clint found his own tree on the opposite corner.

Standoff.

"What do we do?" asked Brook.

Serge ducked as a bullet whizzed by. "Wait for God again."

Splat, splat, splat.

"What's with all those fish?" asked Reevis. "It's like that movie *Magnolia* with the frogs."

"Except that was surreal symbolism from the book of Exodus," said Serge. "This is actually happening."

"But where did they come from?"

"Probably sucked up by those." Serge pointed past the southern-most point, where the moon revealed vague shadows from a pair of sinewy waterspouts dancing just off the coast.

"Oh," said Reevis. "Like *Sharknado.*"

Clang.

A crab trap bounced in the street.

Clang.

A Rhode Island license plate.

Clang.

A prosthetic leg with a Willie Nelson bumper sticker.

"What the hell?" said Reevis.

More bullets flew by.

"It's just Key West." Serge reached around the tree to return fire. "Dear God, one more favor . . ."

Crash.

A giant green block fell from the sky and exploded in the intersection halfway between Clint and Serge.

One street over, someone sounded the traditional island alarm. *"Marijuana bale!"*

The stampede was impressive and undaunted by gunfire.

"The road's completely blocked!" said Brook.

"Run!"

Chapter **FORTY-THREE**

DUVAL STREET

Giant dung beetles rolled their brown ball into a parking lot and popped beers.

Serge raced around the corner with Brook and Reevis.

"Where do we go now?" asked the cheerleader.

"Not back to your room at the Southern Cross," said Serge. "That's the first place he'll check."

"Maybe it's the second place," said Reevis.

"What do you mean?"

"Don't look back now."

Serge looked. "Cripes! He's only a block away behind that giant float about penises. Or penii?"

Brook tugged his arm. "This might be a good time to get out your gun."

"Don't have it," said Serge, weaving between disco dinosaurs.

"Where is it?"

"Same old story: Potheads crashed into me. Feel like some more running?"

Didn't have to ask twice. They executed an up-the-middle, heads-down football offense from 1958. Elbows and lowered shoulders, not worrying about forward vision. Then, abruptly, no resistance. An expanse of street had unexpectedly opened up. They had been charging so hard against the tide that their momentum carried them into the middle of the clearing.

They looked up at the reason for the extra space.

"Why don't you love me anymore?" asked the Woman in Red.

"Molly, put down the gun and I promise we'll talk about it over lunch tomorrow."

"No." She stomped her right heel. "This time my needs come first!"

"Baby, I'm kind of busy with something right now. We're being chased by a hired killer."

"That's just like you." Mascara streaked down her cheeks. "Always putting your career ahead of our marriage."

Instantly, a second clearing opened up on the other side.

Clint Racine raised his gun.

Serge, Brook and Reevis were in the center of it all. They turned around in a full circle in the middle of the street, nowhere to run, alone in no-man's-land except for a few drunks who wandered through the triangulated lines of fire. Others on the sidewalk cheered at what they thought was a stage show for their entertainment.

Molly waved her pistol offhandedly. "Who's that guy?"

"Oh, him," said Serge. "Just wants to murder me is all."

"What!" Molly saw Clint aiming his gun and swung her own pistol. "Don't you fucking point that gun at my husband!"

"Thanks," said Serge.

The pistol swung back toward him. "Don't you try to sweet-talk me!"

From the sidewalks: *Shoot him! Shoot him!*

"Ahem." Serge looked at Molly and angled his head. "The guy with the gun?"

Her pistol swung again. "Stop aiming that at my man!"

"Shoot him!..."

Serge slapped his forehead. "This could go on forever."

More drunks wandered into the line of fire. Coleman and Ziggy strolled up.

"Yo, Serge," said Ziggy. ". . . Oh, I see you've got your hands full. We'll be going."

"No, stay here," said Serge. "Perfect timing."

"Molly," said Coleman. "Sorry about the guest towels."

Her gun swung his way.

"Shoot him! . . ."

"It's that guy from The Hangover*! . . ."*

"Man, she never forgets," said Coleman.

"Just shut up and give me back my tote bag."

"I was tired of carrying it anyway."

Molly returned her pistol's aim to Serge. "You even complained about how expensive the guest towels were. You said you could get blown for that much."

"But only in certain countries." Serge reached into the bag.

A red-faced Clint Racine stiffened his shooting arm. "I'm sick of this bullshit. To hell with all of you."

"Shoot him! . . ."

A few stumbling Hemingways staggered across the street, momentarily preventing clear shots. It was all the time Serge needed.

He reached in the tote bag and pulled out a giant weapon that matched his *Scarface* costume.

"Say hello to my little friend!"

The crowd gasped as Serge crouched and fired the T-shirt gun.

The already unstable mob lost any remaining sanity: charging, screaming, clawing, gouging eyes. *"Over here!" "We want one!"*

Serge fired again and again.

Sidewalk people crammed back into the road, fingers wiggling over their heads as T-shirts arced across the sky. The frenzy increased, clothes ripped, splashed drinks smearing body paint. Someone leaped from a balcony—*"I got one!"*—and took out three butterflies. The Hemingways began running.

"Give me the fucking T-shirt!" yelled Edith.

"Let go of my hair!" screamed Ethel. "I just got a permanent."

Serge caught the draft behind the Ernest look-alikes, still pulling pre-wrapped T-shirts from his tote bag and firing behind him on the go. The celebration pulsed forward with him, faster and faster, until it took on a life of its own, gaining mass and momentum. Almost a stampede, but not quite.

Molly fled for the safety of the doorway to Margaritaville. And Clint . . . Where was Clint?

Footprints on his arms and legs. "Get off me, you bastards!" Lying on his back, he managed to free an arm and raise his gun straight up.

Bang, bang, bang, bang . . .

Okay, now it was a stampede. All wings and tits and crazy hats. Clint pulled away but lost his gun, watching it get kicked down the street. A sleeve tore off his arm, and he decided to retreat.

Serge and his posse broke off from the Hemingways and found shelter in the entrance of the La Concha.

"What are you looking for?" asked Brook.

"Clint. He's out there," said Serge. "We have to go after him."

"Wouldn't it be better to run in the opposite direction?"

Serge shook his head. "He's no threat to me and Coleman because of our mobility. But you and Reevis will be easy targets when you go back to your regular lives."

"You really think he'd come after us?"

"I know the type." Serge raised his chin and scanned the street. "If he gets away, he'll go dark into deep hiding until he can ambush. So this is our best shot . . ."

Reevis pointed at a head that had just popped up on the opposite sidewalk. "There he is!"

"Let's rock!"

Clint ducked down a side road and sprinted for Simonton Street. He reached the corner and glanced back to see Serge peeling off Duval. A quiet motorized whine came up the street. A human moth on a moped. Clint suddenly jumped off the curb and threw out a stiff arm, clotheslining the rider in the neck and flipping him backward onto the ground. The empty scooter wove erratically another twenty yards before plowing through a row of trash cans.

Serge quickly made up ground, rounding the corner and barreling down on Clint, who looked back frantically as he arrived at the garbage bins. He righted the moped, jumped on and turned the key.

Serge was right on top of him. He reached out to snag Clint's collar, but the scooter zipped away.

Brook and the rest of the gang soon arrived to find Serge standing forlorn in the street, watching the moped become smaller and smaller in the darkness.

"What happened?" asked Reevis.

"He got away."

In the distance, a barely audible pop.

"Look!" said Ziggy.

The tiny moped began wobbling until it drove directly into the bumper of a parked car, sending Clint over the handlebars and onto the vehicle's hood. Clint pushed himself up from the cracked windshield and fell to the ground with a thud. He woozily sat up in the road, eyes moving from a punctured moped tire to the crushed shell of a giant African land snail. *"Mmmmm, got to get up . . ."*

With significant drive, Clint made it to his feet and began limping away like Frankenstein toward Truman Avenue.

"Where's he going?" asked Reevis.

"I know where." Serge turned around with a smile. "You can all go back to the motel now."

"But you said it wasn't safe," said Brook. "It's the first place he'll look."

"I've got it from here." Serge sprinted across the street and vanished into an anonymous alley.

Chapter FORTY-FOUR

TRUMAN AVENUE

A shoe scraped the pavement as Clint Racine dragged a bum leg up the street.

He signaled for a cab, but it was full of painted people heading back to the franchise motels on the far end of Key West.

U.S. Highway 1 starts in Fort Kent, Maine, and 2,377 miles later reaches its southernmost stretch on Truman Avenue. It is the most popular tourist gateway to Old Town, and the obvious emergency egress for anyone not intimately familiar with the island. Clint's hand waved at the street. Another cab full of costumes breezed by.

Clint was experiencing twin waves of relief and pain the farther he got from the festival madness. He limped along an ancient stone wall of coquina running right up against the sidewalk. He was home free. He saw two more pink taxis and held out his hand.

On the other side of the stone wall stood a magnificent fire-red royal poinciana whose broad, flattened old-growth canopy created a massive umbrella over the grounds of the Basilica of St. Mary's Star of the Sea.

Among the historic features of the church and neighboring old convent—accessible from a long winding path off Truman—is an ancient grotto for Our Lady of Lourdes. Anyone can drop in twenty-four hours a day, but few do. At night, colorful votive candles flicker in the darkness of the cave. Even if you weren't raised Catholic, it's well worth the visit. And Serge had been an altar boy. His head popped up behind the candles.

Clint pitifully shuffled along. He passed a used-book store and a Cuban sandwich counter—his hand permanently outstretched toward the street in a futile attempt to signal cab after packed cab. Because you can't get a cab at Fantasy Fest.

After crossing the intersection with Grinnell, Clint decided to stop and make a stand. The pain radiating from his hip was now just too much; he would simply stay put and wait as long as it took for a taxi. His luck instantly changed. A pink car pulled to the curb.

Clint limped forward. From behind, a forearm wrapped around his neck in a choke hold and dragged him backward through the open corner door of Don's Place.

The bartender named Lubs looked up from the draft spigots. "Serge! No! Not in here! Not again!"

"Wouldn't think of it." Clint's heels skipped across the floor as Serge dragged him past a long line of occupied bar stools. "This is just a transfer station."

"Then make it quick," yelled the barkeep. "A lot of people have to pee."

Serge pulled Clint into the men's room and locked the door. Another bartender, named Boomer, hung an out-of-service sign from the knob.

A jingling sound, the theme of *Flipper*.

Serge opened his cell. "How's it going? I'm almost done, and then we can really have some fun!"

"Uh, Serge," said Reevis. "We got a little problem here."

"Really?" Serge tore off another piece of duct tape. "Well, it's got to pale against what we've already been through today."

Reevis stared into the black hole at the end of a Smith & Wesson barrel aimed between his eyes. "Actually, it's kind of a priority."

Serge tightened a plastic strap around Clint's ankles. "So what is it?"

"Your wife's here. She somehow found our room."

Serge's shoulders sagged from the buzzkill. "Okay, I can see the picture now. Just tell her to stop pointing the gun at you and hand her the phone."

Reevis's voice turned away. "He wants to talk to you."

"He does?" She grabbed the cell.

"Molly, listen. Will you leave those people alone if I agree to go out on a date?"

"You really mean that? So you do still love me? I knew it!"

"Let's not get ahead of ourselves." Another piece of tape ripped. "We'll see how it goes."

"Where are you going to take me? What are we going to do?"

"I want it to be a surprise." Serge kicked already bruised ribs. "Can you drive over and meet me behind Don's? And pick up a few things?"

"I'm on my way."

A banana-yellow Eldorado convertible cut the lights as it pulled off Grinnell and into the gravel behind the bar.

Molly jumped out and threw her arms around Serge's neck for a big wet kiss. "I knew you still cared."

Serge pulled her arms away. "It's just a date."

She grinned mischievously. "I know how you really feel . . . So what are we going to do on our *date*?"

"First"—Serge pointed back at a bound-and-gagged Clint Racine lying in the dark along the rear of the building—"help me get him in your trunk."

Molly grabbed the hostage's feet. "It's so good to be back together."

Serge grabbed him under the armpits. "It's just a date."

Thunk. In he went. Serge slammed the trunk. "I'll drive."

The Cadillac crossed the Cow Key Channel Bridge to Stock Island; Molly scooted all the way over, snuggling into Serge.

"I need a little more room to drive here," said Serge.

"You do? I'll give you some room." She unzipped his pants...

Ten minutes later, the Eldorado rolled quietly up an isolated driveway on Boca Chica. The couple got out, and Serge sliced open the crime-scene seals on the door of a rusty trailer.

Molly helped carry Clint inside. "Have you been eating well?"

"Of course: 7-Elevens are everywhere."

They dropped the captive on a lumpy mattress in the back. The pair stood at opposite ends of the bed, fastening Clint down spread-eagled.

Molly clicked a pair of handcuffs shut. "Ever think about children?"

Serge tied an ankle. "All the time, just not mine."

They went back out to the car for the rest of the equipment.

"What do you need me to do?"

Serge screwed an eyelet into the wall next to the bed. "Spray silicone on the petcock valve and attach it to the propane tank."

Molly grabbed the canister. "I'll also file the gasket to decrease torque."

"Good thinking." Serge threaded a piece of string through the eyelet and ran it across the room to the valve's lever.

"Where's the candle?" asked Molly.

"In my duffel."

She set it on a shelf and lit the wick. "This should be high enough. I found the cutest little place on Sugarloaf. Want to take a look at it later?"

Serge strained to crank open the propane tank's main valve. "Might not hurt to take a peek."

Clint thrashed and tried to scream under the tape across his mouth.

Molly tested the tautness of the string running across the room. Then she stood back and appraised the rest of their work. "I think that's just about it."

Serge knelt next to Clint. "Here's the deal. The valve on that propane tank is way too hard to open for my needs, so I already opened it in advance. But don't worry: There's no gas coming out because I attached a little petcock valve that's closed for now. But it's got a hair trigger, which is why it's dangerous to tie string to the handle and run it tight across the top of your bed to that bolt on the wall . . . Dang it, your thrashing just opened the valve . . . Molly, would you be a sweetie and close that for me?"

Clint stopped wiggling, but the tape-muted screams continued.

Serge tapped Clint lightly in the middle of his chest. "As you can see, the string's resting right on you, also not very safe. However, if you can remain perfectly still and don't breathe too deeply, there's a good chance they'll find you in time."

"He's looking at the candle," said Molly. "I'm guessing he doesn't know that propane is heavier than air, and if he accidentally trips the string and releases the gas, it will begin to fill the room from the floor up until it reaches the ignition source of the flame. That love nest on Sugarloaf has the perfect room for a nursery."

Serge rechecked the eyelet at the end of the trip wire. "We'd probably need to take parenting classes."

Molly looked around the trailer at the implements of death and began panting hard through flared nostrils.

Serge patted Clint on the head. "Sweet dreams." He stood and turned. "Molly, why are you pointing that gun at me?"

"You motherfucker!"

Serge whipped out his own gun from his waistband. "You conniving bitch!"

Molly pulled back the hammer with her thumb. "Drop your gun or I'll fucking kill you right now!"

"Not a chance!" Serge tightened his index finger around the trigger. "Should have never trusted a treacherous cunt like you!"

Clint screamed even louder beneath the tape. Both guns simultaneously swung toward his head. "Shut up!"

Then the couple aimed at each other again.

"Get ready to die, cocksucker!"

"Eat shit, you whore!"

"Ready?" said Molly.

"Think so," said Serge.

They dropped their weapons and tore each other's clothes off. Molly socked Serge in the jaw and threw him to the floor.

Serge seized her hips. "You always did like the top."

Molly rode him like a bronco, her head whipping side to side, curly red locks flying.

"Oh yes! Oh God! Oh yes! . . ."

"Your bucking just hit the string," said Serge. "Turn off the gas."

". . . Oh yes! Oh God! . . ." She reached over and twisted a valve. *". . . Harder! Harder! Yes! . . ."*

Two minutes later, they got dressed.

"You still have it," said Molly.

"You're even better."

"Been doing Pilates."

She took his arm in hers and they strolled out of the trailer.

Epilogue

KEY WEST

Knock, knock, knock.

Brook checked the motel room peephole and turned to the others. "It's just Serge."

She opened the door. "You're safe!"

"Of course."

He walked into the room.

Then Molly.

The others gasped and jumped back.

"Don't worry," said Serge. "Everything's cool."

"What happened to Clint?" asked Reevis.

"Better you not know. But you won't have to look over your shoulder anymore."

"That's a relief," said Brook.

Serge plopped down in a wicker chair. "So what have you kids been up to since I left?"

"Me and Coleman designed this great bong from a Styrofoam fishing float—"

"Not you, Ziggy." Serge pointed the other way. "I was talking to them."

Brook stared down, a wet washcloth in her hand. "I've been putting ice on Reevis's finger. He's also got a bunch of bruises all over his stomach and chest. Clint worked him over good before he called us, the asshole."

"I'll be fine," said the reporter.

"You just let me take care of you," said Brook, wrapping more cubes in the cloth.

Serge stood back up. "So what's everyone's plans?"

"Power party," said Ziggy. "I've decided to chill down here a couple more days."

"Brook?"

"Huh?" Pressing the ice pack to Reevis's ribs.

Serge glanced over at Molly, impatiently tapping a foot in the doorway.

"Uh, listen, Brook," said Serge. "I don't really know how to say this. Just put the blame on me—it's all my fault. You see, Molly and I . . ."

Brook dabbed Reevis's forehead with another damp cloth. "Oh, you poor sweet boy."

"I'm twenty-six," said the reporter.

". . . Anyway," said Serge. "Molly and I were talking on the drive back, and we've decided—"

"You got another bruise back here," Brook told Reevis. ". . . What were you saying, Serge?"

Serge just smiled and turned to Molly. "Let's split."

The couple headed down the stairs. A third set of footsteps clomped behind them. Molly looked back. "Coleman's coming with us?"

"I swear it will be different this time."

BOCA CHICA

Frantic eyes darted back and forth from a string to a candle.

From the front of the trailer came a creaking noise that Clint couldn't quite make out. Then more little sounds. Clint raised his head. Nothing was there . . . *Wait, what's that down near the floor in the bedroom's doorway?*

Under the tape: *"Mmmmm! Mmmmmm! Mmmmm!"*

Something hopped up on the foot of the bed.

"Mmmmmm! Mmmmmm! . . ."

Clint was eye to eye with a giant green iguana as it slither-crawled over his legs and toward his chest in search of warmth. Of course, the string was in the way. A petcock valve turned. Clint began spazzing violently. The startled iguana scampered off the bed and climbed back out the doggie door as a '76 Cobra flew by on U.S. 1.

Molly snuggled into Serge and put her head on his shoulder.

Coleman was alone in the backseat eating Cracker Jacks and a Klondike Bar.

Fleetwood Mac played softly on the radio.

Molly began rubbing Serge's chest under his shirt. "It's so good to be back together."

". . . You can go your own way . . ."

"Absolutely," said Serge. "In fact, while we were loading the car, I snuck off to Fast Buck Freddie's and bought you a special gift."

"Fast Buck? I love that store!" said Molly. "What did you get me?"

"Something romantic and sentimental," said Serge. "It'll be different this time. You'll see."

Molly looked around with anticipatory glee. "Where is it?"

"The backseat." Serge glanced in the rearview. "Coleman, can you hand me that bag?"

"What?"

"The bag."

"Sure thing."

"Coleman! . . . No! . . . Hand me the whole bag; don't stick your hands in it!"

"Here you go."

Serge took the gift from Coleman and sulked. He passed it to Molly. "Set of guest towels. They have sea horsies."

"They're all fucked up! Chocolate and caramel smeared every-where!"

"I'm sure they can easily be washed," said Serge.

"That's because you never *did* the wash! I'll need stain fighter, and let it set, and put the washer on a special cycle! . . ."

"Molly—"

"I am not a doormat! I am not your maid! Do you know how much the work of a wife is worth? I try to keep a clean house! Sixty-eight thousand dollars is how much! . . ."

"Molly—"

"You take me for granted! You men are all alike! You'll never change! When are you going to get rid of those disgusting sneakers! . . ."

The Ford muscle car screeched to a stop on a desolate shoulder of the road. A door opened. Molly flew to the ground, followed by her purse. The car took off.

She quickly got up and grabbed her handbag.

In the background, a fireball rose in the night sky over Boca Chica as Molly emptied her .38 in the direction of a '76 Cobra disappearing up the Overseas Highway.

ABOUT THE AUTHOR

TIM DORSEY was a reporter and editor for the *Tampa Tribune* from 1987 to 1999, and is the author of seventeen novels: *Tiger Shrimp Tango, The Riptide Ultra-Glide, When Elves Attack, Pineapple Grenade, Electric Barracuda, Gator A-Go-Go, Nuclear Jellyfish, Atomic Lobster, Hurricane Punch, The Big Bamboo, Torpedo Juice, Cadillac Beach, The Stingray Shuffle, Triggerfish Twist, Orange Crush, Hammerhead Ranch Motel,* and *Florida Roadkill.* He lives in Tampa, Florida.

BOOKS BY TIM DORSEY

COMING IN WINTER 2016
Coconut Cowboy
A Novel
Available in Hardcover and eBook

Channeling his inner *Easy Rider*, Serge Storms saddles up for his most epic, lethal, and hilarious road trip ever as he revvs off to find the lost American Dream . . . starting in the Florida Panhandle.

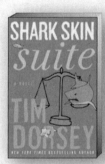
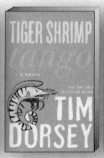

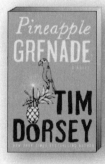
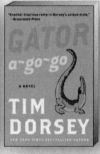
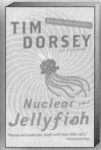

Available in Paperback and eBook
wherever books are sold.